VEINS OF SAPPHIRE, HEARTS OF STEEL

The Destiny of Terraqua Trilogy

By A.K. Neane

WASTELANDS
FROST KING
SHADOW OUTPOST
CAPES CROWN
NORTH NEGALL
SILVERTHORN RANGE
ORLONDIA
LUMINA LAKE
ORLONDIA CENTER
SILVERWOOD
GRIMSC RAVIN
MELUSINE MOUNT
FAEDAMIR
MOUNT KHORDRUM
AQUASIA
MITHRIA MINES
CRYSTAL REEF
KHAZHAD KEEP
FORGE PEAK
MAGNAR DELVE
SEREIA CREST
GOLAC

BANEBERG PORT
OSTSPIRE
ATTERIS
NEGALL
SOUTH NEGALL
EMBERFIELD VALLEY
BRONDOR HOLD
SOUTHERN REACH
ALKEM DALE
SYLVAN ENCLAVE
MITHRENDIL
GALADHWEN
TAURETH

To Roni, for being the mother I always needed but never had. You are the greatest gift I've ever been given, and this book brought us together.

To Kayla, the best friend who loves and supports me unconditionally—never judging, even through our differences.

To my BookTok community, your support has blown my mind and filled my heart with gratitude.

To all the pieces of myself left between these pages—may you finally find peace.

And to you, dear reader, may you find joy, hope, sorrow, love, empathy, determination, desire, peace, and solace in these words. Thank you for allowing me to share my story with you.

Trigger Warnning

Your mental health is important to me, and so is the opportunity to share stories that might resonate deeply—or occasionally hit a nerve. Yes, this is fiction set in a fantastical world, but it draws from real parts of myself—some beautiful, some messy, some a bit broken, and some that I've stitched back together. You'll find moments here that may feel a bit too real, like navigating the dark and jagged corners of the human heart, with love, compassion, and humor, to light the way.

This journey includes themes of trauma, grief, identity, and resilience, sprinkled with the strength it takes to find ourselves and keep going. Please take what serves you and leave the rest. And if the journey gets too intense, it's okay to step away. Your peace of mind comes first.

I have done my best to include all potential triggers, but I understand that I may not have covered everything. If you come across a trigger that hasn't been listed, feel free to reach out.

If you are in distress or need support, the U.S. National Mental Health Crisis Hotline is available 24/7. You can connect with a trained crisis counselor in the way that feels most comfortable for you:

📞 Call: Dial 988

📱 Text: Send 988 or 838255

💻 Chat: Visit 988lifeline.org

You are not alone. Support is always available.

This book contains mature and potentially triggering themes, including:
-Graphic sex scenes
-Graphic sexual use of items
(i.e. knife, wax, belt, water)
-Tentacle erotica
-Queer identities, romance, and sex
-Graphic sexual assault (SA)
-memories of groping, fondling, and
grooming by a peer at various ages.
-Physical assault
-Emotional abuse
-Themes of duty, war, and personal sacrifice
-Gore and violence
-Enslavement
-Self harm
-Grief
-Killing and death of loved ones
-Strong language
-Alcoholic drinking and drunkenness
-Infidelity -Between side characters.
-Occult rituals
-Fantasy religious systems with multiple deities
-Forced incapacitation (via magical drain or leech)
-Description of ptsd symptoms
-Description of anxiety attacks
-Mentions of cigar use and scent

Pronunciation Guide

PLACES-

Terraqua -TARE-uh-kwuh
Orlondia - Or-LON-dee-uh
Faedamir -Fay-duh-meer.
Negall - Nuh-gawl.
Atteris - AHT-teh-ris
Golacia - Goh-LAY-shuh
Sylvan - SIL-vuhn
Galadhwen - Gah-LAHD-hwen
Taureth - TOW-reth
Mithrendil - MITH-ren-dil

NAMES-

Orlond - or-LON-d
Aurelia / Aure - aw-RAIL-yuh / R-ree
Demajanio - de-ma-HE-nee-oh
Cliodnha - klee -O-nuh.
Azuraitha / Azura - AS-ur-RAW-thuh / AS-ur-ruh
Meles Tari - Mee-less TAH-ree
Cambria - KAM-bree-uh
Reinferd / Rein - RAYN-furd / RAY-n
Rielle - Ree-ELL
Kepple - KEP-uhl
Zardarian - Zar-DARE-ee-an
Voraxius - vaw-RAX-ee-us

GLOSSARY PDF
DOWNLOAD
Playlist On
Spotify

table of contents

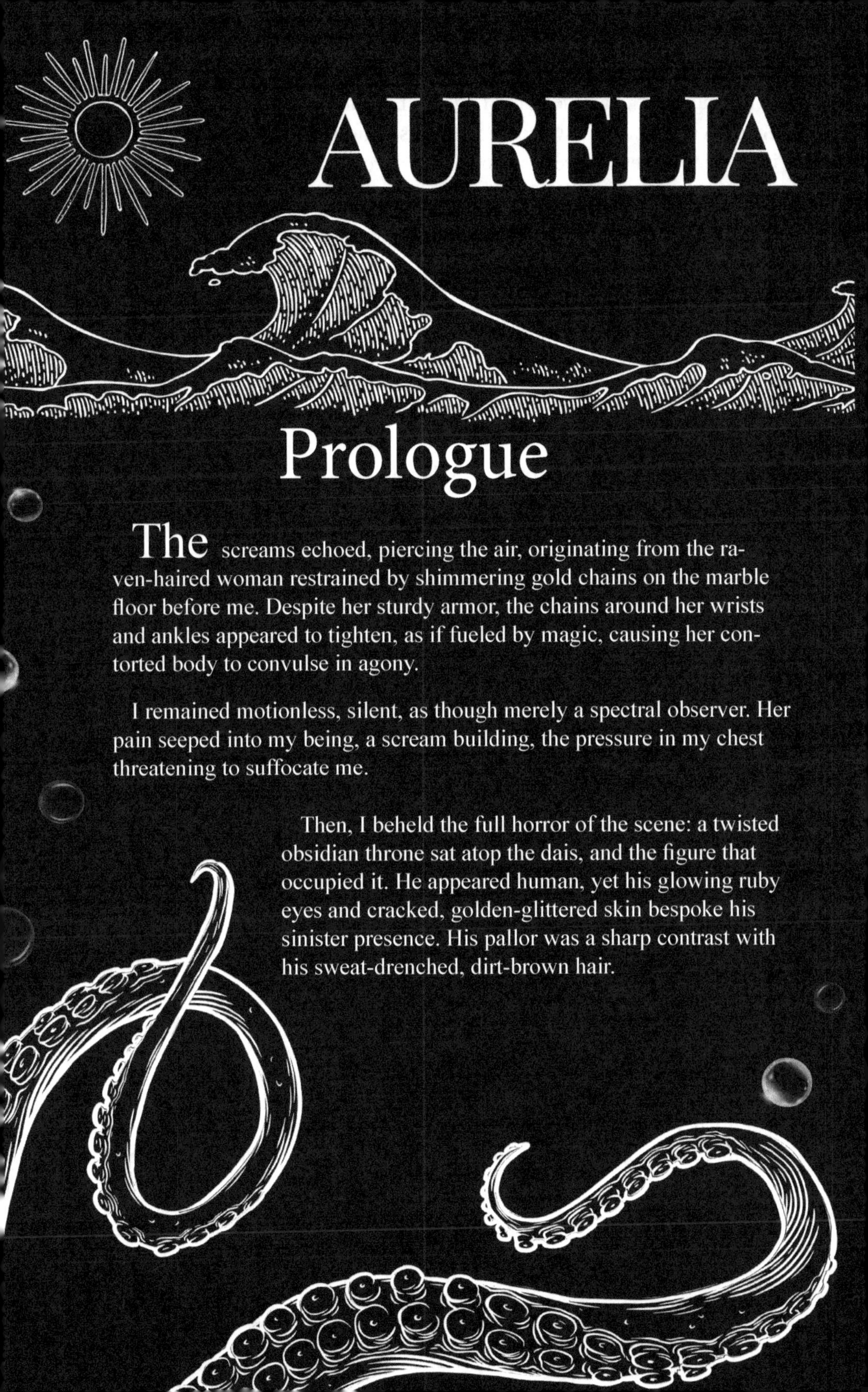

AURELIA

Prologue

The screams echoed, piercing the air, originating from the raven-haired woman restrained by shimmering gold chains on the marble floor before me. Despite her sturdy armor, the chains around her wrists and ankles appeared to tighten, as if fueled by magic, causing her contorted body to convulse in agony.

I remained motionless, silent, as though merely a spectral observer. Her pain seeped into my being, a scream building, the pressure in my chest threatening to suffocate me.

Then, I beheld the full horror of the scene: a twisted obsidian throne sat atop the dais, and the figure that occupied it. He appeared human, yet his glowing ruby eyes and cracked, golden-glittered skin bespoke his sinister presence. His pallor was a sharp contrast with his sweat-drenched, dirt-brown hair.

The throbbing orb he held emanated power, drawing life and magic from its surroundings. With each scream of agony from the woman, I felt her suffering intensify within me. She was dying, this resilient woman, and I was powerless to intervene. Waves of grief and sorrow washed over me, bitter on my tongue, the taste of metal lingering.

As she screamed once more, her life slipping away, the man laughed, his voice laced with cruelty. "You thought you could defeat me… *alone?*" His taunt met only with another agonized cry from the woman, her strength waning with each passing moment.

My eyes burned, yet no tears fell. I screamed, yet no sound escaped my lips. I felt only her pain, her regret, her profound isolation. She had fought this battle alone, unaware of my presence, unaware that I yearned to aid her. I struggled to speak, to move, but my body remained inert, a mere vessel.

Jolting awake, I sat up, breathing heavily and my body drenched in sweat. My night shirt felt damp as it clung to my skin and my legs tangled up in my bedding. It had been a dream. The reminder, though, didn't squelch my fear or ease my mind because my dreams held the potential to manifest into reality. *When did this occur? Was it occurring now, as it had during my mother's death?* I didn't know if this was a glimpse of the past or the future.

The salt filled breeze wafting through my open window offered a grounding comfort, dissipating the lingering ache in my chest. I wiped the tears from my face, my cheeks stinging at the touch, my throat sore, as breathing rasped, my heart still racing. I wiped the wetness from my mouth and I looked down at the red streak that now marred my hand.

Rising from my bed, I felt the cool stone floor beneath my bare feet, the moonlight bathing my childhood room in hues of blue and silver. I walked towards the basin on my oak vanity, I washed my hands and face. Closing my eyes, I sought to calm myself, to banish the haunting images and emotions I so vividly witnessed. Leaning my weight against the sturdy structure, my mind wandered.

Thoughts of my impending marriage to a noble of Orlandia, urged by my father, flooded my mind. I would do whatever was necessary to end this war, for if this dream held any truth, the realm faced a greater peril than we had imagined.

Draping myself in my silk robe, I approached the window, gazing out over the rocky terrain and crashing waves toward the distant, mountainous volcano. The silver moon illuminated the landscape, casting an ethereal glow. A full moon, my mother had taught me, heightened our powers, and urged vigilance in our dreams. Even now, her words resonated, her presence felt keenly, especially on nights like this, when my foresight dreams came to haunt me.

Turning away from the window, I walked over to my desk and waved a hand, powering the light with my magic. The lamp glowed an amber hue over the golden-edged papers that had been laid out there for days. Closing my eyes, I inhaled deeply, savoring the cool, sea-scented air, and let it out with a sigh. Despite being the Princess of a vast kingdom, the ability to make up my mind seemed to elude me.

Turning my attention from the dossiers spread before me—the candidates selected by my father for my arranged marriage—I acknowledged that, at least, I had some choice, more than most, I suppose. However, the truth was, I didn't want to marry.

I believed myself more than capable of running this kingdom independently. My father agreed to my capability, but he insisted that the marriage was a means to ensure the longevity of the alliance we needed to forge.

Narrowing my focus on to one particular dossier, the one I had examined countless times. The name inscribed on it was a mouthful, "Or-la Or-lon, Princess of Or-lon-dia." Despite its complexity, her listed attributes left an impression—one full of strength and resilience. I recall reading over and over her dossier, her education, skills, and interests; *how could one piece of paper determine the fate of my entire life?*

Picking up the rose and sandalwood scented, gold-embossed page yet again, I observed the sparkling flecks of sapphire dust on its front. Once more, I immersed myself in the details about this woman whom I hadn't even met yet.

"Trained in hand-to-hand combat, sword fighting, and archery," I read aloud. It struck me that more women should be taught how to defend themselves at least, but also should be capable of engaging in battle. Orlondia boasted many great warriors, and its military ranked among the largest in all of the realm of Terraqua. Undoubtedly, being a princess meant Orla had delved into military strategies and undergone training in various forms of combat. While I had also received combat training, I was certain she possessed more extensive knowledge.

"Only living heir to the kingdom of Orlondia," I continued reading. *That made two of us. Did she also feel the weighty pressure of ensuring the prosperity of her kingdom, like what rested on my shoulders?*

On paper, she had everything desirable to be well-suited to ruling a kingdom. *How was I to marry and rule two kingdoms with someone I didn't know?* I sighed and tossed the page back onto the desk, watching it float across the other papers.

As my gaze shifted from the dossiers, I turned my attention once again out one of my windows, this time to a small part of my vast kingdom of Faedamir. In the distance, I could see some of our many ships that would likely be sent to aid in the war we were now a part of. The conflict had little effect on our islands so far, but we had noticed an increase in trade routes being cut off and more of our merchant ships raided. Not to mention the growing number of refugees each day.

The call to aid pleaded for the deployment of our fleet of military ships and a steady supply of our runic magic-imbued weapons. All in exchange for more favorable trade terms and our influence in the decisions of another significant kingdom. According to my father, it was a strategic and beneficial move on both economic and political fronts. However, my insistence on only marrying a woman complicated this typical arrangement.

Glancing back at the desk, I was already certain of one candidate I would not choose—the lone male dossier in the bunch. *"Just in case,"* my father remarked when he handed them to me the day before. Difficult or not, he was keenly aware of my firm stance on the matter. I had explicitly told him I would marry a woman who would never be with me or love me, versus a man who I could never want.

Abruptly, anger surged within me. I moved swiftly, sifting through the dossiers to locate the one titled "Reinferd Grathlend, Prince of Negall." I had no intention of choosing him, and I tossed it into the fireplace and set it alight with a small spark of magic. I watched it crackle and burn, the embers pulling me into a trance. A wave of loneliness and the feeling of being misunderstood flooded over me.

Catching the scent of roses and sandalwood drew me back to my desk. I picked up Orla's dossier again, and with a final deep breath, I made my choice.

ORLA

Chapter 1

"This wasn't my choice, just so you know." I crossed my arms over my chest, the metal of my gauntlet tinging against the steel of my chest plate. My magic churned in chaos, reflected in the swirl of purple and dark blue in my eyes. I turned away from the gorgeous woman standing along the patio railing, trying to distance myself from the intensity of the moment.

She appeared calm, placing a hand on the stone railing as the cool autumn breeze swept through the balcony. I stole a glance at her, my resolve faltering as my gaze landed on her long copper curls, deeply sun-kissed skin, and those sea-glass green eyes framed by a kind smile that seemed impossibly genuine.

"I do understand that," came her lark-like voice—Princess Aurelia Demajanio, heir to the kingdom of Faedamir. Her words drew me back to her, and I realized I couldn't tear my eyes away. My gaze trailed over her silken sapphire gown, the fabric hugging every graceful curve. She was taller than most women but would still fit just under my chin. That thought alone sent a flicker of something unfamiliar through me.

I struggled to hold on to my anger at the situation, but the spark of chemistry between us was undeniable. Despite my reservations, I knew—no, feared—that I was already smitten.

"For the record, I had very little choice in this matter too," she continued, her voice steady. Princess Aurelia moved gracefully along the balcony's edge, her fingers brushing over the begonias blooming in abundance. Even as her tone turned serious, her words seemed to enchant me. "Princess Orla, I understand this arrangement may feel awkward, but marriages to solidify treaties have been a tradition for centuries across the realm."

I remained silent, my eyes fixed on her hands as she fidgeted with the delicate petals. Her movements seemed both calculated and nervous. "My father's decision in this arrangement is tied to the fact that I'll be ruling our kingdom very soon. His health has been failing for years, and he knows his time is coming to an end. He wanted to ensure that this alliance would endure after I become queen." I could hear the sorrow in her voice as she mentioned her father's health.

Her voice softened, carrying a note of boldness that made it hard for me not to smile. "One thing he understands, however, is that I'm a lesbian. He would have preferred an alliance that also ensured the continuation of our royal line, but he respects my strong views on bearing my own children. Thankfully, he didn't force me into a marriage with a man. Still, I realize your situation might not be as understanding." She looked up at me, and I could see her genuine concern, even though she spoke matter-of-factly.

She looked up, her sea-glass eyes meeting mine with genuine concern. Her blunt honesty left me momentarily speechless. I turned toward the garden below, searching for something—anything—to anchor myself. The vibrant greenery was tinged with the warm hues of fall, and the scent of flowers tickled my nose. Slowly, I exhaled, feeling my magic settle as the dark blue in my eyes faded to lavender.

Breathing in deeply the crisp fall air and the scent of the garden. I wanted to reassure her, but I could not seem to find the words. Instead, my mind wandered as I tried to avoid my conflicting emotions. The memory of the day my parents presented the proposal was etched vividly in my mind.

I recalled being summoned to my father's office, King Oric Orlon. His tone was grave as he began, "Orla, we've received a response to our request for aid." My magic stirred uneasily, and my eyes shifted from lavender to sky blue, betraying my concern.

The aid we sought was crucial. Faedamir possessed the most formidable navy fleet, and their dwarven enchanted weapons were invaluable. The King of Frostspire in the far north was pushing borders more aggressively, turning all trade routes hostile, signaling the looming impact of this nearly fifteen year long war had on the entire realm of Terraqua.

King Rowan Demajanio of Faedamir had sent my father new terms in response to the proposed arrangement in exchange for their assistance. I stood restlessly, waiting for my father to continue.

Instead, my mother, Queen Helena, spoke tenderly, "Darling, King Rowan is requesting a marriage treaty."

Confusion clouded my thoughts. *Did he not have a daughter? Maybe King Rowan will consider a Duke, or another allied royal like Prince Reinferd. There was no way they would consider me.*

Though not unheard of in our history, it was rare for two princesses to be considered for a marriage treaty. My parents knew I didn't want to marry at all. They remained unaware, however, that it was more my unwillingness to marry a man that led me to that decision. I waited in silence for them to explain.

My father continued, explaining that King Rowan had requested dossiers to be sent for consideration by his daughter, Princess Aurelia. All to be women candidates save for one male, and only with the highest royal titles in our kingdom. My eyes widened to the brightest sky blue, surprised by this odd request.

I was caught off guard by what my father stated next. "You will be considered as a candidate," my father said, his tone firm. "Offering our sole heir to the throne looks favorable, and despite your reluctance to marry, this arrangement could prove mutually beneficial to our kingdoms. You would gain influence over Faedamir and all its holdings. Including its fleet and forge."

Anger simmered as I considered the implications of this unexpected and forced proposal. My magic churned again and my eyes turned the darkest sapphire. Yet, I knew I couldn't refuse outright.

"Um, Princess Orla?" Aurelia's soft voice brought me out of my thoughts and back to her. I blinked, finding her watching me closely and my eyes finished, shifting to my neutral lavender.

"Should we sit and have our tea?" I motioned to the lace-covered table, adorned with the delicate porcelain tea set my mother had selected for the occasion. Little silver trays held an assortment of tiny cakes and cookies, their sweetness mingled faintly with the crisp evening air.

A soft fall breeze stirred, unmistakable for Orlondia this time of year, which swept around me as I approached the iron table and chairs. I eased into one of the cold, black chairs, the chill biting through the chain mail under my shirt and the leather of my pants. Despite the lingering warmth of the day's sun, the metal's coolness sent a shiver darting up my spine.

Princess Aurelia sat gracefully across from me, her presence both calming and unsettling. I watched her and I let out a deep breath before I began. "I never expected to be part of an arrangement like this. I will honor the agreement because it's my duty, not because it's a fate I would have chosen for myself. Though I'm truly surprised that you, out of all your options, chose me." I felt my cheeks heat as I admitted part of the truth.

I looked down at the detailed frosting of the tiny cakes before I met her gaze once more. "Princess Aurelia, you came here so we could get to know—"

She interrupted me, with a small, genuine smile, "Please call me Aure; nearly everyone does. And I hope you don't mind if I just call you Orla." Her cheeks glowed a rosy hue as she looked at the ground for a moment, her beautiful green eyes glinting with shyness.

I blinked, momentarily caught off guard by her openness, before replying, "Oh, no, I don't mind. This is an informal setting, after all."

I reached for one of the tiny cakes, my nerves prompting me to take a larger bite than I intended. As the sweetness melted on my tongue, I realized she was watching me with a grin, barely holding back a laugh. Embarrassed, I quickly grabbed a napkin, covering my mouth as I chewed.

The silence between us stretched, teetering on awkwardness, until Aure broke it with a question. "So, what are your current responsibilities in your kingdom?"

Amazed that she had started with such a relevant question, I pondered a moment. I likely would have begun by asking about her favorite food. She seemed very well put together and intelligent, which admittedly, I admired.

I set the napkin down carefully and responded, "Well, honestly, my involvement in the day-to-day running of the kingdom is minimal. My father has me assist with research and paperwork, but I've been eager to take on more responsibility. It feels like he's holding back, as though he plans to rule forever."

My magic stirred, and I felt my eyes shift to a fierce violet as I glanced toward the garden below. "I have ideas for my kingdom—plans to strengthen it, especially in how we confront this war against the North."

Aure sipped her tea, her attention unwavering. Her focused gaze unsettled me, making me feel exposed, as if she could see straight through my words. I hesitated, wondering if I had revealed too much. Why did she make me feel safe, like I could tell her anything? I couldn't fully trust that, though; she might perceive it as a weakness.

Shifting in my chair, I softened my tone, letting my magic settle as my eyes faded back to lavender. "I do a lot of research, and I love learning new things. For the last fifteen years, my focus has been on my education and combat training. My studies have largely revolved around the war over the past five years. Have you had many educational opportunities?"

Aure smiled as she delicately set her teacup down on the matching gold-and-blue saucer, folding her hands in her lap. "Well, I can tell you're very well-educated. I've been fortunate to have many opportunities myself, and I'm immensely grateful for them. Education is a gift, wouldn't you agree? It opens doors, broadens horizons. Knowledge, I believe, is invaluable."

I nodded, a small smirk tugging at my lips. "Absolutely. Knowledge is crucial—especially when governing a Kingdom or two."

Her eyes lit up with enthusiasm as she leaned forward slightly. "Yes, I firmly believe that a strong kingdom is an educated one. Knowledge should be accessible and free to anyone willing to pursue it. What are your thoughts on education for your subjects?"

I met her gaze and felt a flicker of admiration. "I think every subject should have access to free education. People deserve the chance to grow intellectually and physically. It's a government's responsibility to provide the means for them to do so."

She nodded eagerly, her voice tinged with frustration as she continued, "One thing I deeply disagree with is the Kingdom of Frostspire's stance on education. It baffles me they have outlawed even basic education for the lower classes as a means of control. Only the wealthy have access to schooling, and they heavily regulate literature, banning any books the King disagrees with. It's one of the many reasons I'm glad my father allied against them and supported Orlondia's war effort."

As I watched her grow more impassioned, I felt a sense of resolve. I allowed for a small smile to curve my lips. "I'm grateful for my alliances against the North as well. Everyone should have the opportunity to learn and grow. Ignorance only serves to weaken a kingdom."

Her posture softened slightly, and she offered a warm smile. "I'm glad we agree on this."

I turned to her, my tone resolute. "The Kingdom of Frostspire is backward in many ways. They treat their subjects poorly, keeping them in the dark about everything that matters. The rich live comfortably while the rest are left to suffer. No kingdom should endure what the Northerners do."

Aure's expression grew somber as she said, "If there's anything we can do to lessen their suffering, I'd gladly give everything I have. Laws are important for maintaining order, but it's been proven time and time again that education brings stability, success, and peace among the masses. I can see why you're so eager to involve yourself in your kingdom's affairs."

Her voice softened as she added, "I've had more opportunities than most in that regard. My father has always relied heavily on me, especially in the last five years, as his health has kept him away from many of his duties.

Her words stirred a pang of sorrow within me as I listened to her share such personal details with me. I couldn't help but wonder why she was opening up to me in this way, so soon. Unsure of how to respond, I forced a small, hopefully reassuring smile, though it felt awkward and out of place.

Instead of speaking, I let my gaze drift over the sprawling garden, where the vibrant greens of summer had shifted into the warm yellows and reds of autumn. The sight was easier to focus on than the vulnerability Aure had just shared.

After a lingering pause, I glanced back at her, and our eyes met. Her seaglass-green gaze held mine, and I found myself momentarily lost in its depth. Her lips twitched, the hint of a smile forming, before she broke the silence. "Can I ask you about your eyes? I know your dossier mentioned that you're magic-born, but..." She hesitated, leaving the sentence unfinished.

I interrupted gently, nodding. "Yes, I'm magic-born. Though, honestly, it feels a bit anticlimactic." A self-deprecating laugh slipped past my lips. "My magic is mostly just my eyes—they change color with my mood. It's not exactly convenient since it makes my emotions hard to hide, but I've learned to keep calm. They usually stay within a range of purple to blue."

Aure's expression softened, and she spoke shyly. "Well, they're very beautiful and unique. I'd love to paint them sometime."

Heat crept into my cheeks, and I felt my magic stir as my eyes shifted to a softer lavender hue. She noticed and smiled, then asked, "Is one of your parents magic-born?"

I shook my head. "Oh, no—or at least, not that I know of. They've always said there's some magic-born in our bloodline somewhere, and that's how I ended up with a bit of magic."

She tilted her head, curiosity sparking in her expression. "Do you know which bloodline? I haven't heard of your gift among the Siren bloodlines, and you're obviously not dwarven." Her smile grew faintly teasing, and I could guess she was referring to my height.

Running my fingers through my hair, I answered curtly, "I'm not really sure. My mother once mentioned something about Fae in her ancestry."

Aure nodded thoughtfully. "That would make sense. If it's a Fae gift, it might have some empathic traits. But… that's your only magic?" Her tone carried a note of confusion, and I suddenly worried she might have expected more from me.

My eyes shifted toward sapphire blue as my tone grew curt. "Yes, that is all the magic I possess." Aure looked shocked at my sudden change in tone. Trying to recover, I forced a smile and softened my voice. "What are some of your interests or hobbies, Aure?" I felt the surge of magic as my eyes faded back to purple.

She hesitated briefly; her discomfort evident, but then spoke quietly. "Well, I enjoy reading and learning new things. One of my passion projects is to help establish well-equipped libraries across all regions of my kingdom and in those of our allies."

Intrigued, I leaned forward slightly. "That sounds wonderful. I know a few people here in Orlondia who could help with that. I'm sure they'd value your insight and be eager to assist if you wanted to expand your project here."

Aure's face lit up, excitement filling her voice. "Oh, thank you! That would be amazing." She paused briefly, her tone growing more tentative. "Would you consider joining me at an opening or book-reading event sometime?"

I felt my cheeks warm, my magic stirring softly as I smiled. "I think I'd enjoy that."

Her blush deepened slightly as she added, "They're usually pretty fun events. I think you'll like them."

Tipping my teacup, I studied the tiny leaves clinging to the bottom before noticing Aure had finished her tea as well. She seemed restless, standing and stretching her arms casually before asking, "So, do you have any projects right now, political or otherwise?"

Setting aside my cup, I stood and walked alongside her, our strides naturally falling in sync. "I do," I replied, my tone thoughtful. "I've been advocating for a more inclusive role for women in governing our kingdom. While a few women hold high-ranking positions, there's still too much misogyny and sexism ingrained in the system. I'm working to expand opportunities and dismantle those barriers."

I wanted that to be entirely true, but despite my efforts, I often hesitated in moments when I longed to be bolder—especially around my father, King Oric. Yet Aure had a way of effortlessly drawing out my innermost thoughts and desires, a talent that left me both unnerved and intrigued.

"I see," Aure said, her tone thoughtful, a faint frown tugging at her lips. "It's disappointing to hear that's still such a prevalent issue here. I believe everyone should be given the opportunity to lead and contribute, regardless of gender or background. It's not just about breaking barriers for women but about creating a system where no one is excluded from decision-making based on who they are."

Her words reignited a wave of deep-seated frustration within me. "Yes, most men I've known are insufferably arrogant, convinced they're always right, and expecting women to follow their orders without question."

Aure's tone turned sharp as she replied, "That arrogance is a symptom of imbalance. In my view, every rank and position in a kingdom should reflect the diversity of its people. Leadership and representation should include everyone—women, men, and those beyond the binary—so that no perspective is left unheard."

I nodded, her conviction resonating with me. "I like the sound of that. I only wish it were something my father would consider implementing."

I smiled, grateful for the chance to have an honest, meaningful dialogue. Aure's presence felt like a refreshing change—a glimpse of the world as it could be, rather than as it was.

We descended the balcony steps into the garden below, the soft crunch of gravel beneath our feet accompanying the fading light of day. I watched as Aure paused by a marigold, her touch delicate as she brushed the vibrant blossom with her fingertips. She glanced back at me, her eyes thoughtful, before we continued down the path together.

"It's inspiring to see someone with your perspective and influence advocating for change," she said, her voice carrying easily in the tranquil evening air.

I responded with quiet humility, "Thank you, Aure. I believe that by challenging the status quo, we can create a more just and equitable society. Unfortunately, I haven't been able to sway my father as much as I'd hoped. Our marriage treaty is proof of that."

She turned to me, her expression pensive but sincere. "Orla, I value your honesty and your commitment to progress. Even though this isn't the way either of us envisioned, I truly believe we could accomplish great things together."

For a moment, her words kindled a spark of excitement in me, and I met her gaze with a flicker of hope. But just as quickly, reluctance surfaced. My jaw tightened, and with a surge of anger I felt my eyes shifting to a deep cobalt blue. "I may be going along with this, Aure, but that doesn't mean I'm happy about it. Let's not pretend this is going to be some kind of fairy tale."

The smile that had lit her face moments before faded, the warmth between us dimming as the air grew charged with tension. "I'm not pretending it is," she replied, her tone sharp, each word cutting like the frigid wind.

The sun dipped lower, casting a warm amber glow over the garden, but it did little to ease the sudden chill between us.

I turned away, struggling to regain my composure as the conflicting emotions within me churned. Behind me, Aure hesitated, her bashful tone breaking the silence. She glanced at the horizon, where the sun was now barely a sliver. "Um, before we turn in for the night, I have something for you."

Surprise mingled with a growing warmth in my chest as I turned back to her. "You didn't need to get me anything," I replied softly.

Without another word, we walked back into the palace parlor, stepping through the arched doors that led from the balcony.

Inside, her personal guard stood by her luggage—an impressive collection of trunks and boxes waiting to be moved to her guest quarters. I glanced at the array, silently marveling at the sheer volume of items she had brought with her.

From the pile, Aure pulled a long wooden box, its length nearly matching her height. Her smile brightened, and her eyes sparkled with excitement as she held it out to me. "Here, Orla, open it," she urged, practically vibrating with anticipation.

Taking the hinged box carefully, I opened it slowly. As the lid lifted, the light caught the object within, gleaming brilliantly. I gasped softly, staring in awe at the most exquisitely detailed broadsword I had ever seen. Its intricate decorations shimmered with artistry and craftsmanship beyond anything I could have imagined.

"I forged it myself," Aure said eagerly, her voice tinged with pride. "Well, with help from my dwarven teacher. I do a lot of art and crafting, but you seemed like the kind of woman who'd appreciate a sword over some jeweled trinket."

I stood mesmerized, my fingers brushing the flawless surface of the blade. Overwhelmed by the emotions swirling inside me, my eyes shifted between shades of purple and blue. "It's… beautiful," I murmured, my voice barely above a whisper. I hesitated before adding, "But I've never wielded a two-handed sword before."

For a moment, surprise flashed across her face, but it quickly melted into a warm smile. She turned to her royal guard, placing a hand on the woman's arm. "Cambria here is my personal guard and usually trains me in combat. She's excellent with broadswords. I'm sure she wouldn't mind showing you a few techniques in a training session or two. Would you, Cam?"

Cambria bowed deeply, her tone firm and respectful. "It would be my honor, Your Highness."

I hesitated, unsure but trying not to let it show. "Okay… will you be there too, Aure?" I offered her a small, polite smile.

Beaming, she turned to me. "Of course! It's a date. Would Pyros morning at dawn work for you? It's in just a few days and is my usual weekly day for combat training."

I nodded, though my stomach tightened into a nervous knot. Straightening my posture, I said, "Yes, that works. I suppose I should send for someone to take you and your things to your guest quarters." My fingers brushed the sword one last time before I closed the box and set it gently on the table.

Aure's gaze softened as she replied, "That would be very helpful. It's been a long day, and I'm starting to feel the weight of it."

I called for servants, who arrived promptly to begin moving her trunks and boxes. A small parade of attendants filed out of the room, winding through the foyer and up the grand staircase toward the east wing. For a moment, we stood in silence, watching them go. Realizing my manners, I turned to her. "Would you like me to show you to your rooms?"

She hesitated before responding, her voice tentative. "If it's not too much trouble, thank you."

Falling into step behind the last servant, I waited for Aure and Cambria to follow. We walked together, just behind the procession. I noticed Aure's gaze sweeping over the vast columns in the foyer and the art that adorned the walls—tapestries and paintings depicting vibrant animals, prairies, and serene ponds. Her fingers trailed along the thick oak banister, just behind mine, as we ascended the grand staircase.

We entered the west wing, the wooden-floored halls lined with relics and rich décor. The high ceilings amplified the glow of the lamps, their amber light casting elongated shadows that flickered across the closed doors as we passed.

At last, we reached a set of double doors at the end of the hall. Pushing them open revealed a spacious parlor-style room with a table and chairs, several sofas, and a chaise arranged on one side. Shelves lined another wall, holding books, while a small wooden desk trimmed in gold stood nearby. Beyond the parlor, another set of double doors opened into the bedroom, dominated by a large plush bed piled high with pillows and furs. The servants carefully arranged her trunks and boxes by the wardrobe before filing out.

I watched as Aure turned in a slow circle, taking everything in. Her wide-eyed wonder brought a smile to my lips, and I couldn't help but chuckle. "Do you like it?"

She stopped and met my gaze, her expression warm. "Orla, it's wonderful. I think I'll be very comfortable here. Thank you."

Feeling a bit awkward, I replied, "You're welcome. I hope you have a good night. See you soon." I gave a slight bow and turned to leave. As I passed Cambria, her eyes swept over me, her expression unreadable. I hurried past her, feeling my cheeks warm.

"Good night, Orla. See you soon," Aure called from the bedroom, waving at me.

I didn't turn back, my steps quickening down the hall. My hands trembled as I reached my own room. Letting out a sigh, I stepped inside the familiar comfort of my sanctuary. Closing the door behind me, I leaned against it, my emotions swirling. Finally, I allowed myself to relax, preparing to turn in for the night.

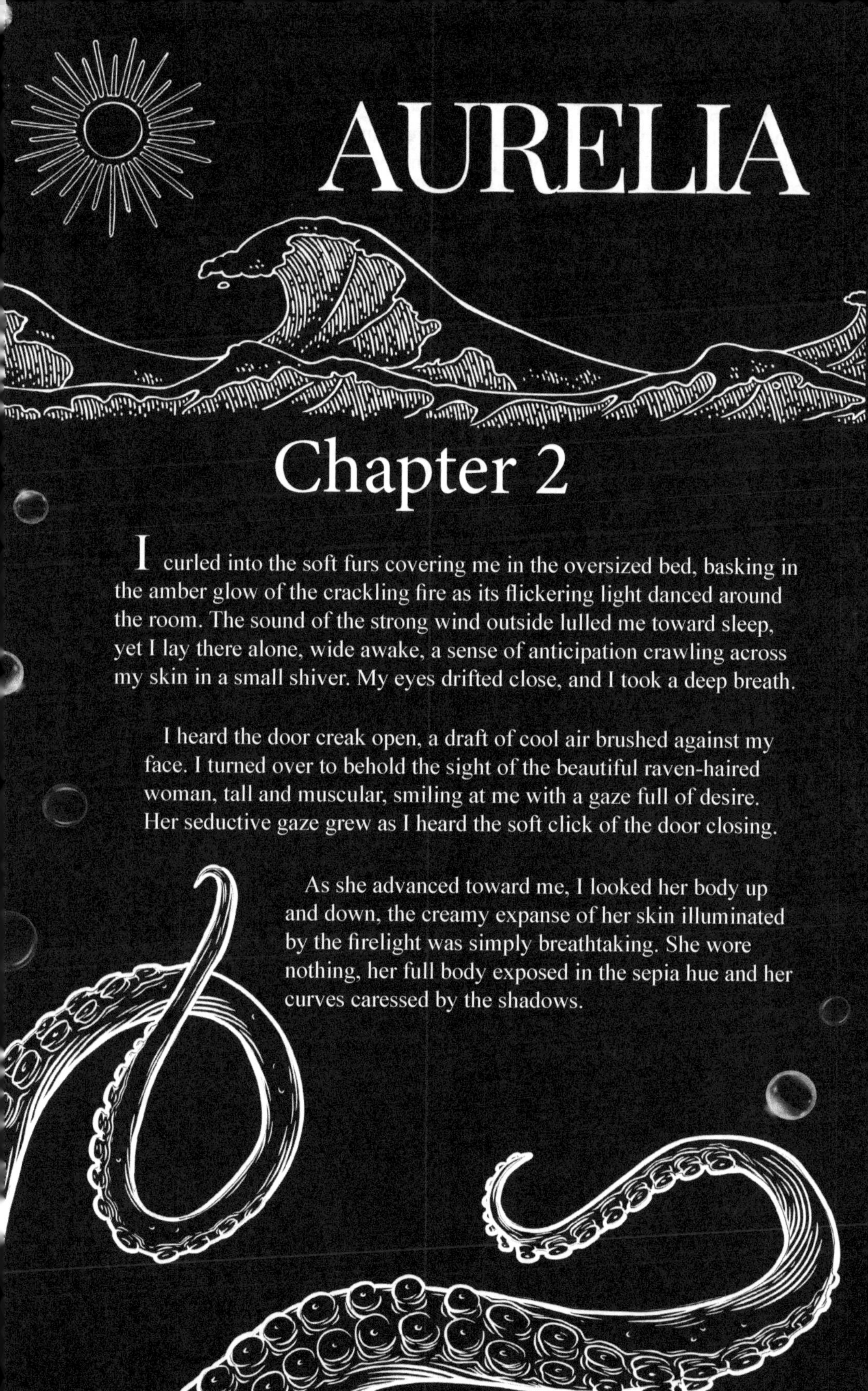

AURELIA

Chapter 2

I curled into the soft furs covering me in the oversized bed, basking in the amber glow of the crackling fire as its flickering light danced around the room. The sound of the strong wind outside lulled me toward sleep, yet I lay there alone, wide awake, a sense of anticipation crawling across my skin in a small shiver. My eyes drifted close, and I took a deep breath.

I heard the door creak open, a draft of cool air brushed against my face. I turned over to behold the sight of the beautiful raven-haired woman, tall and muscular, smiling at me with a gaze full of desire. Her seductive gaze grew as I heard the soft click of the door closing.

As she advanced toward me, I looked her body up and down, the creamy expanse of her skin illuminated by the firelight was simply breathtaking. She wore nothing, her full body exposed in the sepia hue and her curves caressed by the shadows.

My breath quickened, and my heart raced as Orla's gaze met mine, magnetic and intense. Her hand reached out, fingers grazing my cheek, and I leaned into her touch instinctively. My eyes fluttered shut as a soft breath escaped my lips, the warmth of her skin igniting a fire within me.

"How can you possibly be so cold under all those furs, Meles Tari?" she teased, her voice low and laced with amusement.

I grinned in return, playful despite the heat pooling in my core. "And how are you not freezing, standing there naked like that?"

With a chuckle, I pulled back the covers and scooted over, making room for her beneath the furs. She climbed onto the bed, her body brushing against mine as I replaced the silken layers over us both.

Her hand gripped my hip gently but firmly, pulling me close. I nuzzled under her chin, her fingers drawing slow, teasing paths up my spine. I kissed the side of her neck as she let out a soft breath. Her scent—rose and sandalwood—filled my senses, intoxicating me. Smirking, I bit my lower lip softly as I felt her hand slide down to the crease of my ass. She grabbed it with possessive tenderness. Her hand then pulled my top leg over hers and threaded hers between my thighs.

Our eyes met, her gaze now a swirling magenta. My body responded instinctively, a soft moan escaping my lips as she cupped my soft, lush breast in her hand and dipped her head towards it, licking me from my collarbone towards the peak of my firming nipple. I shuddered as her lips enclosed around the swell and drew my nipple into her mouth between her teeth, drawing a quick breath in response.

Her lips curled into a smile as her tongue twirled around my eager nipple. Liquid heat filled my center, and a rush of desire ran up my spine as I arched into her touch, moaning. I gripped the sheets beneath me as she slowly moved, not only her mouth sucking me in but also her leg between mine, her hand now firmly holding the crest of my ass.

Orla tangled her other hand in my hair on the back of my head and with her body, she pushed me onto my back. Her lips claimed mine in an all-consuming kiss, our tongues exploring the depths of one another. Her hand held my head gently as her other trailed up my side in soft, teasing touches. The warmth spreading from her hands to every part of me she touched sent a surge of desire curling in my stomach.

My hands settled on her strong hips as she slowly churned them, pointedly moving not only herself against my upper thigh but the leg that she still had solid between mine. Her groan mixing between our kisses sparked my breath to hitch as I felt the wet from her slicking my thigh.

My breathing was heavy. I broke our kiss to quench my need for air, biting my lower lip again. Her smirk grew as she reached between us and found the hot sticky depth between my legs, her middle finger finding its mark, the focal point of my pleasure, a pulsating nub of sensation yearning for her embrace.

I couldn't contain the low murmurs of desire escaping my lips as her touch continued to stir the flames of want and need. She moved more fiercely against me, my need to return the pleasure filled me as my hand slipped from her hip to my thigh as I teased it between us, garnering a groan from her.

I felt her pressing harder, and she dipped, enclosing her mouth around mine in a passionate kiss. Our bodies move in perfect harmony, each touch a symphony of sensation that was building toward a crescendo of shared ecstasy.

Breathlessly, I looked deeply into her eyes, into the swirling magenta color, as I moaned louder, feeling close to the edge.

"Please don't stop," the plea was a whisper against her mouth. Her forehead pressed against mine, her smile an inch from me, and her movements were response enough for me. She slipped her hand lower, pressing into me. My mouth parted as I felt another moan escape me, my breath heady.

The tension coiled tighter and tighter until I could take no more. My back arched into her touch as I lost all sense of rhythm.

"Please," I begged, my voice only a husky whisper, and she captured my mouth again in a fervent kiss, her movements driving me closer to the brink.

I awoke with a start, breathless and hot, aching in my whole body, desire deep inside, and everything starved for the touch that I so vividly dreamt. The remnants of it clung to me like a heavy fog, clouding my mind as I sat up in bed, unable to catch my breath.

Gripping the blanket beneath me, I attempted to regain control of my racing heart and swirling thoughts. The room felt unfamiliar, shadows cast by the firelight twisting into shapes that seemed to mock my unease. I wiped the dampness from my face, my chest heaving as I tried to steady my breathing.

It hadn't been that long since I last had a foresight dream, those haunting visions that both terrified and intrigued me. Some of my people, the Siren, view them as a curse, a burden that weighs heavily on those who possess the magical gift. Others see them as a blessing, a glimpse into the mysteries of the future that only a few are privileged to witness. At this moment, I aligned more with the former, feeling the weight of my abilities pressing down on me like an oppressive force.

I loosened my grip on the bedding as my breathing gradually returned to normal. I couldn't shake the lingering desire for her, Orla, that still burned deep inside me. Despite the uncertainty and trepidation that flooded my mind, her presence lingered like a ghost in the recesses of my thoughts, a constant reminder of the tangled web of emotions that bound us together.

The events of the dream replayed in my mind, each detail etched into my memory with painful clarity. The intimacy and intensity of it left me feeling raw and exposed, my emotions swirling in a tumultuous sea of longing and confusion. *Would we ever find that type of bliss in each other, or was it just a fleeting illusion that taunted me with its unattainable promise?*

No matter the amount of hope or joy I felt, my visions have never ended well or happily before. This dream, though, didn't seem like any I have ever had. That beautiful and intoxicating person in my dream appeared and smelled like Orla. But it was a very different version of her. That dream version was nothing like the woman I had only met a few days before.

Her anger and resentment towards our forced union was palpable, lurking beneath the surface of her composed facade of duty and civility, like a dormant volcano waiting to erupt. It was evident that she is devoted to her kingdom and is honorable. Despite her outward defiance, there was a vulnerability in her eyes that spoke volumes, a silent plea for understanding and acceptance that tugged at my heartstrings.

However, after our first conversation, she had been aloof and found excuses not to entertain me or even merely have a conversation. I should have expected as much with my father's demands of King Oric. I hated that the need for such an arrangement was even still necessary, but our history had been full of various marriage contracts for allyship, which was the custom for thousands of years. Most had become positive stories in our history.

I sat on the edge of the bed, the night chill invaded me. I shivered as a draft swept through the room, the cold seeping into my bones like an unwelcome intruder. I was not accustomed to the harsh climate of this foreign land, its icy grip a constant reminder of my status as an outsider in this unfamiliar kingdom.

A spark of magic pulsed through me, drawing my attention to the glowing marks down my left arm—the signet rune of my bond with Azuraitha, my Sea Dragon. The dream must have triggered the signet rune, which only activated when I truly needed her or sought her presence.

I opened my conscious space to a flood of concern and curiosity. *"Aure, our bond awoke me. Are you alright?"* The melodious voice resonated in my mind, a comfort I had grown accustomed to since bonding with my beloved Azura. Her worry warmed me, yet it also stirred guilt.

I vividly recalled my mother's teachings about Sea Dragons from my childhood. She described them as the guardians of the Siren and lifelong companions, their bond with us sacred and unbreakable. Her voice was always gentle yet filled with reverence as she shared our people's traditions with me.

"Aure," she once said, her tone both instructive and tender, "every Siren has the opportunity to bond with a Sea Dragon who is ready to find its mate. They serve as our guardians, and we, in turn, ensure the continuation of their bloodlines. This bond is something that is created during an Auqarune rite, forged through the mixing of blood and magic to create matching signet runes inked onto both bodies. It's a bond for life, a rite of passage into adulthood for both Siren and dragon. It transcends mere companionship."

Her ocean-blue eyes sparkled as she added, "Remember, my love, Sea Dragons can only find their lifelong mate with the aid of our Siren's song. I will pass this sacred knowledge to you during your coming-of-age rituals, your Enkindling, just as it was passed to me."

I remembered looking up at her with wide, eager eyes, curiosity bubbling inside me. "When will I get to bond with a Sea Dragon, Momma?" I asked, my voice was full of excitement.

She had smiled warmly, pulling me into her embrace. "Typically around the age of sixteen, darling. That's when our inherent gifts begin to manifest—that is the Enkindling. Soon enough, you'll be so grown up." Her voice softened, and she gently tucked one of my curls of hair behind my ear. "But for now, just enjoy being a child, won't you?"

Even now, I felt a deep gratitude for the wisdom she had shared, not just hers but also that of the Siren Elders who stood by her. Their teachings remained etched in my heart, a steady compass guiding me through the tides of my destiny.

I worked to steady my breathing, sending waves of calm and reassurance down the mental bond to Azura. *"Yes, I will be alright,"* I conveyed softly, willing her to feel the conviction I struggled to summon. Her concern pressed against my mind, but I knew it wouldn't end well for either of us if she continued to fret. The distance between us made everything harder—normally, I confided in her about everything—but she needed her rest, especially now.

A soft knock at the door pulled me from my thoughts. I turned to see Cambria slipping inside, her movements quiet and precise, a look of concern etched into her features.

"Azura, Cam is here. Please rest and don't worry about me," I sent through the bond, my mental voice as firm as I could manage. I felt Azura's lingering annoyance and unease before her presence faded, the glow of my signet dimming as she reluctantly withdrew.

Turning back to Cam, I watched her approach with a silent grace honed by years of service. Her steady presence was a balm to my frayed nerves, though I could still sense the weight of her worry as she drew closer.

Her presence brought a small measure of comfort to the turmoil swirling inside me. Cambria draped a warm quilt around my shoulders and sat beside me on the bed, her movements deliberate and steady. She sighed softly, her voice low and soothing. "I heard you."

Her words, though meant to calm, only deepened the tension gripping my chest. "Did you have another dream?" she asked.

I clenched the quilt tighter, heat rushing to my cheeks. Unable to meet her gaze, I nodded silently, the storm of emotions bubbling inside me too tangled to articulate. How could I explain the conflicting waves of desire and despair that consumed me with each passing moment?

Cam softly took a seat beside me on the bed and tilted her head slightly, her eyes filled with genuine concern. "How bad was it this time?"

I looked away, unable to face her gentle scrutiny. My eyes drifted to the tall glass windows, their muted stars offering a momentary reprieve from the chaos within me. The faint, silvery light painted the room in hushed tones.

I didn't want to admit, not even to myself, that this dream felt different— more vivid, more intimate—than any I'd experienced before. And I certainly couldn't share that truth with Cam.

As I sat there, feeling the crushing weight of loneliness, memories from the first foresight dream I ever had surged to the forefront of my mind. They crashed over me like a tidal wave, raw and relentless. That memory had become etched into the very fabric of my being, a haunting reminder of life's fragility and the inexorable flow of fate.

In that moment, my memories flooded back to a little over ten years ago—a time when my world shattered by tragedy and loss. That night, it wasn't just a dream. It was a haunting glimpse into the event that would devastate my entire being — the death of my mother. Even now, I could feel the crushing weight of it, the overwhelming sense of helplessness as I watched the events unfold, unable to alter the course of fate.

I was nearly sixteen then, my powers still in their infancy, barely grasping the depth of what I possessed. Yet, in that dream, I saw everything as though I stood there, a silent witness to the unraveling of a life so dear to me, my mother, the Queen Cliodhna of Faedamir.

My mother was more than just a leader; she was the embodiment of our people's strength and wisdom. As a powerful Siren, her presence commanded respect, and her gifts were revered by all who knew her. From her, I inherited not only my lineage but also the weighty responsibility to carry forward our traditions and safeguard our legacy.

In the lore of our kind, the passing of knowledge from parent to child, elder to babe, is sacred. Our magic, ancient and potent, flows through our veins regardless of the purity of our bloodline. Even a drop of Siren blood has been said to carry the gifts—and burdens—of our heritage. Unlike some magical races, such as the enigmatic Fae or the industrious Dwarfs, who often view mixed ancestry with disdain, our Siren heritage embraces diversity. Our magic knows no bounds of blood percentage; we welcome all who carry even the faintest trace of our blood.

Despite the mingling of Human ancestry through my father, I was undeniably tied to my Siren heritage. Raised by the elders, I was nurtured in my abilities and guided in the ways of our magic. Now, I stand poised to assume the mantle of leadership my mother once carried—the role of High Priestess and leader of the Siren. But with this immense weight of expectation and destiny, uncertainty lingers.

The dream that haunted my youth, foretelling the loss of my mother, serves as a constant reminder of the unpredictability of my magic. Through many challenges, I have grown more confident in my abilities, gaining control over most of my powers as I step closer to my destiny as the Queen of the Western Isles. Yet, my dreams remain the most unpredictable—and the most difficult— aspect of my magic to accept.

My parents created a kingdom rooted in diversity and harmony, and I have always felt a strong desire to honor their legacy. I long to be everything my mother hoped I would become. But as I sit here, lost in memories of the past and fears for the future, I can't help but wish she were here now to guide me through these metaphorical stormy seas.

Cambria's gentle touch brought me back to the present, her quiet presence a balm to my frayed nerves. Her unwavering support anchored me amid the chaos of my emotions, a beacon of light cutting through the darkness that threatened to consume me.

Tears threatened to spill as I whispered, my voice thick with emotion, "I miss my mother, Cam. She would know what to do with everything."

Cam's hand moved gently across my back, her touch steady and grounding. My heart swelled with gratitude for her unwavering presence, a steady anchor in my turbulent world.

"I know, my Princess," she said softly, her voice carrying the weight of understanding. "But you are not alone."

She wrapped an arm around me, warmth seeping into my chilled skin. I leaned into her embrace, letting the comfort of her steady support wash over me. For a moment, I allowed myself to feel gratitude for this loyal friend who stood by me without question, her strength bolstering my own.

As Cam rested her chin lightly on my head, she murmured, "I'm always here for you, Aure. Whatever you need."

I pulled back slightly, meeting her gaze with a warm smile. "I know, Cam. I just don't know how to deal with this whole thing." I hesitated, searching for the right words. "I like Orla a lot; however, she seems so angry. It feels like she won't even try to get to know me. I understand our arrangement isn't ideal, but…"

My voice faltered, and I sighed. "I feel connected to her in a way I haven't felt with anyone before."

I paused, wrestling with emotions I struggled to articulate. *I can't explain it to make sense of it myself, let alone to anyone else, especially her.* I couldn't explain the inexplicable pull I felt toward Orla—the way it both excited and terrified me.

Cam holds me in silence, her embrace a comforting anchor in the storm of my emotions. Finally, she spoke, her voice calm and steady. "My Princess, try to rest before the day begins. Perhaps one day, Princess Orla will see you as I do."

Her words carried a quiet confidence that I clung to. Cam offered me a small smile, nodding as she stood. I watched her retreat toward the door, her steps silent and measured.

As I lay back in my bed, exhaustion settled over me like a heavy blanket. The door clicked shut, and I let my eyes drift close, finding solace in the stillness of the room. For the first time in what felt like an eternity, sleep came easily, unbroken by dreams.

ORLA

Chapter 3

The sun began to rise casting the front lawn of the castle in hues of pink and gold. Dew glistened on the blades of grass. The tranquil ambiance of the brisk early morning held the promise of a peaceful day that the sounds of our clanking swords would soon contrast.

With the beautiful gold broadsword in hand, a gift I held reluctantly, I stood ready for combat training. The morning light danced on the blade as Aurelia and her Royal Guard, Cam, approached.

"Good morning, Meles Tari," My lips curled into a half smirk, my tone full of sass as I gave a curt bow to Aurelia who seemed more than surprised by my greeting. Perhaps she knew some of the ancient Fae language herself.

"Good morning, Orla," Aurelia replied tersely.

Cam bowed toward me and greeted, "Your Highness." Before she assumed the poised stance of a skilled instructor ready to guide us. I observed Aurelia growing a mischievous glint in her eyes as she moved gracefully around us. I was unsure what had sparked this new sense of flirtation.

Cam was fully prepared to guide me through the intricate steps, which I was eager to learn, to expand my knowledge and combat skills. The sword I held was surprisingly light for a broadsword, which felt closer to that of my rapier. I gripped the blade tightly with a mix of determination and anticipation.

Aurelia's presence, however, filled the morning air with an unexpected sweetness that left me feeling nervous. My eyes shifted; they matched the blue of the morning sky from the steady lavender I sought to maintain.

The tension between us built as our blades clashed. Cam's instructions echoed in my mind, but Aurelia's words pulled my attention. "You swing that sword as if settling a score, Orla. Is there a particular adversary in your thoughts?" cooed Aure in a combative melody.

My eyes narrowed and deepened in hue, catching the subtle challenge in her voice. "Perhaps, Meles Tari, I'm envisioning an opponent who insists on complicating matters that should be straightforward."

Cam, with a knowing look, interjected, "In combat, your Highness, hesitation can be as lethal as a poorly aimed strike. Trust your instincts."

I watched Aurelia circle closer, her eyes locked with mine. "Matters like arranged marriages and alliances, I presume?" Her voice hushed with a sound like dripping decadent honey.

The clash of our blades intensified, mirroring my conflicting emotions beneath the surface. "You presume correctly, Princess. But don't mistake reluctance for weakness." I grunted as I stepped forward into a strike she effortlessly blocked.

Cam nodded approvingly, adding, "Reluctance is a natural response to the unknown. Embrace it, and let it fuel your determination."

Aure stepped close again, holding our blades in a lock, and whispered in a voice that carried a hint of amusement. "Reluctance can be a guise for many things, Orla. Perhaps it conceals a desire you're not willing to admit."

I gritted my teeth, frustration bubbling beneath my controlled exterior, my eyes betraying me by flashing cobalt. "Desire has no place in matters of duty. It only complicates what should be straightforward."

Cam, with a reassuring tone, chimed in, "Desire, when harnessed, can be a powerful driving force. It adds depth to your actions and purpose."

Aurelia's gaze held a challenge, a spark of defiance mingling with an undeniable attraction. "Duty without desire is a cold existence, Orla. Even in combat, one must find the fire within."

As the blades met in a rhythmic dance, Cam continued to instruct me with precision. It seemed Aure couldn't resist adding more to the proceedings, though. "Feel the sword, Orla. Let it become an extension of yourself," she suggested, her voice carrying softness in contrast to the sharp tone she had been giving me.

Catching a hint of an underlying flirtation, I shot Aurelia a guarded glance. "Is that a lesson on swordsmanship or matters of the heart, Princess?"

Aurelia stepped close, locking blades once more with me in the gentle dawn light. "Perhaps both, my dear. The dance of blades is not unlike the dance of hearts—one must be attuned to the nuances." Reluctantly I played along, following her lead, the unspoken connection between us deepening with every move.

Cam, though focused on the training, interjected, her voice firm yet laced with wisdom. "Strength lies in acknowledging one's inner conflicts, Your Highness. It's the essence of mastering swordplay and perhaps also the complexities of the heart." As the two of us continued the intricate dance, Cam's guidance became a steady presence.

Cam shouted over the beat of our sparring, "Your Highness, feel the rhythm of the blade, but also the rhythm of your own heartbeat. Your strength is not just in the swing, but in the intention behind it."

Aurelia seized the moment again, adding her own cryptic layer. "Intentions can be elusive, Cam. Sometimes, they hide behind duty and reluctance." As we continued the dance of blades, the atmosphere crackled with both conflict and a magnetic pull.

The sunrise bore witness to a training session that transcended the physical. Delving into the realms of anger, attraction, and the unspoken complexities of our intertwined destinies. In the quiet moments between strikes, I couldn't deny the truth in Aurelia's words, leaving me to grapple not only with the weight of steel but also with the unresolved emotions within myself.

As the training came to an end, I was left breathless but exhilarated, however conflicted still. I walked away from the lawn to put my sword in its box as servants brought out refreshments of water and fruit on silver trays, offering it to the princess and her guard. Cam refused refreshments and instead started to walk towards me.

Her approach bore the weight of unspoken questions, her eyes a canvas of concern and suspicion. "Your Highness," she began, her voice a low murmur carrying a hint of caution. "There's a guardedness about you. What are you truly fighting against?"

I opened the box, but her words caused my fingers to tighten around the hilt of my blade, its reassuring weight grounding me amid uncertainty. As my emotions swelled, I felt a spark of magic surging through the blade, but I ignored it.

"I fight against obligations," my tone flat, the admission hanging in the air, before I added. "And against a future dictated by political alliances rather than personal choice."

Cam's perceptive eyes met mine, and I felt her scrutiny delving deeper. "And what about the woman observing us?" She glanced toward Aure. "Do you feel any connection with her?"

A pause lingered as I navigated the labyrinth of my thoughts. "Our connection is one of duty," I finally confessed. "not of choice. An arrangement for the greater good, or so they all claim."

Cam, fiercely protective of Aurelia, scrutinized my response with a tinge of jealousy. "She may be a princess, but she's more than a pawn in a political game. There's a fire in her, a spark that refuses to be extinguished. Have you not felt it? She aims to be a great ruler."

Vulnerability flickered through me, I could feel my eyes swirl blue and purple, a glimpse beneath the façade. "I've seen her fire, yes, but I have felt only conflicting currents from her," I stated. "But duty has been my steadfast anchor."

Aure approached, her presence bridging the unspoken tensions. Cam's protective stance softened into a casual smile, concealing the depths of our conversation.

The tension dissipated like morning mist as Frank Lavaburn, one of my Royal Guards with a knack for getting us into strange situations, loudly sauntered onto the lawn. His presence was a great relief for me. Being half Dwarf, he was taller than most Dwarfs, even for his small stature, a fact he won't soon let you forget. The infectious sound of his laughter seemed to echo through the castle grounds.

"Orla, my favorite partner in crime!" Frank bellowed, his eyes sparkling with mischief as he approached. "I heard there was some top-notch swordplay happenin', and I couldn't resist joinin' the party. Though it seems I have missed the lot of it."

Relief washed over me, a welcome reprieve from the weighty exchanges that had transpired moments ago. "Frank, you couldn't have come at a better time." A genuine smile playing on my lips. "Allow me to introduce Her Highness Princess Aurelia of Faedamir and her personal royal guard and combat instructor, Cambria. Please meet Frank Lavaburn, the castle's resident prankster, and a surprisingly skilled warrior."

Frank bowed low to Aurelia, who smiled curtly at him. "All the pleasure of meetin' you, your Highness," he grinned.

Cam's eyes narrowed in scrutiny as she sized up Frank. His flamboyant demeanor and flirtatious grin seemed to catch her off guard, a stark contrast to the intensity she seemed to adorn. Frank, undeterred by her guarded demeanor, extended a hand in greeting.

"Pleasure to meet you as well, lovely Lady of the Swords," Frank crooned, his charm oozing like a full honeycomb. "If I may be so bold, you and your Princess' beauty is a sight for sore eyes amongst all the rough creatures here."

Cam's response was a measured nod, her skepticism unyielding. I couldn't help but chuckle at the dichotomy between the two. The serious, stoic-composed Cam and the irreverent, charismatic Frank.

"Frank, we were just finishing up here," I explained, eager to redirect the focus. "Cam guided Aure and me in some rather intense training."

Frank's eyes twinkled with mischief. "Well, I hate I missed out on all the fun. How about a round in the sparrin' ring, Orla? Or are you too worn out? I've been itchin' for a small challenge, and it seems our new friends here," he winked at Cam. "Could use a bit of entertainment."

Cam's expression shifted from guarded to incredulous, clearly unprepared for Frank's unorthodox approach. I seized the opportunity to divert attention and diffuse the tension.

"A sparring round or two sounds like just the thing I need to cool down, Frank," I agreed, shooting a grateful glance his way. "Let's head to the training grounds. Aure, you and Cam are welcome to join us if you care to see where we train our renowned warriors." Aure gave an eager nod and nudged a reluctant Cam.

The sparring ring, our perennial battlefield, welcomed the clash of fists. The intricate dance of hand-to-hand combat began to unfold beneath the watchful eyes of Cam and Aurelia.

Frank, with his flamboyant charm and surprisingly adept combat skills, circled me with a confident grin. "Ready for a taste of Lavaburn's brilliance?" Frank quipped, his eyes gleaming with playful arrogance.

I rolled my eyes, a smirk playing on my lips. "Brilliance might be a stretch, but I'm always up for a challenge, Frank."

As the first strike rang out, our movements were a flurry of precision and counterattacks. Frank's agility belied his stout frame; each dodge and parry was executed with a finesse that defied expectations. Despite his penchant for jest, he was a formidable opponent, and the sparring match promised to be anything but predictable.

Frank had been my long-time companion and comrade, now standing opposite me, a mischievous glint in his eyes that matched his cocky grin. We had sparred countless times before, our movements a seamless fusion of familiarity and rivalry.

Cam observed us with a scrutinizing gaze, her stoic demeanor giving away little. Beside her, Aure watched with a mixture of fascination and amusement, her eyes flickering between the two of us. I couldn't help but wonder how much of Aure's fascination was directed at the sparring and how much lingered on the enigmatic royal guard by her side.

"Come on, Orla! Loosen up a bit," he teased, effortlessly dodging my swift jab. "You're gettin' hitched to a real beauty, and you've got this perpetual frown like the world's about to end."

I shot him an exasperated look, blocking his incoming strike. "Frank, this isn't exactly the time for celebration. It is simply my duty, and I've got responsibilities to uphold."

He chuckled, a sound as hearty as his stature was diminutive. "Responsibilities, shmonsibilities. You've got the chance to spend your days with a stunnin' woman whose head over heels for you. Lighten up!" I shot him a confused glance as I looked over at Aure, cheering for me. Suddenly, I got hit by Frank's right hook and landed on my ass.

"Well, well, looks like Lavaburn's brilliance strikes again," he declared, a triumphant smirk spreading across his face.

I chuckled, conceding defeat for the moment. "Impressive, Frank. I suppose your brilliance isn't entirely overstated." As I grabbed his outstretched hand hopping back to my feet.

Our banter continued as we danced around each other, the rhythm of our sparring punctuated by Frank's playful comments. Amidst the agility and precision of our movements, he seized every opportunity to nudge me toward his more carefree perspective.

"You know, Orla, I've got a sixth sense for these things," Frank said, feigning a secretive tone. "Love's a complicated business, and I reckon you're caught up in a storm of emotions. Why don't you spill the beans to old Lavaburn?"

I rolled my eyes, a mixture of irritation and amusement. "Frank, you're impossible. Can't a person have some privacy?"

He winked, his grin widening. "Privacy's overrated. Besides, I'm the best listener this side of the castle. Confide in me, Orla. Sometimes, sharin' the load makes the journey easier."

In the pauses between strikes, I found myself confiding in Frank about the conflicting emotions swirling within me. "It's not that simple, Frank. Yes, Aurelia is beautiful, and I'm honored by this duty, but it feels like I'm caught between tradition and the desires of my heart."

Frank nodded knowingly, his eyes glancing toward Aure with an air of mischief. "Well, maybe she is more of what your heart desires than you care to admit. Spice up the routine of duty a bit, you know?"

I sighed, feeling the weight of both duty and desire. "It's not about showing off. It's about navigating uncharted waters. Also, feelings and desires aren't my concern right now."

Frank, ever the showman, grinned and executed a series of flashy moves, deliberately drawing Cam's attention. "Beautiful Lady of swords, feast your eyes on the Lavaburn brilliance! Maybe you need a bit of this in your life."

As Frank continued his display, I couldn't help but smile at his antics. In the midst of the physical exertion and the lively banter, I found a temporary reprieve from the complexities of my emotions.

As we caught our breath, I noticed Cam's measured expression and Aure's infectious laughter. Little did I know, Frank's playful encouragement and flashy performance would become a catalyst for introspection, challenging me to consider a path that balanced duty and personal fulfillment.

As I exited the ring, breathless and exhilarated, Aurelia approached, and the magnetic energy between us was undeniable. Her presence stirred a whirlwind of emotions within me, challenging my efforts to maintain composure. I felt as my eyes betrayed me, shifting blue, revealing the depth of my feelings.

As Aure smiled at me, her words brought a warmth that I can't help but reciprocate with a smile of my own. "You're a skilled warrior with excellent form, Orla."

"Thank you," I responded sincerely. "You're quite skilled yourself."

"Broadswords, daggers, and archery. Those are my three combat areas. You seemed to be far more versed in combat than me." Aure replied as a soft smile played across her lips.

"I've had plenty of practice, thanks to this never-ending war," I reply with a hint of bitterness.

She frowned. "Is there no plan for resolution to the war with Frostspire?"

My tone sharpens as my magic swelled and my eyes turned cobalt blue. "The end will only come when we bring down the King of Frostspire from his tower and feed him to his wolves," I assert firmly.

Aurelia's expression grows concerned. "So, there's no hope for a peace treaty, then?" She asked.

I meet her gaze squarely. "He'll never agree to any humane terms," I replied curtly.

Aurelia's gentle touch on my hand surprises me, her thumb tracing soothing circles that have me momentarily frozen in surprise. "If there is no way for peace, then together we will stand strong and defeat the evil bearing down upon us, even if it means killing the King of the North," she declares with resolve.

Her words and touch brought a sense of resolve to my heart, reminding me I am not alone in this war. Yet, the flood of emotions overwhelmed me, and I gently pulled away, squeezing her hand in acknowledgment.

I turned to find Frank on his knees in front of a bewildered Cam, and Aure followed my amused gaze, erupting into laughter at the scene before us. I shook my head and whispered to Aurelia, "He's relentless. He won't stop until Cam either kicks him on his ass or gives in." We shared a chuckle, the momentary levity was a welcome relief amidst the gravity of our conversation.

I smile as I reminisce about my first encounter with my best friend, Frank. It was shortly after my 19th birthday, and I had just wrapped up a long day of training in the barracks. I decided to unwind at the local pub, which had grown common for me at the time.

Surprisingly, I found Frank, a rather tall Dwarf, engaged in a brawl with three burly men from my guard. Despite being outnumbered, he was holding his own, effortlessly dispatching his opponents while casually sipping ale between blows. I stood there in shock, watching him crack jokes and jaws alike.

After the dust settled and the men lay defeated, Frank sauntered over to me, his demeanor brimming with confidence. "Hey there, pretty Lady, did you enjoy the show?" he quipped.

I couldn't help but laugh. "I think you should consider joining my royal guards," I replied, half-jokingly.

His response, however, lacked the same levity, his combat prowess evident as he remarked, "Would it make it easier for me to gain entry to your bed chamber if I did?"

Despite his audacious comment, I chuckled, running my hand through my short hair. "Fuck no," I retorted, "but we could certainly use skilled warriors like yourself in this war that has started with the North."

Frank downed the rest of his drink and turned to me, a hint of curiosity in his eyes. "Alright, buy me another ale, and let's discuss what your army is willin' to pay for my services," he said with a grin. That began a friendship that had endured the passing years, growing stronger with each shared victory and hardship.

Frank's nudge of my arm jolted me out of my thoughts as Cam whispered something to Aure, who then turned to me, offering a slight bow. "I am needed elsewhere now. Thank you both for a delightful morning. I hope to see you again soon, Orla." She spoke politely before she and Cam made their way towards the palace.

I glanced at Frank and let out a sigh. "Is it too early for ale?" I asked, half-serious.

Frank chuckled in response. "It's never too early for ale, but I doubt the pub is open at this hour. We might have to settle for ale in your quarters," he suggested with a grin.

I laughed and teased, "Still trying to find your way into my bed chambers, are we?"

He shook his head, a playful glint in his eyes. "Fuck no," he retorted, and we both shared a hearty laugh.

AURELIA

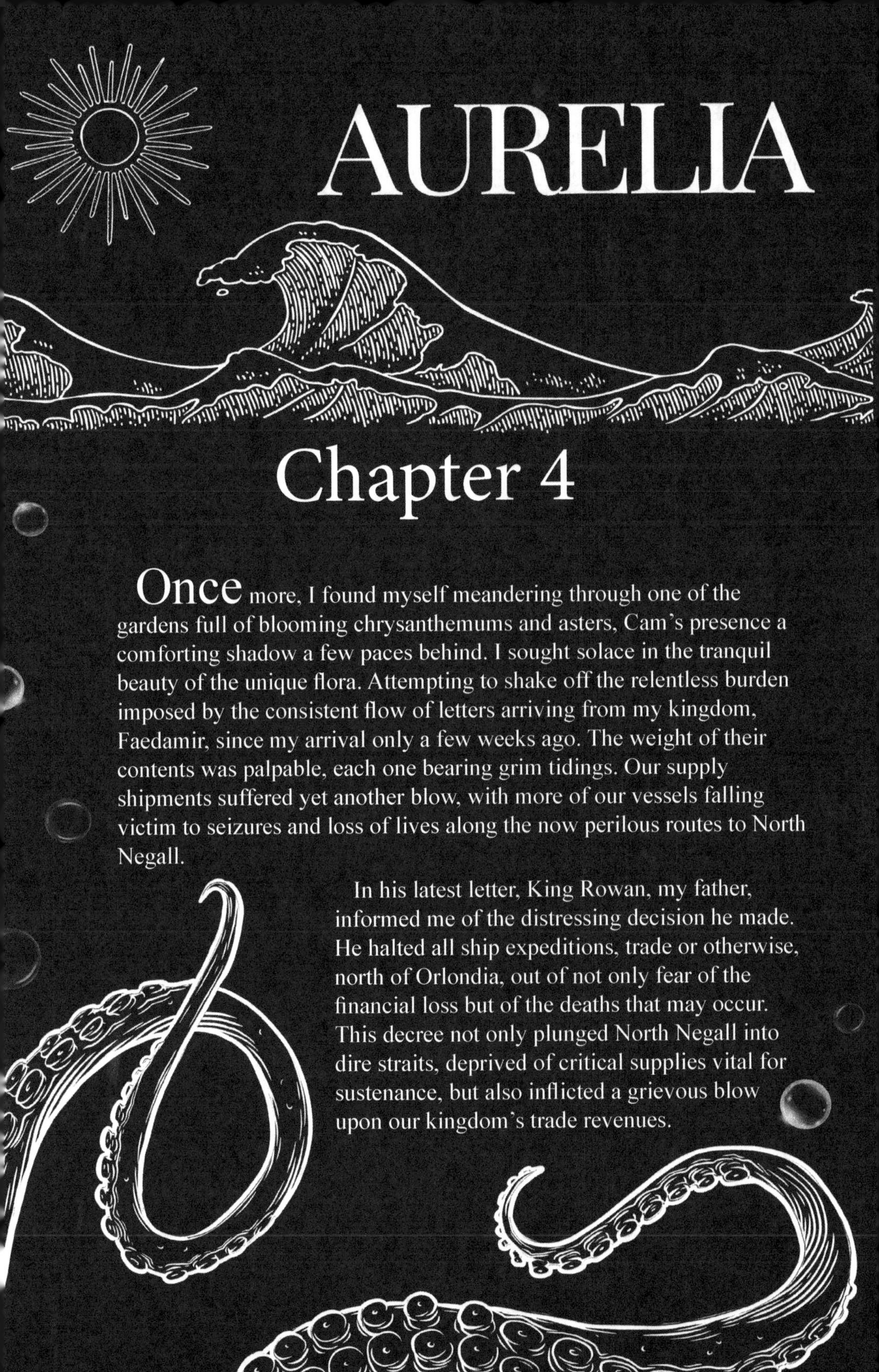

Chapter 4

Once more, I found myself meandering through one of the gardens full of blooming chrysanthemums and asters, Cam's presence a comforting shadow a few paces behind. I sought solace in the tranquil beauty of the unique flora. Attempting to shake off the relentless burden imposed by the consistent flow of letters arriving from my kingdom, Faedamir, since my arrival only a few weeks ago. The weight of their contents was palpable, each one bearing grim tidings. Our supply shipments suffered yet another blow, with more of our vessels falling victim to seizures and loss of lives along the now perilous routes to North Negall.

In his latest letter, King Rowan, my father, informed me of the distressing decision he made. He halted all ship expeditions, trade or otherwise, north of Orlondia, out of not only fear of the financial loss but of the deaths that may occur. This decree not only plunged North Negall into dire straits, deprived of critical supplies vital for sustenance, but also inflicted a grievous blow upon our kingdom's trade revenues.

The cessation of voyages to the northern regions dictated that we must now exclusively offload our cargo at the ports of Orlandia and the southern Kingdoms, further complicating an already intricate logistical web. The subsequent overland transportation of supplies to North Negall would undoubtedly exacerbate the financial strain, rendering it doubtful that our northern allies could afford the escalated costs.

The grim prospect of unsold goods loomed large, casting a shadow over the economic stability of our realm. Nevertheless, I recognized that the preservation of life surpasses any economic cost, no matter how great.

As I immersed myself in the serene and fragrant surroundings, I felt a gentle surge of magic brightening a glow across the signet rune on my left forearm. The subtle pulse signaling the awakening of the bond I share with Azura, as I answered the familiar call within my mind. *"I can sense your concern even from afar again, Aure. Are you truly all right?"*

I missed the comfort of being closer to Azura, swimming with her was our daily ritual. The feel of her gliding alongside me as we swam, her speed in the water always exhilarated me. She was large and beautiful, her scaled body always made me jealous that she never needed to fuse with clothes. The length of her strong, finned, serpent-like tail was nearly the size of most of our fishing boats. Though she had Human facial features, she retained a creature-like body and head with frills and horns mixing with locks of shimmering golden hair. Her arms, full of muscle and claws instead of nails along her five fingers. She was among the smallest of her race, but she was not small compared to me, being more than five times my height.

"Aure?" Azuraitha's voice echoed through our bond once more.

"I'm sorry," I replied, sensing the unease in her tone. *"My thoughts have been wandering a lot lately. I'm well though; it's just this war and worrying about my father... Is he doing okay?"*

The nervousness in her voice was palpable as she responded, *"Yes, though he tires easily and sleeps often. I dislike you being so far from me."*

A pang of sorrow washed over me. *"I miss you, but you know I'm safe here, right?"*

"I can sense that," she acknowledged. *"Yes, but I wish I had wings like the dragons of myth instead of being stuck in the water."*

I chuckled. *"And where would you fly, Azura? To the mountains of Golacia? Or all the way to the Sylvan Enclave?"*

Irritation tenges her sigh as she replied, *"I would go wherever you go, wherever I pleased."* I laughed aloud, momentarily startling Cam, who, although accustomed to my internal conversations with Azura, seemed unaware until that moment of my communication.

"All right, Azura, I believe you," a small smile grew across my lips. *"But unfortunately, you're sea-bound, and I'd hate to startle the Humans here by having you lounging in their ship ports."* A sense of disappointment, but understanding, flowed through our bond.

"What is it like to be mated?" I asked, surprised by the question that arose in my mind.

It took a moment for her to respond. *"It's hard to put into words. It's like discovering a part of yourself you never knew was missing. It's both annoying and frustrating, yet utterly amazing. It's like becoming whole in a way you never realized you were incomplete before. But you couldn't imagine ever living without it again."* Her response carried a wave of emotion and introspection.

"I'm not sure I'll ever feel that with someone," I admitted, sadness etching my tone. Considering the conversation I briefly had with Orla about her magic and magic in general, it made me concerned that she wouldn't understand how much magic was a part of my world.

I brushed the magical bond in my mind with a thought towards Azura. *"I want to share a memory with you. Can you sense what magic I was seeing there in Orla?"* I shared the memory of our conversation upon my arrival, and our evening tea together. The sense of a replay coming across my bond with her unsettled me a bit.

"I've never encountered the magic I saw in your memory, perhaps Fae, but it feels incredibly blocked or perhaps not fully awakened. Maybe there is some form of binding on her, or she hasn't gone through her rites of passage. It's hard to really know; so little is shared about the Fae. They rarely travel and keep their knowledge to themselves. The fact that she has Fae blood at all surprises me this far west of the Sylvan Enclave." My nervousness was heightened by the unease I sensed from Azura, causing me to shiver. *"Aure, I must rest now. I will let you know if I can find out anything about the Fae and will keep an eye on your father. Stay safe."*

Azura sent a comforting warm feeling to me as I replied, *"Be well, Azura, and thank you."* I touch the open buds of a purple aster, the feel of its feather-like petals grounding me, calming me. The color of the flower reminds me of Orla's eyes when she seemed at peace and calm. Her eyes were so beautiful, and I felt as though I wanted to study every variation and hue like it was a map to her soul.

I was worried, though. *How would she respond to learning about my magic and its integral part of who I am? Would she think I was using magic to manipulate her into feeling attraction to me?* I could sense she already struggled with allowing her feelings to be a part of her beyond her control. *Would she feel betrayed to learn of my bond with my dragon and fear that any of our intimacy wouldn't stay between us?*

The stark absence of common-place magic in Orlandia was jarring to experience; its scarcity created an unsettling feeling in me that bordered on fear of discovery. There was a stark contrast to Faedamir, where the islands have always embraced a culture of inclusivity and collaboration among various races—be they Human, Fae, Siren, Dwarf, or Sea Dragon—magic is simply an integral aspect of daily life. There, it flows as freely as the air we breathe, woven into the fabric of existence like a vibrant tapestry. Even among full Humans, who lack innate magical abilities, the use of enchantments or runic items is as routine as eating.

Yet, here in Orlandia, I couldn't shake the feeling that beneath the surface lay an undercurrent of jealousy and fear toward magic. It loomed ominously, casting a shadow over interactions and conversations, suffocating the very essence of acceptance. Since my arrival, not a single person has inquired or even considered I was magic born. Their assumption remains firmly rooted in the belief that I am Human, a presumption created by my appearance, which, as a Siren, closely resembles that of a Human. Most Sirens do, unless we invoke our Siren song, then our nature is shown in the change of our appearance.

The sound of fast-approaching footsteps and Cam's swift movement to stand between me and the interloper startled me from my thoughts. The young boy, with tousled brown hair and a too-thin face, seemed frightened as he halted in front of Cam, who towered over the lad. "A... a letter for Her Highness," he stuttered, bowing his head and holding out a gold envelope towards us.

I smiled at him, placing my hand on Cam's shoulder, though she never loosened her stern look. I reached out, taking the letter from him. "Thank you... What is your name, sir?" I said with a calm and regal tone, aiming to set the boy at ease.

Without raising his head, he replied, "Ned, Your Grace," his voice quiet with surprise.

"Thank you, Ned," I reiterated. With that, Ned turned and ran off back towards the palace.

"I don't like that they always know where to find you." Cam whispered in a guarded tone.

"It's a palace, Cam, and I am royalty. What do you expect?" I said casually as I examined the golden envelope and the blue wax seal that closed it. I gently opened it to reveal an elegant black lace and pearl vellum invitation.

I read the golden scrolled text out loud, "You are cordially invited to a celebration of the arrival and introduction of Princess Aurelia Demajanio of Faedamir, the Western Isles, at the Diplomats of the Alliance social held by the DOA." I read the other details to myself and then folded the paper, carefully sliding it back into its envelope.

The brisk fall wind caught the edges of my skirt, sending a shiver through me as silence settled around us for a moment. "Do you know who all attends these "Diplomats of the Alliance" social events, Cam?" I inquired tightly, hoping she had more knowledge of what this was about.

Cam's face remained stern, her tone tinged with annoyance as she replied, "The lack of information given to me has been startling, to be honest. I've gained more insights at the army barracks and from Frank than I have from any of the other royal appointments. I had hoped that there would be a better sense of schedule and concern for your safety. Considering, you're the sole heir to a vast kingdom and we are at war. Sometimes, it feels like an afterthought here at the palace."

I grimaced and nodded in agreement. It had indeed been frustratingly slow-paced for a kingdom embroiled in war. Initially, I had attributed the lack of introduction and time spent with Orla or any of the royal family to their presumed busyness with wartime duties. However, perhaps this alliance had indeed taken a backseat amidst the chaos.

Resigned, I turned quickly towards the palace, my skirt catching around my legs in my haste. Determined to find Orla no matter her whereabouts, I wished to talk to her, and as my betrothed, it was my right to demand this if need be. With a confused but dutiful Cam following my brisk pace, I stormed into the palace as if it were the front lines of battle, my usual grace eluding me in my fury.

I gently gripped the arm of the first servant I encountered, a young woman whose slight frame bordered on frailty. Letting my magic flare just enough to infuse my voice with soothing reassurance, I sought the information I desperately desired. "Tell me, where can I find Princess Orla?" I asked, my voice melodic and soft.

Mesmerized by my words, the young woman blushed, her cheeks taking on a rosy hue. "In her chambers, Your Highness... I can show you," she replied quietly.

With a slight touch of my hand, I ran it along her arm, I responded, "Yes, please do." As the servant turned and led the way to Orla's chambers, I followed closely, still shadowed by the silent, yet undoubtedly annoyed Cam.

The servant led us down the familiar halls and up the grand staircase, heading towards the west wing where my accommodations lay. It struck me then—*had Orla been this close all along, yet our paths had never crossed by chance?*

The servant halted in front of a set of closed double doors, just a few rooms away from ours. I sucked in a sharp, annoyed breath, feeling the tension mounting. With a bow, the meek young woman asked. "Anything else, Your Highness?"

I offered her a smile and replied simply, "No, thank you," dismissing her back to her duties.

Once she was out of sight, Cam leaned in close to me, her voice a whisper of caution. "Is this truly the conflict you want right now?"

I shot her a less-than-kind look, my anger evident on my face. "Conflict? I simply want to talk with her," I said, trying to keep my voice low. I continued somewhat flippantly, "Why don't you and your opinions go get some rest in your chambers and leave me alone to talk with Orla?"

Cam raised her eyebrows in a mix of surprise and contempt. Ultimately, she bowed and silently turned away, leaving me standing alone in front of the imposing dark brown wooden doors. I took a deep breath, my gaze drifting over the ornate carvings that adorned the door, matching the intricate details of the surrounding area. After a few moments of gathering my courage, I knocked firmly on the door.

I heard muffled rustling and the sound of booted feet approaching, then finally, the door opened. I was met with a surprised Orla standing there, her eyes shifting from a lavender purple to a bright sky blue. I couldn't help but smile as I watched the swirl of magic in her eyes. I swallowed hard, suddenly feeling both too dry and too wet all at once.

Orla tilted her head slightly to the right and with a soft voice said, "Um... Princess Aurelia, this is a surprise. Is there something you need?" Her gaze seemed to linger on me, then sweep up and down the hall, as if assessing the situation.

I found my voice, though my composure still eluded me. "Yes, I wish to speak with you, now, if it isn't too much of a bother." I stood, impatience growing within me as I observed her every move.

Her posture was always one of being on guard, alert, and tense, as though she stood ready to fight, to move, to act. It was as if she wore invisible armor, even though I had never seen her quite like this. Today, she wore heavy leather boots with tight-fitting black trousers and a loose pastel blue linen shirt that flowed over her strong, athletic muscles, softening her hard, angular features. This was the first time I had seen her without her uniformed leathers and metal armor plates. She was just as stunning as she had been in my dreams. *Why did she take my breath away?*

I lingered only for a moment as she graciously moved aside from the door, welcoming me into her private domain with a subtle sweep of her arm. Nodding slightly, I entered, my skirt swishing softly with each step across the room's polished wooden floor. The snugness of my bodice seemed more noticeable now, contrasting with the airiness of the chamber that greeted me.

Taking in the room's elegant furnishings and fixtures, I observed that while the space wasn't as grand as the one I stayed in, it had a small open lounging area that possessed a certain charm. Every wall boasted shelves laden with a vast array of books, reaching from floor to ceiling.

Two small sofas faced each other, between the only space free of books, which was occupied by a modest black stone fireplace. The flickering light of the fire cast dancing shadows upon the walls, bathing the space in a warm, amber glow. Opposite the fireplace, a large pine desk stood adorned with scattered books, papers, maps, and trinkets, a testament to Orla's intellectual pursuits and worldly interests. Positioned before the desk, was a sturdy wooden chest that seemed to serve both as seating and storage, its surface adorned with intricate carvings.

Noticing a slightly ajar door, I glimpsed what appeared to be a modest bed chamber. A single bed covered in large furs, unadorned yet inviting, occupied the center, while articles of clothing, armor, and weaponry lay strewn about, hinting at Orla's practical nature and the demands of her station. The lived-in feel of the room drew a genuine smile from me, offering a glimpse into Orla's personality and providing a sense of intimacy. It was clear that this space was her sanctuary, and I had been invited in, however momentary it would be.

As Orla closed the door behind us, granting us the first semblance of privacy since our meeting, a surge of nervous energy coursed through me, causing my stomach to flutter uncomfortably. I watched the subtle shift in her eyes back to their soft lavender hue, indicating her return to calm and no longer feeling the flare of surprise.

She spoke, breaking the silence of the space. "You wish to talk with me? What about?" Her tone was a bit unreadable, seeming flat but inquisitive, as though there was no feeling, no concern, or even expectation behind it.

My annoyance returned to me. How could she be so aloof with me? Did she truly not care about the situation, even though she clearly seemed passionate about her duty to her kingdom?

I handed her the golden envelope with the invitation inside for her to read. Perhaps she could explain what this was and why I hadn't been consulted prior to invitations being sent out.

Trying hard to keep my tone level I stated, "I received this. I wish to know what to expect and who will be attending. It appears to be in my honor, yet no one had even consulted me before sending these out. Apparently, I am viewed no better than a mere toy or prize to be shown off." I crossed my arms.

Her eyebrows arched in surprise, and her eyes flashed cobalt with intensity, silently acknowledging the gravity of the situation. Retrieving the delicate paper from its ornate enclosure, she studied it with a focus, her silence punctuating the weight of my inquiry.

A torrent of questions flooded my mind. *Had she not received one of her own? Had she truly not been a part of the planning of this "celebration"? Was she not a part of the mentioned "Alliance"?*

After a silence that seemed to stretch longer than it was, her tone remained even and flat, yet her eyes retained their deep cobalt hue, which reminded me of the sapphire gems I had worked with in the forge.

"I have many questions for my father," she mused aloud to me, her voice carrying a hint of contemplation. "Because no, I did not receive one of these invitations, and I have never been a part of any such 'Alliance' meetings with diplomats or anyone else for that matter."

Slowly and deliberately, she returned the paper to its place in the envelope, exhaling as if releasing a pent-up breath. Meeting my gaze, she handed it back. "You are right, though. We need to talk. Please, sit. Would you like a drink?"

She moved gracefully to a small table next to one of the sofas, where bottles containing various liquids in an array of colors were arranged next to beautifully crystal-etched glass cups.

Pausing for a moment, I hesitated before making my way to the sofa opposite her. "Do you have any wine?" I sought the comfort of a familiar beverage, craving its warmth on this chilly evening. Though the heat from the fire had eased the chill in my arms and hands.

Orla poured a rich crimson liquid from a tall glass bottle into two of the clear cups, bringing out the intricate designs etched onto them. Handing one to me, she sat down and took a sip of her drink. Following suit, I tasted the fluid, its floral and berry flavors dancing on my tongue, leaving a lingering spice in my mouth after I swallowed, which warmed my throat and stomach. I looked up to find her studying me for a moment, seemingly contemplating her words before speaking.

"I must admit that despite my insistence to be more involved in the workings of my kingdom, I have faced much resistance. From my father, in particular," she confessed, her eyes unwavering in their deep blue intensity.

As she glanced towards the fire, a sense of shame tinged her words. "In the past, admittedly, I have largely ignored or attempted to let go of such matters. But even with this arrangement, I have been treated as merely another piece on my father's chessboard. This is not what I want for my life – being used for someone else's purpose." Her vulnerability hung in the air, and I felt a surge of empathy, longing to reach out and comfort her. Yet, I remained still, knowing that any physical gesture might only add to her unease.

Instead, I thoughtfully suggested, "Why don't we attend this together?" I waved the envelope before setting it on the wooden table next to me.

"Together?" she echoed flatly, but her eyes slowly streaked with lighter blues.

I smiled. "Yes, I have attended many diplomatic events in my kingdom, so I am accustomed to navigating such social gatherings. Going together shows that we are truly a united front. It will also give you access that has been so needlessly refused to you before, without the pushback you have received." A slow smirk crept across my face, "your father won't be able to deny your involvement because of our arrangement."

Her lips twitched, a hint of amusement growing evident in her sly smile. "Agreed," she said simply.

I watched her take another sip from her glass, and I gathered the courage to broach another topic that troubled me. I looked into my glass, swirling the liquid inside before taking a rather large gulp of it.

Finally, I tentatively stated, "There is another topic I wish to discuss with you, but I feel worried it will upset you. However, it is important to our relationship and to my kingdom."

I could see worry silently cross her expression, but she remained flat, distant almost. I bristled at her lack of emotional expression. How could she remain so detached? Everything but her eyes—the mix of blue hues of her iris's was like the storms I had witnessed in the sea, beautiful but dangerous.

I slowly and quietly began, my nerves feeling raw. "You are aware that I am Magic-born, yes?"

Her detached and flat demeanor changed as shock and surprise clearly gripped her. She jolted, stiffening, her eyes going a solid and bright sky blue.

Just breathe in and out. At least her eyes hadn't darkened to the depth of blue I had observed when her anger and fury surfaced. I breathed deeply, feeling my chest rise and fall with each breath, awaiting her response, her questions.

She repositioned herself and took her final drink from her glass before muttering, "I see."

My anger sparked deep inside me, I sat forward and snapped out. "Is that all you have to say? Do you not have questions? Or concerns? Do you even know what I am?" I placed my unfinished drink on the table next to me, and fisted the skirt of my dress, clenching my hands tightly around the soft fabric.

"Yes," Orla said flatly through clenched teeth.

"Yes, to what?" I seethed. At that, she stood and began pacing, to my surprise.

She turned abruptly towards me as her words flooded out. "Yes, I have questions. So many questions, and concerns. It's more that I only have limited book knowledge of magic. It isn't that I haven't heard the stories of the Western Isles in the pubs around the ports or in the limited texts we have on your kingdom. It's not that I haven't seen or even used some items that come from your kingdom. I know magic is used and is considered common, I suppose. I just don't know what that is like. Here, magic is not openly taught. It is kept for those who can afford it or those who wish to use it as a means of power over others. Most of my kingdom views it as evil, or at least that is what is said among our cities and villages. Yes, we are home to a few Sirens in our coastal and port towns, and even less in the city. We rarely encounter Fae, I have never even met one. Mainly our cities are mixed with Humans and Dwarfs. As you know Humans are not magic born, so here, magic is not common." She sighed as she ran her hand through her short raven black hair.

As I silently let my anger ease, her words poured out, washing over me. I reached out, grabbing her hand and pulled her towards me and the sofa. I guided her into a position beside me, her shock perhaps the only thing that allowed me to do so. Her heat, her strong body, her nearness calmed me.

"I can understand that," I started quietly, folding her hand in mine, resisting the urge to use my magic. "Magic wasn't always common in Faedamir either. Not really until my mother, Queen Cliodnha, was a Siren—the high priestess of the Sirens, in fact, which is basically like a tribal leader. Her marriage to my father, a Human and King of Faedamir, finally united the isles. However, the Sirens and the Sea Dragons have always been native to the Western Isles of Faedimir long before it was ever a kingdom. Magic for their culture is as common as breathing."

Shock continued to play across Orla's face as she quietly asked, "What is a Sea… Dragon?"

A rich, deep laugh erupted from me, shaking my whole body. "They have kept you sheltered, haven't they?" My amusement quickly faltered, though, as Orla pulled her hand from mine, looking again toward the fire, the redness rising up her neck and flushing her cheeks.

My empathy grew, and with a smile, I touched her hand calmly and gently, saying, "I am sorry, I didn't mean to make you feel ashamed or anything. I just can't imagine being as educated as you are and not knowing about a whole race within the realm, albeit a small population. However, it is a bit concerning since we are to be so involved in each other's lives and kingdoms."

Orla turned to face me and nodded. "I dislike feeling so uninformed. Information brings me a sense of comfort and, I guess, even a sense of control over myself, which feels so lacking all the time. However, I truly do wish to know more about the Sea Dragons. Do they have wings like the myths?"

The joy I felt inside from her inquisitiveness and curiosity brought a smile to my face, I explained. "No, they're different, but are believed to be closely related. Though there is little knowledge of the relation between the dragons of myth and Sea Dragons. At full-grown size, they are roughly the size of a small ship, but as with anything, they do vary in size. Some speculate that they are far more closely related to an animal than a race. They don't have the ability or desire to interbreed with any of the other races. Which is a disappointment to some, oddly enough."

I watched her as I spoke, Orla's eyes returning to a lovely lavender hue. I felt more calm myself, and enjoyed the closeness to her.

So, I continued, "However, the Sea Dragons are higher beings like any other race. They have a rich cultural history, the ability to communicate, and to learn. They also have unique complex relationships, with social structures, their own systems of governance, and spirituality." Smiling at how she tilted her head when listening intently warmed me. Nervously, I added, "Sometime at the start of the world, the Siren and Sea Dragon created a unique and symbiotic relationship. Each Sea Dragon, upon their rite of passage into adulthood, must choose a Siren during their rite to bond with and protect. The Siren possesses the only means by which the Sea Dragons can find their mate. The Sea Dragons mate for life, and they are also bonded to their Siren for life."

Sensing more questions running through her mind, I stated. "I have plenty of books I brought with me that I can lend you. There are various topics, including books on the Sea Dragons, Sirens, Magic, and even my kingdom for you to enjoy at your own pace if that helps ease you any."

Those words evoked the most beautiful smile from her, and her eyes flickered with just a hint of pink? Or maybe I was imagining it? Nonetheless, I knew it was getting late, and Cam would be pacing a hole in the floor if I didn't head back soon.

"So, you have magic then?" Orla asked, pulling my attention back to her, "Siren, right? And you have a Sea Dragon?"

Softly, I smiled; goddess, I couldn't help but smile around her. "I don't have a Sea Dragon, but yes, I am bonded with a Sea Dragon, and yes, I am a Siren, and I do have magic."

Her face grew shadowed by worry or maybe it was fear. I bristled at her unease and clear concern. I fidgeted my fingers against the soft material of my gown once again. Unsure how to respond I waited for her to say something, anything that would unfound my fears.

With the awkward silence growing, I stood, hoping to break the tension, but I gained only a small gesture of curiosity from her. With only a slight tilt of her head, she remained still. "It is late, I wish you a good night, Orla," I said, my voice slightly strained.

She gave me a curt nod as she meagerly replied, "Goodnight." I left through the door with her unmoving.

As I made my way back, alone, to my chambers, the corridors seemed unusually quiet, amplifying the whirlwind of thoughts swirling in my mind. Orla's reaction lingered, her expression etched with worry and a hint of something else I couldn't quite decipher.

Was it fear? Confusion? Whatever it was, it left a sense of tension in the air, one that seemed to mirror the currents of uncertainty brewing within me.

Replaying the conversation in my head, I couldn't shake the feeling of inadequacy that gnawed at me. *Did I reveal too much? Was I too forward?* The weight of Orla's unspoken words hung heavy, leaving me grappling with all of my emotions.

Reaching the ornately carved door to my chambers, I leaned my back against it for a moment closing my eyes. The support and sturdiness of the door lent itself to finding my center, my calm, before walking into a certain confrontation with Cam. Running my fingers over the rough and smoothness of the intricate design in the wood, soothed me. Finally, with a breathy sigh turning myself, I opened and walked through the door.

ORLA

Chapter 5

The hush of midnight approached as I scrutinized my reflection in the full-length mirror. I modeled a ruby gown that reached my ankles except for the thigh-high slit on one side. The tight bodice seemed to constrict my ribs and present my cleavage to the world. My fingers bore into the silken material as I tried to pull it higher, while then pulling the dress down. I tugged, trying in vain to alleviate the discomfort of my crawling skin. Why did this dress feel more suffocating than my full metal armor? I turned left, then right, judging my reflection—a person I couldn't quite reconcile as myself. With a sigh, I grabbed my dagger and thigh sheathe, securing them under the gown. No one should notice, but I refused to attend this event unarmed.

Two nights ago now, I think it was, Aure had all but pushed her way into my chambers, angered by this invitation to a social event made in her honor. I hadn't wanted to burden her with the fact that I knew nothing about this group of diplomats claiming affiliation with our alliance. Initially upset about being excluded yet again, now that she, too, would be part of something I wasn't.

Yet she invited me to accompany her, presenting a united front as equals. I had never been equal, either above or below, but never equal. My magic stirred and my eyes shifted to deep cobalt as anger, fear, and trepidation surfaced, but I quickly suppressed those emotions, willing my eyes to return to violet as I nodded in the mirror, somewhat satisfied.

A light knock on my door interrupted my thoughts, and I drew in a deep breath before opening it. A smile lit up my face as I beheld Aure, resplendent in an emerald green gown that shimmered in the candlelight. The iridescent smooth fabric billowed in layers of ruffles from her hips down. From her hips up the corset bodice was black lace with crystals beaded into a design that seemed to be tailored to her curves. My mouth felt dry as I realized how stunning she looked.

I became aware that my simple yet flowy silk dress paled in comparison, but it was one of two dresses I owned. My other gown was what I wore at any royal function, and I hated it even more than this one.

Realizing I was staring at her, I inquired, "Are you ready? We don't have far, I don't believe." I offered my hand somewhat awkwardly, but she smiled and took it. I led the way through shadowy corridors and hallways until we reached a small banquet hall on the castle's lower level.

The gold inlay on the door glittered in the low lamplight of the entrance. With a turn of the crystal knob, I opened the heavy door, revealing a grand room alive with music and murmuring voices. Wait, this was a masquerade event; notably, we didn't have masks. I could sense Aure's clear discomfort and weariness to this whole situation.

A woman approached us dressed in a pearlescent cream lace gown. She wore a mask firmly shaped around her nose, eyes, and forehead with golden scrollwork against black porcelain, giving the appearance of a face wearing a crown. She smiled gracefully as she floated toward us, arms and hands opened wide as though she planned to embrace us. I took a single step back, brushing my hand along my sheath and dagger.

"Aurelia, dearest,"The woman cooed as she embraced a surprised, but cordial, Aure.

I watched the woman take her mask off and Aure smiled as she stated, "Madame Koi." They embraced again, this time less stiffly.

Aure turned to me. "This is my betrothed, Princess Orla. Orla, this is Madame Koi, Faedamir's most successful diplomat and personal family friend of mine. Madame Koi used to be one of my Mother's closest ladies of sorts."

She seemed to say the last bit with a slight chuckle, and then Madame Koi embraced me. I froze in place as I felt her tight hug.

She released me and said, "Welcome, both…" She eyed me smiling slyly, "…of you to the Diplomats of the Alliance. This is our monthly social. I will introduce you to a few people I think you should talk with and then before we eat I will present you, eh both of you, to the group. Otherwise, you are free to mingle and enjoy the festivities as you like."

I lost track of the conversation between Aure and Madame Koi as I took in the enchanting room. The main hall was intimate yet beautiful, adorned with floor-to-ceiling painted murals framed in glittering gold. Large mirrors were strategically placed between each artistic scene, amplifying the room's grandeur. Gold-trimmed arches led to alcoves down the length of the hall, creating an illusion of space and adding to its majestic atmosphere.

The matching gold-trimmed ceiling caught my eye, leading my gaze to the stunning sight above. A deep blue painted dome adorned with glittering flecks caught the candlelight, creating the illusion of a starry night sky. It was as though we were standing beneath an open celestial canopy, surrounded by a galaxy of shimmering stars. The golden theme became apparent as I observed the small group of about thirty or so people, all adorned in black masks trimmed with gold of various shapes and styles. Each mask was beautiful and extravagant in its own right, adding an air of mystery and sophistication to the gathering. Men and women alike danced, drank, and engaged in lively conversations while a few unusual pairs discreetly slipped away into the private alcoves.

As we moved through the crowd, I couldn't help but notice the warm reception we received. Every gaze that we met granted us a smile and a slight bow, conveying a sense of genuine welcome and acceptance. It was a stark contrast to the usual formality of royal gatherings, and I found myself feeling surprisingly at ease in this unfamiliar setting.

I followed closely behind Aure as Madame Koi led us toward a rather tall and dark man. He wore tight, dark blue trousers adorned with intricate scrolls of leather and a loose cream shirt that draped over his muscular arms and chest. Engaged in a heated debate with him was a short, stocky Dwarf with flushed cheeks, his beard cascading down his chest in a tangled mass. The Dwarf's eyes were obscured by a thin gold mask, shaped like a miniature mountain scape.

I watched as the Dwarf took another long drink of his wine before launching into a tirade. "The Northern government can't be placated! They must be demolished. We can't leave any of their royalty alive at the end of this war.

That is the ONLY way to end their tyranny!" His voice echoed through the hall, filled with fervor and anger. With a sudden force, he slammed his wine glass to the floor, shattering it and sending its contents spilling across the marble tiles. With a growl he stormed out of the hall in a blaze of fury.

Aure leaned close, whispering to me, "The man who was shouting, I recognized him as Duke Kinsmere of the Golacia Mountain Dwarf Clan. He can be quite temperamental." She rolled her eyes, a hint of exasperation in her voice.

Servants moved silently to clean the red bloody looking mess, their efficient actions almost making the outburst seem like a mere blip in the evening's affairs.

The tall man turned and smiled warmly at us, and Madame Koi beamed. "Oh Rein, I have the most lovely ladies for you to meet. Her Highness Princess Aurelia of Faedamir and Her Highness Princess Orla of Orlondia."

His charming smile never faded as he bowed and kissed Aure's hand, and I extended my hand to shake his. As he greeted me, a dimple showed, indicating his slight amusement, and he firmly shook my hand. "The honor is mine to behold such wonderful women. I am Prince Reinferd Grathlend of Negall."

I smiled in return, but I noticed Aure stiffen at his full name, though she nodded and bowed politely. "Pleasure to meet you," Aure said simply, turning slightly to engage in hushed tones with Madame Koi.

"You can just call me Rein. I am sorry you had to witness the Duke's outburst earlier," Reinferd said to me, his voice warm and apologetic. "Like most in his kingdom, he has a short fuse and a big temper. We can count on him to loudly storm out at least once per event." He chuckled, his brown eyes resembling warm milk chocolate under his half-mask, which appeared like a golden vine with thorns and leaves growing across his face. The black porcelain backdrop of the mask was only a few shades darker than his rich, dark skin.

"I see. I can't say I disagree with his statements though," I tell Rein, curious about his stance on handling the war since his kingdom has been the most affected.

Rein ran his hand through short, curly locks of black hair. "Yes, I can see how that would feel satisfying to end the ruling tyrant, but my concern is for the people's well-being and the lives that are being lost." I nodded in agreement listening.

He grew passionate as he continued, "We have lost all access to ocean trade due to the raiding of ships, and the number of refugees coming through our borders is overwhelming us. Not that we don't wish to offer safety and freedom to these people. However, we lack the resources and space to properly handle the influx of so many. Not to mention all of the troops and armies that have to pass through to the front lines. Getting into Frostspire is a landscape nightmare. The rugged cliffs and tall, ice-packed peaks make it nearly impassable for any army, so mostly we are stuck holding a border that is being pushed back every day."

My worry grew evident on my face as I felt my eyes shift to deep blue. *Why hasn't my father shared any of this with me? Why are we not sending more aid, and why is so much of our army still here, wasted in the barracks?* With concern in my tone, I asked him, "In your opinion, what should we try to do?"

Rein frowned, a somber look growing on his face. "If there really is no negotiations to be had with the King of Frostspire, then I believe a small precision strike would suffice. It is rumored that King Frostbane has an adult daughter, so if we could simply assassinate him, then perhaps his daughter would be a better ruler and open to change, thus ending the war peacefully."

Madame Koi turned towards me now, interrupting us, her tone playful, "Orla, is Rein boring you with his idealistic fantasies of peace?" Unsure how to respond to her teasing nonchalance about Rein's ideas, I shake my head, the annoyance clear on Rein's face fading a little when he notes my reaction.

Aure stepped closer to me and looped her arm around mine, pulling me close. The touch and possessive nature of the action surprised me. "Please excuse us, Prince Reinferd, but we have other introductions before we eat. Thank you for your time; it truly was a pleasure to meet you," Aure politely excused us as she guided me away.

My eyes widened with surprise, I felt their hue brighten to a vivid sky blue. I've never experienced anyone being so concerned about my presence before. I rather enjoyed knowing I was wanted, even needed. I wondered, though, about Aure's reactions to Rein. He seemed like someone I could forge a close friendship with, and I thought his opinions on the war had merit. Besides the fact that I was also slightly jealous of his defined muscles. *Did she have a history with him, or did she not truly want to ally with Negall?*

My mind flooded with thoughts and questions. I could sense Aure was not as I had seen her in any other setting; she was more on edge and alert, and her smile was fake—it did not reach her eyes like it usually did. I didn't understand. This place is so full of wonder and beauty, and the people all seemed wonderful. I felt like I was finally able to be a true part of this war. I had learned the thoughts and opinions of people who truly make all the decisions.

Aure brought us to a stop where Madame Koi had beckoned us, upon which she promptly introduced us to a couple standing next to her. A woman adorned with an artistic array of fabrics that seemed to translate as a gown, but all the various fabrics and designs seemed to simply form a pile around her body. Next to her was the rather shifty average man who wore a crisp and elegant jacket and trousers, upon his flush pale face sat a black mask with a weight scale designed in gold.

After presenting us to them, Madame Koi continued, "This is Baroness Lyra Aveline of Capes Crown, Orlondia, and Baron Luke Rothgar of the Southern Reach. Both are critical in the trade treaties because each is a merchant in their own right. Baron Rothgar is an influential international trade figure known for his shrewd business dealings and political connections. Baroness Lyra is a patron of the arts, influential in cultural exchanges, and fosters creativity across the kingdoms."

Both bowed to us. Only Baroness Lyra lifted her mask of black and gold mismatched shapes, smiling. She said, "Please, won't you both just call me Lyra? I despise the labels of the titles we are forced to use for status."

I felt a curiosity rise within me, eager to learn more about her and the type of trade she conducted, but before I could inquire further, someone approached Baroness Lyra and whispered in her ear.

She turned back to us. "Excuse me, it was lovely to meet you both, Your Highnesses." She then sauntered away and I lost her in the crowd.

Being left standing with an all too quiet Baron Rothgar, we simply walked toward the refreshments. Aure was still leading me by the arm. It was such a comfortable and simple thing. I had never been able to be touched with such ease. At times, I almost forgot I was anchored to her. In the past, in such situations, my mind and nerves usually have too much effect for me to be anything but awkward.

I picked up a glass flute filled with some sort of shimmering, sweet beverage and handed one to Aure. As I drank, the room seemed to come alive with brightness and energy. Looking out over the crowd, I felt a surge of excitement. "Aure, isn't this wonderful? People truly coming together for change in the war," I exclaimed, eager for her agreement.

However, my enthusiasm was met with a cool yet concerned expression from Aure, who offered only a quick, chaste smile in response. What was her actual problem? Leaning closer to me, Aure whispered, setting down her untouched flute, "This is a very informal setting for most of the people here. There's no record of their talks, and it's hard to even tell who is actually present." My cheeks flushed at her words, but I brushed off her apprehension. I believed this gathering was a sign of progress, something desperately needed after nine years of war, especially the last five, which had seen our most concerted efforts.

After finishing my second flute of wine, I leaned heavily into Aure's space. "Did you know this wine is a Dwarven specialty, Eruric wine? And it's scrub…scum, scrumptiously… It's good," I slurred, my tongue fumbling over the familiar word.

Aure tilted her head, a sweet, small smile breaking through her trepidation. "Yes, it's often made from the rare crystal fruit that grows in the Mountains of Golacia. It's quite strong. We should get you something to eat."

She guided me to the table filled with pastries, breads, and small bite-sized hors d'oeuvres. I picked up a buttery, cheese-topped roll and devoured it enthusiastically. Gods, it was so good—and warm. I felt my senses returning to me and my head clearing some.

Aure and I were then introduced to a string of people, but I struggled to keep track. How had I never met most of them before? I recognized Sir Tristan Gareth and Lord Alden, both of whom seemed surprised by my presence, which annoyed me. I wasn't some child hanging on Lord Alden's leg or playing with sticks to spar with Tristan. It baffled me how they could ignore my right to be actively involved in this war when I saw them day after day.

As the crowd began to gather around the table, servants had already laid out a feast of various dishes, the long polished wood adorned with a cornucopia of food and decor. The decadence of it all seemed out-of-place given the context of war.

Madame Koi projected her voice loudly over the murmurs, as though with magic. "I am honored to present, her Majesty Princess Aurelia Demanjanio of Faedmir, our esteemed guest tonight, accompanied by her betrothed, Princess Orla of Orlondia, who honors us with her company. If you haven't already greeted them, please do so throughout the night. Now, let us enjoy our meal." A twisting sensation gripped my gut, more than just from drinking wine on an empty stomach. I was always an afterthought, even in my own kingdom.

About to take a seat, I noticed Aure scanning the no longer attentive crowd. She leaned over to me and in a hushed tone said, "I'm leaving. I've had more than enough of this masquerade. You can stay if you want."

Uncertain how to respond to her disdain, I seated myself at the table and nodded at her, the only response that came to mind. I wanted to stay and be a part of this, even if she didn't. Understanding her reasons for not wanting to be here eluded me, and I wasn't going to ask her to stay. I didn't even bother to watch her as she walked out the door.

Sitting with an empty seat beside me, I filled my gold-etched plate with a few of the foods I recognized, like ham meat and sweet rolls.

Rein sat next to me, filling his plate as well, he spoke to me in hushed tones. "I saw Princess Aurelia leave, was she unwell?"

My mouth was awkwardly full of food, which seemed to happen every time I ate around people. I shrugged as I swallowed before saying, "She seemed put off by this whole affair. I am not really sure I understand why, I see a lot of opportunities here."

Rein nodded thoughtfully, his gaze scanning the room as if searching for something beyond the surface. "Indeed, there's more to these gatherings than meets the eye," he replied, his tone cautious yet intrigued. "It's easy to get caught up in the festivities and overlook the underlying currents of politics and intrigue."

I furrowed my brow, intrigued by his words. "What do you mean?" I asked, curious to hear his perspective on the matter.

He paused, considering his response carefully before continuing. "Well, alliances are forged, deals struck, and secrets exchanged in these halls," Rein explained, his voice lowered to a conspiratorial whisper. "But one must tread carefully, for not all intentions are noble, and not all alliances are as they appear."

He took a small drink then smiled at me, before speaking again, "Still, amidst the shadows, there's also hope. Opportunities arise for positive change, alliances that can bring about peace, and secrets that, when revealed, may lead to greater understanding."

I nodded, heartened by his balanced perspective. It was a reminder that even in the midst of uncertainty, there were glimmers of possibility. "Thank you for the insight," I said sincerely, feeling a renewed sense of optimism.

Rein smiled warmly, his dark eyes reflecting a mixture of camaraderie and determination. "Of course, Your Grace. We must navigate these waters together, keeping our eyes open to both the risks and the opportunities."

I casually responded, "Please just call me Orla, no need for titles among friends."

He nodded, gracing me with a large smile and his dimples appeared. After a few moments of eating. He mused, his voice held a hint of amusement, as he revealed. "My mother, Queen Nilah, would die if she could see me here."

Curious, I raised an eyebrow, my eyes shifting to sky blue as I inquired. "Why is that? Does she not wish for you to be a part of the war?"

Rein grew somber as he let out a deep breath. "After my father's death at the front lines, she had to make a lot of decisions for our kingdom, as I was just a child, and so was my brother; he was unable to rule alone."

I finished another bite of my meat and said, "Rein, I never realized you were raised by just your mother. What was it like growing up in Negall?"

Rein paused, his expression softening. "It was... unique, to say the least. I don't remember much of my father, so my mother has been everything to me my whole life. Being raised by a single parent in the royal court came with its own set of challenges. She felt the weight of the kingdom on her shoulders, you know?" Nodding, I took another bite and listened. "She wanted to protect us from all the dangers of the world, so she kept us sheltered within the palace walls."

"That sounds incredibly isolating," I could empathize with him.

His gaze deepened onto his plate. "It was. I didn't have many friends growing up. My mother was always worried about assassination attempts or kidnappings, so she kept me under constant guard."

I looked at him, trying to be comforting. "It must have been difficult not being able to experience the world like other children."

He moved the unfinished food around his plate with his fork. "It was. I envied the other kids who could run and play outside without a care in the world. Which we did often before we lost my father, but my mother always told me I needed to think of our safety. She loved us fiercely, but sometimes I wished she would have let me live a little."

I gave a reassuring pat on his shoulder. "I can imagine. But it sounds like she did what she thought was best for your brother and you out of love."

"She did. And I'll always be grateful for her sacrifices. I know she loves me more than anything," he continued, opening up, "but as I grew older, I began to feel confined by the walls of the palace. I longed to explore the world beyond, to experience life outside the constraints of royalty. Now I'm determined to see the world beyond the palace walls, to make my own mark on Negall."

I offer a supportive smile. "And now here you are, charting your own path. I admire your determination, Rein. I'm sure your mother is proud of who you've become. You've grown into a strong leader, despite the challenges you faced."

As the room emptied out, Rein looked at me with gratitude. "Thank you, Orla. That means a lot coming from you."

I nodded, impressed with Rein and the openness he had shown me. Pushing the empty plate away from me, I glanced around the room, realizing it has nearly cleared out completely. "Well, Rein, I do hope we can navigate these waters together, as you say... building relationships and alliances," I said with a small smirk, then glanced toward the door. "However, I think I should go check on Aure. Thank you for sharing with me."

I stood up leaving my napkin on the table, as Rein also stood up with me. He bowed his head, and gave me a warm smile. "The honor has been mine, Orla. Goodnight."

I walked out of the room, full of more questions than answers. As I traversed the dim corridor, I noticed a shadowy figure lurking in a dark alcove ahead. The tall silhouette was pressing someone against the wall, barely discernible in the darkness.

An uneasy feeling crept over me, and my skin prickled with goosebumps. As I drew closer, my senses heightened, and I instinctively reached my hand down the slit of my gown to my dagger and clutched the hilt, freeing it. A familiar scent of citrus and coconut filled the air, and the figures came into clearer view.

I caught sight of green ruffles against the stone wall, and my breath lodged in my throat. The predatory stance of the shadowy figure and the hand cupped over the mouth of the other person sent alarm bells ringing in my mind. My pace quickened as I made plans to confront them.

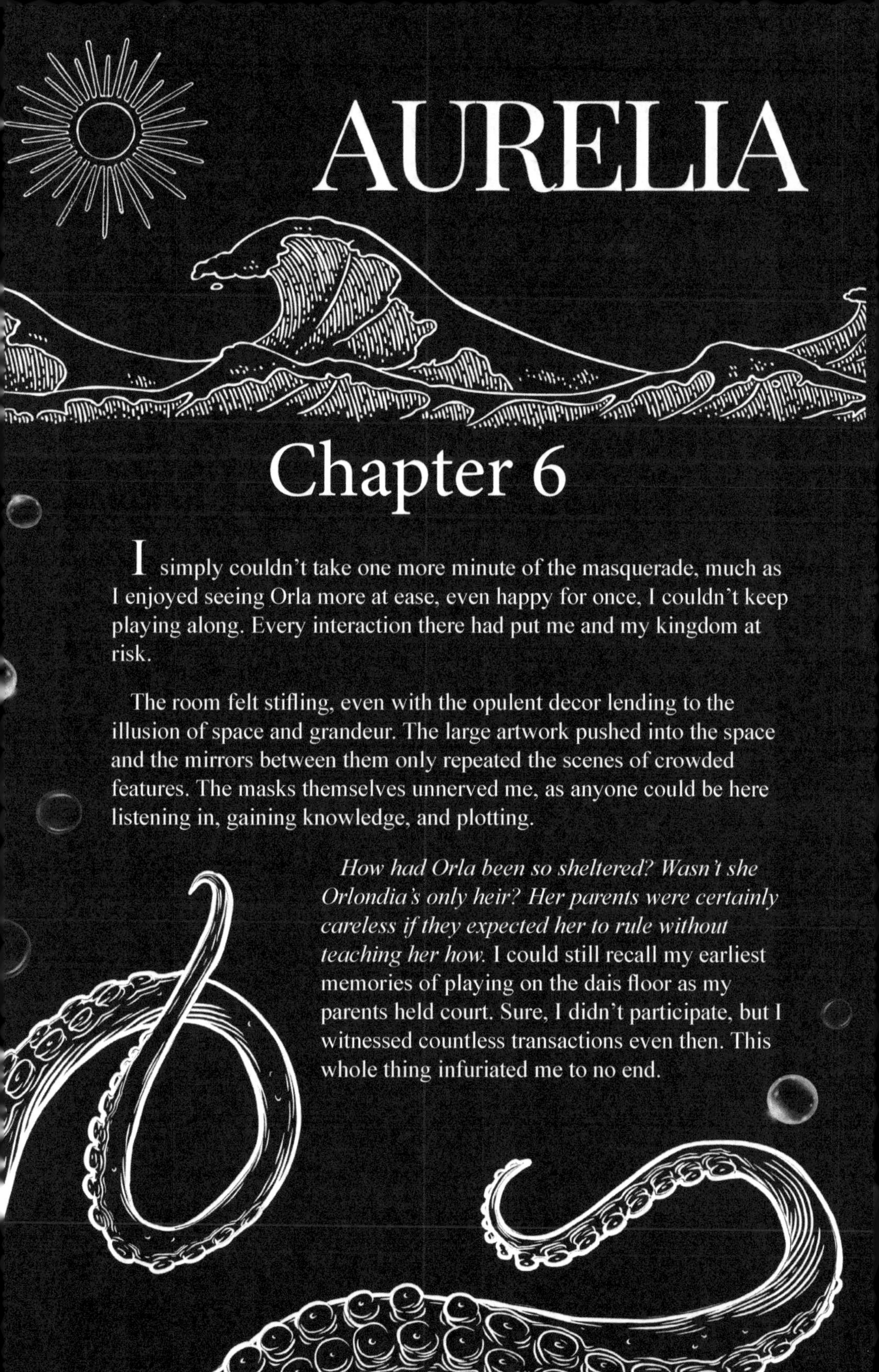

AURELIA

Chapter 6

I simply couldn't take one more minute of the masquerade, much as I enjoyed seeing Orla more at ease, even happy for once, I couldn't keep playing along. Every interaction there had put me and my kingdom at risk.

The room felt stifling, even with the opulent decor lending to the illusion of space and grandeur. The large artwork pushed into the space and the mirrors between them only repeated the scenes of crowded features. The masks themselves unnerved me, as anyone could be here listening in, gaining knowledge, and plotting.

How had Orla been so sheltered? Wasn't she Orlondia's only heir? Her parents were certainly careless if they expected her to rule without teaching her how. I could still recall my earliest memories of playing on the dais floor as my parents held court. Sure, I didn't participate, but I witnessed countless transactions even then. This whole thing infuriated me to no end.

Madame Koi finished our introduction, and finally, I could slip out with little notice. I glanced over the crowd, now engrossed in their conversations, and seated comfortably at the opulent wood table filled with food and flowers. The sheer decadence of it soured my stomach.

Leaning down, I spoke so only Orla could hear my words. "I am leaving. I have had more than enough of this masquerade. You can stay if you want."

Her eyes flashed blue, reminding me of the summer clear skies that I would lose myself in back home on the warm afternoons.

I hoped she would join me, perhaps for another private conversation or to walk me back to my quarters. However, her silence spoke volumes. She simply nodded, her eyes returning to lavender as she barely glanced at me, taking her seat and her decision made.

Frustration bubbled within me as I fisted my hands into the silken ruffles of my gown and turned toward the door.

My exit didn't go completely unnoticed, much to my dismay. Stepping out of the large double doors into the dimly lit corridor, I found myself approached by a tall, somewhat older man. His oil-sleeked brown hair was slicked back, and he sported a tightly trimmed beard. Unlike many others at the masquerade, he didn't wear a mask, instead opting for a military uniform similar to those worn by the palace guards.

As he reached me and stepped in front of me, a forced smile graced his lips as he bowed his head. "Your Grace, I am General Roderick Magnus, leader of Orlondia's military. I would like to have a word with you if I may." He gestured toward a small alcove along the corridor.

Not wanting to offend someone who held such power here, I nodded in agreement and turned toward the alcove.

The simple candlelight did little to provide a clear view of our surroundings, which I supposed was the point. It would allow talks and meetings to be conducted without drawing too much attention. The General followed closely behind me, in an uncomfortably intimate way that I had encountered all too often.

I quickly found a seat in one of the small plush chairs and gestured for him to sit across from me. He bowed his head in acknowledgment and took the indicated seat. Silence fell over us, lasting only a moment before the General spoke in a flat but hushed tone.

"I am very interested in learning more about the weapons your kingdom creates and is providing us as part of our alliance." The last word was drawn out in a way that unnerved me, but I smiled politely. I had been well-prepared to explain before ever coming to Orlondia, as I knew our magic-imbued Runic Weapons would be a common topic of discussion among the Humans here.

"Of course, General, what would you like to know?" I shifted in the chair, feeling a bit uncomfortable having this discussion here, alone. His face lit up with the eagerness of a child learning how to use their magic for the first time.

"Will they work for anyone?" His simple question was probably a fairly common one, since humans aren't capable of even wielding lesser magic. Runic Items however, can be forged to allow someone to wield all kinds of powerful magic; it all depends on how the item was created and charged. How I would explain this to the General though would have to be done carefully.

"Yes, unlike Runic Weapons of the Dwarfs from Golicia, our unique forging process allows them to work for anyone who uses it, including Humans," I replied, offering one of my practiced lines.

The General's eagerness seemed to only grow. "To what quantity can you produce such items? Are we able to forge them here in Orlondia with your aid? Is there a limit to how many different kinds of magic someone can use at once?" His questions flowed like a flood rushing through a desert. A nervous chuckle escaped my lips as I tried to collect the answers I would give him while protecting my sacred knowledge.

However invaluable these enchanted objects may be, they owe their existence to the symbiotic relationship between the Siren and their bonded Sea Dragons. Along with the expertise of the Dwarves in capturing and channeling magic through Runic inscriptions.

Sea Dragons, unknown to most, are integral to the enchantments crafted in collaboration with the Siren and Dwarves in Forge Peak. This unique blend of magic is not found anywhere else in the realm.

I knew I would need to be as diplomatic as possible with my answers and show genuine empathy as I explained things. I started with the answers he would likely find most displeasing.

Frowning, I wore a look of empathy on my face. "Unfortunately, our process is unique because of a variety of factors, one of which is the location being Forge Peak, an active volcano among the Western Isles and part of my kingdom, Faedamir."

I smiled, trying to emphasize the positive aspects of our process. "However, we can produce simple weapons like arrowheads and daggers rather quickly that can pierce any armor or magical ward. These would still need to be used by skilled warriors to be effective in battle, but can be produced in very large quantities." I watched the General ponder my answers, hoping I could satisfy some of his curiosity without giving away too much.

I decided to offer more information to address his active thoughts. "When we use our unique process of forging a Runic object, it becomes accessible to any wielder, albeit with certain limitations. The stored magic may require periodic recharging for specific enchantments to remain effective. For instance, a Runic gemstone embedded in a necklace could enhance the wearer's beauty, projecting a captivating aura visible to all."

I tried not to fidget, but my fingers slowly felt the fabric of my ruffles. I continued with my smile soft and tone sweet. "Similarly, a Rune of strength inscribed on a forged sword may grant the wielder the ability to deliver more forceful strikes. While protective Runic armor provides defense against many magical assaults. One could use a variety of Runic items because the item serves as the vessel for the stored magic. Unlike Dwarven Runic items, which are made to channel their specific magic through the item, making it nearly impossible for any other magic type to use such an item."

General Magnus nodded thoughtfully, absorbing the information. "Fascinating," he murmured, his gaze flickering with newfound understanding. "And what of the limitations you mentioned? How often does one need to recharge these enchantments?"

I leaned forward, my expression earnest. "The frequency of recharging depends on the potency of the enchantment and the frequency of its use. For instance, a simple enhancement like the beauty aura may require recharging every few weeks, while more complex enchantments, such as those imbued in weapons or armor, may last for several months before needing replenishment."

He nodded, mulling over the details. "And how is the recharging process conducted?"

I paused, considering my response carefully. "The recharging process involves exposing the Runic object to a source of magical energy, typically through rituals performed by skilled enchanters. This energy replenishes the enchantments stored within the object, ensuring their continued effectiveness."

General Magnus absorbed this information, his brow furrowed in concentration. "It seems your kingdom possesses formidable resources indeed," he remarked, his tone respectful.

I inclined my head graciously. "We take great pride in our craftsmanship and magical expertise. Our goal is to forge alliances based on mutual benefit and cooperation."

He nodded, a hint of admiration in his eyes. "Well, Your Grace, I appreciate your candor and willingness to share your knowledge. Our partnership with Faedamir holds great promise for the future of Orlondia."

He stood and bowed slightly. I offered him a warm smile despite my wariness. "The feeling is mutual, General Magnus."

"I am sure we will have many more discussions on this matter in the future as our need here is great, and we do truly appreciate your willing alliance." He turned and disappeared down the corridor leaving me alone in the dark quiet, as I gathered my breath and sense of calm.

I rose from my seat, smoothing down my ruffles to cascade around me once more. The sound of my fingers running along the iridescent material was a stark contrast to the otherwise quiet, shadowy space. With a deep breath, I prepared to leave the small alcove.

However, my moment of peace was shattered as I suddenly became aware of a figure lurking in the shadows. His eyes gleamed with an unnatural intensity as he watched me, his movements swift and purposeful.

Before I could react, the man lunged forward, his hands seizing my shoulders firmly and pinning me against the rough stone wall of the alcove. His sweat-covered hand clamped tightly over my mouth, stifling any chance of a scream.

My heart hammered in my chest, drowning out all other sounds as panic threatened to consume me. The man's breath was ragged, his skin clammy, and his features frail as he held me there, staring into my eyes.

I would not be easily subdued. I struggled against his grip, my hands searching desperately for something—anything—to use as a weapon. With every ounce of strength I possessed, I fought back against the unnaturally strong assailant, determined not to let fear overpower me.

His grip was unwavering as I writhed between the barrier of his body and the unyielding wall. I sensed an unusual magic flowing through him, but not from him. This realization gave me a moment of pause under his unmoving hold, but I knew I had to act swiftly to escape this perilous situation.

Feeling the urgency of my predicament, I tried to summon my own magic, but to my horror, it felt as though it too was ensnared, trapped by some invisible force. My magic hummed to life beneath my skin but felt bound somehow unreachable.

My signet glowed brightly upon my arm, a beacon of my bond to Azura, but when I reached for the power shared with me, I found nothing. Panic surged through me, icy tendrils of fear coursing through my veins, my breaths coming fast and shallow, my eyes widening with terror. Who was this man? And what sinister force was at work here?

Slowly, he advanced his free hand, now clutching a shimmering blue dagger, toward my throat. Despite all my knowledge, training, and the immense power of my magic, I felt utterly helpless in that moment.

The realization of my impending fate washed over me like a cold wave, drowning out any hope of escape. I was going to die in this stifling alcove, at this wretched party I hadn't even wanted to attend.

The thought left me longing for the comforting presence of my mother, whom I was certain I would soon be reunited with. My body slackened as I stopped fighting, and grew resolved in my fate.

Small tears fell from my eyes, offering a strange sense of comfort and relief amidst the chaos of this moment. I closed my eyes, expecting the worst, but the pressure fell away, my body dropped, my feet firm on the floor. My body trembled, yet I remained standing, rooted in disbelief.

I opened my eyes. My cheeks streaked with tears as I looked around. I saw the assailant lying bloodied and crumpled on the stone floor, a testament to the swift justice that was just dealt. My gaze lifted to meet a pair of captivating sea-storm black and cobalt eyes. They belonged to the woman clad in a striking red dress that matched the color of the blood pooling at our feet. It was Orla who stood there.

Without hesitation, I rushed into her chest and wrapped my arms around her as relief flooded me and my tears fell anew. Her single arm enveloped me, offering silent reassurance as she wiped clean her blade against the skirt of her gown and sheathed it underneath.

Gods, how had I not thought to wear any kind of weapon to this thing and she had, in her own palace. I vowed never again would I be so stupid, because clearly, my magic was not good enough against whatever the hell that was.

I tilted my head, gazing up at her with a mixture of uncertainty and gratitude. "Orla," I murmured, her name encapsulating a question, a statement, and a sense of relief all at once.

She met my gaze, her eyes swirling with a color storm of emotions as she whispered my name in return. "Aure?" Her concern was palpable, her voice barely above a whisper. "Are you hurt?"

Shaking my head against her chest, I replied, "No, I don't think I am, but..." My voice trailed off as I glanced back at the motionless figure on the floor, a shiver coursing through me. "Something wasn't right about him."

Orla's eyebrows furrowed, a hint of amusement dancing in her eyes as she quirked a smile, but it faded just as quickly. "Other than him trying to kill you?"

I pulled back slightly, meeting her gaze with a determined expression. "Yes. I wasn't able to break free of him. No matter what I did, even with my magic." My voice wavered slightly as I confessed, "I couldn't even connect to Azura through our bond. Nothing I have ever heard of can do that, Orla."

My magic surged through me like a floodgate had opened, as my bond signet glowed red hot, and Azura's presence was all-consuming. Her thoughts filled me. *"AURE! What happened?"* I closed my eyes, steadying myself against Orla as I held my connection to Azura in my mind.

"I don't know— a man, and Orla." My words escaped my mind, so I sent the memory through the connection and felt the warmth of comfort coming through our bond wash over me.

Azura's deep concern and equal affections accompanied her words. *"I thought you died. I could no longer feel our bond. There is dark magic here."*

Orla stared at me for a moment as I lingered against her, my eyes closed. Once I opened them, I moved away from her as I felt more steady on my feet.

Turning away from me, she crouched down next to the lifeless corpse, her fingers lightly brushing against his clothes as she examined him. After a moment, she looked back up at me. "He appears to be Human, I think. But we have someone who can perform a full examination on him."

A servant girl walked down the corridor and looked into the alcove. Her scream echoed off the stone walls as she froze in place, her eyes wide with horror at the scene before her. Orla rose abruptly, her posture commanding as she addressed the girl.

"Fetch the royal guard immediately, and Frank, you know who I mean?" Her tone brooked no argument, and the girl nodded frantically before darting off down the corridor.

Taking a step backward, I sank into one of the nearby plush velvet-covered chairs. I tried to steady my racing heart. *"You are safe now, it will be ok. I am right here if you need me."* Azura's calm and comforting words embraced my senses. Her silent presence felt as I tried to come to terms with what happened.

Orla returned to my side, her presence a reassuring anchor. "Let's keep the information about the magic between us, Frank, and Cam," she whispered, her voice urgent yet controlled. "We don't need the General or my father sticking their noses into you or your magic." I nodded in agreement as more people began to flood into the corridor.

Losing myself in the aftermath of the ordeal, the pain was throbbing in my body as the adrenaline rush faded away. I gingerly touched my bruised shoulders and winced at the tenderness, then reached up to feel the soreness on my face.

My gaze drifted towards Orla, who was engrossed in conversation with guards, orchestrating the response to the incident. People had been turned away, and the alcove was now cordoned off by vigilant guards.

As the servants brought in more lights, I shivered involuntarily, the cold air seeping into my bones. Orla, who had been stealing glances in my direction, somehow appeared before me, crouching down to my eye level and placing a gentle hand on my bare shoulders. "Aure, are you cold? You feel cold," she murmured. I nod, my attention still fixated on the lifeless body on the floor.

Orla wrapped a soft woolen blanket around me, its comforting warmth enveloping me like a protective embrace. I was momentarily puzzled. *Where did she get a blanket?* Though, I was just grateful for the small gesture of care. "Thank you," I managed to whisper, my voice barely more than a hoarse murmur.

Over her shoulder, I caught sight of Cam storming past the crowd, her hand resting on the hilt of her sword, a silent warning to anyone who might impede her progress. Frank followed closely behind her, his expression grim. Cam, reached us, stepping forward in front of Orla and put herself between us. Orla stepped back, allowing my guard and friend the access to me that she sought.

Cam embodied a protective presence as she knelt down beside me, her keen eyes assessing my condition. "I am fine, Cam, really," I reassured her with a small smile. Meanwhile, Frank positioned himself beside Orla, and together they approached the scene where the body lay.

Cam shook her head in response to my reassurance. "You are not fine, Aurelia. You're hurt, and..." Her voice trailed off as she glanced over at the grim scene before us. "I should not have let you go alone," she admitted with a tinge of regret evident in her voice.

Turning back to me, Cam gently took my face in her hands, her expression a mix of remorse and guilt. Her lips pressed together in a thin line as she silently conveyed her concern.

As Cam's hands cradled my face, a wave of gratitude washed over me. Despite her regrets, her presence was a comfort. "Cam, it's not your fault," I insisted, reaching up to touch her hand.

She sighed, her gaze lingering on mine for a moment before she nodded in reluctant acceptance. She let go of me and stood. "We'll talk about it later," she promised, her tone firm yet gentle.

Turning to Orla and Frank, Cam motioned for them to join us. "We need to figure out what happened here," she declared, her voice carrying the weight of authority.

Orla nodded in agreement, her expression grave. "Agreed. And we need to tell you two something more, in private, as soon as possible," she added, her eyes full of concern. I nodded, feeling a mixture of exhaustion and apprehension settling over me.

With a heavy sigh, I glanced around at the gathered guards and servants, their faces etched with concern and curiosity. The weight of what had transpired settled upon me like a heavy cloak, but I knew I couldn't dwell on it now.

Turning back to the others, I offered a reassuring smile. "We'll figure this out together," I comforted, my voice carrying a hint of determination. Cam nodded in agreement, her eyes reflecting a mixture of resolve and concern. Frank, unusually stoic, grunted in acknowledgment.

As the others moved to investigate the scene, I leaned back against the chair, enveloped in a blanket of uncertainty. My mind raced with questions and possibilities, but one thing was clear. We needed answers if we ever hoped to not only win this war but also stay alive doing so.

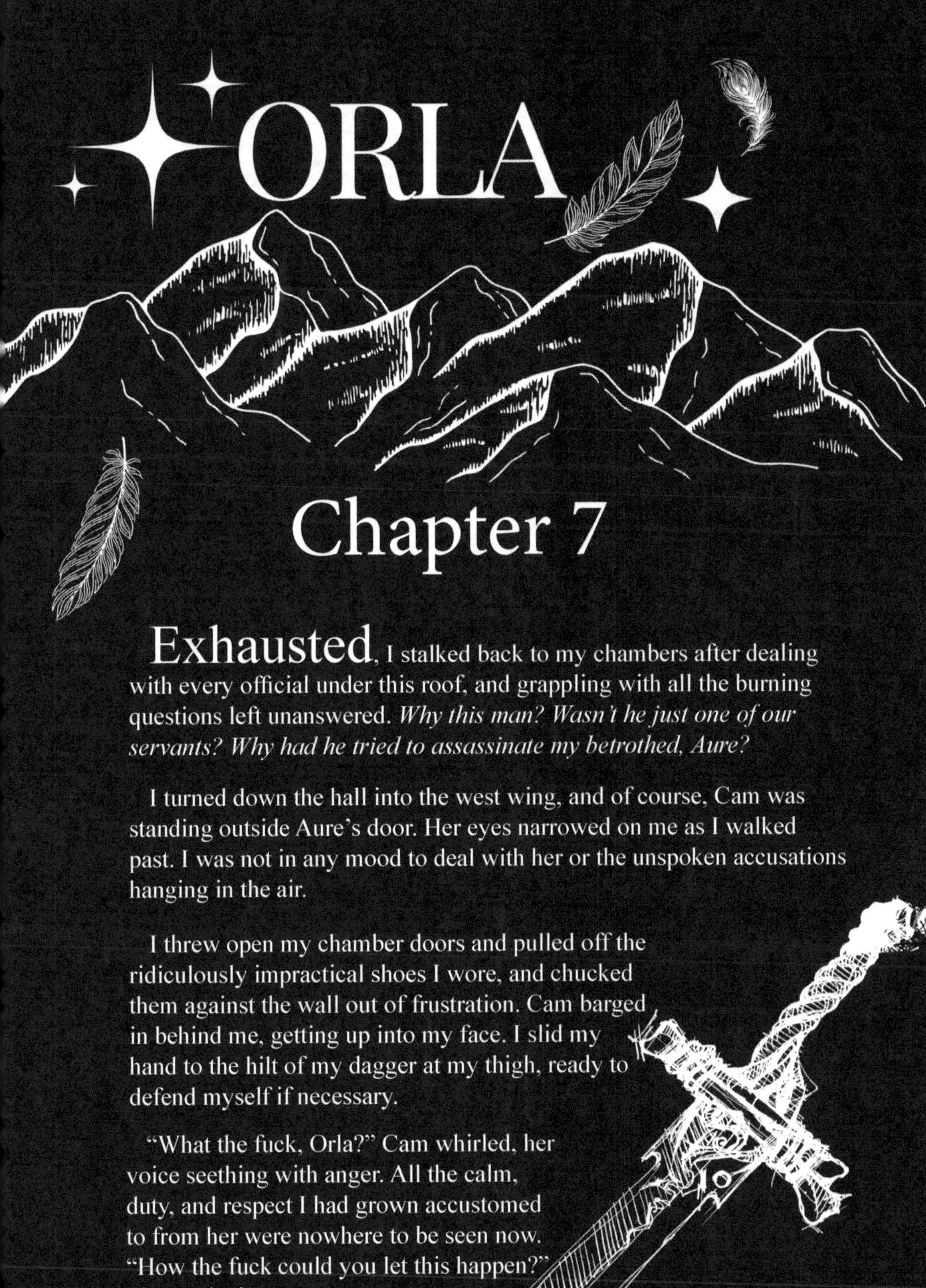

Chapter 7

Exhausted, I stalked back to my chambers after dealing with every official under this roof, and grappling with all the burning questions left unanswered. *Why this man? Wasn't he just one of our servants? Why had he tried to assassinate my betrothed, Aure?*

I turned down the hall into the west wing, and of course, Cam was standing outside Aure's door. Her eyes narrowed on me as I walked past. I was not in any mood to deal with her or the unspoken accusations hanging in the air.

I threw open my chamber doors and pulled off the ridiculously impractical shoes I wore, and chucked them against the wall out of frustration. Cam barged in behind me, getting up into my face. I slid my hand to the hilt of my dagger at my thigh, ready to defend myself if necessary.

"What the fuck, Orla?" Cam whirled, her voice seething with anger. All the calm, duty, and respect I had grown accustomed to from her were nowhere to be seen now. "How the fuck could you let this happen?" She seethed.

"I didn't, and I have the blood on me to prove it," I shot back. I gestured down to my blood-soaked dress. My eyes turned a blue so deep they almost appeared black.

But Cam didn't back down. "You shouldn't have even needed to do that. And how long did he have her? Those bruises on her neck are deep." I gritted my teeth.

I knew all too well what those bruises looked like. I had studied them and all the others on her for hours while Aure sat there after the assault had happened. All the while, the head of the guard questioned her, and the Healers looked over her. She hadn't let the Healers do much. I watched the haunted look in her eyes. She had been so vulnerable without her magic, a weapon, or any other way to defend against such an attack.

What had he wanted, and why was he able to block her magic? I hated seeing Aure, the strong woman I knew, brought down like this. Even though I wanted answers, I didn't for one minute regret killing the fucking bastard.

"Cam, you don't have to tell me how badly she got hurt. I was there. I killed him. I saved her. Where the fuck were you, her personal guard?" I said, my tone cruel and judgmental. Cam stiffened and crossed her arms, my hand never leaving the hilt of my dagger.

Slowly, Cam admitted, "she insisted she would be fine, that I could take the night off. She didn't want to appear suspicious of the diplomats. This alliance is important to her," she gritted out. "And you are important to her."

My heart skipped, momentarily shocked at the boldness of the last statement, but of course, I was important. I was only important to her plan, her kingdom, and the success of this alliance.

Cam turned, running her hand across the hilt of her blade, before speaking again softer. "Look, I don't feel like I have enough information here. You're right, I should have never let either of you go alone, even in the palace. Even though both of you can defend yourselves, I should have never let her go without at least a weapon. I didn't realize it was a concern." She sighed. "It's different back home in Faedamir. It's safer."

She glanced down the hall toward Aure's chambers through my still-open door. I relaxed just a bit and spoke flatly. "I know it's different. I am always armed, always. It's not like this has happened before. I just… don't trust anyone."

Cam nodded. "Have they figured out what he was yet?"

I shook my head. "No. I do not know how he was able to keep her from using her magic, either. To be honest, though, I don't know much about magic in general. I think Frank knows more, but he doesn't really talk about it, and I have never seen him use it." Cam shot me a look of surprise, but said nothing.

She walked over to me and pulled my left hand up, placing something in it. "Take this" It was a small teardrop sapphire pendant on a silver chain.

I held it up to the light, my eyebrows raised. "Um, I don't like you like that, Cam," I joked.

Cam shook her head and sighed as a thin smile showed through. "No, this is a runic pendant called a Rebounder. It should give you protection from one blow, be it magical or physical. It will reflect it back to whoever dealt it. Wear it, please. You are…" she paused letting out a breath, then continued, "important." With that, she walked out, back to her post in the hallway. I closed my door and looked at the necklace once more before putting it around my neck.

I tore off my gown and tossed it into the crackling fire, watching it burn as I walked into the shower. I had to get this gross feeling off of me. The hot water steamed the room, and I closed my eyes, feeling its heat invade my body as I toyed with the pendant around my neck. I felt something buzzing in it, a familiar feeling. It was almost like I could see the threads of magic, even with my eyes closed. I dropped it back into place and started to scrub everywhere on my body, letting the water wash away the remnants of the night.

I knew sleep wasn't going to be an option because I was expected to be in my father's office in just a few hours. I finished up in the bathroom and got dressed in my full leathers, but no metal armor plates today. My father hated that I didn't wear something more appropriate already, but he always had a fit when I wore any kind of military uniform or armor. I wasn't sure what he would expect from me since I never wore dresses unless forced, even as a child. King Oric wasn't known for his tact or his gender equality, and my mother did nothing but placate to his personal misogyny. She played the always-subdued and dutiful wife. I don't think I had ever even seen them fight. My mother always simply agreed, even in her silence.

I felt my sides and sheaths where I had placed my six daggers, making sure everything was as it should be. I sighed and walked quietly down the hall past a now-sleeping Cam and the closed door of the woman who vexed me. I just couldn't figure her out, and it intrigued me but also frustrated me. I passed servants, guards, and the bustle of people with duties in the palace before coming to a stop in front of the large double doors. They were on the main level, in the center of the palace, next to our very lavish throne room. This office felt just as grand and ancient as the rest of the palace.

The doors had worn carvings and metal inlays of gold and copper depicting humanoid creatures five times the size of the human figures. Some with wings, some with fish-like tails, and others that looked like stalking tree creatures. I had never really paid the carvings much mind before, but now I noticed they seemed to depict a variety of people and beings. I wondered if the creatures with fins were Sea Dragons. They were one thing I had only learned existed because of Aure and this alliance. It made me so mad that I hadn't been educated about these things long ago.

I pulled the heavy door open and walked in to find my father sitting at a huge oak desk, poring over maps, books, and papers cluttering most of it. He looked up and saw me, then looked back down. "Nice of you to finally grace me with your presence, Daughter," he said gruffly.

I rolled my cobalt eyes as I shut the door behind me. "Is there any news about the assailant from last night?" I asked, hoping to gain anything from him.

He didn't bother to look up. "The investigators assure me he was simply an over-excited servant looking to take advantage of your beautiful bride-to-be. You should keep her on a shorter leash."

I pushed down my anger, trying to keep my eyes purple as I breathed slowly and controlled. "I see. Am I to assume now that I'm marrying a woman, you will view me as you would a son?" I trained my voice to stay level, though I wanted nothing more than to have a full-out fight with him.

He looked up at me, a quirked, unsettling smile on his lips, before saying, "Do you plan on fucking her with your own cock?" He watched for my reaction, relishing in my discomfort and disdain. Still smiling, he looked back to his maps. "I thought so... No, you are still very much my 'daughter'." A statement that sounded more like an unfortunate fact than any kind of adoration. My teeth gritted together with the sound of release in my ears. I breathed evenly through my nose, willing my eyes not to betray me as they rushed a deep purple hue.

I decided to pry for more information instead and asked, "Are they sure the man wasn't from Frostspire? Or sent by the north?"

My father gave me a puzzled look as he stopped short of what he was doing. "Why would you ask such a ridiculous question, Orla?" He eyed me suspiciously. "We haven't had any enemy movement past North Negall. How and why would they send a single assassin for her?" Why indeed? But this attack didn't appear like a simple rape gone wrong. I knew it, Aure knew it, Cam and Frank knew it.

I walked over to my father's shelves full of books, all of which I had read at least once. "True, I suppose." I ran my fingers along their spines. "Unrelated, why do we not have any books on magic in here?"

Again, he sized me up and down. "So bold lately. Why would we? We don't have magic ourselves and can't use magic. Why would we need books about it?" He watched me as I kept my posture loose, trying not to give anything away. "Orla, are you gaining any sort of magic?"

I tried not to stiffen at the question as I paused and turned, giving a small smile. "Don't be silly, father. I only have a small drop of Fae in my blood, right?"

He nodded as he continued to watch me intently for a few moments. Finally, he looked back down at the map. "Will you find me the book of census taxes for Negall from five years ago and the one for last year, please?" I sighed, feeling resigned once again to the mundane task of fetching books and reading out loud, seemingly useless data.

After what felt like days and not hours, I lay in my bed, exhausted, wearing a long shirt beneath the furs and blankets in my cozy little nest of a bed. I watched the flickering light of the fireplace dance along the ceiling as though it was dueling with the shadows.

I ran my fingers along the pendant for what had to be the thousandth time today, pulling it along the chain back and forth, feeling the hum of magic inside it. As my eyes fluttered closed, my thoughts inevitably drifted to Aure, her presence felt like a gravitational pull, drawing me toward her door which remained tantalizingly close, yet impossibly distant.

My feet fell firmly along the stone floor as I pushed open the door to her room. Aure sat peacefully on the sofa, engrossed in a book. Her beautiful curves guided my gaze down her body. I could not help but lick my lips as heat filled my core, proof of my desire for her. I approached her, my body moving on its own.

I smirked down at her, now close enough to read the pages. Aure turned, noticing my presence as she looked up into my eyes. Her eyes sparkled a soft green like the moss that clung to the palace exterior. Her smile made my breath catch in my throat. I pushed her book down to her lap with a single finger.

"Hi," I greeted her softly, my voice filled with warmth and affection.

Returning my smile, she chuckled softly. "Hi."

Leaning closer, I whispered in her ear, "How wet are you for me?" Her blush only fueled my need further. I reached out, gently brushing back a stray copper curl from her face, my touch light and tender. She leaned into my hand, a silent invitation for more affection.

My fingers traced the curve of her cheek, savoring the softness of her skin. Feeling a rush of emotion, my fingers tangled in her curls at the back of her head and I gripped her, my touch both firm and gentle. As I pulled her closer, the book slipped from her lap, its soft thud against the stone floor the only sound in the quiet room.

I brushed my lips softly against her cheek and across her lips before claiming her mouth with mine. Her lips parted for me as an eager invitation for my tongue, and I accepted with a full exploration. Her scent of citrus and coconut enveloped me as the sweet taste of her mouth indulged my want.

I gripped her ass with my free hand, pulling her even closer to me, which granted me a small moan from her. Her breathless pace increased as she flicked her tongue along my teeth in response. I flinched at the sharp pleasurable pain of her biting my lower lip. I held her so close that with each of her heavy breaths, her breasts and nipples moved up and down my own. Holding her firmly, my fingers pressed into her plush skin through her silk nightshirt.

I let my hand fall from the back of her head, my lips swollen from our kissing. Breaking the kiss, I leaned in and brushed my lips against her neck, my voice husky. "How much do you want me, Meles Tri?" Her whimper and shudder was the reply I received. I let my fingers draw small circles on her upper thigh. "Use your words." I whispered the command against her ear.

She gripped my shoulder as she admitted, "So much, Orla."

With a quiet teasing tone, I asked, "Do you want me to make you cum, Meles Tari?" She let out a slight whimper at my words. She nodded, I brushed my fingers up higher along her thigh moving my hand between our warm bodies. Her body shivered in response to my advance as a soft moan escaped her lips. I smiled, taking her open mouth into mine with a ravenous kiss.

Her eyes fluttered closed as I consumed her, my need for her growing like a hunger in the pit of my stomach. My fingers found their mark against her soft, velvety skin and the pooled wetness there.

She gasped into our kiss as I tightened my hold on her, as if I was trying to melt us into a single being. Her soft sounds fueled my pace as I found a rhythm in teasing and playing with her clit, bringing more liquid heat to my fingertips.

She leaned closer, allowing me to take the weight of her in my arm, my muscles taut like a bow. I felt so powerful, and desire filled me with a single goal in mind: to hear her lips part in ecstasy with my name on them. The waves of uncontrolled quivering caused a smile to play across my lips. Knowing that my goal was within reach, my movements increased.

I kissed down the sweet-salty skin of her neck, nipping and sucking there. Her moans grew louder and her breath ragged. She began to chant my name like she was summoning a goddess. "Orla," it started softly through a moan. "Orla." It grew louder and breathless until.

"ORLA!" Frank shouted my name, jolting me awake, sitting up so fast the room spun. My cheeks heated and my room slowly came into focus. Frank threw my leathers at me, "Get dressed. We have an infirmary to break into."

I groaned at him and pulled my shirt snuggly over my head. "I am going to kill you, Frank." I muttered, slipping to the edge of my bed and tugging on the skin-tight leather leggings up then over my hips.

Frank fussed with a pot and cups on a tray at my desk past my bedroom door, which he hadn't bothered to close. Rolling my violet eyes at him, I smiled. Despite him being annoying, I felt grateful for his loyalty and friendship.

"Did you hear me, Frank?" I shouted a bit louder, wiggling my toes into my leather boots.

The strong scent of brewed chicory root and anise wafted to me. "Yeah, yeah, yeah, ya gonna kill me or somethin' along those lines," he muttered as he held a full steaming cup to his bearded lips blowing on it and sending ripples across the chestnut liquid.

"Smells amazing, Frank. Just the thing I need to get motivated." I ignored the urge to replay the unsettling dream with its vividness and the feeling of reality it brought. I had never experienced anything like it. Embarrassingly, I could still feel the heady throbbing in my center and the pool of hot wetness there.

I had to shake it off. I didn't have time to think about the dream or my feelings about it. Not when we had to figure out why this random man tried to kill Aure. I couldn't. No, I wouldn't let that happen again. She was mine and for whatever that meant between us, I would let no one touch her like that again.

Walking into the sitting area, I turned toward Frank as he handed me a full cup of tea. "Is Cam still on watch in the hallway?" I asked as I sipped the hot tea. It filled my mouth and throat with a warmth that spread throughout my body.

Frank nodded as he drank his cup of tea. "She was sleepin' there. I covered her with one of your throws." He smirked a bit as he glanced toward the closed door, as if he could see her through it.

Finishing my cup quickly, I nodded. "We will have to let her know so she can be alert while we are gone."

Setting my cup back on the tray, I turned, touching each of my daggers, and counting them in their places. Six. I looked at the door, my hand mindlessly going to the teardrop sapphire pendant around my neck. Running it back and forth along its steel chain, the buzzing magic soothing me.

Frank cocked his head, watching my hand. "What is that?" I froze in place like a child with their hand in a cookie jar.

"A Runic pendant." My simple answer was void of information that I didn't even have myself.

"Is it from your girly?" I shrugged, dropping the pendant back in place, as I wasn't sure if it was actually from Aure or Cam.

He approached me, leaning close to the gem and appraising it. "Ah, a rebounder, huh? Looks to be a true Faedamir gem." A smirk grew across his lips as his mustache followed the line, proving his wryness. "Those come in handy in a fight, or a good prank."

"So you know of them?" I wondered how much we had not spoken about, even though we had gotten close these last few years.

"Eh, not one quite like that, but as children, we played with Dwarven rebounder stones all the time. Loads of fun if you set up the prank right, but one like that will be useful in the event of an unexpected fight. It could be the thing that gives you the upper hand." A smile formed as I thought of little Frank running around the cavernous city of Golacia pranking everyone he could.

Frank opened the door and bowed, gesturing toward it. "After you, Your Grace." I shook my head, walking through the door towards the waking Cam.

Frank, close on my heels, and stopped next to Cam. His voice was full of charm as he stated, "M'Lady we are off to find answers from our mysterious assailant. Please be vigilant." He grabbed Cam's hand and kissed it and she glared at him, but nodded.

"We will be back in a few hours. Please keep Aure here until we get back." My voice was full of concern.

"Are you sure you don't want our help?" Cam asked with her own concerned tone.

I felt my eyes as they shifted to blue. I spoke firmly but hushed. "I think it is best if just Frank and I go this time. If we find something we need help with, we can always come back and get you."

Reluctantly, she nodded and slipped into the room. We continued on our way to the closed infirmary where they kept the man's body—the man I killed. I had only ever killed once before, and that was an accident during training.

Unlike before, it was surprising how little I felt about doing such a thing. The accident had wrecked me for months. At the time, I had considered simply giving in to my parents' wishes for me to stay far away from the military and battle. Then Frank came into my life, and he helped me see that sometimes shit just happens, and we have to take the bad with the good. I still regret what happened to the young man during that training, but at the end of the day, it was an accident.

This, though... I had no regrets. I didn't even think before slitting that man's throat. He had her; he was hurting her; he was going to kill her. She was mine and he was touching what was mine.

We arrived at the infirmary, and with Frank's deft hands, the lock yielded easily. Silently slipping into the dark room, we shut the door behind us and lit a small lamp. Its soft glow cast eerie shadows across the cold, lifeless body lying exposed on the table. The examination that had been conducted was undeniable by the marks left gaping across the torso of the bloodless corpse.

Frank's smirk broke the silence, his jest cutting through the somber atmosphere. "How about this stiff, Orla? I think he might have a hard on for the way you handled him," he quipped, gesturing towards the body with a teasing glint in his eye.

Suppressing a chuckle, I shot back, "Well, Frank, I think he might prefer you warming him up instead."

Frank began his inspection, his hands tracing the contours of the body. He started with the arms across the chest and then legs. I let out a soft giggle, unsure of what he was doing. The question formed on my tongue when an inked mark appeared with a glow and charged sound on the man's thigh. Stepping closer, I couldn't help but gasp in astonishment at the intricate symbol etched glowing into the skin.

"What is that, Frank?" I whispered, my voice filled with shock and intrigue.

"Don't touch him, Orla!" Frank said quickly and harshly, his warning strict.

I kept my distance but watched the humming mark as Frank took his blade and struggled to cut through the flesh, crossing out the symbol. He let out a large breath, as if a weight had been lifted off him. The only thing visible now was the bloodless gash left behind from the blade.

"It makes so much sense now. I think I have seen this before." Frank spat out. Confused, I almost spoke, but the sound of approaching voices made us look at each other. He put out the lamp, and we both swiftly moved into action, fleeing in the opposite direction of the interlopers.

We navigated the dimly lit corridors, our footsteps echoing softly against the stone walls. The urgency of our situation quickened our pace as we made our way toward Cam and Aurelia. As we approached Aurelia's chambers, Cam emerged from the shadows, her expression tense with concern. "What happened?" she asked, her eyes darted between us.

Frank quickly summarized our discovery in the infirmary, his voice low but urgent. "The assailant was marked with the symbol of the Order of the Golden Rose. It seems they're involved in this somehow."

Aurelia's eyes widened in alarm, her hand instinctively reaching for the hilt of her dagger. "What is The Order of the Golden Rose? And why would they target me?"

"I have only ever heard rumors of the order. I don't know why you would be the target, but I aim to find out," Frank admitted grimly. "We need to be vigilant. They could strike again at any moment."

Cam nodded, her jaw set with determination. "We'll need to increase security measures immediately. And Orla, we can't afford any more risks. You need to stay close to Aurelia so we can better navigate this."

I nodded in agreement, the weight of responsibility settling heavily on my shoulders. "I agree," I replied, my voice resolute and my eyes violet. "We won't let anything happen to her."

Together, we would form a united front, ready to face whatever threats the Order of the Golden Rose might unleash. Were they working with Frostspire or did they have their own agenda? With Aurelia's safety as our top priority, I stood prepared to defend her at any cost.

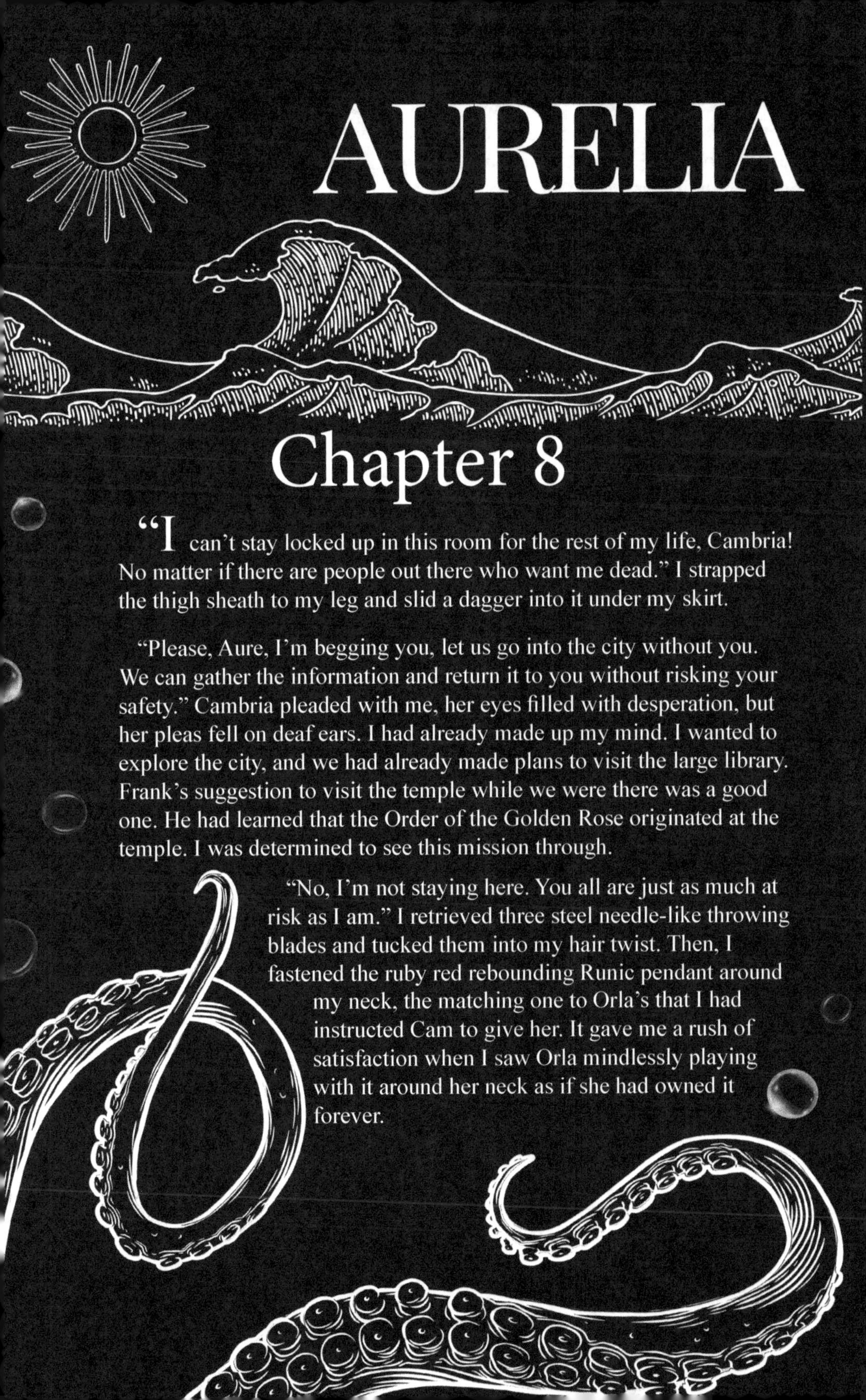

AURELIA

Chapter 8

"I can't stay locked up in this room for the rest of my life, Cambria! No matter if there are people out there who want me dead." I strapped the thigh sheath to my leg and slid a dagger into it under my skirt.

"Please, Aure, I'm begging you, let us go into the city without you. We can gather the information and return it to you without risking your safety." Cambria pleaded with me, her eyes filled with desperation, but her pleas fell on deaf ears. I had already made up my mind. I wanted to explore the city, and we had already made plans to visit the large library. Frank's suggestion to visit the temple while we were there was a good one. He had learned that the Order of the Golden Rose originated at the temple. I was determined to see this mission through.

"No, I'm not staying here. You all are just as much at risk as I am." I retrieved three steel needle-like throwing blades and tucked them into my hair twist. Then, I fastened the ruby red rebounding Runic pendant around my neck, the matching one to Orla's that I had instructed Cam to give her. It gave me a rush of satisfaction when I saw Orla mindlessly playing with it around her neck as if she had owned it forever.

After Orla and Frank returned to my chambers to share what they had uncovered about the assassin, we worked together to piece the puzzle together. Drawing on my experience and Frank's knowledge, we deduced that the Order of the Golden Rose must be using a siphon Rune inked with blood magic on their person.

Siphon Runes are powerful, complicated, and ancient. It's possible that this group has possessed the knowledge for a long time. We needed to learn more about whether they had allied with Frostspire or what other motivations they had for wanting me dead.

Cam pressed her lips into a fine line, and I knew I had won. She wouldn't question me further. As her Princess, she understood I could command her to stand down. She stood by the door in her full armor, which gleamed in the morning sunlight streaming in through the windows. I knew she wouldn't let me out of arm's reach, and that was fine.

A knock sounded behind Cam. I watched as she cautiously cracked the door, her hand resting on the hilt of her blade. As she caught sight of Orla and Frank, her tense stance relaxed, and she swung the door open fully. Damn, Orla always looked stunning in her skin-tight leathers. Even in her more casual attire, the sight of her still sent a thrill through me, tying knots in my stomach.

Orla smiled at me, and I felt heat rush to my cheeks as I gazed into her bright lavender eyes. She closed the distance between us, and I held my breath, releasing it slowly as she stood next to me. Her eyes dropped to the pendant around my neck and then lower. "Is that a rebounder?" she asked with a smile.

"Yep," I couldn't help but smirk, noticing that she had also checked me out. "Are we ready?" I announced loudly, spotting Frank chatting quietly with an unamused Cam. All eyes shifted to me. Frank nodded, while Cam crossed her arms with a sigh.

"I think so. Do you have everything you need?" Orla inquired, not so subtly hinting that I should ensure I had armed myself. Lifting my skirt just high enough to reveal the dagger sheathed there, I flashed it towards her, a small smile curling my lips.

Her grin widened, and she nodded in approval. "Let's go then." She led the way, followed by Frank. I trailed behind them as Cam shadowed my every move. I was excited to finally see more than just this garish palace. The streets were full and crowded with people of all kinds, mostly Human. I noted the Dwarfs and a few Fae among them. There were peddlers and beggars, children and soldiers. It was an overwhelming scene that stole my breath. I had never been around so many people at once. The bright, new-looking tall buildings mixed with ruined, crumbled stones only added to the feeling of suffocation.

Arriving in the evening, I had spent the trip to the palace from the dock inside a carriage, shielded from the crowds. However, now we attempted to blend into the chaos of colors and people. The smell of weeks-old fish and urine accosted me as I tried not to breathe through my nose. Orla, Frank, and even Cam seemed unaffected by this place.

We weaved through the crowds and came upon steps that led to a huge stone structure holding a domed roof supported by marble pillars. I stopped short, needing to crane my neck to see the top of the building, which was carved entirely out of marbled stone with statues of creatures I had never seen or heard of. I felt so small in comparison; my kingdom felt small in comparison.

How would Orla and I ever rule two kingdoms when hers was so vast and grand? Dizziness overwhelmed me as thoughts poured in from everywhere. Cam placed her hand on my arm, steadying me. "We need to keep up," she whispered into my ear, nodding towards Frank and Orla, who had already made their way up most of the stairs.

I swallowed hard and rushed through the maze of people, Cam still on my heels. Guards stood at each entrance door as people passed in and out. We caught up to Orla and Frank as they stood near a door, chatting with the guard there. Frank continued laughing and speaking with him.

Orla turned to me and leaned close so I could hear her. "This is our largest and oldest library in all of Orlondia. We can look through any book here, but it is the rule that we don't remove anything. We can copy out what we need on paper. It has been that way from the start. It safeguards the information here."

Passing through the door into the huge space, I knew it was big, but I wasn't ready to see it. The floor-to-ceiling shelves and round balconies left the center open to the glass dome above. Every wall held books and scrolls, and people wandered throughout. Children sat in groups in partly walled-off areas, studying with teachers.

Orla navigated the space with the ease of someone well-acquainted with this place. Of course she was. She had said she spent lots of her time studying. I watched Orla approach a person in a simple shirt and trousers with thick round glasses sliding down a slender nose. They were tall and lean, with short blonde hair holding a large leather-bound book under one arm. They smiled as Orla spoke, and nodded, then squinted.

Orla finally turned, smiling. "Kepple, this is Princess Aurelia and her Personal Guard, Cambria."

Kepple bowed, their toothy grin bright. "Kepple Thelxiesia, Your Grace. I am also a Siren, born in Faedamir. However, my mother traveled back to Orlondia when I was young. It is such an honor to meet my future queen."

My shock must have been evident on my face. They stated with slight amusement, "I know. How could I love being so far from the water and our home? I love the library though, and the books here are just a part of me. Which is why I take great pride in caring for this place."

They pushed their glasses back into place before continuing. "Orla tells me you need information on the Order of the Golden Rose, and that perhaps you could help in our efforts to bring books to the outer provinces and towns?"

Smiling, I nodded slightly. Kepple must have never completed their rite, living here. If they had any magic, it would be dormant. My heart lurched at that thought. I couldn't imagine not being bonded or not having my magic. Not having access to my magic during my assault still sent shivers down my spine.

Kepple turned and walked toward a gated area with a lock on it. We all followed close behind. Taking a ring of keys, they fiddled with the lock on the gate and opened it, and we filed through.

"We only have a single book, a journal, that I know of that says anything in reference to the Order. The group seems to be very secretive." Kepple explained as we entered a restricted section of the library that held ancient scrolls and weathered books.

We gathered around a table and I noticed how Orla stood on one side of me and Cam was on the other, just behind me. I couldn't help my heart beat a little bit faster, but I also felt annoyed at how protective they both were being of me.

Kepple opened a tattered, old-looking leather-bound book with scrolled handwriting inside. "Here," they said, pointing to a passage. "It states: 'I was taken to the caverns below the temple tonight. There was a large group of people gathered who called themselves The Order of the Golden Rose. My recruitment was considered imperative to their cause, as I am close to the king and my influence in Orlondia. They didn't know, however, that I am a Siren, one unbonded and without access to my magic. I am not Human. Apparently, that is a requirement to join— to be Human and wish to rid this world of all magic and magic-born. I don't agree. I was lucky to be able to talk my way out of joining and wasn't suspected. Thus far no attempt on my life has been made. However, it is clear they are doing untold evil to advance their cause. I don't know to what extent they have gone or will go to reach this end. I warned our king, and we have set to end this cult, but I fear we won't be successful."

Shadows loomed over us as we all realized that this underground organization must have been biding their time and working in secret for a very long time. I watched Orła run her hand through her hair, her eyes swirling cobalt. Gods, the colors her eyes made mesmerized me, igniting an urge in me to turn and kiss her. Instead, I clenched my fists against my skirt.

"As if we need another damn enemy right now," Orla voiced what we all were thinking.

Frank tilted his head to the side, and with a smirk, he said, "Well, at least our pants aren't on fire." We all looked at him and laughter roared out of us. Kepple tried to shush us while giggling. Finally catching our breath, we all turned serious again.

Kepple silently closed the book and walked to a glass case, carefully stowing it away. I sighed, feeling the tension mounting inside me. The ongoing war with Frostspire often felt distant and easy to overlook. However, the realization that I was a target, likely because of my magic, sent a wave of unease coursing through me. My stomach twisted into knots, and a sense of nausea settled over me like a thick fog.

I am brought back to the moment by lighthearted laughter. I then noticed Prince Reinferd hugging Orla, and she returned his embrace. I shifted and moved closer to Orla, and stood right next to her, our arms brushed against each other.

Reinferd looked at me with a small, polite smile that graced his features, his demeanor exuded warmth and congeniality. "Princess Aurelia, it is truly a pleasant surprise to encounter you and your companions here," he greeted with a respectful bow, his voice carrying a hint of genuine friendliness.

Returning the gesture with a nod, I attempt to maintain my composure, masking the twinge of unease that flares within me. "It's likewise, Prince Reinferd," I reply, my tone cordial despite the subtle tension prickling beneath the surface. I struggle to suppress the rising curiosity about the easy rapport he shares with Orla. Offering a polite inquiry, I continue, "What brings you to this part of the Grand Library today?" Though my words convey polite interest, my eyes betray a flicker of apprehension, silently questioning the underlying motive behind his visit.

Reinferd's expression brightens with a genial smile as he responds, "Oh, I was simply browsing through the library, seeking some respite from the day's affairs." His gaze shifts between Orla and me, his eyes lingering on Orla with a hint of warmth. "But stumbling upon such esteemed company is a delightful surprise indeed."

My heart sank as Reinferd's gaze lingered a moment too long on Orla. Jealousy stirred within me, though I tried to suppress it. "Orla," Reinferd began, his tone warm and inviting. "Would you and Princess Aurelia care to join me for a private lunch at the royal gardens later this week?"

His invitation caught me off guard, and I stole a quick glance at Orla, searching for any sign of agreement or hesitation. However, Orla's response was swift and gracious. "Of course, Rein," she replied with a warm smile. "A private lunch sounds delightful. Thank you for the invitation."

I forced a smile, nodding in agreement. "Yes, thank you, Prince Reinferd. A private lunch sounds lovely." Internally, I cursed my own weakness.

Why did I care so much about the budding friendship between Orla and Reinferd? Was it the fear of losing Orla's companionship to someone else, or was it something deeper, more personal? As Reinferd departed, I couldn't shake the feeling of unease that settled in my chest.

Kepple approached me, their demeanor more composed than before. "Princess Aurelia," they began, their tone respectful. "I wanted to discuss with you a matter regarding the expansion of our kingdom's libraries."

Intrigued, I turned to them, gesturing for them to continue. They straightened their posture, their expression earnest. "In recent months, there has been a push to establish smaller libraries in the outer villages and provinces," Kepple explained. "The idea is to make knowledge more accessible to those living in remote areas, ensuring that everyone, regardless of their location, has the opportunity to benefit from our vast collection of books and scrolls."

I nodded, impressed by the initiative. "That sounds similar to what I have strived to do in my own kingdom," I remarked, recalling my own experiences.

Kepple's eyes gleamed with enthusiasm. "Indeed, Your Highness, Orla informed me about your expertise. We require help in organizing and overseeing the establishment of these libraries. Your support and guidance would be invaluable in ensuring the success of this endeavor."

I considered their words carefully, recognizing the significance of such a project. "Count me in," I replied with determination. "I will do whatever I can to aid you and this kingdom." We delved into the logistics of the project, and our enthusiasm grew.

Orła's interruption broke the momentum. "I see you two finally ended up on the topic of libraries, but it's time for us to go, Aure," Orła remarked with a smirk.

Reluctant to leave the discussion, I embraced Kepple, showing my gratitude. "You know where to find me. Let's discuss this more soon," I promised.

As we made our way toward the grand temple, Frank led the way with confidence, his stride purposeful. Orla paced him as I followed close at her heels and Cam became my shadow once more. The streets were just as busy as they had been this morning, but now the sun had grown warm and the smells overwhelmingly pungent.

Orla stopped abruptly, and I fell into her. She caught me before I fell to the ground, her stance sturdy, our bodies tangled, our eyes met and her lips parted. My heart started beating faster and my own lips parted as she pulled me up closer to her. Then I was standing again. She looked at me with a smirk forming at the edge of her lips and whispered, "Careful, Meles Tari."

My breath caught in my throat and biting my lower lip, I nodded. "Yeah, sorry." *What was I thinking? She isn't going to kiss me, let alone here in the middle of the crowded street.*

I finally looked up at why she had stopped. The Temple was in front of us now, and a sense of awe washed over me at the sight of its majestic architecture. The structure stood tall and imposing, its ancient stone walls adorned with intricate carvings that spoke of a rich history.

We approached the temple's entrance. I couldn't help but feel a sense of anticipation building within me as we drew nearer to the temple's threshold. We entered the temple, and a hushed silence enveloped us, broken only by the echo of our footsteps against the stone floor. The interior was bright, with shafts of sunlight streaming through the stained glass windows, casting ethereal hues across the marble floors.

Orla paused, her gaze sweeping over the grandeur of the temple's interior. "This place is ancient and we do not know who might be here," she murmured, her voice barely above a whisper. "We must tread carefully." With a nod of agreement, we pressed onward, our senses heightened as we explored the ancient halls and chambers of the temple.

I trailed behind her, taking in the sights and sounds of our surroundings. The air was heavy with the scent of incense, and I could feel a strange energy pulsing through the very walls of the temple. As we ventured deeper into the heart of the temple, we came upon a vast chamber bathed in a soft, golden light. Ornate tapestries adorned the walls, depicting scenes of ancient battles and mythical creatures. In the center of the chamber stood a towering statue of a goddess, her serene visage gazing down upon us with an air of benevolence.

Orla approached the statue. I noticed her eyes were a soft lavender and she seemed to study the intricate details carved into the stone. "This must be the central shrine of Lunara," her voice barely above a whisper.

I tilted my head curiously, looking up at the dark marble statue of a woman full of curves. She appeared to wear a skin-tight gown with carved celestial designs across it painted in gold. It shimmered in the sunlight; the reflections danced along the floor. She held what looked to be a crescent moon carved out of a white milky stone. It was beautiful. I had never been to a temple like this. Our rituals took place in sacred waters among the Sea Dragons.

"We aren't going to find anythin' gawkin' at some fake lady. Come on, let's try findin' a way underneath this cold slab of rock." Frank shook his head at us, heading for a dark corridor. I wondered if we would actually find anything here.

I glanced at the others. Cambria, with her keen eyes, was already scanning the shadows for hidden mechanisms, while Orla had pulled out a pad of paper and pencil as she started scribbling notes. I hesitated, feeling the pull of the statue as if it wanted to tell me something. "Just a minute, Frank," I called out. "There's something about this statue. Look at the base. There are inscriptions."

Frank stopped and turned back, squinting at the base of the statue. "Probably some weird poem."

Kneeling down, I ran my fingers over the worn words etched in the smooth marble. The inscriptions were in an ancient language, one I thought Orla could likely decipher. "Orla, can you read this?" I asked.

Orla's eyes, swirling violet, leaned in, mumbling to herself as she read the text. "It's a dedication to Lunara, the Moon Goddess. It speaks of a hidden chamber beneath her gaze, where her most devout followers would gather. There's also a riddle here: 'The path to Lunara's heart is found where her light touches last.'"

"Where her light touches last," Cambria echoed, looking around the room. "That must mean something about the way the light interacts with the statue."

We all stood back and observed the statue again. The sunlight streaming through the high windows created intricate patterns on the floor, but there was one spot where the light seemed to linger longer. At the statue's feet, the last beam of light illuminated a small, barely noticeable indentation in the stone floor.

"That has to be it," I said, excitement building in my chest. "We need to press that spot." Frank, raising an eyebrow but now intrigued, joined us at the base of the statue. I reached out and pressed the indentation. There was a soft click, and the statue began to shift. Slowly, the marble woman and her crescent moon moved aside, revealing a spiral staircase descending into darkness.

"Well, I'll be damned! The fake lady has manners." Frank exclaimed in genuine surprise, his smile widening. "Looks like you were right." Taking a deep breath, Orla led the way down the staircase. I followed, my hand resting on the cool stone wall for support. The air grew cooler and damper as we descended, and the sound of dripping water echoed through the passage. The stairs seemed endless, winding deeper into the earth than I had anticipated.

Finally, we reached the bottom, stepping into a vast underground chamber. It was illuminated by soft, bluish light emanating from bioluminescent fungi that clung to the walls. In the center of the chamber stood an altar, and on it, a large, intricately carved chest. Cambria moved forward cautiously, scanning for traps, while Orla examined the walls for more inscriptions. Frank looked as eager as a child on his birthday.

"Do you think it's safe to open?" I asked Cambria.

She nodded, her sharp eyes detected no immediate danger. "I think so. Just be careful."

With a mixture of anticipation and trepidation, I approached the altar and slowly lifted the lid of the chest. Inside, nestled in velvet, was a silver dagger with a hilt shaped like the crescent moon, glowing softly with an otherworldly light. Alongside it was a bottle of dark crimson liquid.

Orla's eyes widened, turning a deep cobalt. "What is that?" Her tone was full of concern.

I reached out and touched the dagger, feeling its cool surface pulse gently under my touch. "It feels runic but different… I think it's charged with dark magic," I whispered. "I have never seen or felt anything like this." As we stood in awe of our discovery, the sound of footsteps echoed down the staircase. We turned, hearts racing, as the silhouette of a figure emerged from the shadows above.

"Who's there?" Frank called out, his hand on the hilt of his sword. The figure stepped into the light, revealing a familiar face. It was Sir Tristan Gareth; I had met him at the masquerade party of the Diplomats of the Alliance. I believe Orla said she had known him since he was a boy.

"Tristan!" Orla exclaimed, a mixture of relief and suspicion in her voice. "What are you doing here?" Tristan looked just as surprised to see us as we were to see him. Without a word, he bolted back up the stairs. Frank and Cambria ran after him, ready for a fight. The chamber grew colder, and a blue light flickered ominously.

Orla and I exchanged wary glances, unsure of what secrets this place truly held. "We need to get out of here," Orla whispered urgently. "This place is waking up, and I don't think it's happy."

I shook my head. "No, not yet. Look." I gestured toward a narrow passageway hidden behind the altar. "Follow me."

Despite her reservations, curiosity got the better of Orla. She followed me through the passage, which appeared to lead to another set of stairs. This time, the descent was shorter, and at the bottom, we found ourselves in a large, dimly lit room.

The atmosphere was thick with the remnants of dark magic. The walls were adorned with faded murals depicting twisted, arcane rituals. Broken ceremonial objects and decayed relics were strewn across the floor. In the center of the room was a large, circular platform with a golden rose emblem engraved into the stone—another symbol of the Order of the Golden Rose. Orla inhaled sharply. "This... this is a ritual room of the Order of the Golden Rose isn't it?"

I looked around as the energy in the room buzzed. "Yes, this must have been where they did their dark magic and forbidden practices."

Quietly Orla said, "This place looks as if it was abandoned long ago."

I looked at her and whispered, "Yes, but I can feel the power they invoked still lingering." We exchanged uncertain glances, the enormity of the complexities sinking in. The remnants of dark magic pulsed around us, a constant reminder of the dangers we face. "Let's go find Frank and Cam," I say finally, wanting to be out of this oppressive place.

With a nod, Orla turns and I follow her back out of the hidden chambers to the temple above. My eyes squinted at the brightness of the light that still streamed in through the windows as we stumbled upon Frank and Cam.

Breathless, I asked, "Did you catch up with him?"

Cam shook her head, and Frank griped, "Bastards' too quick, but he can't hide for long. I will figure out where the weasel goes. One way or another, he will give us answers."

"We should get back to the Palace before the sun goes down. I don't want to navigate these streets in the dark," Cam states to us all as she looks at me, her hand firmly on the hilt of her blade, always ready.

With the feeling of having more questions than answers, I mindlessly follow the others as we leave this place and head back to the sanctuary of the palace. However, it feels even less safe now that someone we know could be a part of this.

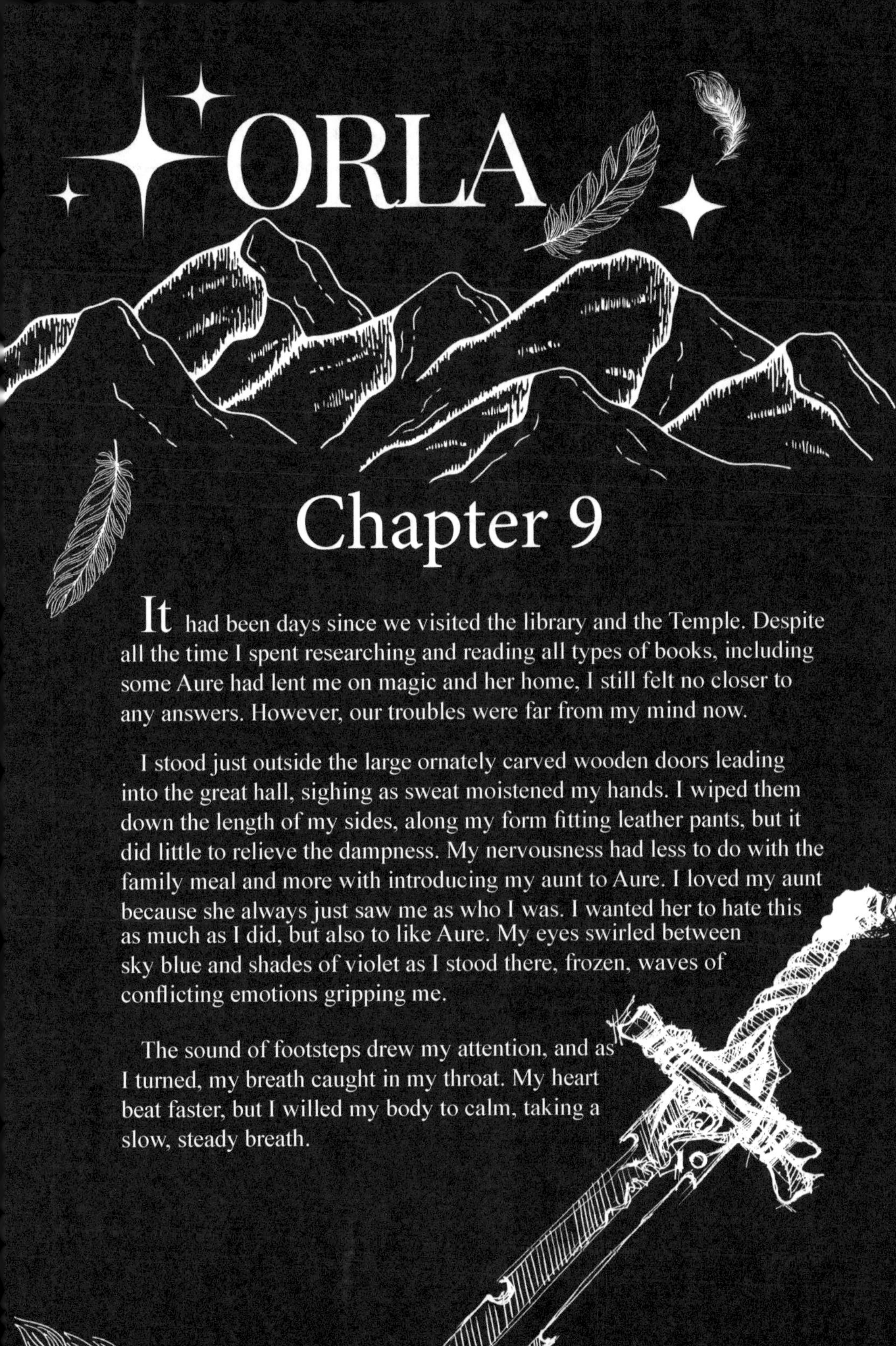

ORLA

Chapter 9

It had been days since we visited the library and the Temple. Despite all the time I spent researching and reading all types of books, including some Aure had lent me on magic and her home, I still felt no closer to any answers. However, our troubles were far from my mind now.

I stood just outside the large ornately carved wooden doors leading into the great hall, sighing as sweat moistened my hands. I wiped them down the length of my sides, along my form fitting leather pants, but it did little to relieve the dampness. My nervousness had less to do with the family meal and more with introducing my aunt to Aure. I loved my aunt because she always just saw me as who I was. I wanted her to hate this as much as I did, but also to like Aure. My eyes swirled between sky blue and shades of violet as I stood there, frozen, waves of conflicting emotions gripping me.

The sound of footsteps drew my attention, and as I turned, my breath caught in my throat. My heart beat faster, but I willed my body to calm, taking a slow, steady breath.

Aure glided closer, the skirt of her gown rippling around her like airy, glittering smoke caressing her hips and the length of her legs with each step. The subtle shade of iridescent blue contrasted with the black trim details of the corset bodice, which fully covered yet still accentuated her curves. Her hair lay in intricate braids around her head like a beaded crown.

She is going to be so fucking distracting, looking like that. I swallowed hard, resisting the instinct to suck my bottom lip between my teeth. Instead of staring longer, I looked down and nodded, keeping my expression unreadable. This wasn't the time to lose resolve. *Orla, this is simply a matter of duty.* I gritted my teeth and my stomach twisted tightly. I reminded myself that she was a Siren, and I had heard the tales of their allure. That was all this was: my weak humanness against her magic.

"Aure, shall we enter?" I said flatly, noting the slight fade in her smile.

"Yes, I suppose we should," she responded in a tone I couldn't quite recognize. *Could she be disappointed or upset with me?* It was of little matter now, though, because with my jaw set, I was determined not to care.

We strolled in, side by side, inches apart but not touching. Looking across the room, my gaze landed on my father sitting at the head of the large dark oak table, polished and shining, despite the marks that showed its true age. My mother and Aunt Lili, though, caught my eye. They stood by the servant's doors, fussing over some trays the maid was holding—likely some part of our dinner.

My aunt was stunning, as always. It was hard to believe that she and my mother were sisters; my mother was so homely compared to the thin yet bountiful curves my aunt possessed. My mother just seemed frail and meek standing next to my aunt. Though my aunt's eyes never shifted colors, they were a deep violet shade that reminded me of a hue my own eyes took on at times. Nothing like my mother's dull brown eyes. I shared more similar features with my aunt than my own mother, but I guessed that the small amount of Fae blood had something to do with it. I didn't think my aunt had magic, though, or at least none that I knew of.

My attention drifted back to Aure, who seemed to step closer to me as I realized my father was staring at us—well, at her. I strode toward my mother and aunt, with Aure on my heels. *Good, she followed me.* I hoped moving behind my father would keep his lingering eyes away from her and on his cup of wine.

"Aunt Lili, it's so good to see you." I smiled boldly with genuine admiration as I embraced her, fully wrapping my arms around her. I pulled her close and an odd hum I hadn't ever noticed vibrated between us. Stepping back, I felt puzzled, though I ignored it as I continued to smile fully.

My aunt's rich smile parted her deep crimson lips. She spoke with such richness it was like a fruit wine. "Oh, my dear Orla, it is so good to see you, too, and— is this her?" Her eyebrow raised as if she was appraising Aure.

"It is so nice to meet you. I am Princess Aurelia of Faedamir," Aure said, extending her hand to my aunt, who responded by pressing her lips into a tight line.

Ignoring Aure's gesture, she remained unmoving. Instead, she spoke harshly, "Your father had some nerve to demand an arrangement like this, and from my niece, no less."

Aure slowly pulled her hand back and plastered on her diplomatic smile. "I wasn't too keen on the idea myself. However, this has been a tradition long before any of us were born." Aure's gaze landed on mine as she continued, "Besides, I have grown rather fond of Orla. I am grateful for the opportunity I have had to get to know her, despite the circumstances."

I watched in awe as Aure effortlessly defended our arrangement. My mother interrupted the tension by meekly stating, "Dinner will be out shortly. We should all take our seats at the table. Please, Lili, come sit with me next to my dear Oric." I turned and nodded to Aure, gesturing her towards the table, our eyes lingering on each other.

We all moved toward our seats on the opposite sides of my father. My mother sat to his right, I sat to his left, Aure sat next to me, and my aunt was next to my mother. My father's greedy, wandering eyes lingered on Aure as she sat, making my teeth grind against each other. My eyes swirled a deep cobalt as I glared at him.

My aunt tilted her head as she observed me. She turned to my father, her voice smooth as silk and sweet as honey, and said, "Oric, darling, tell me, how has the war been going?" His gaze snapped to my aunt, lingering on her tight gown where her breasts peaked along the neckline, seeming to inch closer to release with each breath. I shook my head as my eyes settled back to lavender. *How did that dress not rip at its seams?*

In a booming voice, my father spoke, "I received word just a few hours ago that the north has pushed the line again and has nearly reached the walls around Atteris. Since it is the largest city in North Negall, the front is requesting more troops to be deployed. Along with any other weapons or aid we can send. We can't have Atteris fall to the north; if it does…" My father shook his head, but I saw the gesture as nothing more than a show about the war. It always bothers me. He spends so much time talking about the war and very little actually doing anything actionable.

I noticed the worried look that grew on Aure's face as she listened to my father. The urge to reach over and take her hand to comfort her drove me to find my napkin instead, which I grabbed and fisted under the table.

Leaning towards her, I whispered, "My father likes to make it sound worse than it likely is. If it were urgent, he wouldn't be here having dinner with us; he would deploy troops and arm himself for battle." I hoped my words would soothe her worry and allow her to focus on better things.

However, it gnawed at me, and I wondered if Reinferd had also received the same news and could shed some much-needed light on the topic. I wanted to excuse myself from this dinner and find out, but I stayed rooted to my seat.

Aure spoke with such confidence and care to the table. "Well then, I am glad our treaty has come together at such a critical time." She smiled and placed her napkin on her lap. My father's eyes met Aure's, and he licked his upper lip, brushing against his mustache hair. Aure straightened her back and held his stare, not backing down. I clenched my fists under the table.

Aunt Lili smoothly spoke, "You worry so much, Oric; I know your powerful army will do what is necessary to keep the line." She snapped her fingers at a servant, "More wine for your king and refill mine, too." The servants hurried their pace out of fear. Some started to bring out plates of food, another did as Aunt Lili commanded.

My father nodded as he returned to watch my aunt with lustful eyes. I relaxed some, but rolled my eyes as I observed the scene silently. My father being too friendly with my aunt had been a thing my whole life, and I simply didn't care to know what went on there.

Aure, undeterred by my father or aunt, spoke up. "I can send word to my father tonight to send some of our ships in aid. Also, I believe the first shipment of weapons arrives soon, so you could send them to the front lines as soon as they arrive." Grace radiated from her as she smoothly added to the conversation, seemingly unphased by the flirtatious scene between my aunt Lili and my father, or my father's wandering gaze on her. I never involved myself in these sorts of discussions. My father seemed to only want attention and used the war as his personal hardship to gain sympathy. I pushed my food around my plate.

My father filled his mouth with the roast duck, and he spoke, "HMMM, yes, umh I can't wait to eh, see these weapons." His lips smacked as bits of the duck fell into his beard. He drank from his cup and his lips stained scarlet with the wine. It was enough to turn anyone's stomach.

Aunt Lili's eyes seemed to spark at the mention of the weapons. She looked at Aure, her lips curling into a wide smile. "Aurelia, do tell us more about these infamous weapons of yours."

Aure wiped her mouth with her napkin, smiled and said, "It is only the first of many but this shipment should have magic piercing arrows, and protection amulets and a few other things to provide aid to the front lines."

Aure's simple response seemed to satisfy my Aunt Lili. Though she had a glint in her eyes, Aunt Lili retorted, "Seems like small trinkets, compared to the value of my niece. Is that really all you gave her away for, Oric?" She turned to my father, smirking.

Her boldness shocked me, and I felt my eyes turn sky blue. I looked at Aure, whose face turned beet red, and her lips pressed firmly against each other. My father spit out his drink of wine as he choked on it, and my mother turned a lighter shade and she looked down into her lap.

Softly, my mother spoke, "Please Lili, we all agreed this was the best thing, remember?"

My aunt said, turning to my mother. "Helena, I remember discussing the potential it could have for us to align with Faedamir, but is this really the only way?"

Aure spoke up, "My father wished to seal this alliance in the traditional and binding way. In no way have we intended it to mean that we bought Orla as some sort of object or slave."

My aunt spoke with true passion, "You seem like a lovely young lady, but you don't act like you know anything about wars, kingdoms, strategy, or alliances. I bet you have spent your whole life tucked away on that little island playing queen in your little sand castle."

Aure was calm and firmly looking at my aunt with her large green eyes and a smile. She said with ease, "I may not have ever been in a war, but I have daily negotiated treaties and grievances between a vast variety of people and races. Yes, I do call the beautiful islands of Faedamir my home, but I have traveled to all kinds of places. None as large as Orlandia before, but don't mistake my inexperience as some kind of ignorance of the ways of the world. May I remind you that the first Queens of Negall successfully united their kingdoms in this very same manner during the first great war?"

Gods, I was in awe of how damn beautiful Aure was speaking up like that. I just could never imagine being so bold. I felt the urge to add something. I wanted my aunt to be angry about this, but I didn't want her to take it out on Aure. I didn't know what I wanted. My body buzzed as I ran my fingers across the Sapphire rebounder that hung around my neck, and I pushed my still-full plate away. I looked at my aunt and spoke flatly but loudly, "Aunt Lili, it is my honor to fulfill this duty for my kingdom. We need the aid. I am happy to do my part to help with the war, finally."

My aunt smiled at me, full of affection, "Of course you are, my dear. You are a strong, noble woman." With that, she turned and in hushed tones, she and my parents spoke amongst themselves.

Aure turned to me smiling, then said in a whisper. "Thank you for saying that. I am glad to know we're on the same side." She took another bite of food. My fingers are still teasing with the pendant around my neck. Aure pointed to it and asked, still whispering. "Do you like the pendant I told Cam to give you?"

My hand dropped back to my lap, and I blushed slightly, my magic hummed, and my eyes turned violet. "Uh, yes, I do."

Aure nodded and quietly spoke so only I could hear. "I am glad you like it. I just thought we should be as safe as we can be." She looked over at my family and my aunt turned back to us, smiling.

"So, Orla dear, we are having a big party for your thirtieth birthday in three weeks, right?" I nearly choked on my drink of wine as I swallowed hard, my eyes shifting to bright sky blue.

All eyes turned to me as I covered my mouth with my napkin. Trying to regain my composure, focusing on my breath. Aure looked a bit curious while a small, sweet giggle escaped her. My father grunted and took another bite of his duck, tearing into the flesh like a dog. My mother watched my Aunt Lili intently.

My fingers buzzed and tingled, but I took a deep breath. "Actually, Aunt Lili I was just hoping for a quiet day and maybe hit the tavern or something with a couple people. I don't need some big thing."

"Nonsense, you are the Princess and the heir. Thirty is a big deal, plus we haven't been able to celebrate your betrothal either. You must let me plan a grand event for you." My Aunt Lili spoke with such excitement, I usually couldn't say no to her and once she got an idea in her head, it happened. I looked at my mother. Her smile and stare were unchanged, as though painted on. My father was fully attentive to devouring his meal in the glutenous way he always did.

Reluctantly I smiled and shook my head slightly and responded, "If that would make you happy, aunt."

My aunt's eyes sparkled as she smiled in satisfaction as she clasped her hands together. "Wonderful darling, then it's settled. I will plan the most beautiful birthday. Aurelia, you seem like someone who knows her way around a good party. Care to help me plan the event?"

Aure, always the diplomat, smiled graciously as she nodded and replied, "Of course, Lady Lili, that would be wonderful. Thank you for asking." Her smile didn't reach her eyes, and I noticed her subtle nervousness as she fidgeted with her skirt under the table. I couldn't help but smile at all the little things I was noticing about her. My eyes had fully settled back to lavender as I took a small bite of my food, trying to get something in me.

Everyone had finished around me as the servants cleared the empty plates. Mine still sat mostly untouched. I placed my napkin across the top of my plate so the servants knew to take it as well, which earned me a sideways glance from Aure and a look of concern. Trying to ignore Aure, I turned to see my father staring at my aunt again as they exchanged quiet words and laughter all in front of my steadfast mother.

I had about enough of this for one night and stood, my chair scraping loudly across the stone floor as I did. All eyes turned to me and I pivoted, holding my hand out to Aure.

With my voice bold, I spoke loud enough my family could hear me. "Aurelia, care to join me in getting some fresh air before we retire for the evening?"

Aure smiled fully and beautifully at me as she reached her hand to mine, a small shock sparked between our fingers. I helped her stand and I bowed slightly to my family and said, "Good night."

Aure also bowed slightly before speaking, "It was lovely to meet you Lili, and dinner was incredible, Queen Helena. Thank you for hosting me, Your Grace, King Oric." I gripped her hand tightly in mine as I led her out of the great hall and towards an outside door. The warmth of her hand in mine and the hum of energy that was there made me painfully aware that I never wanted to let go.

Forcing my fingers open, I dropped her hand, stopping in my tracks. "I'm sorry about dinner." I stared down at her hand as she finally relaxed it against her skirts. The unsettling stirring of my eyes swirled with purple and blue, my emotions a crashing storm inside me, flipping my stomach over. My gaze returned to her face as she watched me, and her lips formed a soft smile.

"Dinner was lovely, Orla. There's nothing to apologize about. Your Aunt Lili seems very close to you." I just nod. The way she says my name reminds me of the dream I had and sweat returned to my palms as the desire to pull her into a kiss consumed my mind. Almost as much as it had when I had caught her in my arms just days ago, on our trip into the city. I nearly let my emotions take over that day in front of everyone. Perhaps her magic was growing stronger over me and I just needed more distance.

As if to prove just that to myself, I took a step back, and finally responded, "Yes, my Aunt Lili and I get along well. She is someone I care deeply about."

Nodding, she spoke. "I can tell, and I did really appreciate that you said that you wanted to honor our arrangement. However, I want you to know that I want this treaty to be a partnership between you and me. Even if our marriage never becomes romantic, I truly think we can rule our kingdoms together well, and for the better." She touched my arm so gently it sent shivers up my spine.

My lips parted and my throat felt so tight I could barely get the words out. "I think so too."

My whole body felt on fire, like tiny bees were stinging every part of me. I felt dizzy, my eyes swirled, and my breathing grew fast. Then the world went black.

Ice cold darkness consumed every part of me. I couldn't feel my body, myself, nothing but the consuming blackness. I had the feeling of awareness of the nothingness here, just the icy cold sensation that was deep and painful.

My thoughts raced. *What is happening? Where am I? Am I dead? Aure?* Slowly, I saw the white of my breath, like I was breathing outside in the dead of winter. I felt an intense shiver that ached everywhere. The mixture of sensations overwhelmed me as I wished to close my eyes and wake up from this nightmare. *It has to be a nightmare, right?* I heard a familiar voice but I couldn't remember whose. The soft, sweet melody filled the air around me and fueled the warmth buzzing in me now.

Meles… Meles…hush now and slumber…

Sweet… Sweet… Meles Tari…

Be still. Mother holds you here…

Meles… Meles… hush now and slumber…

Sweet… Sweet… Meles Tari…

One day Meles Tari… you will rise in the warm sun and fly…

Meles… Meles… hush now and slumber…

Sweet… Sweet… Meles Tari…

Slowly the pain subsided, and I was filled with warmth, like a spring morning sun.

The only sound is the melody filling the air around me in an unending rhythm. The darkness faded against the brightest golden light, like your closed eyes against the rising sun, but more gold. The light was just as overwhelming as the darkness had been. Still unable to make out anything other than the all-consuming brightness and warmth I felt now, I faded into the emptiness.

AURELIA

Chapter 10

"ORLA!" my voice cracked as I screamed her name, reaching her just as a burst of magic exploded from her, shaking the whole palace. The color drained from her face as I wrapped my arms around her torso. Her legs gave way, her weight a sudden burden I wasn't fully prepared to bear. My legs buckled beneath me, and we fell to the floor. I took the full brunt of the impact as we landed in a heap on the cold marble floor.

"Orla!" My voice was full of urgency and concern. "Don't do this to me. I can't lose you, too," I breathed the hushed plea.

In the tangled mess of our bodies, I held her to me. Her breath was shallow. I gently caressed her cold face as my signet bond glowed, my magic flaring to life. *Azura, what do I do?* My mind reached out to her.

"Calm, focus, now sense her life force, her magic ." Azura's voice was the calm I needed in that moment. I did as she directed, forcing my breath to steady. I closed my eyes and placed a hand over Orla's heart. It was beating, steady and true. I focused on her energy, the one she held so tightly inside, now a crashing tidal wave flowing through her.

My eyes shot open, wide with shock. *"Azura, she has so much power. How has she not burned up or erupted before?"*

Azura's connection strengthened through me, and her response was startling. *"It feels ancient, like our magic, the Sea Dragons, Aure. Like some of the magic only ever told in the tales when we were young."*

"What do I do?" I looked down at Orla's closed eyes, her chest rising and falling more easily now. I caressed her cheek, feeling the cold chill of her skin still.

"There is little you can do. She has to regain control of her magic, like you did during your enkindling. I know Fae and even Dwarfs go through a similar process during their enkindling . Perhaps this is what it is." Azura's words offered less comfort than I wanted and only raised more questions in my mind. However, I had little time to ponder them because the doors to the great hall burst open, and Lili bolted through.

"What did you do to her?" she seethed, falling to her knees beside us and cupping Orla's face in her hands. Queen Helena walked slowly behind her, pale and trembling, staring at the scene from a distance. "Get me the healers. NOW! You fools," she commanded, and the servants scattered like insects, scurrying out of the hall.

"I did nothing, Lady Lili. She just collapsed on top of me, no less." Lili pulled Orla off me, cradling her as best she could. Orla was taller and muscular, a contrast to Lili's elegant frame. I untangled my legs and dress from Orla's body and sat up next to them. A rush of servants and healers crowded around us, one helping me to my feet.

They carried Orla to the infirmary, and I followed as closely as I could, sticking to the caravan of people. We entered a room that was bright and smelled strongly of witch hazel and pungent alcohol. Wooden chairs lined one wall, and a simple flat bed covered in white linen dominated the center. A cabinet stood along one wall next to a tall table with containers filled with various unknown liquids. I didn't see either of Orla's parents. The healers laid her on the flat white bed and drew a crisp, cream curtain around the space to provide privacy while they worked on her, trying to determine what was wrong.

But I already knew—she would have to do the work and align with her magic. There was nothing anyone could do for her now. Regardless, though, I stayed just out of the way, waiting and watching. Lili refused to let go of her hand as she sat by the bed.

The healer determined Orla was unconscious but stable. They had no idea what had caused it or when she would wake up. Cam entered silently, and I rushed to her, hugging her tightly. I whispered in her ear, "It's her enkindling, at least we think so." I let her go, and her eyes fixed on where Orla lay.

Cam spoke in a hushed tone, "Was that the surge I felt? It was strong." I nodded, glancing at Lili, who was still holding Orla's hand tightly, her focus unwavering.

Turning back to Cam, I asked, "Have you seen King Oric or Queen Helena? I don't understand why they aren't here. Also, does Frank know?"

"I'm not sure. I'll go check and see if I can find him." Cam hurried out of the room, and I walked over to Orla, taking a seat opposite Lili. She looked at me, her intense violet eyes swirling with magic but not changing colors. In that moment, I knew she was magic-born. Her magic felt familiar, yet I couldn't pinpoint her race. She had no pointed ears like the Fae, she was tall like Orla, and she didn't feel like a Siren. It puzzled me. How could I recognize her magic, but not where it came from?

A servant walked in and leaned toward Lady Lili, whispering something in her ear. Her expression shifted from concern to anger, and she glanced at Orla before standing. Looking down at Orla, she said, "Be strong, my dear," gently touching Orla's cheek. Without another glance at me, she left the room, and I was alone with Orla.

I leaned in close to Orla's face; she looked so peaceful lying there. I whispered to her, "You are strong, Orla, and you can get through this. I am right here with you, and I always will be." Overcome with emotion, I kissed the soft skin of her cool cheek. *Do her lips feel just as soft?* I wondered. I pulled back just as I heard footsteps approaching the doorway. Cam entered, followed by Frank, who rushed to the side where Lili had been, taking in the scene.

"Well, well," Frank said, his eyes twinkling with mischief. "If I didn't know better, I'd say I walked into a romantic drama. Next thing you know, you'll be writin' poetry about her eyes and serenadin' her with a lute."

Cam shot him a look, but Frank just grinned. "Hey, don't get me wrong. If I were in a coma, I'd want someone whisperin' sweet nothing and kissin' my cheek, too. Maybe I should start practicin' my swoon, just in case."

Frank then dipped down beside Orla, examining her with exaggerated curiosity. "Orla, Orla," he said in a mockingly dramatic tone, "I never knew you to play the damsel in distress, but I've got to admit, it seems to be workin' for you. Who knew you'd get all this attention?"

Despite the seriousness of the situation, I couldn't help but smile at Frank's antics. Cam rolled her eyes, but even she looked slightly amused.

"Alright, Romeo," Cam said, nudging Frank aside. "Let's focus. Orla needs our help, not our theatrics."

Frank stood up, saluting playfully. "Understood, Cap'n. But seriously, what's the plan?"

I took a deep breath, trying to steady my emotions. "The healer said she's unconscious, but stable. They don't know what caused it or when she'll wake up. I think it's related to her enkindling; her magic is out of control."

Frank's expression turned serious, his playful demeanor slipping away. "Okay, then. Whatever she needs, we're here for her."

Cam nodded, her eyes full of determination. "We won't leave her side."

As I looked at my friends, I felt a surge of hope. With their support, I knew we could help Orla through this, no matter how long it took.

The hours turned into days, and we took turns watching over Orla. Though her parents never visited, her Aunt Lili came by every day. I had duties to attend to, and Cam remained a steadfast shadow as I went about them. Today, I was to meet with the council of Orlondia to discuss various matters, including a wedding date. It felt wrong making these decisions without Orla, but I guess war waits for no one.

As I approached the ornately carved doors of the meeting room, my hand fell upon one of the creatures depicted on it—a Sea Dragon. Had Orla really seen this every day and not known what it was? I traced my finger along the worn lines in the wood, my heart aching for the sea and for Azura. She had been more distant lately, which was expected as she grew closer to laying her egg and sleeping over it. My eyes stung with the tears that threatened to fall, homesickness growing stronger.

Cam touched my shoulder, and I shook my head, coughing to clear my throat and shake off the emotions building inside me. "Let's do this, then," I spoke firmly, though I felt shaky.

We entered the council chamber of Orlondia which was a grand room with a high ceiling, adorned with tapestries depicting the kingdom's rich history. A large wooden table occupied the center, surrounded by chairs. Light filtered through smoked glass windows, casting the room in a hazed but bright light. The atmosphere was tense, reflecting the gravity of the matters to be discussed.

King Oric sat at the head of the table, his expression stern and contemplative. General Magnus, his trusted military advisor, stood nearby, rugged and pragmatic. Prince Reinferd of Negall sat on the king's right, eager to prove himself. Duke Kinsmere, the head of the Golacia Mountain Dwarf Clan, sat next to General Magnus. Madame Koi sat next to my seat across the large table from the king. Various diplomats from allied kingdoms and officials of Orlondia filled the remaining seats.

Cam stood silently behind me, offering a steady presence as I took my place at the table, feeling the weight of representing Orla and our future.

King Oric opened the meeting with a formal greeting. "Thank you all for coming. We have much to discuss today, from the state of our war efforts to the plans for the upcoming wedding."

I shifted in my chair as King Oric mentioned the wedding and not the fact his daughter was currently unconscious. I sat silent, taking everything in.

General Magnus began with a detailed report on the current state of the war. He unrolled a large map of the kingdom, marked with various strategic points and battle sites. "Our forces have held the northern front, even though it was pushed close to the city of Atteris, but we've lost more ground in the west. The enemy's recent advances have put us in a precarious position," he said, pointing to the areas in question. "Here in the north, we managed to repel their last assault, but their numbers are growing. Intelligence suggests they're receiving reinforcements from the east."

Prince Reinferd leaned forward, his eagerness palpable. "We should launch a bold maneuver to outflank them here," he said, pointing to a vulnerable spot on the map. "A swift attack could catch them off guard and turn the tide in our favor."

General Magnus shook his head. "We can't afford to be reckless. Our priority should be to preserve our forces and strengthen our defenses. A failed offensive could leave us even more vulnerable. I don't think you wish to lose Atteris, Prince Reinferd, do you?" Reinferd sat back and crossed his arms over his chest and his jaw set, but he didn't offer any response.

High Chancellor Malachi, head of the Diplomats of the Alliance, added his thoughts. "We must consider our supply lines. A bold attack might spread them too thin, leaving our troops underfed and under-supplied. The enemy could exploit this weakness." His statement granted him several nods of approval from around the table.

King Oric looked contemplative. "We must balance caution with action. While a bold move could be advantageous, we cannot risk the security of our forces and our people. General Magnus, continue to fortify our defenses and monitor enemy movements closely. Prince Reinferd, prepare a contingency plan for an offensive strike should an opportunity present itself." Reinferd nodded, though his frustration was evident.

Diplomats from allied kingdoms shared their contributions to the war effort. "We are sending additional troops and supplies," one diplomat said. "Hasn't our alliance with Fædamir also secured runic weapons and magical training for our soldiers?"

Madame Koi spoke up, "Fædamir's enchanters will join the front lines, providing unique magical support that could be decisive. Their enchantments can fortify our defenses and disrupt enemy formations."

Prince Reinferd, skeptical but intrigued, asked, "How effective are these enchantments in actual combat? We need to be sure they'll hold up under pressure."

Madame Koi responded confidently, "Fædamir's magic is renowned for its potency. Their enchantments have been tested in battle and have proven highly effective. They can turn the tide in our favor if used strategically."

I spoke boldly to outline our specific aid. "We are providing runic weapons, magical training, and Enchanters to support your forces. Our aid can be integrated into your strategies to enhance your capabilities."

General Magnus looked intrigued, but cautious. "Integrating magical support with conventional forces is complex. We need to ensure effective coordination."

I spoke confidently to the room, "From my experience, magical and non-magical forces can work together effectively with proper training and communication. It's essential to have clear lines of command and mutual respect among the troops."

Murmurs swept through the room as I gripped the fabric of my skirt under the table. Cam placed a silent hand on my shoulder, and I took a deep breath, unfocused to the surrounding conversations, until I heard King Oric speak again.

King Oric had transitioned to the topic of the wedding. "We must also discuss the wedding date. It's crucial for political stability and morale."

Several tentative dates were proposed, but I interjected, expressing the importance of waiting for Orla's recovery. "It feels wrong to proceed without Orla. We should wait until she's awake and is well."

Diplomats debated the benefits of the marriage: strengthening alliances, ensuring loyalty, and boosting the kingdom's morale. "The wedding should proceed for the sake of political necessity," one argued.

"But Orla's health must come first," I countered, highlighting the tension between political needs and personal loyalty. "I intend to uphold my agreement with providing aid for the war, even as Orla recovers. I propose a different approach. Since Orla seemed less keen on her birthday being celebrated lavishly, we should simply turn the event into an official announcement of our engagement. This will bring much-needed morale to the kingdoms and give us time to decide on the details of the wedding. That gives us just about two weeks to send out invites and announcements and prepare for the event."

Many around the table nodded in agreement, considering the practicality and symbolism of the proposal.

After a moment of contemplation, King Oric spoke, "It is settled then. We will announce the engagement and hold the ball here. Then we will discuss a date that better suits you, Princess Aurelia, once Orla has recovered fully."

The decision brought me a sense of relief mixed with anticipation. With the path forward clearer, attention turned to the logistics of organizing the engagement announcement and ensuring it would bolster the kingdom's morale during these challenging times.

King Oric summarized the decisions made during the meeting. "We have agreed on our war strategies, integrating Fædamir's aid, and tentative plans for the wedding. Assignments will be given to follow up on these points."

The sense of urgency was clear as King Oric gave his closing remarks. "Thank you all for your contributions. We must act swiftly and decisively. This meeting is adjourned."

As the council dispersed, I lingered, feeling the weight of the decisions made and the uncertainty of the future. The war loomed large, and the absence of Orla felt like a void in the midst of these critical discussions.

Approaching King Oric, I bowed slightly before speaking, "May I have a word with you, Your Highness?" His gaze swept over me, his expression lustful, as he looked me up and down. His stare was hot as he bit his lower lip, I noticed Cam move closer to my side.

He nodded, his lips curling slightly. "Of course, Princess. Anything for you."

Shifting slightly, I asked, "Have you visited Orla, *your daughter*?"

The smirk faded from his face, replaced by a sour expression. "I have no intention of indulging in her childish antics. I've been informed there is nothing wrong with her; she simply refuses to wake."

He stepped closer, his tone mocking. "But if she takes a turn for the worse, don't trouble yourself. We can find you another match, little princess."

His fingers reached out and plucked a lock of my hair between his fingers. Cam instinctively moved forward, hand on her hilt, positioning herself between us. The king raised an eyebrow, his smirk unwavering as he released my hair and stepped back.

Cam intervened firmly, "Your Highness, there are urgent matters elsewhere that require the princess's attention."

Maintaining my composure, I spoke evenly, "Yes, Cam, thank you." I turned to the king and bowed. "Your Highness, I will not consider any suitor other than Orla. You would do well to pray to all the Gods of the realm—for the sake of your kingdom and this war—that she does not take a turn for the worse. The consequences will be on your head. Good day." With that, I left him with a frustrated look on his face.

My mind reeling from the entire council meeting, I stalked towards the infirmary, Cam trailing behind. As I entered the room that had become a familiar sight over the last few days, I stopped in my tracks. Reinferd and Frank were sitting on either side of Orla. Grinding my teeth, I strode forward into the room. "Prince Reinferd, what a surprise," I said sharply.

Both men stood, and Frank moved away from the chair, allowing me to take his spot. Reinferd bowed politely. "Yes, Princess Aurelia. I was concerned and wished to see her. I am glad to see she has such wonderful company."

I settled into the chair where Frank had been sitting, speaking softly as I looked at Orla. "Orla, I'm back, and I have so much to tell you when you wake up." Reinferd sat back down.

Frank headed towards the door, gesturing to Cam. "Come, my Lady of the Swords, let's get some food. I'm sure they'll be fine without us." Cam hesitated, but ultimately followed Frank out of the room, leaving Reinferd and me alone with Orla's still unconscious body.

Reinferd cleared his throat, breaking the heavy silence in the infirmary room. "Princess Aurelia," he began cautiously, "I sense that things between us have been strained. But I want you to know that I care deeply for Orla. She's become a great friend to me."

I glanced up from where I was gently holding Orla's hand. The bitterness and jealousy I felt towards Reinferd and Orla's close friendship surged, but I fought to keep my voice steady. "I see," I replied, my tone cooler than I intended. "You've grown close then?"

He nodded, his expression earnest. "We both have been through a lot. We all have. But she's strong, Princess. She'll pull through this."

I sighed, feeling a pang of guilt for letting jealousy cloud my judgment. "I hope so," I admitted quietly. "I just wish I understood her magic better and understood what she's going through."

"You're doing everything you can," He assured me, leaning forward slightly. "She needs you now, more than ever."

Silence settled between us again, the weight of our worries for Orla hanging palpably in the air. After a moment, he spoke again, softer this time. "Aurelia, I know we don't know each other well yet. But I want you to know that I'm committed to forging a friendship with you too, not just Orla. For both our sakes and for the sake of the realm."

I looked at him, surprised by the sincerity in his voice. Despite my lingering doubts and jealousy, I could see his genuine concern for both Orla and me. "Thank you, Reinferd," I said finally, meeting his gaze. "I appreciate that."

He nodded, a small, understanding smile playing on his lips. "We'll get through this. Together."

I nodded back, feeling a sense of reassurance in his words. Maybe, just maybe, there was room for understanding and trust to grow between us after all.

He paused, then added, "I always hate these rooms, ever since I lost my father when I was young."

I kept my gaze on Orla but nodded. "My father spends many of his days in a room like this. And my mother..." My voice cracked, tears welling and burning my eyes.

He reached out hesitantly, placing a comforting hand on my shoulder. "I'm sorry, Princess. Losing a parent is never easy."

I nodded, grateful for his understanding gesture. "Thank you, Reinferd. It's a pain that never truly goes away."

"I know," he whispered, his voice full of emotion. "My father was a great leader, but the little I remember of him is that he always made time for me. Losing him... it changed everything."

I looked up at him, seeing a vulnerability in his eyes as they welled with tears that mirrored my own grief. "My mother was my guiding light," I admitted, my voice barely above a whisper. "She taught me so much about compassion and strength."

Reinferd nodded, his gaze turning back to Orla. "Orla has talked about how your mother must have been a great woman because you are so strong and kind."

A small smile touched my lips, despite the tears threatening to fall. "She has? I never seem to really know what or how she is truly feeling."

"She cares deeply for you," Reinferd observed gently. "I can see why."

I sighed, feeling a weight lift as we shared our grief and our memories. "Thank you, Prince Reinferd," I said again, this time with more warmth. "For being here, for caring about Orla, and for understanding."

He squeezed my shoulder gently. "We're in this together, Princess. For Orla and for each other." Reinferd stood and smiled warmly. "You can call me Rein. Please."

I watched him head towards the door and replied, "Only if you promise to call me Aure."

He grinned broadly. "Deal. Keep up the good work, Aure. I'll see you again soon."

"I look forward to it, Rein. Take care." I watched him fade down the hall through the open door. The space fell quiet, and the air was cool on my face. I closed my eyes and took a deep breath.

Now alone with Orla, I squeezed her hand tightly. "Okay, maybe you were right about Rein." I smiled down at her.

With my emotions spiraling, a surge of instinct pulled me closer to Orla. The air around us crackled with tension as I leaned in, my heart pounding with uncertainty and longing.

My lips brushed across hers, soft and gentle. Her lips were soft and warm against mine, a fragile connection in the midst of turmoil. As our breaths mingled, a surge of magic erupted from within me, sparked by the intensity of the moment. I felt a rush of energy, almost overwhelming, as if our connection had unlocked something powerful and ancient.

Orla's eyes flew open, wide with surprise and a hint of recognition. The room seemed to pulse with the newfound magic, swirling around us in vibrant hues that mirrored the emotions coursing through me. For a fleeting moment, it was as if time stood still, encapsulated by the raw energy between us.

Just as quickly as it had ignited, the surge subsided, leaving us both breathless and bewildered. I pulled back slightly, my hand trembling as I reached to touch Orla's cheek, searching for any sign of understanding in her gaze.

Her eyes, still wide with the remnants of magic as they swirled with a rainbow of colors. Her gaze held mine for a long, suspended moment. There was a depth there, a silent acknowledgment of something unspoken yet profoundly felt. It was as if, in that brief exchange, we had bridged a gap between us, touching a place where words faltered.

Orla's lips parted, as if she wanted to speak, to convey the tumultuous emotions that had surged between us. But no words came, only a soft exhale that echoed the fading magic around us.

I swallowed hard, my own emotions raw and tangled. The air felt charged, heavy with unspoken truths and possibilities. For a heartbeat, I dared to believe that our connection had changed, deepened in a way that defied explanation.

Uncertainty lingered in the quiet aftermath. I withdrew my hand slowly, breaking the spell of intimacy that had enveloped us. The room, once vibrant with magic, settled into a hushed stillness.

Orla blinked slowly, her expression a mix of confusion and wonder. I searched her eyes, hoping to find clarity in the depths of her gaze. But she remained silent, her thoughts hidden behind a veil of lingering magic.

In that moment, I realized that whatever had passed between us was both profound and fragile. It was a glimpse into a world where our destinies intertwined, where magic and emotion collided in ways we could scarcely comprehend.

As the echoes of our shared moment faded, it left me to confront the reality of our circumstances, though I knew that nothing between us would ever be the same again.

ORLA

Chapter 11

The light subsided, and all the muted colors were out of focus. I felt disembodied, as if in a dream, but it felt more real, like a memory. Trying to focus but the shadows and colors were like viewing the world through a foggy window. My attention was fixed on the familiar voices speaking, I heard them say. "What is this, Oric? It could be a cursed object. Gods, it could destroy us all." *Mother?"*

"Nonsense, Helena. You worry too much, my dear. This is rare and magical. It is valuable." The booming voice was clearly my father.

"I can't believe you brought this back all the way from the wastelands of Frostspire. You are completely ridiculous." She laughed softly. I watched the shadows grow closer and then apart again.

"I am not. I think this might have a dragon in it." His tone grew serious with excitement.

"What makes you think that, love? I mean, I can see it is egg-shaped, but a dragon?" Her voice carried a soft, curious quality.

"Well, just look at the size, and the black scales, they sparkle," He retorted.

"Dragons are just an old myth, Oric. There isn't any way this is a dragon," she stated firmly with a hint of annoyance.

"It also hums with magic. See, touch it, and feel," he insisted.

A moment passed, then a loud cracking sound filled the air, consuming me and plunging my world into darkness again. Out of the depths of shadows, I heard Aure's beautiful voice calling my name. "Orla, you are strong. I will not leave you. You aren't alone." I see a bright blue thread of light and it flows in front of me like it is calling me. I don't know how to follow it though. It disappears, the world covered in a fog not fully dark but not fully bright. I felt a rush of wind, and suddenly the familiar stone halls of my home came into view. I felt like a specter, observing the fuzzy scene.

I saw myself as a toddler running through the halls towards my father's office, pushing the large carved wooden doors open. I heard my small voice speak to the images on the door. "Hi daegons." I toddled into the room, my mother racing after me.

"No, Orla, don't bother your daddy," Helena said. She was too late, and I was already giggling my way past the door into the large room with walls full of books and maps. The tables, taller than my small self, filled with trinkets and papers. My father stood at the wall of maps, sticking bright metal pins into it.

He turned, seeing the toddler me, and my mother out of breath from chasing me. I reached out to my father, and he stood there looking at my mother. "Helena, I have told you before to keep this thing out of here," his voice boomed.

"She is your daughter too, Oric." My mother said softly as she scooped my small self into her arms. I buried my face in her long brown hair.

"Only because you can't seem to give me a real child, Helena. Now leave me." With that, he turned back to his maps and trinkets.

I watched as anger rose inside me. I tried to scream, but no sound came out. I watched as my mother's silent tears rolled down her cheeks. She took the smaller me out of the room. Once again, the entire world faded into darkness.

I lost all sense of time. *Had it been five minutes, five hours, days, months, years?* Through the fog I heard Aure again, this time she seemed so close, like right next to me. Her soft lark voice spoke. "Ok, maybe you were right about Rein."

Everything inside me hummed with energy, a symphony of power and emotion. I felt the pull of magic, a bright sapphire blue light swirling around me, drawing me irresistibly toward the voice that surrounded me. The music of her voice filled the space like a call I couldn't ignore, echoing in my mind and heart. It was everywhere, all at once, permeating every fiber of my being.

Warmth brushed my lips, a gentle heat that sent shivers down my spine. The heat of her breath mingled with mine, a connection that felt both intimate and electrifying. It felt like I was waking from a long, dark slumber. My eyes fluttered open, and I saw only her.

Her eyes, an all-consuming green like vivid tide pools in the summer sun, locked onto mine. They were filled with a depth of emotion that took my breath away. Her soft bronze skin glowed with an ethereal light, and her long copper locks curled around her face like tendrils of flame. The air between us crackled with magic, sparks of energy dancing around us in a radiant display.

The sapphire blue light intensified, wrapping us both in its luminous embrace. I could feel her magic intertwining with mine, a powerful and ancient force that pulsed with life. I had magic now. Our connection felt deeper, the magic flowing between us in a seamless, harmonious dance.

As the magic surged, the room around us seemed to fade away, leaving only the two of us in a cocoon of light and energy. The hum of magic grew louder, a resonant melody that filled the air. The sapphire blue light began to shift, intertwining with flashes of emerald green and fiery copper, creating a mesmerizing display of color and power.

My heart pounded in my chest as the intensity of the moment grew. Her eyes never left mine, and in that gaze, I saw everything—love, hope, strength, and a shared destiny. The warmth of her touch, the magic that crackled around us, and the undeniable connection between us all converged into that single, powerful moment.

Then, with a sudden burst of light, the magic reached its peak. A brilliant flash enveloped us, and I felt a surge of power unlike anything I had ever experienced. The light slowly faded, leaving us both breathless.

I somehow knew, now, that I wanted her to be mine and to be hers in return. Overwhelmed, feeling unsure, and my throat dry, I whispered in a husky voice, "What just happened?"

Aure spoke, "Take it easy, Orla. You've been out for days. Don't sit up too fast." Despite her caution, I felt more than fine—energized, even. My fingers brushed against her hand, and tiny sparks of magic flickered between us, hot and intense. I pulled my hand back, afraid of hurting her.

All I wanted to do was pull her close and kiss her for real, to taste her lips, to explore her mouth completely with mine. *But what if this energy is magic? What if it caused a problem? I needed more information about what this is. I don't want to risk hurting her.* I fisted the blanket tucked neatly around my legs and glanced towards the open door and the empty hall. Yet, her scent lingered in my nostrils, a sweet mix of coconut and fresh citrus.

My jaw tightened as I clenched my teeth, struggling to control my urge and the magnetic pull I felt towards her. I could feel her hand shaking as it rested on my leg. Clearing her throat, she spoke, "Let me get you some water. You must be thirsty." She stood and walked over to a table across the room, where a clear glass pitcher of water infused with mint and lemon sat next to some glass cups. I watched her pour the water, her movements graceful and precise. My gaze swept up and down her body. She wore a simple yet elegant pale yellow dress that flowed seamlessly along her body.

I tried to keep my breathing steady. "Where is everyone?" I asked, looking around the empty space, trying to avoid staring only at her. She handed me a glass of the water and I took a full large gulp, the sensations overwhelming, the cool water fulfilling a need I didn't realize I had. The burst of flavor tickles my tongue, fresh and tangy. I drink more and feel like I can't get enough. I choke a bit, but that doesn't stop me from emptying the glass down my throat.

Aure watched me with a look of concern, twisting her lips. She sat back in the chair beside the bed that I now sat in. I realized then that I was wearing only a loose cotton night shift, and I pulled the blanket up further, covering myself. She answered my question with a sweet calm tone. "I am not entirely sure of everyone's whereabouts, but I do know a healer will be in soon to check on you, as they have regularly done so. They will alert everyone that you are now awake. I wanted to take this time alone, to talk with you for a moment." She reached out her hand to touch me, and I felt the charge of magic start, so I pulled away. *God's, I wanted nothing more than to hold her, kiss her, make her mine.*

"What do you want to talk about, Meles Tari?" I couldn't help myself from smirking as I used the nickname I had given her. *I wonder if she actually knows what it means.*

She tilted her head slightly and then sighed, letting out a long breath. She spoke to me with such gentleness, "I wanted to tell you, I'm pretty sure you went through a magic awakening—your rite of passage, your Enkindling."

My confusion was clear by my expression, my breath caught in my throat, and I only managed to choke out the word, "Magic?"

Folding her hands in her lap, she nodded. "Yes, your magic, Orla. Everyone has their own experience with it emerging and, well, yours is very clearly emerging." The look of confusion never left my face, but maybe that did explain my passing out, the weird dreams I had, all those colors I saw, and the strange energy I felt.

Somewhere deep down, I knew. I think I had always known; it was just one of the many aspects of myself I buried and denied even to myself. Avoiding those uncomfortable things and focusing on what I had in front of me was just easier, safer, more comfortable. I itched my legs, which felt prickled with stinging fire and itchiness. "So, the Fae in me, then?" I spoke, staring again towards the hall.

Aure nodded and then pulled a small mirror from the folds of her skirt, handing it to me. "You've also changed some." Her voice was sweet, caring, but cautious. I slowly gripped the mirror, hesitant. *What? I've changed?*

I lifted the mirror to look at my face, and a gasp escaped me. My eyes, no longer the usual swirl of blue and purple, now looked like a kaleidoscope of a full rainbow, full of all colors. Then, a bright blue of surprise flashed, but only for a moment before getting lost in the rainbow reflecting at me in the mirror. *Okay, I can handle this. My eyes had always been a bit unusual. They are just more colorful now.* I turned my head slightly, still looking in the mirror, and the flash of my ears caught my gaze. "What the actual fuck? Why are my ears pointed?"

Aure chuckled softly. "Yes, many Fae have pointed ears, Orla." I turned my head back and forth. My features looked slightly foreign, like I was staring at a stranger, not my own reflection. Though I could still recognize my features and those I shared with my aunt, anything I ever considered of myself looking like my parents had faded.

Aure's chuckle softened as she saw the bewilderment on my face. "It's a lot to take in, I know. The Healers said this transformation is a sign of your magic coming into full power."

I blinked, trying to process everything. "So, the dreams, the colors, the energy… it was all part of this enkindling?"

Hesitantly, she nodded, her expression gentle. "Yes, we believe it's your Fae magic emerging. I found a few Fae healers and they say it's incredibly rare to see it happen this way, but it is possible when someone tries to suppress their magic."

I rubbed my temples, feeling a mix of awe and confusion. "It's just… so much. How long was I out?"

"Several days," Aure replied, her voice thick with worry. "We were all so concerned. The Healers, Human and Fae alike, did everything they could, but it was your magic that needed to fully awaken."

I looked at her, seeing the strain in her eyes. "Did you stay with me the whole time?"

Aure smiled, and a flush rose to her cheeks, her hand reaching out to brush a strand of hair from my face. I flinched at the spark of magic. "Of course. Well, we took turns. We couldn't leave you. Not when you needed us."

A warm feeling spread through my chest at her words. Before I could respond, the door to the room opened, and two Healers walked in, their expressions a mix of relief and professionalism. One was a tall woman with long silver hair, teal eyes, and pointed ears poke through the braids that held back her flowing lock. The other was a young, equally tall man with a slender frame and an eagerness about him.

"Princess Orla," said the Fae Healer, bowing slightly. "I am Healer Willow, it's good to see you awake. How are you feeling?"

"I feel… different," I admitted, glancing at Aure before looking back at the Healers. "But not bad. Just different."

The other Healer nodded. "That's to be expected. Your transformation has been unique. We need to conduct a few checks to ensure everything is as it should be."

Aure stepped back, giving the Healers room to work. "I'll be right here, Orla."

The Healers began their examination. Healer Willow's hands glowed softly with some sort of magic. The other Healer held his clipboard and performed all the usual health checks.

Something inside me grew anxious at Aure's being so distant. I couldn't help but feel a sense of connection with her that held a magnetic pull. Despite the chaos and confusion, her presence grounded me.

"ORLA!" Frank boomed as he barreled past the Healers, scooping me up into a full bear hug and lifting me slightly from the bed. I hugged him back, his warmth and the familiar musk of ale and cedar a comfort I didn't realize how much I missed. He let me go and sat on the bed next to my legs, not minding anyone else in the room. I noticed Cam had followed him in and now stood right next to Aure, my swirling eyes flicking green for a moment.

Frank spoke excitedly to me. "Them Healers worried you might never wake up, but I knew you wouldn't let anythin' keep you down. Your girl Aure here kept fussin' over you like some new babe." With a wide cheeky grin, he nudged my arm. "I told her just to kiss you and that'd wake you up."

My eyes locked onto Aure's. Both hers and my expressions changed to a mixture of shock and embarrassment as I felt heat rush to my cheeks. Her cheeks turned rosy red, which I was sure matched my own. Cam stared at us, shifting her weight, her jaw tightened.

Frank's grin turned into a wide-mouthed smile, and he chuckled. "Wait. Wait." He leaned in close to me and whispered, "Did she kiss you awake, Princess?" I shoved Frank, and he fell to the floor with a laugh. He stood up, amused. "Wow, I think you may have gotten stronger while you slept, Orla." I looked down at my hands in shock. I just wanted everyone to leave me alone, except Aure. No, Aure too. I buried my face in my hands. *Gods, I just need a minute or a thousand.*

Aure, seeming to sense my need to be alone, spoke in a commanding but gentle tone. "Everyone, let's give Orla some time alone. Everything is a lot to process. Frank, why don't you go find her some GOOD food?"

Frank was reluctant at first, but then said, "Alright, I'll go hunt you down somethin' delicious, though I'm not sure I could find anythin' better than what you already have in this room." I chuckled, and Aure rolled her eyes and shooed him towards the door.

She turned back to me and said, "Cam and I will go make sure your parents have been properly notified." She then turned to the Healers, who murmured quietly amongst themselves. "There will be no more need to examine or interrupt Orla's rest. If we need anything further, we will call for you." They nodded and bowed to us both, then left the room.

Aure took a few steps towards me and pointed to the small bedside table next to me. "There is a bell to ring if you need anything, and I left a few books for you." She turned towards Cam, speaking louder. "Cam, please bring over a glass of water, so she has one nearby." Cam silently did as Aure commanded and set a full glass on the bedside table. Aure moved towards the door, Cam falling into step behind her. At the doorway, she paused and turned to me with a smile. "I am really glad you are awake, and I know you will find your own path through all of this." With that, the room was empty, and I was alone with my thoughts and a flood of emotions.

My attention was pulled to the incredible itchiness of my legs yet again as I scratched up and down along my thighs. My skin was so dry, I needed a shower, but I wasn't even sure where the bathroom was in this part of the palace. I tried to stand up; my legs felt strong but ached like I hadn't moved in too long, which was true. I took a few steps and felt oddly energized for someone who had been unconscious for days.

I noticed a door towards the back of the room and opened it, finding a small bathroom. I turned on the shower and used the facilities while the water heated up. I took off the cotton nightshirt and stepped into the hot, steaming water. The warmth felt incredible as I rubbed the water down my body, scrubbing my itching legs and lower back.

I touched my body, feeling for any differences, until my hands reached my new pointed ears. I explored the new contours of them, noting how sensitive and soft the skin was. The sensation was strange yet fascinating, a reminder of the changes I was still coming to terms with.

What can this magic do? I was curious, but also worried about how everyone in my life would react to this change in me. I stretched my hands out and closed them again, feeling the buzz of energy. Suddenly, a spark of fire burst from my right hand, which was quickly extinguished by the shower water. I jumped back in shock, my heart racing. I finished washing and stepped out of the shower, wrapping a towel around myself, not wanting to put the dirty cotton night shirt on. I stepped back into the room.

I walked toward the neatly made bed. The bedding was clean, someone had changed it—likely a servant. Neatly folded on top of the bedcovers were my leather pants, tan cotton shirt, and undergarments. I dressed, but my pants seemed a bit tight and short.

"Fuck, they shrunk my pants in the wash," I muttered. Still, anything was better than a nightshirt.

After dressing, I plopped onto the bed and grabbed one of the books Aure left for me from the bedside table.

"The History of Magic: Spoken Histories of the Sea Dragons as Recorded by Priestess Hana-Kanna," I read the title out loud to myself. I opened the old book, and the smell of ink on musty paper invaded my senses. Turning to the first chapter, I began to read.

The Myth of Creation

"When Terra was young, the skies, land, and seas lived in complete harmony, and the world was free of all intelligent life. But that did not last, as a star seed from the celestials fell to Terraqua, bringing with it the three giants: those of the sky, the sea, and the land. The three sisters, who brought with them their eggs, sought to live in harmony and peace for a time. However, as each sister's offspring grew more plentiful, they realized that this realm could not sustain them all.

The sister of the sky, cunning and powerful, used her magic to begin a war with the land and sea. Because the sister of the sky kept her magic for herself, her offspring were weak and easily lost any battle they fought. The sister of the sea gave her essence to her offspring, and they grew strong and powerful. For the magic to stay strong the children of the sea would be bound to a single mate of the sea, passing the power to their offspring. Their mate bond foraged through their songs of the sea.

The land sister, with her limited offspring, made them a sacrificial offering to the land, thereby creating a new and abundant life in the form of smaller, lesser beings: the humans, the dwarfs, and the fae. Even these lesser beings could defeat the sister of the skies' children and destroyed them all.

The sister of the sky, consumed by rage and despair at the loss of her offspring, committed a heinous act—she murdered her land sister. In her dying moments, the land sister's magic transferred in part to her new creations: the dwarfs, born from minerals, and the fae, born from trees. However, the Humans, born from the soil, were not blessed with magic.

The sister of the sea feared her sister of the sky. Giving a final sacrifice of herself, she was able to drain her sister's magic, creating the Siren, who held the magic of the sky but for protection had to be anchored to the sea. She created a bond, gifting the mating songs of her children to the Siren.

The sister of the sky did not die; her power only reduced, and she had to rely on herself, now alone. She vowed she would destroy the realm. She searched for her stolen magic among the realm. She seduced her way through Terraqua, regaining her power bit by bit as she drained magic and life force from those she could lure through dreams and life."

I looked up from reading, hearing Frank's heavy, booted steps echoing down the hall. His laugh boomed through the space as he spoke with someone outside. I set the book aside and smiled at my short friend when he appeared in the doorway, a plate full of food in one hand and a mug of ale in the other.

"Orla, you're lookin great. I bet you're famished, though," Frank said with a warm, familiar tone that felt comforting. I nodded in agreement as he sat down at the end of the bed and handed me the plate. Folding my legs beneath me, I took in the sight and smell of the food. The buttery, creamy, salty aroma of the mashed potatoes, the rich, smoky garlic scent of the roast beef with a hint of iron, and the warm, yeasty fragrance of the bread made my mouth water.

I took a bite of the mashed potatoes, savoring the comforting flavors before turning my attention back to Frank. "Frank, what exactly happened while I was out? Do you know anything about this enkindling thing?"

Frank leaned back slightly, his expression softening with concern. "I'm not an expert on magic, especially Fae magic, but from what I gathered, your magic was wakin' up in a big way. Aure called it an 'enkindling.' The Dwarfs call it our Runebirth, cheesy, I know."

"Yeah, I remember her calling it that. Enkindling," I repeated the word, trying to wrap my head around the concept. "Would that explain the weird dreams and the colors I saw? And this... change in my appearance?" I gestured to my pointed ears and the rainbow hues in my eyes.

Frank chuckled, his warm laughter filling the room. "Yeah, likely. I am not sure what you experienced while you were out, but it's like your magic is comin' into its own. Magic awakenings are powerful stuff, Orla. You're handlin' it well, all things considered."

I sighed, feeling the weight of everything. "It's just a lot to take in. I've always known I had Fae blood, but this is something else entirely. I'm worried about how everyone will react."

Frank reached out and patted my leg reassuringly. "Hey, you're still you. Just with a bit more flair now. You've got me in your corner and now Aure too—we're all here for you. We'll figure this out together."

His words brought a sense of comfort I hadn't realized I needed. "Thanks, Frank. I really appreciate it."

He grinned, his eyes twinkling with mischief. "Anytime, Princess. Now, eat up. You need your strength for whatever crazy magic stuff comes next."

I laughed, feeling lighter for the first time since waking up. "You're right. Just as long as I don't accidentally set anything on fire."

Frank raised his mug in a mock toast. "Here's to not settin' anythin' on fire!"

I clinked my fork against his mug, smiling. "To not setting anything on fire."

I took another bite of food, silently eating while Frank drank. After a moment, I asked, "Frank, what was your Runebirth like? We haven't really ever talked about your magic before. Sometimes I forget you even have it."

Frank paused mid-drink, lowering his mug with a thoughtful look. "Ah, my Runebirth. Well, it's something we Dwarfs don't talk about too often. It's a deeply personal experience."

I leaned forward, intrigued. "What was it like for you?"

Frank sighed, leaning back again. "Well, it's different for everyone, but for me, it happened when I was workin' in the mines. I hated bein' so cooped up, but workin' the mines was expected of me. I was just a young lad, barely old enough to swing a pickaxe. One night, I snuck outside the mines, and as I emerged, I fell into the clay mud. Suddenly, the runes started glowin' on the surroundin' ground all around me. The whole place lit up like a festival. I felt this surge of energy, like the earth itself was speakin' to me."

He took another sip of his drink, eyes distant as he remembered. "It was overwhelmin' at first, but then it settled into a sort of hum, like a deep, comfortin vibration. I realized I could sense the different minerals and ores, and I had this instinctive knowledge of how to shape and use them. It's what makes us Dwarfs such good smiths and alchemists. I knew, though, in my bones that I would not be either of them and that my magic agreed."

I nodded, fascinated. "That sounds incredible. Did it scare you?"

Frank chuckled. "Terrified me at first, but I had my brother, even though my clan didn't understand me. My brother helped me understand it, harness it. It's part of who I am now. My brother was the only person who encouraged me to listen to my heart and follow my dreams, which is part of why I am here now."

I finished the last bite of my food and set the empty plate on the bedside table. Frank stood up and picked up the plate and walked towards the door. Smiling at me, he said, "Get some rest, Orla, and try not to burn down the palace." I chuckled as he left me sitting on the bed alone once again.

I lay back on the bed, stretching out and tucking my arms behind my head. I had just barely closed my eyes when the door to the room closed, startling me. I sat up quickly, reaching for my dagger, which wasn't there. Fuck! I saw Tristan standing there with a worried look on his face, along with the caring expression he always had for me. His tousled, dirty blonde hair framed his angled features and always fell slightly over his brown eyes. He took long strides as he approached the bed.

"Orla, I'm so glad you're awake and well." He knelt beside the bed, reached up, and cupped my cheek. I flinched back a bit at his tender touch. My magic prickled beneath my skin. Waves of confusion and warning crashed through me. I was unarmed and didn't want to spook him into any sort of fight.

I forced a smile as I took his hand in mine, removing it from my face and holding it on the bed. "I am awake and I am very well, Tristan." My response granted me his full smile. He moved himself from the floor to sit close beside me on the bed. I slowed my breathing to calm myself as my magic buzzed loudly inside me.

Tristan turned, looking me over, and spoke tenderly with a hint of sorrow. "I haven't been able to visit you. That Siren has had you under watch around the clock." The relief I felt that I hadn't been alone while I was unconscious was now stifled by my emergent feelings from being alone and unarmed. He spoke remorsefully, "She has started to corrupt you with her magic. I'm sorry I didn't warn you sooner, Or." My jaw tightened at the words he spoke and at the childish nickname only used by him.

Just breathe. I took a breath, then responded. "Corrupt me with magic?" Skeptical of his claim, I knew Frank wouldn't lie to me, ever, and Tristan knew nothing of magic.

He gestured to my pointed ears and spoke with passion. "Yes, Or, that Siren Princess is corrupting you with her evil magic to take over the kingdom. Please, we can't let her get away with this. With your help, I can get rid of her for you. It was my mistake last time. I didn't warn you. But together it will work, I promise." I don't know if it was the shock of hearing him confess to treason or if I simply froze trying to process how he justified it. I sat there, speechless.

He continued softly, his voice rich with affection. "I can help free you. I love you. I've waited so long for you to be ready." I wanted to sink into the bed and disappear. It is true I have known since we were kids that Tristan cared for me. I have tried many times to make it clear to him I am not interested and never will be.

I pulled my hand back from his and shifted on the bed, glancing around the room for any kind of weapon. "Tristan, look, you know I don't feel that way about you."

He seemed unfazed by my response. "Or, you remember our first kiss?" He reminisced, focusing on my hand and tracing my fingers with his. Painful heat, like hot fire, followed each of his touches.

I did, in fact, remember. We were only twelve and had been chasing each other through the halls of the palace, playing tag. Once he let me catch him, and he kissed my lips with his. A shiver ran down my spine at the thought. I remembered that at the time I thought his lips had been just as slimy and cold as the toad he had once dared me to kiss when we were eight. "Yes, I do." I whispered and moved my hand to my lap.

"The last time was far better, though, right?" He chuckled at himself and ran his fingers down my cheek, dipping them under my chin. Tristan's energy flowed orange through him and licked at my skin hot like an ember in a fire, seeking to destroy and consume me and my magic. My eyes were ablaze with cobalt blue, and my jaw set. I wanted to headbutt this motherfucker before he ever kissed me again.

The door handle loudly turned. He dropped his hand from my chin and turned to look at the opening door. Aure walked in and he stood quickly, bowing to me. "Think about what I said, your Grace." He smiled at me, then turned, walking past her and out the door. She stood there, a look of confusion and concern on her face.

AURELIA

Chapter 12

I strode down the hall, leaving Orla alone for the first time in days. Nervous energy coursing through me, and I couldn't shake the feeling that something bad was going to happen. The thought of something happening to her was unbearable, but I had to let her rest and collect her thoughts. It was hard to walk away, leaving her there all alone.

Cam followed me, and we turned a corner, finding ourselves alone in the hall. She pushed me against the wall, startling me. Her body felt hot as it pinned mine to the smooth papered surface. She leaned in close, her eyes searching mine.

Twisting one of my curls around her finger, she bit out, "Did you really kiss her?" Her voice was low, her breath hot on my neck. "I thought secret kisses were our thing."

I planted my hand firmly on her chest and pressed, unmoving. "Are you really questioning me, your Princess? Am I not allowed to kiss my own betrothed if I want to?"

In one swift movement, Cam pulled my wrist away from her chest, pinning it to the wall at my side while grabbing my hip with her other hand and pulling us closer. Her lips brushed against the bottom of my ear. "Is this marriage, this Fae Princess, what you really want, Aure?"

The surge of desire in my core was undeniable, but the pull of what I shared with Orla was stronger, calling me back to my senses. Cam's lips brushed my neck, sending a shiver up my spine. "Cam," I breathed softly, barely getting the words out. "I can't…" I swallowed hard. "Do this…" I whispered. The words came slowly as she kissed my neck. I forced my eyes to stay open and, feeling a bit bolder, said louder, "Because, yes, Orla is who I want."

Cam froze for a moment, then took a step back, releasing me. Her jaw set, and she gritted her teeth. "I didn't realize there was more than duty between you two. Are you sure she feels the same way you do, Highness?"

I straightened, meeting her gaze with a mixture of resolve and vulnerability. "Even if she doesn't, I am sure of my choice," I replied, my voice steady. "I know there's something between us, something real. It's not just duty or obligation. It's deeper than that."

I balled my hands into fists, not about to say more about my feelings for Orla or what we share with Cam, my guard. "For me, from the start of this arrangement, I was open and ready for this to be more than just a loveless duty. I won't pretend or ignore what I feel for her."

Cam's eyes flickered with a mix of hurt and anger. "And what if you're wrong?"

"If I am wrong, then that is my risk to take," I said firmly. "I'd rather be honest about my feelings than live a lie. Orla deserves that much."

The hurt was clear in her eyes. I reached for her hand, gripping it in mine. She pulled her hand away and straightened, donning the mask of duty. Her voice strained as she whispered, "As you wish, Your Grace." She bowed her head to me.

My whole body stiffens, and my jaw tightens at her response. I let out a slow breath before I said with a measure of authority. "Cambria, you are my dear friend, and your loyalty to me is something I appreciate beyond measure. I couldn't imagine ruling without your support."

She looked at me stoically, with only a glimmer of her emotions showing through. She took a deep breath, her expression softening slightly. "I just don't want to see you get hurt, Aure."

"I know," I blurted out more harshly than I intended and I pressed my lips together, regaining my calm, before I continued. "And I appreciate your concern, Cam. But this is something I have to do, for myself and for Orla."

She gave a tight nod, stepping back to give me space. "I'll be around if you need me, Your Grace."

I turned away from Cam, unable to bear watching her hurt any further. I just wanted her to understand, but there was no way for her to truly comprehend this thing I couldn't even fully express.

Breaking the awkward silence, Cam spoke again. "I'll go make sure someone has properly informed King Oric that Orla is awake. You have your dagger, right?" I nodded, and Cam bowed before walking down the hall, leaving me alone with my swirling emotions.

 I closed my eyes and reached out to Azura, activating my signet bond. The magic pulsed through my arm, and my signet mark glowed brightly. *"Azura, I need your insight, your strength, your calm."*

I felt a brush of awareness and a tentative calm wash over me. The weight of my Sea Dragon's slumber hit me, and I slumped to the floor, my back against the wall for support. *"Yes?"* Azura's voice came through, drowsy yet alert. *"I am h... what is this new magic in you? Aure, what has happened?"* Her surprise, worry, curiosity, and concern hit me like a tidal wave crashing against an unexpected coast.

"Yes, a few things have happened." I closed my eyes, conversing through my bond, trying to hold on to that thread of green light to Azura through the blinding new thread of blue. *"I kissed Orla, and our magic..."* I struggled to explain. I didn't even know what had happened, and I wasn't sure I wanted to share that moment with Azura. It was our moment. I had kept nothing from Azura before, so why did I feel so possessive of this memory now?

"Aure, I can feel your conflict, your protectiveness. You don't have to share everything with me always. However, can you tell me if in this space you feel or see anything new?" I swallowed hard, my breathing quickening.

"I... I see a blue thread of light. The thread I follow to you has always been green. I have to really focus on our thread to keep our connection strong." I admitted not only to Azura but also to myself. A full sense of relief and love flooded my senses, comforting and calming me. My tight shoulders loosened, and my breathing evened out.

"I believe you have somehow found your mate and have begun a mate bond, which is odd because no other race but the Ancient races have a mate bond."

My eyes widened, and my mouth fell open as shock rippled through me. Surprise and worry surged through me and to Azura. *"These feelings are a mixture of your heart and the thread of fate. It's very similar to our bond, but different in its own ways. Just as you don't have a bond to Voraxius, I won't be bonded to Orla."*

"But how is this even possible? It's not... it isn't what happens to Sirens or Fae. Not with any race other than yours, so how?" I didn't know if I should feel excited or worried. How will I explain this to Orla? What will she even think? What if she blames me for seducing her with my magic? My mind spiraled with anxiety and fears.

"Aure, breathe, just breathe." Azura's voice filled my mind, and a grounding warmth filled me, but it did little to soothe my racing thoughts. *"I honestly don't know, Aure, but I will seek the elders and call the whole clan together if you like to find out how this is possible. However, this is your bond, and it is up to you who knows and what you choose to do with it. I am always here. Sleeping or not, hatching my egg or not, I will always be here for you."* I touched my arm, feeling the magic of my signet humming beneath the glowing mark on my skin.

"Thank you, Azura. Please ask the elders if something like this is even possible, but try not to reveal it's about me. I... I am not sure I'm ready to share this yet." My head swims with a sudden flood of fear, anxiety, and disgust. Gripping my stomach, I clench my sides, willing myself not to hurl all over. I have lost all sense of Azura and a thrumming pull to Orla wells deep inside me, a need I can't ignore. I pull myself up to my feet as the intensity subsides, and I breathe heavily, still holding my middle.

Bracing myself against the wall, I touch my ruby rebounder pendant and breathe deeply, focusing on my breath as my mother taught me. Closing my eyes, I concentrate on the blue thread of magic in my mind, accepting it, breathing in time with its pulse, and following it to Orla. In my mind, I feel her emotions—her fear, her anxiety, her disgust. I send my own calm toward her through this strong and strange connection, as I have practiced with Azura.

After finding my center, I know I need to get closer to Orla, to check on her. Now steady on my feet, I straighten and walk with quick, determined steps until I reach the closed door to the infirmary. I twist the knob and step in. Tristan sits close to Orla, his finger beneath her chin. My stomach drops, and rage builds inside me like a silent hurricane about to be unleashed. I sense all the water-based elements in the room that my magic threatens to call to my aid, to punish this man who dares to touch what is mine. My lips quiver as I struggle to contain not just my own emotions, but also Orla's.

This touch isn't one she wants, and my rage isn't born of jealousy, but of vengeance. I clench my hands into fists beside me. Tristan stands abruptly, dropping his hand from her chin, a lustful smile playing across his face. He dips his head in a bow to Orla as he speaks, "Think about what I said, Your Grace." Turning towards me at the door, he looks me up and down, disdain replacing his earlier lust. As he passes, he grits out in a hushed growl, "I won't let you get away with this."

As he walks out the door, I release my magic, slamming the door behind him and shaking the room with a burst of mist.

"It's not what it looked like, Aure," Orla blurts out, clearly afraid I'm angry with her or jealous of him. She quickly stands up from the bed and with her long legs strides towards me, closing the distance between us in a few quick steps.

I release my clenched fists, focusing on my breath, willing my body to relax. Instead, my body tightened like a taut bow from her closeness. The anticipation was palpable, my mouth watering as a sweet essence of desire mixed with need. I drew in a sharp breath and bit my lower lip, with Orla standing inches in front of me. The air felt heavy, electric. Goosebumps rose across both my arms, running up my neck and across my chest, causing my nipples to peak. The soft light material of my yellow gown did nothing to hide my response.

Orla's eyes, with a storm of swirling colors, a kaleidoscope I could lose myself in forever. My heart raced, thrumming loudly in my ears. Her scent overwhelmed me, filling my senses with the intoxicating blend of rose and sandalwood. Her hair, still wet and tousled, dripped slightly down her neck.

I wet my lips, longing to taste the droplets of water glistening on her neck. My eyes traveled down to the swells of her full, perky breasts, barely concealed by her loose tan cotton shirt. The skin-tight leathers hugged her tight, muscular ass, leaving nothing to the imagination. The thin line of the crease between her thighs stole the last breath from my lungs.

Every fiber of my being was acutely aware of her presence. The space between us felt charged with unspoken words and unfulfilled longing. My breath hitched as her eyes roamed over me, taking in every detail. The intensity of her gaze sent shivers down my spine, igniting a fire within me.

She reached out, her hand trembling slightly as it brushed against my arm. The touch was electric, sending a jolt of heat through my veins. I closed my eyes, savoring the sensation, the connection between us almost tangible.

"Aure," she whispered, her voice a blend of desperation and desire. "I'm sorry...for everything." Her words hung in the air, heavy with emotion. I could feel the weight of her fear and anxiety that created the turmoil in her heart. My own emotions mirrored hers through our bond, the overwhelming sensation leading to my deep, insatiable need for her.

"You have nothing to be sorry for," I replied, my voice barely more than a breath. "I know nothing happened, Orla." I wanted to reassure her, to ease her fear that was a thick smoke around us.

The distance between us dissolved as she stepped closer, her body pressing against mine. The warmth of her touch and the rhythm of her heartbeat felt so right, so inevitable. Her hot breath against my lips stirred a liquid heat in my core and the wetness growing between my thighs. The scent of a rich, savory meal mingled with ale lingered on her slightly parted mouth.

I couldn't hold back any longer. I leaned in to capture her lips with mine—

The door burst open with a loud bang, and Lady Lili stormed into the room, her face etched with worry. "Orla! My sweetness, how are you feeling? You should be in bed not up and about!"

Orla and I jumped apart, the intense moment shattered. My heart pounded wildly as I struggled to regain my composure. Aunt Lili's presence was like a bucket of cold water, dousing the fire that had burned so fiercely between us.

My cheeks flushed as Lady Lili pushed past me to capture Orla in a tight embrace. Orla returned the hug, albeit awkwardly. I stepped back further, giving them space. Lady Lili fussed over Orla. "I am fine, Aunt Lili," Orla stated, stepping back from her.

Our gazes locked, and I could sense her unease, but couldn't place what had caused it. I excused myself to let Orla spend time with her aunt. "I'm heading to the docks to oversee the arrival of the shipment of weapons from Faedamir. Will you be okay here, Orla?"

Lili answered before Orla could. "She has been just fine in her palace for twenty-nine years before you came along, Your Highness." The look of judgment on her face was unmasked and clear.

I simply nodded in response to Lady Lili. I wasn't about to start an argument now; it wouldn't change her mind about me, anyway. Orla gave me a small, apologetic smile and a quick nod in return.

I left the room, softly closing the door behind me. I regained my breath while the remnants of our moment still lingered in my mind and on my skin. The draw and pull of our bond is still strong within me. I had to get out of my head and focus on the task at hand. I couldn't afford to walk around like a lovesick puppy all day.

Finally on the docks, I closed my eyes, breathing deeply the comforting scent of the sea air, the salt-filled moisture coating my lips. This smell always reminded me of home. However, the biting cold wind pierced through even my woolen dress and fur shawl almost as hard as Cam's glare from behind me. I could feel the chill of the air deep in my bones, a sensation I was unaccustomed to and didn't think I could ever get used to. A shiver skittered across my body, and I wrapped the fur tighter around my shoulders and arms.

I let out a sigh and looked out across the cresting waves and crashing sea. The ships and boats in the dock rocked violently in a chaotic rhythm with each swell. In the distance, the large carrack approached the docks, battling its way against the rough currents.

I watched the carrack grow closer and gasped as fear gripped me, its hull battered and scarred from a recent battle. The sails were torn in places, and smoke still lingered in the surrounding air. It was clear the ship had faced a fierce attack, likely from Frostspire forces. My heart tightened with worry; the shipment of weapons and supplies, along with the Faedamir Enchanters, had been crucial to our cause. Losing them would be a devastating blow.

The carrack finally reached the dock, and the crew hurriedly threw ropes to the waiting dockhands, securing the ship in place. They lowered the gangplank with a loud thud, and the crew began to unload their cargo. Among them, I saw the exhausted and sweat covered faces of the Faedamir Enchanters, their eyes reflecting the battle they had endured. I worried as I watched the injured being carried off the ship, some on stretchers, others leaning heavily on their comrades.

Captain Cole, a rugged sun baked man with a grizzled graying beard and piercing blue eyes, descended the gangplank. He walked with a noticeable limp, a fresh wound on his left leg wrapped hastily in blood-soaked bandages. Despite his injuries, his eyes lit up when he saw me.

"Aure! My Queen!" he called out, his voice hoarse but strong. "We nearly lost it all, but we managed to fend off da Frostspire bastards."

I rushed to his side, helping him to steady himself. "Captain Cole." I sighed but gave him a soft smile, he knew I hated him calling me queen. "Thank Nereus, you made it. I am surprised you kept that clunker of a ship of yours in one piece. How bad is it?"

He grimaced, glancing back at his ship. "We lost a good number of people. Da bastards were relentless. They came at us with everything they had." His voice dropped to a whisper. "Including Fae soldiers, Aure." I froze, stopping our progress toward the awaiting wagons. He continued eagerly, "But we fought back hard and kept safe da weapons and supplies. Our enchanters… they were crucial. Their magic turned da tide in our favor. Though one of da Fae begged us to keep him as a prisoner."

I looked at the enchanters, who held the quiet determination of the warriors they were. "We owe them a great debt," I said, my voice filled with gratitude.

Captain Cole nodded. "Aye, we do. But right now, we need to get da injured to da infirmary and unload da supplies. Every moment counts. And Aure, we need to question our 'prisoner'."

I nodded in agreement, then turned to the nearby soldiers and dockworkers. "Help the injured and secure the supplies into the wagons," I commanded. Turning back to Captain Cole, I added, "We'll need to debrief and plan our next move."

As the men and women sprang into action, I stayed by Captain Cole's side, supporting him the rest of the way to the Healers and the wagons that would take us back to the palace. Cole winced as he sat down on the back of the wagon, a healer examining his leg.

I surveyed the scene, watching the injured being carried off the ship. The smell of blood and sweat mingled with the sea air, making my stomach churn. The reality of the war hit me hard, bile creeping up my throat and burning my tongue. With these weapons and enchanters now in Orlondia, did we have a fighting chance against Frostspire?

Cam's eyes locked onto mine from where she was speaking with some of the crew and enchanters. Her face was pale and grave, her brow furrowed in worry, and her lips pressed into a firm line. I gestured for Cam to come over, and she quickly approached. "Yes, Aure, how is Captain Cole doing?"

I pulled my fur shawl tight again and spoke in hushed tones. "He is strong and will be fine. I need you to oversee the transport of a prisoner. Take him to my chambers, along with a couple of trusted guards from our ship. Cam, don't let anyone from Orlondia know. Be as discreet and safe as possible. The prisoner is a Fae." Cam's eyes widened at my last statement, but she nodded silently. "I will stay with Captain Cole and then meet you there." I informed her. She sighed, then moved quickly and quietly like a wraith. She disappeared into the ship for the discrete transfer of our Fae prisoner.

The chaotic scene at the docks gradually subsided as the soldiers and dockworkers efficiently managed the unloading of supplies and the injured. My eyes caught sight of a hot pink streak among those loading crates onto the wagons, and my heart filled with warmth as I recognized my fiery childhood friend, Rielle. She saw me and squealed, her petite frame zipping toward me. We collided in a crash of giggles and limbs. Her arms wrapped around my waist and head landed on my chest. She held me tightly as I fussed with the cluster of long, hot pink braids cascading down around her shoulders.

"What have you done to your hair, Rielle?" I asked, a smile now permanently plastered on my face.

She pushed me back and examined me. "Don't tease me about my hair. What have you done to your magic? It's all…" She gestured her hand in a swirling motion from my head to my toes. "…a swirl of colors."

I smirked. "It's a bit of a story for a later time. I can't believe they sent you."

She put her hands on her hips and proudly stated, "I am the best Enchantress you've got, my Queen. Of course, they sent me."

I rolled my eyes and retorted, "I bet you weren't your father's first choice."

"Ugh! He doesn't control me or what I do. He's lucky I even requested this posting. I could have just boarded the ship without so much as a word."

I nudged her. "Yeah right. I've seen you get all blubbery when he has to leave. I doubt you would have ever just left without a word."

"Maybe, maybe not, my Queen." She twisted her lips into a defiant smirk and crossed her arms over her ample breasts. For a Dwarf, family meant everything, even though Rielle tried not to let her soft side show.

"Reille, you should be more careful how you speak to our Queen." Captain Cole stated, holding back a snicker, and we both rolled our eyes at him. We each went to either side of him to help him into our wagon. "No, need to fuss over me ladies, truly." Though he still winced from his injury, he wobbled as he boarded our wagon. "We will show them bastards what real warriors look like." He murmured, though his voice betrayed a hint of doubt. I offered him a reassuring smile, though my own worries mirrored his.

The ride back to the palace was tense, the weight of our recent battle hanging heavy in the air. The streets of Orlondia were eerily quiet, the usual bustle subdued by the news of the attack. As we approached the palace gates, I could feel the eyes of the guards on us, their expressions a mix of concern and curiosity.

Once inside the palace, I directed the Healers to take Captain Cole to the infirmary for further treatment. "Join us when you can. The servants can show you to my chambers." I told him. He nodded, clearly exhausted, and allowed the Healers to lead him away.

Rielle and I made our way to my room, heart pounding with anticipation and anxiety. As we entered, I found Cam already there, along with two trusted guards and the Fae prisoner. The prisoner, though bound, looked more desperate than defiant. His face was pale with violet eyes, and long pointed ears. His hair was a mess of black oily strands and his unkept beard had grown patchy across his neck and chin. He appeared tall and lanky and looked as though his once athletic body had gone through months of starvation.

Cam approached me, her expression serious. "We managed to get him here without incident," she reported quietly. "What's our next move?"

Reille interjected, "I could start with his toes, and my knife."

I took a deep breath, glancing at the prisoner. "We need to find out what he knows about Frostspire's plans. But first, we need to ensure no one else knows he's here. The fewer people who know about this, the better."

"But the things I can do with his toes will definitely get him talking." Reille mused with a giddy smile.

The prisoner looked up, his eyes filled with a mixture of fear and hope. "Please," he begged, his voice trembling. "There is no need to do anything to my toes. I will help you any way I can. The tyrant king of Frostspire enslaved me. He's been abducting Fae for the Sylvan enclave, enslaving us. I escaped during the battle and begged your soldiers to bring me to you. Thank you and your guards for not killing me."

My anger turned to fear and empathy, I turned to Cam. "Make sure the to post our guards discreetly outside my chambers. No one comes in or out without my permission."

Cam nodded and moved to give the orders. I approached the prisoner, my resolve hardening. "We'll start with your name," I said, keeping my voice steady. "And then you'll tell us everything you know about Frostspire."

The Fae looked relieved, though still wary. "My name is Eamon," he said softly. I notice how he watches Rielle as she flips her dagger in her hand. "And I'll tell you everything I know. The king of Frostspire has been capturing Fae, using some kind of dark magic on us. Many of us continue to obey him out of fear for ourselves or our loved ones. He's planning something terrible, and he won't stop until he has what he wants."

A surge of determination and concern flooded me. "We'll do everything we can to stop the king of Frostspire," I promised.

Rielle walked up behind Eamon, dagger in hand, leaned over and pressed it to his throat. "Be sure you don't lie to my queen, Frostspire scum." The color drained from Eamon's face as he began to shake.

I placed my hand on Rielle's arm. "Rielle, that isn't necessary. Eamon is telling the truth; I can tell." Turning to Eamon, I softened my tone. "Would you like some food?"

Rielle reluctantly removed the blade and stepped back. Eamon swallowed hard and slowly nodded. I cut the rope binding him with my dagger. He rubbed his wrists with shaky hands as Rielle grabbed a bowl of fruit from one of the many tables in the room and handed it to him. Eamon eagerly devoured the fruit, his hands trembling slightly as he ate.

Cam now stood next to Rielle as we warily watched Eamon finish the whole bowl of fruit. I sat down on the sofa across from where they had placed Eamon in a wooden chair. "Cam, can you please get some more food for Eamon? And Cam, also, get Orla and Frank. I think they should meet our newest arrival."

Cam didn't look pleased about my command, but she nodded and left. Rielle plopped herself onto the sofa next to me and whispered, "I am a little disappointed that we don't get to torture him." I jabbed her in the side, and she giggled.

ORLA

Chapter 13

I sat on my plush chair by the window, the sound of the cold fall rain pattering against the glass. Soft, stormy sunlight filtered through the gauzy curtains, casting delicate patterns across the room. I tried to focus on the book in my lap, but my mind kept drifting back to the day's events: my conversation with Aunt Lili and that moment with Aure. The knock at the door was a welcome distraction.

"Come in," I called, my voice steady despite the turmoil inside. The door creaked open, and Cam stepped in, her expression hard and unreadable. I watched as she closed the door behind her and walked over, her footsteps soft on the plush carpet rug that covered the wood flooring of my chambers.

"Princess Aurelia has summoned you, Your Grace." She said through gritted teeth, her gaze pointed.

I set the book aside and stood up, feeling the hilt of my hidden blade as I brushed my hands down my pants. "Summoned?" I repeated, arching an eyebrow and crossing my arms across my chest. I took a step forward, meeting her gaze.

With a clipped tone, her lips curled on one side, and she replied, "Yes, summoned."

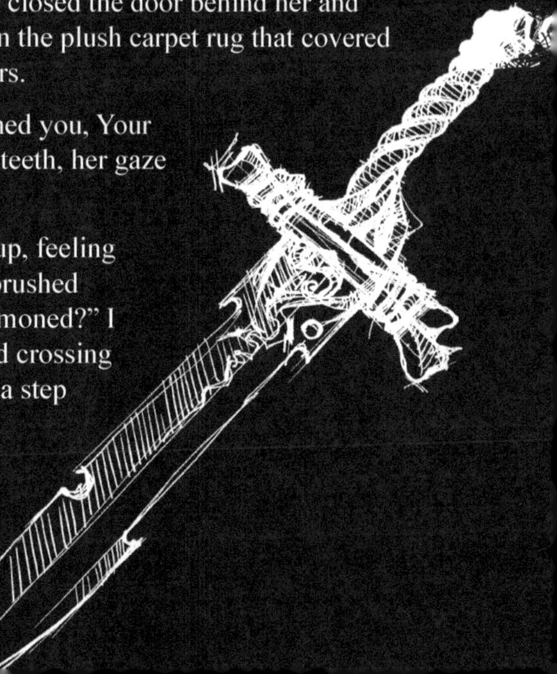

Anger simmered just below the surface as my eyes flashed to cobalt. I quickly closed the distance and stood face to face with her. "What did you just say to me, guard?" Asserting my authority in a way I often had with the soldiers under me.

The room stood silent, with only the sound of the rain hitting the window. Thunder erupted loudly outside as my magic charged to my fingertips. A small smile grew on Cam's face as she poured out her venomous words. "Your Grace, I made myself quite clear. There's no need to plead with me, like Aure does each time I make her moan my name."

I ground my teeth silently, my fists tightening into balls. I took a step back as a cascade of loud thunder rumbled overhead. I turned my back to her as the sense of possessiveness flooded me. *She has actually been with Aure. What the fuck?* The room flashed brightly as lightning stuck close outside, thunder crashing through the palace. Unable to contain the storm inside me, I whirled and punched her flat in the jaw.

Cam stumbled back, the sound of our bones clashing and her loud exhale echoing in my head. A bolt of pain shot up my arm from my knuckles. Giving me a satisfying thrill. I watched Cam wipe the rivulet of crimson blood flowing from her bottom lip.

She straightened, her expression a mix of shock and anger. "You'll regret that," she hissed. She regained her footing and stood glaring at me.

I took a deep breath, my voice cold and firm. "I regret nothing. And you will show respect to Princess Aurelia and me." My heart was pounding, but my resolve was unwavering. I had made my point clear, and I would not tolerate disrespect, no matter the cost.

Cam held her jaw gingerly as she glared back at me. "Respect?" she echoed, a hint of sarcasm in her voice. "You want me to respect someone who's been nothing but a distraction to Aure?"

I felt a surge of irritation. "A distraction? I have done nothing more than my duty. My title alone deserves your restraint at the very least, Cambria."

She scoffed. "You're one to talk about restraint. Is that what you had when you just hit me?" She continued to nurse her wound dramatically, making a point of showing her hurt.

I walked over to a basket near my bathroom door and grabbed two small towels. I smiled as I turned back to Cam. "Yes, actually, that was restraint. I could have done way more damage with a blade." I wiped my bruised knuckles, then wrapped them in one towel and tossed her the other.

Cam caught the towel and held it to her mouth to help stop the bleeding. Her expression softening a fraction. "I just don't want to see Aure get hurt. She's risking too much."

I sighed, trying to move my hand that was swelling. I stated firmly, "That is something for her to decide and is none of your concern. Have you bothered to discuss this with her instead of confronting me? Maybe your motive here is more about jealousy than concern for her well-being."

Cam sighed, the anger in her eyes giving way to a flicker of hurt. "I only want what's best for her. Just... be careful. For Aure's sake. "

I took a step closer to her, my tone softening. "Cam, I don't want to be your enemy. I want to be your friend. I don't want to hurt Aure or disrupt your friendship with her. She means a lot to both of us."

Cam's eyes flickered with uncertainty, the hard edges of her demeanor softening slightly. "It's not that simple. You've already changed things between us."

I tilted my head and smirked, still in a serious tone, and said. "Well, if what you said to me earlier was true. I hope I have changed things between you two, because you even so much as touch her ever again, you won't have to worry about my restraint being a problem."

I tossed the towel toward my dirty laundry basket. I turned toward the door. "Now, if you have finished, I am pretty sure Aure doesn't want to wait on either of us. Lead the way." I gestured toward the door.

Cam gave me one last glare, but she turned and walked towards the door, her movements stiff but less tense. She opened the door to find a startled Frank standing ready to knock. Frozen in shock for a moment, and he took in the sight of her. He gently tapped Cam on the shoulder instead of knocking in mid-air, earning himself a glare and a huff in response. "Aure needs you too, Frank. Follow us," she said sharply.

Frank and I exchanged a quick glance. I shook my head. "Don't ask." I whispered. We followed Cam down the corridor. The soft thud of our footsteps echoed through the palace halls, punctuating the tension that hung in the air. My mind raced with questions and concerns as we made our way toward Aure's chambers.

We arrived at the heavy wooden door where two armed guards stood. Cam nodded to them once before pushing the door open. Inside the room was a mix of organized chaos. The first thing I noticed was a petite Dwarven woman sprawled casually on the sofa, her vibrant pink braids contrasting with the dark upholstery. She exuded an air of fierceness and skill, preoccupying herself by flicking a dagger in the air and catching it again. A tall, lithe man who looked tense and out of place sat on a wooden chair in front of Aure's desk, consuming a plate of food with single-minded focus.

Aure, sitting at her desk, looked up as we entered, her eyes lighting up with a mix of relief and determination. She stood. "Finally, Cam, what took so long? You knew this was important."

Cam looked down, shifting her weight uneasily. Aure's expression turned to concern when she caught sight of Cam's swollen lip and bruised jaw. I simply smiled at Aure and shook my head slightly, keeping my swollen hand tucked behind my back.

Without warning, the pink-haired Dwarf flicked her blade into its sheath, stood, and ran straight toward me, embracing me in a tight and slightly awkward hug. "You must be Princess Orla," the woman nearly squealed. Pushing me back at arm's length, her head reaching only to my middle, she continued, "Ooooh, yes, your magic is something alright."

Aure's smile widened, her eyes sparkling with amusement as she introduced us. "Orla, Frank, this is Rielle, one of my oldest friends and an amazing Enchantress. She just arrived on the transport ship from Faedamir. We received a large shipment of weapons, supplies, and Enchanters for the front-lines."

Rielle stepped back, her vibrant pink braids swaying as she beamed up at me. "It's a pleasure to meet you, Princess Orla." She said with a mischievous glint in her eyes. "I've heard so much about you."

Before I could respond, Frank chuckled softly. "Seems like you've got quite the reputation, Orla."

I rolled my eyes playfully. "Hopefully, all good things."

Rielle laughed, a bright, infectious sound. "Oh, definitely. I was just saying to Aure how it's about time I met the woman she has decided to spend the rest of her life with."

Aure's cheeks flushed slightly, but she maintained her composure. "Rielle, you always know how to make an entrance."

Frank crossed his arms with a smile full of mirth, eyeing Reille quipped. "So Aure, where did you find this feisty little pixie?"

Reille whirled and stood right next to Frank, her dagger in hand and against his thigh. Smirking, "Pixie!?! Dwarf, Human, or Dragon, I could bring you down to your knees faster than you could call me pixie again, halfling."

He let out a low growl and looked down at her, full of delight. "I would enjoy seein you try any day of the week," he looked around the room. "Not sure our present company would appreciate such a display, though." He gave her a wink.

I cleared my throat, drawing their attention. Reille shifted, then moved back to the sofa. "And who's this?" I asked, nodding toward the tall, tense man sitting in the chair.

Aure's expression turned serious. "This is Eamon. He's a Fae who escaped Frostspire. There was an attack on our transport ship by Frostspire forces. Captain Cole and his crew fought off the attack with the valuable help of the Enchanters on board. Eamon surrendered himself to them, begging them to take him as a prisoner. He has valuable information on Frostspire and their king's plans."

Eamon looked up from his plate, his eyes wary but determined. "King Malachor Frostbane enslaved me, like he has many of my people," he said quietly. "He's been using dark magic to control and kill us. He still has many Fae there trapped. We were forced to serve him and his devout acolytes out of fear for our lives and the lives of our loved ones." His eyes dropped to the floor, his whole body deflated. "I have no one left to lose. So I pretended to be a Devout and join as a solider bound to raiding parties, hoping to surrender myself to anyone else, so hopefully I can help save my people."

The room fell silent as we absorbed his words. The weight of the situation pressed heavily on my chest. I took a deep breath and met Aure's gaze, her eyes reflecting the same concern and resolve I felt.

"We need to act quickly," I said, my voice steady. "If what Eamon says is true, we must find a way to free the Fae and stop the king's plans." I felt a closeness to him and the other captive Fae. Righteous indignation fueled me, and my eyes shift orange.

I studied Eamon for a moment. *Is this what I look like now?* I noticed a shimmer to his skin, even though his pallor was dull and gaunt. He had pointed ears, but somehow different from mine. All his features were angular and sharper, even his teeth appeared sharper almost fanged.

Aure nodded. "Agreed, we need to help the Fae. But we must be cautious. Frostspire is powerful, and we can't afford any mistakes."

Frank slowly made his way to the sofa and sat next to Rielle. I walked toward Eamon and placed a reassuring hand on his shoulder. "We will do everything we can to help save your people." His eyes darted up and down, looking me over as he craned his head to the left slightly. I looked at Aure. "We need to share this with my father and the war council, Aure."

Aure looked up at me with worry and concern etched into the crease on her face and she chewed her lower lip. "I am unsure that is wise. I know the war council needs this information. I am just not sure how they will take us having a solider of Frostspire free among us, but I don't wish to hold Eamon prisoner either."

I placed a hand on the desk and leaned down, meeting her at eye level, and whispered. "We need to do this. We are a united front now, and this is important to the war effort. I believe him, and I am sure there will be many questions, but we can figure this out together." I inched my fingers on the desk towards hers and the tips of our fingers touched with a bright buzzing spark snapped between us. I left my hand there, feeling the new pulse of energy flowing through the contact. She smiled at me and I smiled back at her.

Cam, who had been standing silently by the door, spoke up. "Aure, we should move to a more secure location to discuss this further. I agree, the whole alliance needs to know."

Aure glanced at Cam, looking her over, and frowned but didn't comment. Instead, she nodded. "Fine, but I am concerned about how far this news travels. This could be vital to our gaining the upper hand in this war. We know so little about Frostspire and the inner kingdom there. However, let's head to the throne room. Orla, will you present Eamon to your father? Then we can strategize there, after we gather the war council and Captain Cole."

I nodded, my mind already racing with thoughts of how to present this to my father and the council. "Let's move quickly," I said, turning to Eamon. "Are you well enough to walk?"

Eamon nodded, standing up weakly with a slight wobble. "I'm fine," he said, though his voice lacked conviction. I motioned for Frank to help him. Stepping forward, Frank offered Eamon a steadying arm. We all moved towards the door, the weight of the moment heavy on our shoulders.

The journey to the throne room was tense and silent, each of us lost in our thoughts. The grandeur of the palace seemed almost oppressive, its rich opulence a stark contrast to the grim reality of our situation.

As we approached the throne room, the guards opened the massive doors, revealing my father seated on his throne, deep in discussion with several members of the war council. His gaze shifted to us as we entered, his eyes narrowing slightly at the sight of Eamon.

"King Oric, Father," I began, my voice steady. "We have urgent news."

The council members quieted, their attention focused on us. My father sat there sipping his wine, then loudly and with a wave of his hand. "Speak, Princess Orla. What news do you bring?"

I took a deep breath and stepped forward, motioning for Eamon to do the same. "This is Eamon, a Fae from Frostspire. He surrendered on the supply transport after the attack. He brings critical information about King Frostbane's plans and Frostspire. Eamon, can you please share with our King the information you brought us?"

Eamon, looking slightly intimidated and shaking, stepped forward, his voice cracking as he spoke. "Your Majesty, King Frostbane —"

King Oric held up his hand, palm facing us. "Wait, this Fae was part of the attack on our supply ship?" he boomed, interrupting Eamon mid-sentence.

I stepped next to Eamon, holding my arms behind my back, my voice cautious and slow. "Yes, Father. He surrendered to Captain Cole aboard the transport after they had won the battle." I watched my father, his eyes narrowing slightly as he sat up straighter. His hand remained suspended in the air, anger stirring inside him. I held my breath. The moment felt like hours but passed in a heartbeat.

"Tristan." The command, loud and firm, came as a singular, angered word from my father's mouth. He closed his open hand into a fist. My eyes grew wide as Tristan, who had been standing guard next to my father, moved with purposeful steps and shocking speed. A bright, sharp blade glinted in his hand as he curved it under Eamon's chin.

Before I could process what was happening, a deep flood of gore cascaded down the front of Eamon. His limp body crumbled to the floor, lying in a growing pool of ruby-red blood. My whole body vibrated with rage, and the entire palace shook. Tristan knelt over the lifeless body, wiping his blade on Eamon's clothes.

Aure grasped me from behind, holding me close against her, the throbbing energy of magic slowly reducing its intensity. Cam stepped protectively in front of us as Rielle and Frank moved between Tristan and me. The room filled with the sound of women screaming, breaking into sobs, and rushed footsteps echoing through the space. None of the war council members moved. My father waved his hand, and three other unphased guards quickly

167

removed Eamon's body from the room. Silent maids with buckets and rags began the busy work of cleaning the mess.

I turned to my father, my voice trembling with controlled fury. "How could you? He was our key to understanding Frostspire's plans!"

King Oric's gaze remained icy. "A traitor is a traitor, Orla. We cannot trust the words of our enemies."

Aure stepped forward, her voice firm but respectful. "Your Majesty, with all due respect, Eamon had valuable information that could have helped us."

My father's eyes flickered with a hint of uncertainty as they met Aure's, but his pride remained resolute. "This discussion is over. We must not fall victim to the enemy's manipulations. There are better ways to gather the intelligence we need. Orla, you know I don't indulge in these childish antics. Power and control are the only currencies that matter in this world."

I fell into line and grew silent, like the good soldier I was trained to be. My eyes remained deep black, my rage simmering, and my skin crawling. I would not risk Aure's well-being to this man. I would find another way to win this war and free the Fae, my kin. Eamon's death would not be in vain. We would find a way to stop Frostspire, no matter the cost.

I pulled away from Aure and turned, walking out of the throne room. Once I was free of its suffocating walls, I ran. I ran out the palace doors, down the front tiered manicured lawns, past all the people, all the things, and the stifling place I called home.

AURELIA

Chapter 14

I sat alone in my dimly lit chambers at the polished wooden desk. The fire crackled softly in the hearth, casting flickering shadows on the walls lined with books and trinkets I had arranged to make myself feel at home. Rain fell hard against the glass of the windows as the shadows grew and faded again with the flashes of bright lightning, the thunder rumbling outside. My fingers traced the edges of a worn map of Terraqua spread out on the table before me.

I couldn't shake the image of Eamon's bloody, lifeless body from my mind, nor the look of betrayal in Orla's eyes. The events in the throne room had shaken me to the core. Bile crept up my throat again, and I swallowed the burning liquid back down. I refused to let my stomach betray my resolve. This was just the start of the horrors war would bring. I had to stay strong and not show any weakness. The thought that I had used my magic on Orla in that moment to force her magic to restrain itself alone turned my stomach sour.

The door creaked open, and I looked up to see Rielle entering the room. Her face was a mixture of concern and resolve. Her fierce stance was a comfort amidst the somber atmosphere.

"Aure," She gave me a small smile as she took a seat opposite me. "Are you alright?"

I nodded, though the tightness in my chest betrayed my calm exterior. "I'm fine, Rielle. It's Orla I'm worried about. And Eamon... he didn't deserve that."

Her expression hardened. "King Oric is a fucking bastard. Even if he did what he believed was right. Clearly, he values strength and power above all else."

With a sigh, I touched the ruby pendant around my neck. "But there has to be another way. We can't keep killing people, especially those who come to us for help."

Her voice was laced with anger and concern. "I still can't believe King Oric killed Eamon like that. It was so ruthless. I mean, I know I wanted to torture him, but that was completely unnecessary and not even strategic."

My expression turned grim. "King Oric has always been ruthless and brash. But this... this was different. He didn't just kill a prisoner; he destroyed a potential ally. Orla must be devastated. She believes in justice and mercy. It was her idea to bring Eamon to her father. This must be tearing her apart."

She leaned forward, her voice low and earnest. "Yes, but with war comes death, and Orla knows that. If we want to control the way this war is going, we have to do it wisely. King Oric doesn't seem like someone who will tolerate any form of dissent, especially not from you and not even from his own daughter, Orla."

My eyes met hers, which caused a spark of determination to ignite within me. "Then we'll have to find a way to do this without him knowing. We'll gather our own allies, seek out the information we need, and put an end to Frostspire's tyranny without his help."

Hesitating for only a moment before she nodded. "Alright, let's do it. I know I'm the first one to start a rebellion, but I don't want you to risk too much."

I stood up and twisted my hair into a loose bun at the back of my neck, securing it with a pointed silver stick. "We'll be careful. But we can't let fear stop us. Too much is at stake."

She smiled, full of determination. "I completely agree with you, and if you need me to, I will gut the old bloat for you. Just give me the word and it will be done."

My expression remained serious. "I'll keep that in mind, but right now, we need to focus on Orla. She's out there, probably dealing with the shock of her father's actions. We need to make sure she's okay."

She nodded. "I know you want her to know she's not alone in this, but she might just need the space right now, my Queen."

I rolled my eyes, my frustration evident in my tone. "You know I am not your queen yet, Rielle. That was my mother's title, and I haven't earned it."

Her face softened, and she nudged my arm gently across the desk. "You've earned that title many times over the last few years. Just because your mother held it doesn't make yours any less valuable or true. You will never replace her, but you will be the queen Faedamir and this whole realm needs right now. That doesn't change that Queen Cliodhna was an amazing queen and mother. She would be so proud of you, Aure."

I sighed, absorbing her words. The weight of responsibility pressed heavily on my shoulders, but her reassurance provided a small measure of comfort. "Thank you, Rielle. I just wish I could have saved my mother, that I could have warned her."

She looked at me, her eyes full of concern and determination. "You need to let that go, Aure. Do you remember what your mother used to say to us when we were children?"

I hesitated, then nodded slowly. "'The past is a lesson, the present is a choice, and the future is not set in stone.'"

She smiled warmly. "Exactly. She wouldn't want you to be weighed down by regret. She'd want you to lead with the same strength and wisdom she did. And you are, Aure. You're doing that every day."

I managed a small smile, appreciating her unwavering support. "Thank you. I am so glad you're here right now." I smiled at my friend. Thunder crashed loudly overhead, and I jumped, startled. With our peace broken, my mind pulled back to Orla and how she left everything, my nerves bubbling inside me full. I couldn't stay seated any longer.

I stood up and started to pace, the soft rug keeping my movement silent despite the force behind each step. "I wish I knew where Orla went or where to look for her. She ran out of the palace completely and off the grounds in this storm. She was so fast." I paused and sighed. "How am I going to make this right? I… I used my magic on her, Rielle... I didn't feel like I had any other choice. Also, Azura believes somehow we have a mate bond." I looked straight into her shocked eyes.

She tilted her head as she watched me, her lips curled into a knowing smile. "Honestly, that makes sense. Your magic has threads of hers, and the same with her magic. It's like that of mate-bonded Sea Dragons. Which looks different from the siren bond to a Sea Dragon; that looks like a single thread that is separate for each but connects them together, a new magic all its own. But with mate bonds, the magic weaves together until the bond is sealed, then the magic seamlessly mixes. At least that's how I would describe it. It's beautiful to see. I know my gift is unique in seeing people's magic that way." She grabbed my hand and pulled me to the plush sofa, and we sat together. "Have you told Orla?"

I bit my lower lip nervously and shook my head. "No."

"You do know that at some point you will have to show her your true form and sing your song, though, right?" Rielle squeezed my hands that she held tightly in her lap, a comfort I was grateful for.

A flood of words burst from me, everything I held in so deeply. "I knew one day I would want to, and I hoped we could perhaps have that trust. I just didn't expect I would need to seal a mate bond between us. I don't even know how that will work or if it will work. Back home, we only have to do that once with another siren, and our combined magic seals our Sea Dragons mate bond. I don't even know how this is possible. Sea Dragons never mate outside of their own kind. We are not even of the same race. I have no Fae in me, but I don't think mate bonds happen with them, either. However, unless we travel to the Sylvan Enclave, we won't be able to speak to any Fae elder who might know. And if Frostspire has Fae slaves, then it stands to reason that they have been raiding the Sylvan coasts for some time now. How did we not know? How did no one realize, and how did they not seek our aid?"

"Look, I know there are more questions than answers right now, but have you even told Orla how you feel about her?" Rielle tried to quell my fears and anxiety.

I looked away, pulling my hand back into my own lap squeezing them together tightly until my knuckles turned white. "Not yet, and Cam... she is so upset with me right now. Also, I do not know what happened between her and Orla, but something happened. I think it's all my fault. I should have been more clear with Cam before we even came here. I just didn't want to lose her. You know, it was just for fun between Cam and me."

She twisted her lips in a smirk. "I know it was for you, but Cam is too loyal for just fun. I warned you about that then. I am really not surprised she lost resolve with you."

"Yes, it was fun, and I was just exploring life. You know all too well she wasn't the first or the only woman I was with before. I thought she knew better." I sighed and I whispered confiding in her. "She got so jealous. She tried to come on to me and kiss me. Right after Orla woke up from her Enkindling. I told Cam no and sent her away, but it's just a mess. I haven't even had time to talk to Orla about that yet, either. What would I say anyway? Oh yeah, by the way, we are now mated, but I almost kissed my guard in the hallway right after I kissed you awake. How does that even come out with a good ending, let alone not in some kind of argument? I just don't even know what to do." Rielle's eyes grew large, and pulled her dagger out playfully, fidgeting with it.

A knock on the door interrupted our intimate conversation. Rielle popped up, dagger still in hand, pressing it at the ready to the back of the door and cracked it open. "Can I help you, Cam?" Rielle said pointedly.

"Rielle, let her in," I said, rolling my eyes.

"So long as she keeps her hands and lips to herself," Rielle snarked at Cam before stepping aside to let her in. Rielle returned to her seat next to me, leaving Cam awkwardly standing above us.

"Um, Frank went after Orla. He said something about finding her where she always goes, but he didn't specify where that was. I thought you would want to know." Cam spoke cautiously, her eyes flicking to me. I noticed the blue and purple bruise along her jawline and the scabbing split in her lip.

I pointed to her face. "So, are you going to tell me what happened to you on your way to Orla and Frank earlier?"

Cam looked down at the floor, shuffling uncomfortably before meeting my gaze with anger and hurt flickering in her eyes. "I spoke out of turn to her grace, Majesty," she said, her tone clipped.

"So Orla struck you?" I asked, struggling to restrain my magic as rage bubbled within me. I would not tolerate anyone, not even my mate, assaulting my people.

Rielle struggled to hide a smirk. "So were you two fighting over Aure like a pair of juvenile boys?" Cam shot Rielle with a glare that wasn't easily concealed.

I shook my head and held up my hand. "Enough from both of you. Cambria, answer my question."

"Yes, she struck me." Cam crossed her arms. The fire in the hearth flared hot and large, and I grit my teeth until my jaw ached. Did no one here in Orlondia have any restraint?

Rielle let out a small giggle. "What did you say 'out of turn,' Cam? That's not like little miss perfect soldier."

That wasn't like Cam, and now I wanted to know what she had said too. Cam didn't answer, and my patience was wearing thin. "Cam, answer Rielle's question."

Cam kept her mouth in a thin line and finally responded. "I simply informed her that you required her presence."

Rielle and I exchanged looks. Would Orla really strike out at someone just because they didn't address her properly? I sighed. "Fine, I will talk to Orla about it. You are dismissed, Cam. Rielle will stay with me for now."

Cam nodded curtly and left the room, closing the door behind her with a quiet click. The tension lingered, and I could feel Rielle's eyes on me as I tried to process everything.

Rielle broke the silence. "Aure, you need to be careful. There's a lot going on here, and we don't have all the information."

"I know," I said, rubbing my temples. "Orla's out there, and I need to find her. We need to make sure she's okay, especially after everything."

She nodded. "I know that is what you want, but you need to give her some time. Frank's already gone after her, and she likely needs a moment alone to process everything."

I sighed, feeling torn. "You're right. She's probably overwhelmed. But it's hard not to worry about her."

She placed a comforting hand on my shoulder. "She'll be alright. Orla's strong. In the meantime, tell me more about this upcoming engagement party." She pointed to a large stack of parchments on the short oval table in front of the sofa. She was always good at redirecting me when I needed it.

I nodded, trying to push my worries aside. "Oh, yeah, we are announcing our engagement publicly on Orla's 30th birthday. It's in nine days. We need everything to go smoothly."

"What are you working on now?" She picked up the top sheets of parchment and examined them.

"We have sent out the invite and the guest list has been finalized, but there are a few details we need to iron out. For one, the seating arrangements. I need to be strategic about who sits where." I said, pointing out the diagram of the seating.

"Of course," she agreed, leaning back against the plush sofa.

I continued while looking over the seating chart. "I want to place our strongest allies closest to us. And monitor anyone who might pose a threat."

She smirked. "Sounds like you're already getting the hang of this political game."

I laughed softly, despite the lingering tension. "I suppose I am. But it's more than a game. It's about securing Faedamir's future, and mine with Orla."

"True," she spoke in a serious tone. Glancing at the seating chart, her fingers tapping thoughtfully on the parchment. "This looks good, but we need to ensure every detail is perfect. We can't afford any mistakes."

I nodded, feeling the weight of the upcoming event pressing down on me. "You're right. Let's go over it again tomorrow. For now, I think we both need some rest."

She gave me a small, reassuring smile. "Agreed. We've had a long day. Try to get some sleep, Aure. We'll tackle this with fresh eyes in the morning. I am really excited you have found someone that you love to be with. It is the hope we all need right now."

She hugged me tightly, then headed toward the door. I watched her leave and close the door softly behind her. The room felt even quieter. The crackling fire and slowing patter of rain on the glass were the only sounds.

I changed into my soft, silky nightgown and washed my face. I moved to the bed, my body heavy with exhaustion. I slipped under the covers, the warmth of the blankets a comfort to the turmoil in my mind.

As I closed my eyes, the events of the day played over and over in my head. Eamon's lifeless body, Orla's pained expression, the tension with Cam... it was all too much. I took a deep breath, trying to push the thoughts away and let sleep take over.

Slowly, the world around me began to fade. The lulling sounds of the storm grew distant. My mind drifted into a realm where reality and possibilities intertwined.

I found myself standing in a vast, open field bathed in moonlight. The air was cool and filled with the scent of night-blooming flowers. In the distance, a majestic forest loomed, its trees whispering secrets to the wind. The full moon hung low in the sky, casting a silver glow over everything.

I took a step forward, feeling the soft grass beneath my feet. Each step seemed to pull me deeper into the dream, the real world fading away. As I walked, I heard soft, melodic humming. It was a hauntingly beautiful tune, familiar yet strange.

I followed the sound, my heart pounding with a mix of curiosity and apprehension. The humming grew louder, guiding me to a clearing in the forest. There, in the center of the clearing, stood Orla. Her back was to me, but instead of her usually short clipped hairstyle, now she had long hair cascading down her back in waves of silver and gold.

"Orla?" I called out, my voice echoing in the stillness.

She turned slowly, her eyes shimmering with a light that seemed otherworldly. Despite her smile, a melancholy seemed to seep from her. "Aure, you came."

I stepped closer, feeling a strange pull towards her. "Of course I came. I've been so worried about you."

Orla's smile faded, replaced by a look of sorrow. "I know. And I'm sorry for everything. But there are things you don't understand, things that even I'm still trying to grasp."

Before I could respond, the surrounding scene shifted. The moonlight dimmed, and the forest grew darker. Shadows danced around us, and the air turned cold. Orla's form blurred, her image flickering like a candle in the wind.

"Orla, wait!" I reached out, but she was already slipping away, her voice a distant echo.

"Aure, you must ..."

The darkness swallowed her words, and I was now alone in the clearing. The dreamscape twisted and churned, pulling me deeper into its depths. Faces and places flashed before my eyes—King Oric's cruel smile, Cam's angry gaze, the flicker of ancient magic.

Suddenly, the scene changed again. I found myself in a dark, decrepit throne room, the air thick with the scent of decay and dark magic. A figure stood at the far end, cloaked in shadows. His presence radiated malevolency and power, making my skin crawl.

Orla was there too, kneeling before the figure, her face pale and eyes wide with fear. She tried to stand, but dark tendrils of magic wrapped around her, holding her in place. The figure raised his hand, holding an orb formed from pure darkness. Power and magic were being drawn into it, as I watched it drain life directly from Orla's heart.

Orla looked up at him and she spoke weakly, "You will never have her." The man now had golden light cracking through his skin and he pulled out a long obsidian blade.

"No!" I screamed, trying to run towards her, but my feet felt like they were stuck in quicksand. I watched in horror as the blade plunged into Orla's chest, her scream echoing through the chamber. Her body convulsed, and then she fell limp, her eyes glazing over. She lay on the marble floor, as lifeless as Eamon had been.

The dark figure turned towards me, his eyes glowed with a sinister ruby red light. "You cannot save her, Aure. She is mine." Came a voice I thought I recognized.

With a final, mocking laugh, the figure and the throne room dissolved into darkness, leaving me alone with the image of Orla's lifeless body burned into my mind.

I awoke with a start, my heart racing and my body drenched in sweat. The fire in the hearth had burned low, and the room was shrouded in shadows. I sat up, trying to shake off the lingering sense of dread.

Orla's dying scream echoed in my ears, and I knew the dream was more than just a nightmare. My foresight dreams had become so strange, but I knew this was a warning. I had to find Orla, I needed to know she was safe.

ORLA

Chapter 15

I didn't care that my clothes were soaked through from the pouring rain or that lightning struck the ground behind me with deafening thunder. I ran, my feet hitting the wet stone and then dirt. I noticed nothing but the images replaying in my head of Tristan stepping behind Eamon and slitting his throat. The smell of iron from the putrid fluid that gurgled out and washed Eamon's body in a sea of scarlet consumed me.

My whole body vibrated as I ran, the torrent of rain flooded the world around me. I reached the edge of the forest surrounding the barracks. No one in their right mind was out in this storm. Overwhelmed by everything, I faced the blackened sky and screamed. Something ripped through my core as lightning danced across the darkness above me.

My father's mocking words ruminated in my mind. *"Orla, you know I don't indulge in these childish antics."* The memories of every time he had said that to me inundated my thoughts.

I threw my hands out and shouted to the whole of Terra, "ENOUGH!" A wave of energy and wind rippled out around me, shaking the trees and breaking their limbs. The rain paused, frozen in place for a moment, then settled into a slow drizzle. I fell to my knees, sobbing.

I closed my eyes to regain my equanimity. I reached for the rebounder stone that sat around my neck and held it tightly, focusing on my breathing. I felt for the buzz inside it which soothed me. I hummed the tune I only knew from my dreams. The storm eased.

I shivered from the cold seeping in. I stood and walked to the pub where I sought refuge from my family, my duty, and myself. The wooden cottage pub's warm glow beckoned through the rain, promising solace from the turmoil inside and out. I approached, sounds filled the air. Laughter and clinking glasses grew louder, enticing to give me the respite I longed for.

Pushing the creaky worn door open, I stepped inside. The warmth hit me immediately, along with the comforting smell of wood smoke, baked bread, and ale. Patrons turned to look at me, a drenched and muddy stranger, before returning to their conversations. I made my way to an empty corner table, shaking off the rain as best I could. I sank into the worn leather seat, trying to find some semblance of peace.

A barmaid approached with a sympathetic smile. "Rough night, love?" she asked, setting down a steaming mug of mulled wine in front of me.

I nodded, managing a small smile. "You could say that."

She patted my shoulder gently. "This one's on the house. You look like you need it."

"Thank you," I murmured, wrapping my hands around the warm mug. I took a sip, feeling the heat spread through me, chasing away the chill.

I glanced around the room, taking in the familiar faces. Regulars, locals, all seeking refuge from their own troubles. For a moment, I allowed myself to be just another weary soul in need of comfort.

My thoughts, however, wouldn't let me rest. The images of Eamon and the weight of my father's words pressed down on me. I reached for the rebounder stone again, its calming energy a small anchor in the storm of my mind.

The door opened again, and a gust of wind blew through the pub. I looked up to see Cambria standing in the doorway. She looked drenched and exhausted, her usual composure replaced by a furrowed brow. She glanced around the crowded room, and I turned my body, hoping she wouldn't see me. She made her way to the bar and ordered a drink, downing it quickly before ordering another. She sat at the bar, staring into her glass, lost in thought.

I watched her, unsure whether to approach or give her space. I had often seen her as restrained and phlegmatic, but tonight, she seemed weighed down by large burdens. The barmaid refilled her glass. She took a deep swig, grimaced, and her shoulders slumped.

I felt a pang of sympathy, but hesitated to intrude. After a moment, I stood, grabbed my mostly full mug, and walked over to her. "Cambria," I said in a hushed tone. My voice barely carried over the murmur of the pub. "I didn't expect to see you here."

She looked up, startled, and then recognition flickered in her eyes. She gave a tight, but polite, nod. "Orla. Didn't see you there. What are you doing here?"

"I needed some time away," I admitted. I didn't know why I cared to even engage with Cam, but a small part of me felt sorry for her and the position she was in. "Seems like you did too."

She nodded, then swallowed down her drink. "Yeah, it's been a rough day. I thought I'd find some peace here."

"Same here." I took another small sip of my drink. We sat in silence for a while, the unspoken weight of our respective burdens hanging between us.

The barmaid refilled her glass again, and she stared at the amber liquid. After a few moments, she broke the silence. "Do you ever feel like... no matter how hard you try, it's never enough?"

I nodded, understanding her sentiment all too well. "All the time. Especially with everything going on now. It's like we're constantly fighting battles on multiple fronts."

She sighed, swirling her drink. "I joined the military to make a difference, to protect our people, and to protect Aure. But sometimes, it feels like I am just a pawn in someone else's game."

I looked at her, seeing the depth of her struggle. "I understand. I joined for similar reasons. My father's expectations, the pressure to live up to being the sole heir to this kingdom... it's a lot to carry."

Her eyes softened with empathy. "Honestly, I know you will be an incredible queen one day. You're strong and just, Orla. You have a resilience that's rare." She smirked, then whispered. "Also, you have a mean right hook. Fighting your own battles makes you valiant."

I smiled faintly, appreciating her words. "Thank you, Cam. You're strong too. I've seen you fight. You have a lot of determination and courage. It's inspiring. You're a great warrior. Just stop trying to steal my lady, alright?" I snickered and nudged her playfully.

Her eyes widened slightly at my playful jab, but then she laughed, a genuine sound that eased some of the tension between us. "I know my place now. I wasn't trying to steal her. Okay, maybe I was kind of. I just... didn't know how to handle everything. Those lines of duty, loyalty, and desire kind of blur. Regardless, Aure has made her choice very clear, which I will respect and honor."

I smiled and studied Cam for a moment, knowing she spoke the truth. "Well, just so long as you remember who she is marrying, I will let it go."

With a grin, her expression softened. "I know, I know. I will." She took another drink and sighed. "You know, sometimes it feels like we're all fighting for a lost cause? When will we see the end with peace, stability, and a future that's not drenched in blood?"

I nodded, the weight of her words sinking in. "Yeah, it's hard to see the end when we're in the thick of it. But we have to believe it's possible. That's what keeps us going, right?"

Her gaze grew distant, her fingers tracing the rim of her glass. "Yeah. Do you ever think about what it'll be like when it's all over? When the fighting and death stops?"

I took a deep breath, considering her question. "Sometimes. I imagine a world where we can rebuild, where people can live without fear. Where we can honor the memories of those we've lost by creating something better."

She gave me a slow nod, her lips pressed into a flat line. "It's hard to picture. I've been a guard for so long, and this war seems never ending. It's almost like I've forgotten how to be anything else."

I placed a hand on her shoulder. "You're more than just a soldier, Cam. You're a leader, a friend. And when this is over, you'll find new ways to be all of those things. We all will."

She looked at me, a small, hopeful smile tugging at her lips. "I hope so. I really do."

We sat in silence for a moment, the weight of our shared burdens hanging between us. She finished her drink. The pub emptied gradually as it grew quiet and the storm outside was now a distant rumble. It was a rare moment of peace, and I savored it, knowing how fleeting these moments could be.

She signaled the barmaid to place the bottle of rum she had been drinking on the counter. The barmaid placed it with a hard clunk in front of us, and she handed the barmaid a few coins. She poured herself another generous glass, then offered me some. I shook my head and took the last sip of my mulled wine.

She broke the silence with a soft voice. "Do you ever miss it? The simplicity of training, before all the politics and the battles?"

I smiled wistfully. "Yeah, I do. There was a time when it was just about honing our skills, pushing our limits. It felt...pure, in a way. But we can't go back. We've grown, and our responsibilities have grown with us."

She nodded. "True. I guess that's the price we pay for trying to make a difference."

The loud, explosive sound of the door hitting the wall drew my attention. I saw a haggard Frank barge through the opening, his eyes wide with worry. He scanned the room frantically until his gaze landed on me. Relief washed over his face as he hurried over and his lips curled into a grin as he eyed us..

"Ladies, I didn't know this pub had become the new military strategy room," Frank said, walking over to our table with an easy charm. "Orla, you had me worried sick. Thought you'd be halfway to the next kingdom by now. But seein' you both here, lookin like drowned cats, has really made my day."

Cam looked at Frank full of mirth. "Frank, you found us," she said in giddy amusement.

He mused, "It's not every day I get to see the mighty Orla and Cam, soaked to the bone, havin' a heart-to-heart over a pint."

She chuckled, raising her glass to him. "Sit down, Frank, join us."

He pulled up a chair, his demeanor lightening further. "Well, alrighty then, I am happy to rescue two of the fiercest warriors I know from their own thoughts. Should I be worried about a mutiny?"

With a faint smile playing on my lips, I rolled my eyes at him. "No mutiny here, just some much-needed conversation."

She chuckled, shaking her head. "You're safe for now, Frank. We were just building bridges. And maybe plotting a little," she added with a wink.

Frank waved the barmaid over and she handed him a tankard of ale. "What are we drinkin to? Friendship? Battles won and lost? Or just survivin' another day?"

I smiled, raising my empty mug. "How about to surviving another day and the battles yet to come?"

Cam raised her half-full glass eagerly, nearly slipping off her stool as she stumbled to the side. "To surviving," she cheered with a giggle.

Frank raised his tankard. "To survivin' another day," he echoed. We clinked our glasses together.

Frank took a drink, and I set my mug down on the bar, exchanging looks with him as Cam finished off her glass. Given how much she was drinking, I decided not to have any more tonight.

Cam leaned over toward Frank, speaking much louder than she likely intended. "Frank, do you have a map?" He looked back at her, arching his eyebrow in confusion. She giggled and awkwardly placed her hand on his chest. "Because I keep getting lost in your eyes."

With a laugh and a sidelong glance at me, Frank said, "Okay, Miss Cam, I think it's time we all call it a night. Wouldn't you agree, Orla?"

I caught Cam as she wobbled on the stool, trying not to fall onto Frank from leaning too far. "Cam, I think we should get you to bed. It's been a long day for everyone."

Frank nodded and stood up. "I'll go find a way to get her back to the palace without stumbling the whole way there." I gave him a grateful nod and wrapped my arm under Cam's shoulders.

She grinned at me before patting my head. "You are my best friend now."

We walked out of the little pub together, amusement playing across my lips. "Okay, Cam."

We stepped into the rain-soaked night. Frank had hurried ahead to find a carriage or some means of transport. The storm had calmed to a steady drizzle, the earlier chaos giving way to a serene gloom. Cam mumbled incoherently, her weight leaning heavily against me, and I struggled to keep her upright.

Frank returned quickly, a small covered carriage trailing behind him. "Got us a ride," he said, opening the door and helping us both inside.

Once settled, I looked over at Cam, her eyes fluttering closed. "She's had a rough night," I murmured to Frank.

He nodded, his face lined with concern. "We all have. I've been looking for you, Orla. I haven't ever seen you run away from everything like that before."

I sighed, feeling the weight of the evening settle over me. "I needed some space. Everything that happened today... it was a lot."

Frank's eyes softened. "I understand. But you don't have to go through it alone. We're all here for you."

I offered a faint smile. "Thank you, Frank. It means a lot."

The carriage rattled along the cobblestone streets, the sound of the wheels a soothing rhythm against the silence. As we approached the palace, the grandeur of its towers loomed above us, the familiar sight bringing a mix of comfort and dread.

Once inside, Cam and I made our way up the grand staircase toward the west wing hall. The storm had subsided, and only the cold filled the halls of the palace with a promise of the winter that would soon be coming. I couldn't believe I was half-carrying a very drunk and loudly singing off-key ex-girlfriend of the woman I was madly in love with to her bed. I shook my head at the absurdity of the situation.

I just admitted to myself that I love Aure. How could I be in love with her when we still knew so little about each other and with so much going on? I couldn't sit here denying my feelings, though, because I had lost control and hit someone over her. My stomach turned as I looked down at Cam's bruise, a fractal pattern of purples, blues, yellows, and greens.

She hiccuped and leaned heavily on me, her voice slurring. "You know, Orla, you're... you're not so bad. I mean, for someone who... who..."

I sighed, adjusting my grip to keep her steady. "Never mind, Cam. Let's just get you to bed."

She giggled and stumbled. "I really messed up, didn't I?"

I tightened my hold on her. "We all make mistakes. Just... let's get through tonight, okay?"

We made our way down the corridor. Aure stepped out of her chamber, tightly holding a fur robe around herself. Her soft footsteps with her bare feet sent a thrill through me, and she turned toward us, her eyes widening in concern when she spotted us.

"Orla, I have been so worried." Aure rushed towards us but stopping short in front of Cam and I. "What happened? Why is Cam—"

"She's fine, just had a bit too much to drink," I interrupted, trying to reassure Aure. "I'll get her settled, and then we can talk."

Cam lurched forward towards Aure. I kept my firm grip on her so we didn't
fall forward. "Aure, you picked a good one, she is my bestest friend now.
You has to be good to each, a'right… we got to all love ea'other cause zese
barstards are out for blood. Otay? Otay!"

Aure's eyes softened as she looked at Cam, then at me. "Alright, let's get
her to bed. She can sleep it off on the couch in my chambers."

We guided Cam into the room, where Aure helped me settle her on the sofa.
Cam mumbled incoherently as she drifted off to sleep.

Once she was resting peacefully, Aure turned to me, concern etched on her
face. "Orla, what's going on? Why is Cam like this?"

I sighed, running a hand through my wet hair. "It's been a rough night for
everyone. Emotions are running high, and I think she just needed to escape
for a bit. We all do sometimes. Let's go talk in my room. I don't want to wake
Cam. She needs rest."

Aure nodded, her worry still palpable. I led her down the dimly lit corridor.
It was in the early hours of the morning now. The sun peeked through the
windows, painting hues of pink and orange on the stone walls. The silence
between us was thick with unspoken words, the tension building with each
step.

As we entered my chambers, I closed the door softly, trying to keep the
atmosphere calm. I motioned for Aure to sit on the chaise lounge while I took
a chair opposite her. The room, usually a sanctuary of dark woods and deep
purples, felt tense and uneasy tonight.

Aure spoke first, her voice strained. "I don't understand, Orla. Cam was
hurt, and she said you punched her. Why would you do that?" Her eyes were
searching, pleading for an explanation that made sense.

I took a deep breath, the events of the day replaying in my mind. "Aure, it's
not that simple. Cam provoked me. She said some things that crossed the line
and things got heated. It wasn't just a random act of violence."

Aure's eyes widened, her tone incredulous. "Provoked you? Enough to hit
her? What could she possibly have said?"

I hesitated, the memory of Cam's taunts stinging fresh. "She made some
very personal, very hurtful comments about you and HER to me. She was out
of line, Aure."

"But you hit her!" Aure's voice rose, anger and confusion mingling. "She's loyal to us both, Orla. She's been my guard, my friend, for years. How could you?"

My frustration bubbled up, matching hers. "Loyalty doesn't give her the right to disrespect me or you. She wasn't acting like a friend to either of us. She was reckless, and she put herself first before her duty and loyalty. I may have acted rashly, but I don't regret it."

Aure's expression hardened, her eyes flashing with indignation. "You could have handled it differently. Violence isn't the answer, Orla. It never is."

I stood up, unable to stay seated under the weight of her accusations. "Do you think I wanted to hit her? Do you think I didn't want to talk it out with her? With you? Sometimes, there aren't words to express all your emotions, Aure. Sometimes, action is the only option."

Aure stood as well, her posture tense. "But you didn't even explain to me what happened. I'm hearing this from Cam, and she's telling me there was no cause for this. I don't know who to believe."

The room seemed to close in around us, our emotions echoing off the walls. I struggled to find the words that would bridge the gap between us, the words that would make her understand.

"Aure," I said, my voice softening, "I didn't want this. I didn't want any of this. But I made a choice, and I chose to protect you the only way I knew how."

"Orla, I need to trust you." Her eyes softened slightly, but the hurt was still there. "I need to know we are in this together."

"Trust? How am I supposed to trust you when Cam is sleeping on your couch right now? She is always with you and clearly there is a past between you two. Did you ever consider how that would look?" Fire burned deep inside me. I took a step forward as I confronted her standing in her space.

She met my gaze with challenge as her cheeks turned the shade of beets. "It's not like we are virgins or something, we all have a past. I didn't question you about Tristan."

She backed up a few steps, and I would let her retreat from me or this conversation. "There is nothing to be said about that slimy little frog of a man. He was a detestable, entitled brat as a child, and he hasn't gotten any better. The only thing that was ever between us was in his delusions."

"Well, if not him, I am sure there have been others." She backed up again until her back reached the wall, and I smiled as I followed her steps.

"No, Aure, there hasn't been anyone before you." I strategically placed my hand on the wall behind her, barely brushing past her shoulder and hair. An electric shock sung through my arm at our closeness as the heat raced through my body. I leaned in close to her, our breaths mingling. Her scent of coconuts and citrus consumed my senses.

I took my other hand, and gently I brushed a small ringlet of her hair from her face. My breath caught in my throat, and my heart pounded in my ears as everything else in the room seemed to disappear.

I ran my finger down the side of her cheek, savoring the sensation of her soft skin mixed with the static charge I felt. Tracing her jaw, she gave me a lustrous smile. Aure's breath hitched, her eyes fluttering closed for a moment before meeting mine again.

I scanned her luminous green eyes, mesmerized by all of her. I leaned in closer to her. The feeling overwhelmed by the energy between us where our bodies met, even through our clothes.

My fingers lingered on the bottom of her chin, and tipped her face towards me slowly, giving her a chance to change her mind. When she didn't pull away, I closed the distance, my lips brushing against hers with a tenderness that belied the storm of emotions within me. The kiss was soft at first, tentative, as if we were both afraid to break the fragile spell that had woven around us.

But then, the tension that had been building between us erupted. Aure's hands moved to my waist, pulling me closer as our kiss deepened, our tongues exploring the deep recesses of each other's mouths. I could feel the warmth of her body against mine, the soft curves of her form fitting perfectly against me.

The world outside ceased to exist. There was only Aure and the intoxicating feeling of her lips on mine, the way her breath mingled with mine, the electric current that seemed to pulse through every point of contact. I never want this to end.

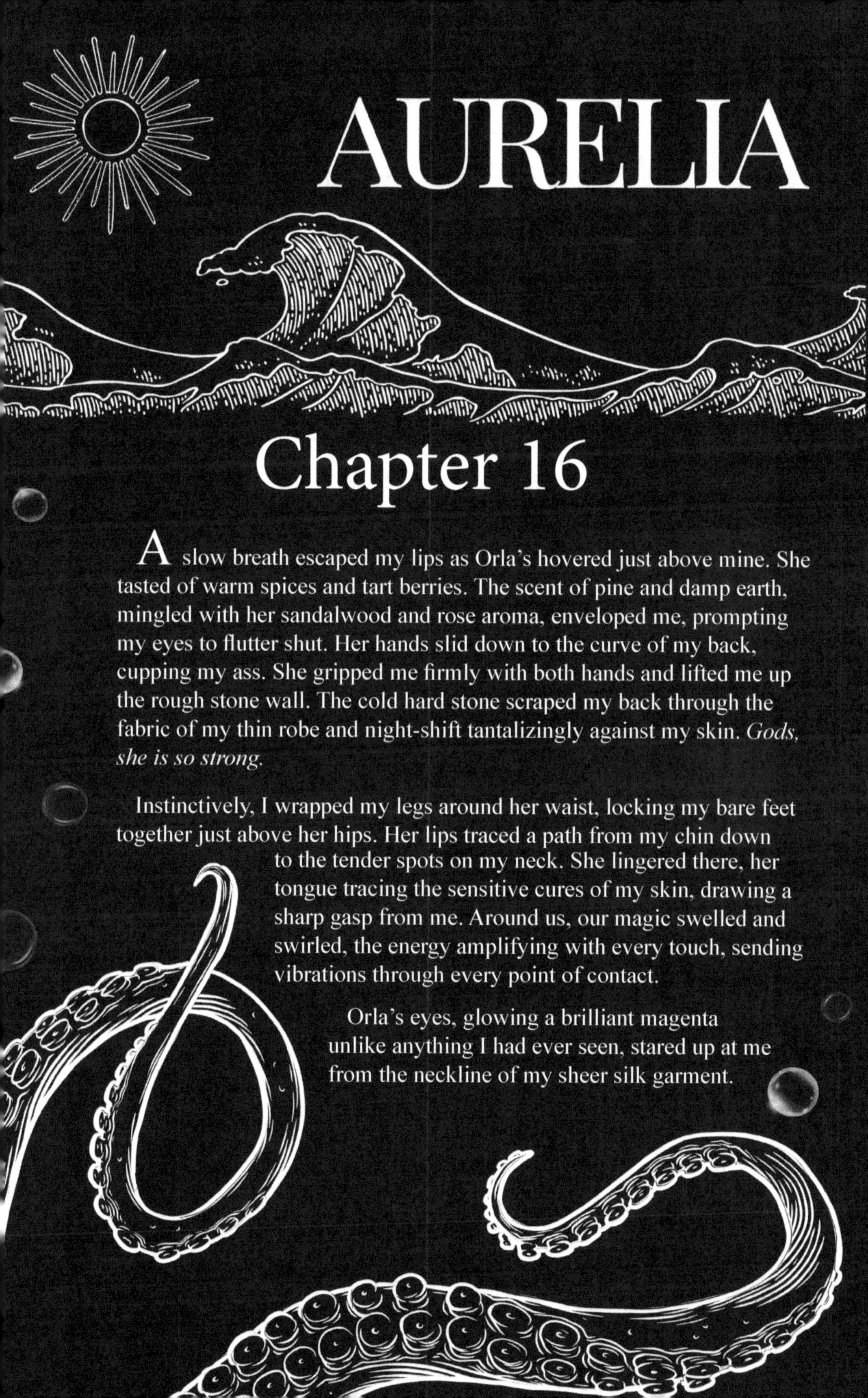

AURELIA

Chapter 16

A slow breath escaped my lips as Orla's hovered just above mine. She tasted of warm spices and tart berries. The scent of pine and damp earth, mingled with her sandalwood and rose aroma, enveloped me, prompting my eyes to flutter shut. Her hands slid down to the curve of my back, cupping my ass. She gripped me firmly with both hands and lifted me up the rough stone wall. The cold hard stone scraped my back through the fabric of my thin robe and night-shift tantalizingly against my skin. *Gods, she is so strong.*

Instinctively, I wrapped my legs around her waist, locking my bare feet together just above her hips. Her lips traced a path from my chin down to the tender spots on my neck. She lingered there, her tongue tracing the sensitive cures of my skin, drawing a sharp gasp from me. Around us, our magic swelled and swirled, the energy amplifying with every touch, sending vibrations through every point of contact.

Orla's eyes, glowing a brilliant magenta unlike anything I had ever seen, stared up at me from the neckline of my sheer silk garment.

A smirk played on her lips as her low voice teased, "If you'd rather not be my first, I could always even the score and see if my 'bestest friend' is up for a bit of fun instead."

Heat rushed to my cheeks, and I squirmed in her firm grip. "Completely unnecessary idea, you little brat." I tried to sound stern, but my voice wavered. She giggled, her head dipping between my breasts. I gasped as she gently pulled a small amount of the soft skin of my left breast into her mouth, biting down slowly, her teeth grazing my flesh.

A moan escaped my lips as I arched into her, my hair tangling against the wall. My fingers curled into the tight, solid muscles of her shoulders, feeling the dampness of her rain-soaked clothes seeping through my thin robe and shift, sending a chill through me. "Orla," I breathed, my voice barely above a whisper.

She paused, lifting her gaze to meet mine. "Yes, Meles Tari?" she murmured, her voice laced with both tenderness and desire.

"You're making me wet," I purred, a smile curling on my lips as I ran my fingers through her still damp hair.

The satisfied grin she gave me in return only ignited the heat building in my core, a deep ache growing within me. I could feel myself growing slick with desire. "Isn't that exactly what you wanted?" she taunted, her voice low and full of promise.

I leaned into her, pressing my lips against hers, giving in to my need to taste her again. She responded with equal passion, and I melted fully into her embrace. When I finally broke the kiss, I whispered softly into her ear, "I meant our clothes."

Her eyes flickered briefly to sky blue, and I couldn't help but let out a small giggle. Resting my head on her shoulder, I suggested, "We could get out of them and head over to your bed."

Her eyes held mine for a moment longer, the sky blue fading back to a deep, intense shade of violet. She didn't need to say a word; the heat in her gaze was enough to set my pulse racing. Slowly, she turned us, carrying me, and without breaking eye contact, she walked toward the open bed chamber.

The soft glow of moonlight filtered through the curtains, casting a gentle light across the room. The atmosphere felt charged with the pulse of our magic. Every step we took seemed to heighten the anticipation between us. When we reached the bed, she let my feet drop to the floor. Her fingers trailed lightly down my arms, leaving a trail of tingling warmth in their wake.

With deliberate slowness, she reached for the clasp of my robe, her fingers brushing against my skin as she loosened it. The fabric slipped from my shoulders and pooled at my feet, leaving me standing in just my shift, the cool air of the room sending a shiver across my skin. Her gaze traveled over me, her eyes darkening with desire.

"I've been waiting for this moment." Her voice was husky as she reached for the hem of my shift. I raised my arms, letting her lift the delicate fabric over my head, leaving me bare before her.

I reached for her, my hands moving to the fastenings of her rain-soaked clothes. As I peeled away each layer, her damp garments fell to the floor, revealing the toned, beautiful body beneath. The heat between us intensified, the last of the barriers between us falling away.

My fingers danced across the scars and imperfections in her skin, the clear sign she had always been tough. I found a small inked drawing of a crystal above her hipbone and touched it softly. She smirked as I did, her eyes growing with mischief.

When we were both fully exposed to each other, she cupped my face in her hands, her thumbs brushing softly over my cheeks. "You're breathtaking," she whispered, and the sincerity in her voice made my heart swell.

Without another word, she pulled me close, the warmth of her body pressing against mine as we sank onto the bed together, the cool sheets a welcome sensation to the fire burning between us.

Kissing me deeply, she rolled us over until I was on my back and she was on top, her weight a gentle but firm presence against my body. My skin grew hot, acutely aware of every place where we connected. Lifting herself slightly, she grinned down at me. "I want you to show me what you like."

She took my hand in hers, guiding it slowly down my stomach toward the curve of my hip bone. Her other hand moved to part my legs as she settled herself between them. Her gaze never wavered from mine, her eyes swirling with shades of pink and purple, full of anticipation and want.

Our hands moved together, gliding down my pelvis and dipping lower between my thighs, brushing against the sensitive skin. My fingers grazed the heat of my core, sending a shiver through me. She settled back on her knees, kneeling between my splayed legs. Slowly, she released my hand, leaving it resting against my wet, aching pussy.

Her hands moved to my ankles, gently pushing my feet up as she bent my knees high. In a low, breathy voice, she issued a firm demand, "Show me, Meles Tari. How do you make yourself cum?"

My breath grew heavy as I slowly drew my fingers toward my clit, encircling it with deliberate, teasing strokes. My back arched into my own movements, and I could feel the weight of her heated gaze on me, filled with raw lust. My fingers grew slick with the hot, wet desire spilling from me, intensifying every sensation. I had never felt so exposed, so vulnerable—and yet, so incredibly comfortable.

A small moan escaped my lips as my hips moved in rhythm with my strokes. The amused grin she wore only heightened my desire to show her just how much she aroused me. Thoughts that weren't my own floated into my mind: *"I want to taste every bit of you."* Startled by what had to be Orla's thoughts, I didn't stop—instead, I felt a surge of excitement.

Without a word, she leaned forward, placing her head between my legs, hovering just above my hand with a wry look in her eyes. She nudged my fingers aside as I continued, moving a bit faster now, a small whimper escaping me. Gods, she was such a fucking tease. She kissed my fingers, then slid her tongue around them, her warm, wet tongue brushing my clit before gliding lower.

My whole body shuddered, "Oh Gods," I moaned, my voice trembling. *Fuck, I wanted to cum all over her face, and at this rate, I was going to do just that.*

Her tongue reached my entrance, and she slowly pushed it inside, curling it up toward my G-spot. I grabbed the sheets with my free hand, my hips bucking to meet her mouth. Between short, ragged breaths, I crooned, "I'm going to cum, Orla…ohh, don't stop, please." Her tongue flicked and moved faster, pushing deeper, and then she sucked and devoured me like I was her favorite meal.

My legs squeezed around her, my toes curling as I ran my hand through her hair, holding her in place as waves of ecstasy consumed me. Moaning loudly, my body convulsed, my pussy throbbing as every muscle tensed and relaxed over and over again.

Even as I let go and my body lay there, completely undone, her mouth didn't stop. She continued her slow, deliberate work, her tongue gently exploring every last inch of my hot, wet pussy. My body trembled with aftershocks, the sensitivity almost overwhelming, yet I couldn't bring myself to pull away. She licked every drop of my cum from me, sending little electric waves through my sensitive body, drawing out every last bit of pleasure until I was breathless and weak.

Finally, with one last gentle kiss, she lifted her head, her eyes meeting mine with a look that was both triumphant and adoring. The intensity of what we'd just shared lingered between us, heavy and charged, but there was something more—something softer, more vulnerable.

Orla slowly crawled up beside me, her warm body pressing against mine as she wrapped her arms around me. I felt her breath on my neck, steady and calming. "You're incredible," she whispered, her voice soft and filled with genuine affection.

I leaned into her touch, pressing a kiss just under her ear, my fingers softly trailing down her arm. Our magic sparked between us, a current of energy that made my breath hitch. In a smooth, soft voice, I whispered my need between each taste of her skin. "I think it's my turn to make you feel good."

With a firm but gentle push, I guided her onto her back, my lips finding hers in a claiming kiss, tasting myself mingled with the sweetness of her. I flicked my tongue deep into her mouth as I straddled her hips, pressing more passion into our kiss. Her muffled moan urged me to take more, to explore every inch of her mouth with mine. I was going to claim this woman in every possible way. She had no idea of the primal desire she had unleashed within me.

As our kiss deepened, I could feel her body respond beneath mine, a shiver running through her that matched the hunger growing inside me. I broke the kiss, trailing my lips down her neck, tasting the pulse that beat wildly under her skin. My hands moved with purpose, sliding over her curves, tracing the lines of her body as I reveled in the softness of her ivory skin.

I shifted slightly, my fingers brushing against her firm breasts and down her tight, toned abs. Teasing my fingers back upward as I caressed both of her tits. She arched into me, her breath coming faster, a silent plea for more. The sight of her beneath me, vulnerable and wanting, only fueled the fire inside me.

"You're so beautiful," I murmured against the skin between her breasts, my voice low and filled with reverence. I wanted to memorize every inch of her, to know her in a way no one else ever had. My hands slipped low between us, finally making contact with the warm wetness of her core. I relished the feel of her, the way her body responded to my touch as if it had been waiting for this moment.

With deliberate slowness, I kissed a trail down her chest and over her abs, my hands continuing their exploration of every hot wet inch of her pussy.

Every sigh, every moan that escaped her lips was a symphony to my ears, encouraging me to take my time, to savor every second of her response.

As I encircled her clitoris, I paused, lifting my head to meet her gaze, biting my lower lip. Her eyes were heavy with desire, a silent invitation that mirrored the longing burning inside me. Slowly, I began to tease the sensitive nub between my finger and thumb, relishing the way her breath caught before she let out a breathless moan.

I took a moment to simply drink in the sight of her, the way her body glowed in the dim light, the rise and fall of her chest as she breathed. I leaned down, my lips brushing against her the curve of her pelvis as I whispered, "I'm going to take care of you. Let me show you how much I want you."

With that, I moved lower, my lips exploring every inch of her body, drawing out every reaction, every gasp of pleasure. I wanted to make her feel everything I felt—the passion, the desire, the deep connection that pulsed between us like a living thing. This wasn't just about claiming her body; it was about claiming her heart, showing her that she was mine in every possible way.

As I reached the apex of her thighs, I glanced up at her, watching as her magenta eyes fluttered closed, her breath hitching in anticipation. I pressed a final, tender kiss to her hip before letting my mouth find her center, tasting her, feeling her arch beneath me as I lost myself in the sweet, intoxicating flavor of her.

Her hands tangled in my hair, urging me closer. I licked slowly up the length of her wet pussy, my tongue swirling around her clit before I sucked it gently between my lips. The guttural moan that escaped her sent a surge of deep, lustful satisfaction through me, twisting low in my stomach. I sucked harder, feeling the pulse of her desire, and pressed a single, soft finger against her entrance, teasing her as she writhed beneath me.

I pressed my finger gently inside her, I felt her body respond, tightening around me with a mixture of need and urgency. I moved slowly at first, teasing her with each shallow thrust, while my tongue continued its focused attention on her clit. The combination of her moans and the way her hips rocked against me drove me to push deeper inside her, craving more. She was so fucking incredibly tight, and the thought of being the first to touch her like this made me feel intoxicated with greedy lust.

I slipped another finger inside her, curling them upward as I searched for that perfect spot. "Meles Tari," she groaned, the sound of her voice sending a thrill through me. One day, I'd hold her down and make her tell me the meaning of that damn nickname, but right now, all I wanted was to make her explode all over me.

With the next thrust, I pushed deeper, feeling her body stretch and open to my movements. A sharp whimper escaped her lips as she surrendered to the sensation. The slick mixture of blood and cum coated my fingers, and I continued to tease her clit with my mouth, determined to drive her over the edge.

Her hands tightened in my hair, her breathing growing more erratic as I increased the pace of my thrusts, each movement curling toward her G-spot. The intensity between us surged, driving her closer to the brink. I could feel her body trembling, the tension coiling tighter within her as she climbed higher and higher, teetering on the edge of ecstasy.

I flicked my tongue faster over her clit, sucking it between my lips while my fingers worked in sync with my mouth, each movement designed to push her closer to that sweet oblivion. "Come for me, Orla," I whispered against her, my voice rough with desire, the words a command and a plea all at once.

Her response was immediate, her body arching off the bed as she cried out my name, "Aure" the sound of her release filling the room. I didn't let up, continuing to stroke and suck, drawing out every last shudder, every wave of pleasure that coursed through her. Her orgasm seemed to go on forever, her body trembling beneath me as I gave her everything I had.

Once her body softened into the sheets, I gently withdrew my fingers and placed one last kiss on her now swollen clit, savoring the way she shivered beneath me. I licked my fingers clean of her and savored the mix of her cum and blood. I moved up her body, kissing a trail along her skin until I reached her lips. The kiss was soft, almost reverent, as I cradled her face in my hands, allowing her to taste herself on my lips.

When I pulled back, her eyes fluttered open, the magenta glow now softened, her gaze filled with a mixture of love and exhaustion. I smiled down at her, wiping a bit of sweat off her brow. "You're incredible," I whispered, my voice filled with awe at what we had just shared.

She smiled weakly, her breath still coming in shallow pants as she reached up to cup my face. "That was…amazing," she murmured, her voice laced with satisfaction and warmth.

I leaned into her, our foreheads touched, and I let out a contented sigh. My fingers traced lazy patterns along her back, relishing the feeling of being so close to her, so utterly connected. "I've never felt anything like that before," I admitted, my voice barely above a whisper.

She smiled, a tender, knowing smile that made my heart flutter. "Neither have I," she replied, her lips brushing softly against mine in a gentle, lingering kiss.

For a long while, we simply lay there, holding each other, the world outside forgotten. In that moment, there was no war, no duty—just us, wrapped up in each other, safe and content in the aftermath of our passion.

As sleep tugged at the edges of my consciousness, I felt Orla's hand in mine, her thumb stroking gently over my knuckles. I drifted off as the warmth of her embrace lulled me into a peaceful slumber.

"She is mine, and you will not have her," growled the gruff voice of the man holding a cold steel blade to my throat. My eyes widened in shock.

"Tristan?" I croaked, my voice dry and raspy. My mouth felt parched, as if it were filled with cotton, and I dared not move, feeling the sharp knife painfully pressed against my skin. The wicked glint in his eyes and the smirk curling on his lips were all too familiar—I would remember that look anywhere.

"You've corrupted her with your vile magic. Look at her," he sneered, yanking my hair and forcing my head to the side, where Orla lay sleeping. Her eyes slowly opened, but she didn't move, staring at me as if she didn't even see him. "I should kill her right in front of you before I end your life, you wicked siren queen."

I reached for my magic, but I couldn't feel it. Panic seeped into my veins, cold as ice. My breath grew shallow, and I couldn't move—I was powerless, unable to even form words. Fear gripped me in every possible way. *Not again. No, this can't be happening again. Fuck.* I desperately searched for the threads of magic, reaching out to Azura, to my bond with Orla—anything—but nothing came. The emptiness was suffocating.

Tristan moved swiftly, gripping Orla by the back of her head just as he had done with Eamon, pressing the knife to her throat. I lay there paralyzed, helpless, every part of my body aching in agony as I watched. "You did this to her. It's your fault she has to die," Tristan taunted, his voice dripping with malice. Orla's mouth opened in a silent scream, her terror palpable, but no sound escaped her lips.

Then he did it. The knife sliced slowly through her throat, the act horrifyingly soundless. Deep purple liquid cascaded down her bare breasts as her eyes turned gray and lifeless. My entire body vibrated with a bottomless void of energy, and a scream tore from my throat, deafening in my ears as my heart raced wildly.

I watched in horror as he smiled, her purple blood staining his hands. "You're next," he sneered, his voice a chilling promise. His hot, sticky fingers wrapped around my throat, squeezing tight. I choked, my breath strangled, panic flooding me. *Fuck, I can't breathe—this is it. How did we let him win? Fuck.* Sorrow and defeat washed over me as I struggled, desperate to gasp for air, my body still immovable, trapped in helplessness.

✦ ORLA

Chapter 17

Loud screaming jerked me awake, and I found Aure's sweat-covered body clinging to mine. The echo of her cries, combined with the lingering terror of my own horrifying dream, sent my heart racing. Still gripped by fear, I shook Aure gently but urgently. "Aure, wake up. Wake up, please," I pleaded, my voice trembling with concern.

Tears streamed down her face as waves of magic pulsed off her, making the air around us hum with energy. Her signet tattoo on her forearm glowed brightly, casting an eerie light across the room. Her body was tense, rigid, as I continued trying to wake her. Then, suddenly, her eyes shot open, and she stared at me in horror, her breath coming in rapid, shallow pants. Slowly, she uncurled her fingers from my arms and tried to sit up. Her bloodshot eyes stared past me, fixated on the wall, as an unsettling silence settled between us.

"Aure?" I gently brushed a few copper curls away from her face, where they had stuck to the sticky sweat on her skin.

She caught my hand, holding it gently to her cheek for a moment before speaking. "I'm sorry," she murmured, her voice laced with exhaustion. "I had another terrifying foresight dream." She pulled my hand into her lap, gripping it tightly now. "I had to tell Azura that everything was alright. I woke her."

Confusion knitted my brow, and my eyes shifted from sky blue to a deeper, darker shade. "Your bond woke her?" I asked, my voice tinged with curiosity and concern. I'd read a lot about the connection between a bonded Siren and Sea Dragon—how they could communicate through a form of telepathy, but only when one of them activated the signet by desire or need.

She nodded, her voice soft and troubled. "I must have been very distressed, and my magic activated our bond." She clung to my hand as if it was a lifeline, her grip tightening as though she needed to anchor herself in reality. I didn't mind that her nails dug into my flesh. The pain was a reminder that I was here, in the waking world, and not trapped in my own nightmare.

Dreams had never been something I paid much attention to before, but lately, they seemed more real than the world around me. This last one was different, though—haunting in a way that left me unsettled. I watched myself in it, not as a participant, but as a helpless spectator, powerless to change the course of events.

"I…" Tears began to spill down her beautifully bronzed and rosy cheeks, her voice cracking as she tried to speak. "I keep dreaming of your death," she choked out, the words barely more than a whisper.

Without hesitation, I scooped her into my arms, holding her still-naked body against my bare chest. My fingers tangled gently in her curls as I tried to soothe her.

"Shhh… Meles Tari. I'm here, and I'm very much alive," I crooned, though comforting others had never been my strong suit, and the awkwardness of the moment didn't escape me. But I knew she needed to feel me, to hear my heart beating against hers. And truthfully, I needed her close too. "I had a nightmare tonight too… we both died," I whispered into her hair, breathing in her scent. Gods, why did she have to smell so damn good?

She looked up at me, shock etched across her features. "What do you mean you had a nightmare where we both died?" Her eyes searched mine, as if trying to find some hidden truth in my expression.

My voice dropped to a hushed tone, as if I didn't want the walls to hear us. "Tristan stood over you, right here in this bed, and threatened you. Then I watched him kill me… but it wasn't really me because I was just watching it all unfold, like I was an outsider. And my blood was purple. I don't bleed purple," I added with a nervous giggle.

Her head tilted as she straightened, moving out of my arms, her eyes distant as if she were piecing together a puzzle. Then her gaze dropped to my breasts and the peaked nipples, and a flush crept up her cheeks. Biting her lower lip, she mused, "You're far too distracting for this conversation, looking like that."

I couldn't resist twisting my lips into a mischievous smile before leaning in and nipping at her neck. "I'm not the only one who's distracting," I breathed into her ear, then teasingly licked the edge of it.

She let out a playful squeak as she pushed me back and tossed a blanket over me. Heat built in my core, and the memories of everything we'd done just a few hours ago sent wetness pooling between my thighs again. Fuck, I never wanted to stop tasting her, touching her, being with her.

"We need to have a serious conversation, and I can't do that with your tits staring at me, Orla," she said, her voice a mix of frustration and teasing.

I growled softly in amusement, peeking my head out from under the blanket but keeping myself covered. I noticed her wrapping a blanket around herself too, and my heart sank a bit in disappointment. I loved just looking at her naked body—the curves, the plush softness that invited me to lick and bite every inch of her. The thought sent a thrill through me, but I knew we needed to focus.

"Okay, so you know that as a Siren, when I dream, I'm seeing a possible future, right?" she asked, her emerald green eyes darker than usual, likely due to the dim lighting.

I nodded, looking into her eyes as I scooted closer, wrapping my arm around her and pulling her back against the pillows with me. "Yes, I know you have foresight dreams. I've been reading the books you lent me." I lazily twirled one of her curls around my finger. "But I'm not going to die. Not anytime soon," I reassured her, my voice gentle but firm.

She frowned, a hint of annoyance creeping into her tone. "You can't know that. Something's been off with my dreams since I got here. I've had… well, good dreams, but your death keeps changing, and this time…" Her voice trailed off as she hesitated, gathering the courage to continue. "This time, Tristan slit your throat in this bed, and you bled purple blood."

I froze, my fingers halting their idle play with her hair as my eyes shifted to sky blue. *Did we have the same dream? Had I somehow seen her dream?*

She turned and cupped my face in her hands, looking at me with a deep, serious expression. I could feel her fingers trembling as she gently held me. *"Yes, and I think our mate bond is changing my magic somehow,"* she said, though her lips didn't move. Her voice was the same, yet different, echoing clearly in my mind.

"What mate bond?" I asked, louder than I intended, my voice echoing through the quiet space of my room, breaking the stillness. Her face lit up with excitement, and she giggled before leaning in to kiss me.

"It works!" I heard her exclaim, even as her lips continued to move against mine in a deep, passionate kiss. Confusion swirled in my mind, but I pushed it aside, wrapping my arms around her and kissing her back with equal intensity. She could explain all this shit later—right now, I just wanted to enjoy the taste of her mouth.

I pushed her onto her back, and she squealed in surprise. Moving on top of her, I smirked as I straddled her hips, pinning her to the bed. I grabbed her wrists, holding them firmly above her head. The blanket slipped down around my hips, exposing my torso as I pressed it against hers. Leaning in close, I whispered in her ear, "Now, tell me about this mate bond, Meles Tari."

She looked up into my now-purple eyes and smiled widely. "I don't know how or why, but I'm pretty sure we have an unsealed mate bond. Our magic… it's sort of mixing right now because of it." The thought sent a thrill through me.

A slow smile tugged at my lips as I held her beneath me, feeling her squirm slightly. I tightened my hold on her, leaning in so that our mouths were just inches apart. "So, you're my mate?" I murmured, my voice low and filled with desire. Her hips arched against me, and I couldn't help but notice there was far too much fabric between us.

She bit her lower lip, breathing out softly, "Yes, I think so." I leaned down, pressing a kiss to her neck, drawing a gasp and a soft whimper from her.

Pulling back, I gave her a wicked smile and teased, "You only think you're mine?" I released one of her wrists, plunging my now free hand between us, slipping through the layers of blankets as I searched for her thighs. My hand found her hot, eager cunt, pressing hard against her center through the material that still separated me from her slick, bare skin I craved.

She moaned, "No," arching into my touch, grinding herself against my hand. Her gaze locked with mine, eyes dark with desire. "I am yours, and you are mine," she breathed, her voice a breathless promise as her lips parted in a soft pant.

The pink morning sun filtered through the room, casting a warm glow around us. I leaned down, trailing my tongue along her collarbone, then down toward her lush, ample breast. I sucked the soft skin between my teeth, gently biting, savoring the taste of her. She moaned low, her hips moving in rhythm with my hand, perfectly in sync with the desire building between us.

I growled in frustration at the damn blankets keeping me from her body. Leaning up, I released her other hand and reached for the dagger I kept under my pillow. Her eyebrows shot up in surprise, but I only smirked, bringing the knife gently along her skin, tracing a path toward the blanket that covered her.

I leaned back on my knees, bringing the dagger between us. With one hand, I lifted the blanket off her skin, and with the other, I swiftly sliced through the fabric, splitting it in half to reveal her bare body beneath. I teased the tip of the blade along her breast, tracing it down her stomach, then dipping lower along her inner thigh. The heat in my eyes, glowing a vivid pink, mirrored the excitement in hers. Her breath came in short, ragged pants as she remained carefully still, every inch of her attuned to my touch.

I flipped the dagger in my hand, carefully holding the blade as I ran the hilt from her ass to her clit, dragging it through her hot, slick wetness. She shuddered with a gasp. "You're so wet for me, Meles Tari," I rumbled, my voice low and thick with need. My desire surged as wicked thoughts flashed through my mind. I pressed the hilt of the blade against her entrance, and she moaned, arching into me with a silent plea for more. Smiling, I licked my lips before thrusting it into her. Her breath caught, and she let out a moan. "Gods, Orla. Fuck," she panted.

The blade bit into my hand as I worked the hilt in and out of her, a delicious sting that only heightened my focus. My other hand pressed firmly on her pelvis, keeping her hips from bucking into my movements. My thumb drew slow, deliberate circles around her clit, and she groaned, her voice thick with need. "Orla, you're going to make me cum." Her words spurred me on, driving me to eagerly continue, each thrust and touch pushing her closer to the edge.

Each sound Aure made tightened the coil of tension low in my belly. Her heavy breaths filled the room as she fisted the remnants of the cut blanket on either side of her. I moved my thumb against her clit harder, faster, the hand holding the blade now sticky with a mix of her fluid and my blood. I didn't stop—I wanted to hear her beg before I relented.

"That's it, cum for me," I whispered, my command almost silent, as her body responded. Her legs shook, her thighs clenched, and her entire body convulsed in unison with her scream. I knew pleasure had overtaken her completely.

A smile tugged at the corners of my mouth as I kept the pace, her moans giving way to short, fast pants. "Orla," she pleaded, her voice breathless. "I… Oh Gods." She shuddered as I pushed the hilt deeper, watching her intently.

Biting my lip, I rocked on my knees and dipped my mouth to her pelvis, her legs trembling uncontrollably as I continued to work my thumb tightly over her hot, swollen clit. I licked my thumb and the flesh beneath it, savoring the taste of her sweet honey. "Please," she gasped, her voice breaking as she arched again, hot liquid squirting out of her as she came undone, my mouth catching some of it. Her eyes squeezed shut. "Ohh, please…" she barely managed to speak, "Orla," she breathed, the sound a melody to my ears as my hips writhed in response. She was all mine.

I slowed my movements, keeping the hilt of my dagger fully inside her as my thumb grew lazy. I licked around my thumb, lapping up her cum as she whimpered softly, her body gradually relaxing, though tiny tremors still rippled through her legs. "Orla, please, no more… I can't…" she pleaded, her tone dripping with exhaustion and surrender, satisfying my desire to completely possess her.

Removing my blade, I sat up, leaving my other hand resting on her. Slowly, I brought the hilt to my lips, my gaze locked on hers as I licked it. Her eyes widened in shock, and she quickly sat up, grabbing my wrist. "Orla, look." I paused, glancing down at my hand as she pulled it between us. Dark purple, sticky liquid coated my skin—my blood was purple.

When the fuck did that happen? I've bled before, and my blood has always been red, not purple. "This doesn't mean your dream will come to pass, Aure," I said, trying to sound reassuring. "You said yourself that our bond has messed with your magic. Maybe you're just having regular dreams now." But the serious, disbelieving look on her face told me she wasn't convinced. I pulled my hand away and stood, walking over to the basket of towels. Grabbing one, I began to clean my hand and the dagger, the room heavy with silence as Aure watched me, saying nothing.

The morning sun glinted off the steel in my hand as heat flushed my cheeks, my eyes shifting to cobalt as anger and worry simmered inside me. I tried to will myself calm—I didn't want her to see how upset I was over this. Gods, that was the last thing I wanted.

Her voice was soft, filled with gentle concern. "Yes, my magic is changing, and perhaps it's unpredictable. But Orla, this proves there's some truth to them." I frowned, keeping my back to her, unwilling to show the turmoil on my face.

The smell of tea and bacon wafted into the room, cutting through the tension. A deep, loud chuckle echoed from the other side of the closed bedroom door. "Orla, Cam was all mops and brooms last night, wasn't she?" Frank's booming voice carried through the thick door, breaking the somber mode.

My eyes shot to the door, now a sharp sky blue. Frank had a habit of barging in without so much as a knock to wake me up in the mornings. Usually, he'd bring food and tea for us to share before heading to the barracks for training. He was my best friend—like an older, annoying brother. And since I never had overnight company, I was usually dressed in some sort of sleepwear.

But not today.

The bedroom door began to creak open, and without thinking, I threw the blade, embedding it in the frame just inches from Frank's hand. He froze, eyes wide. "Don't you dare fucking come in here right now, Frank," I snapped, my voice low and warning.

The door quickly retreated, and Aure let out a muffled giggle. I narrowed my eyes at the door, annoyed but amused. Frank's concerned voice came through the wood, "Everythin' alright in there?"

I smirked over at Aure as I grabbed a pair of clean pants from my wardrobe, yanking them on without bothering with underwear. Aure was still searching for her clothes among the blankets, so I tossed her my robe—the one I never really used.

"Just fine, Frank. I'll be out in a minute," I called back, my voice a mix of frustration and embarrassment. Glowering, I couldn't help but feel flustered at being caught literally with my pants down.

I tugged my deep red shirt over my head, tying the waist cinch tight. After slipping on my boots, I headed to the door. Aure wrapped the soft, simple robe around her beautiful curves, and while it closed, it rode up higher than I would have liked, exposing her knees and lower thighs. It would have to do, but if Frank so much as glanced at her legs, I wouldn't be responsible for what I might do to him. I growled softly, wiggling my dagger out of the wood frame and tucking it into my waistband.

"You can't hurt anyone just for looking at me, Orla." I froze, the realization that she was inside my head still something I was getting used to.

I glanced at her with a playful glare, then focused, trying to mentally send back, *"Yes, I can. Because you're mine, remember."*

She stood and walked toward me, rising up on her tiptoes to plant a soft kiss on my nose. "And you are mine," she whispered, her voice filled with warmth.

I caught her chin and kissed her lips hard and fast, a surge of possessive desire flooding through me. Now that I had been with her, I never wanted to stop touching her, kissing her. She was my favorite addiction, and I would burn the world for this woman. I hoped, deep in my soul, that she knew that— and if not, I would show her every day until the end of time or until my dying breath.

I let her go and opened the door, stepping into the outer chambers of my room with Aure trailing behind me, still barefoot. Frank looked up from the plate of food in front of him, a piece of bacon sticking out of his mouth. His bushy eyebrows shot up as he grabbed the bacon, clearly about to say something. I raised my hand, my cheeks flushing red with embarrassment. "Don't even start, Frank."

Aure gracefully settled onto my small, plush sofa, which faced my worn reading chair. A simple wooden table sat between them, holding a single, well-worn book. I picked up one of the two mugs of tea and walked it over to her, carefully handing her the steaming cup. As our fingers brushed against each other, a spark of warmth shot through me, making my heart race.

Frank's eyes darted between Aure and me, a smirk tugging at the corners of his mouth despite my warning. "Well, well," he began, leaning back in his chair with the plate in hand, "I never thought I'd see the day. Orla, finally caught off guard."

I shot him a warning look but couldn't help the small smile that crept onto my face. "You're lucky I didn't throw the dagger any closer."

Frank chuckled, waving the piece of bacon like a white flag. "Please, Orla. I wouldn't dare cross you. I know you have perfect aim."

Aure shot me a playful look from the sofa, her legs tucked beneath her as she settled in. I rolled my eyes, moving back to the table where the smell of tea and bacon lingered in the air. "You're not going to let this go, are you?" I muttered, reaching for the last mug of tea to steady myself.

Frank chuckled, setting the plate down on the table and offering it to Aure with a wink. "Oh, come on, Orla. You can't expect me to just ignore this. It's not every day I walk in on my best friend blushing like a schoolgirl."

Aure smiled softly as she accepted the plate, her gaze flicking to me with a mix of amusement and something deeper. "Thank you, Frank," she said, her tone light, though I could sense the underlying tension as she took a small bite.

I took a deep breath, trying to shake off the embarrassment. "Alright, Frank, enough. We've got more important things to discuss."

Frank's expression shifted, the teasing glint in his eyes fading as he grew more serious. "Fair enough. I'll let it go for now. What do we need to discuss?"

I sat down next to Aure, the warmth of my chicory tea soothing my nerves as I took a sip. My eyes settled into the calm lavender shade I preferred. "Aure, can you please explain what a mate bond is and why you think we have one?"

Aure placed her mug on the table, sighing softly as a pink flush crept into her cheeks. Frank's eyebrows lifted again in surprise, and he shifted awkwardly in his chair, clearly taken aback by the direction of the conversation.

"I… I noticed a change in us after you woke up from your Enkindling," Aure began, her voice tentative. She glanced at Frank, adding pointedly, "Azura, my bonded Sea Dragon, mentioned something to me. She said it resembled what happens during an unsealed mate bond. When the magic of two fated mates begins to mingle and mix, their magic changes, grows stronger, and there's this… magnetism, this undeniable pull, where they feel a constant need for each other."

"I thought only the ancient races had mate bonds," Frank said, his deep voice carrying a hint of skepticism as he regarded Aure with cautious eyes.

"That's what's commonly believed," Aure replied, her tone soft but held a hint of foreboding. "This would be unprecedented. I only know that it feels similar to, but different from, the bond I share with Azura. If it is like the mate bond of the Sea Dragons, though, we'll need to figure out how to seal it in order to regain control over our magic." She paused, taking a bite of bacon as the weight of her words hung in the air.

"How do Sea Dragons seal their mate bond?" I asked, feeling a bit sheepish. Frank leaned back in his chair, folding his hands over his stomach and interlocking his fingers as he listened.

Aure glanced at me, then down at the plate of food. "I… I've only done the ritual once. That's all we ever need to do as a Siren. But I'm not sure if it will work for us… because we aren't Sea Dragons, and well, I…" Her voice trailed off, and I could sense she was holding something back. Did she not trust me? Or was it Frank she was wary of? I had shared everything with her—well, maybe not everything, but enough. She could trust me.

Frank sat up, giving Aure a soft, knowing smile. "It's alright, Your Grace. Orla won't mind, I reckon. I dated a Siren once. She was a graceful little spit of a thing. We had an amazin' fun time in the water." Frank added with a smirk, his eyes hinting at something I couldn't quite grasp. Aure's tension seemed to ease as she smiled back at him. Meanwhile, I was just disgusted to hear about any time Frank had "fun."

"Orla, to perform the ritual, I have to be underwater to sing my Siren song in my 'true form,' which is… well, different from how I look right now." Aure blushed, fidgeting with the hem of the robe, clearly nervous that I might be upset or disgusted by the revelation.

I gently pulled her hand into my lap, setting my empty mug on the table. "You'll always be the most beautiful thing in the world, no matter how you look, Meles Tari," I reassured her. A coy smile tugged at her lips.

"Aww, aren't you two the sweetest pair of peas," Frank teased, slowly clapping his hands together with exaggerated enthusiasm. "I found the tentacles to be the most fun." He shot me a wry grin, and Aure promptly threw a piece of bacon at him.

"Alright, alright, maybe I should leave you two alone to talk," Frank chuckled, dodging the bacon. "But Orla, the Captain does need to speak with you later this morning."

With that, he stood, picking the piece of bacon off the floor and popping it into his mouth before heading to the door. He walked out, closing it behind him with a grin still on his face.

After that, I eyed Aure with a sly grin. "Tentacles?" I teased. She tried to pull her hand away with a huff, but I held on, not letting her escape. "I think I'm going to need details," I added, my grin widening.

"So, I can only do it in the ocean, but when I let my Siren magic take over, part of me shifts—and I have tentacles," she explained, her tone cautious. I tilted my head, raising a single eyebrow. They had to be teasing me; I had never heard of such a thing. She continued, her voice steady. "Imagine a skirt of squishy octopus legs—I have eight, and they're just an addition. The rest of me stays the same, though I also get gills on my neck so I can dive deep and breathe underwater with the Sea Dragons."

"Oh, you're serious," I said, my eyes shifting to sky blue as the reality of her words sank in. An uneasy itch started in my legs, and I absentmindedly scratched at my pants.

She sighed softly. "I wasn't sure how you'd take all this, especially since you haven't been around magic much at all." Her gaze softened as she smoothly shifted the focus onto me. "Have you tried to use any lesser magic yet?"

"Does nearly burning down my room count?" I chuckled, but then my expression turned serious. "I think I need someone to teach me all this." I picked up the book from the table. "There's only so much research can do for me."

A knock sounded at the door, interrupting the moment. We both turned to look before I stood and answered it. Cam, still disheveled, stood in the hallway. "Uh, have you seen Aure this morning?" she asked, her voice laced with uncertainty.

I leaned against the door, keeping it partially closed, and smirked. "Why? Did you do something you regretted last night, Bestest Friend?"

Cam's cheeks flushed. "I… I don't think so. I don't remember everything, but I remember you, me, and Frank. But I woke up in Aure's room, and she wasn't there."

I grinned widely and opened the door fully. "She's safe."

Cam's eyes widened as she took in Aure's choice of wardrobe, her gaze slowly shifting as she stepped inside. "I'm glad you're safe, Your Grace," Cam said with reverence, relief washing over her.

"I am," Aure replied, walking over to me and pressing a kiss to my cheek. "Let me go get ready for the day. We can talk more later, and maybe I'll show you a few things, too." She smirked, a playful glint in her sea-glass green eyes.

My heart raced, and my eyes flashed magenta. I slipped my hand around Aure and gave her ass a playful squeeze. She jumped with a squeak and a giggle. Cam looked taken aback but said nothing as Aure glided out the door to her room.

Cam turned to me, her expression softening. "I'm glad to see you two finally talked and, um, figured things out." With that, she left, closing the door behind her.

My mind raced with everything that had transpired, but I knew there was still so much more to learn. We both had duties to attend to, and as much as I wanted to stay in bed fucking Aure all day, every day, that wasn't a realistic game plan.

I set out to take care of some of those duties, the taste of Aure still lingering on my lips and a smile plastered on my face. My eyes settled into a calm lavender as I headed off to find the Captain of the Guard.

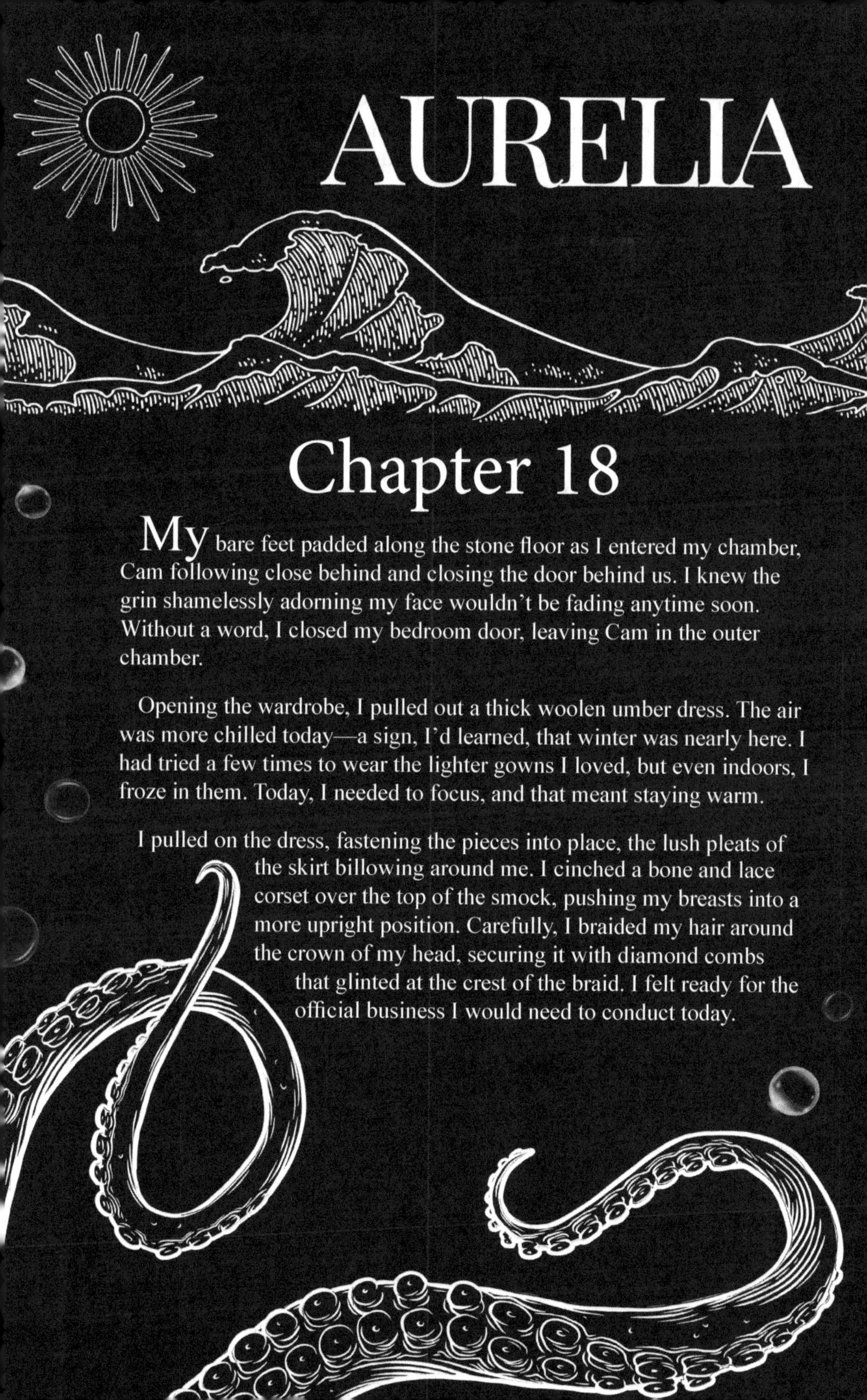

Chapter 18

My bare feet padded along the stone floor as I entered my chamber, Cam following close behind and closing the door behind us. I knew the grin shamelessly adorning my face wouldn't be fading anytime soon. Without a word, I closed my bedroom door, leaving Cam in the outer chamber.

Opening the wardrobe, I pulled out a thick woolen umber dress. The air was more chilled today—a sign, I'd learned, that winter was nearly here. I had tried a few times to wear the lighter gowns I loved, but even indoors, I froze in them. Today, I needed to focus, and that meant staying warm.

I pulled on the dress, fastening the pieces into place, the lush pleats of the skirt billowing around me. I cinched a bone and lace corset over the top of the smock, pushing my breasts into a more upright position. Carefully, I braided my hair around the crown of my head, securing it with diamond combs that glinted at the crest of the braid. I felt ready for the official business I would need to conduct today.

The only jewelry I wore was the ruby Rebounder that hung low around my neck, its presence thrumming with power. I slipped on my flat velvet shoes, their soft warmth comforting around my toes. Gods, my thighs and core still ached from this morning's events. I languished the feeling, closing my eyes and brushing a finger across my lips. It took everything in me not to reach out to Orla through our bond and interrupt her day.

I sighed and returned to the outer chamber, heading to my desk. Cam sat on the small sofa, methodically cleaning her swords. It all felt so mundane—the tasks we busied ourselves with while war raged at our borders and threats lurked around every corner. My thoughts flashed to Orla's soft, sexy, bare body, with its small nicks and scars dotting her skin like the constellations that filled the night sky.

Cam looked up at me, and she gave me a smirk. "You seem distracted." I crumbled a scrap of paper and threw it at her. It landed on the floor, far away from my target. She raised an eyebrow, an amused grin dancing across her lips. She shook her head and returned to her task.

"And so what if I am?" I huffed, my lips twisting in annoyance. Cam merely shrugged, continuing to rub the blade down with oil and a sheepskin cloth. My mind was torn between wanting to scold Cam for what she had told Orla and dismissing her completely for inserting herself between my mate and I. *My mate. What did that even mean?* It sounded so animalistic, so undignified. I had never imagined my marriage would turn out to be so complicated. Sure, I expected hurdles and even some pushback, but I felt a pang of dread at the thought of being with only one person for the rest of my life.

Not that I ever planned to be unfaithful to my commitments; I just relished the adventure and pleasure of exploring all kinds of sexual experiences. Now, I knew I could be happy with just Orla, but a small part of me still hoped she might one day be open to exploring some of those experiences together.

Fuck, how could I even think about that sort of thing right now? We were at war and I had responsibilities. I needed to write to my father, finish the seating arrangements, review the food options with Lady Lili tomorrow afternoon, and prepare statements for the council meeting at the end of the week. That didn't even cover the fact that I needed to speak privately with Captain Cole at some point today about everything that happened to his prisoner while in my care. *Will I ever truly get over Eamon's death?*

The morning sun shone through the window, deceptively warm looking, but the need to keep a fire in my hearth evident to the fact my fingers still felt cold. I took a deep and clearing breath before I pulled out fresh parchment and wrote to my father. I dated the top corner of the page.

Luinith, Day 25, Year 1705

Dearest Father,

I miss you as a boat misses the swells of the ocean while at dock. The
memories of our many years celebrating Morveil Nighte in honor of Mother
have left me feeling terribly homesick. The thought of not being there to help
you set up her altar, to walk the shoreline with you and the others, or feeling
the cool waves against my toes as they sink into the warm sand, fills me with
a deep sense of longing. Not singing with everyone as the waves crash, sending
our thanks and love to the Great Deep when the veil is thin, weighs heavily on
my soul. I do plan to visit the beach here, though I'm unsure if I can endure the
frigid waters to sing to her.

We received the shipment, and thankfully, everyone arrived mostly
unharmed despite skirmishing with Frostspire forces. We briefly had in our
grasp an enslaved Fae, who shared some disturbing news with us. It seems
Frostspire is capturing Fae from the Sylvan Enclave, and I believe King
Frostbane is using dark magic to drain and harness the Fae's magic. I do not
understand how such a thing could work for a human, but there are many
aspects of this war, and King Frostbane himself, that remain a mystery to me.

On a more personal note, I never expected this, but, Daddy, I think I am in
love with Orla. I know I had my reservations about her experience and her role
here, but she is truly the most amazing person. She is fiercely loyal, and she
always stands up for what is right. She is quiet, but when she does speak, her
words are truthful and reflect her true mind.

I hope and ask Melusine that your health has improved and hasn't grown
worse. I look forward to hearing from you soon. Please give my love to everyone
back home. I love you the most.

With all my love,

Your Daughter Aurelia

I glanced over at Cam, who had just finished laying her now clean weapons back in their places, and I finished folding the letter, sealing it with wax. "Will you take this to the docks and ensure it gets sent on the fastest route?" I asked. Cam stood and took the letter from my fingers. I softened my tone, speaking more for my own comfort than hers. "I know you told Orla about our past relationship."

A blush crept over her cheeks. "I did, but I realize now it wasn't my place. I… I'll do better. I'm sorry." Her voice was filled with genuine remorse, and I could see she understood her mistake. Though she hadn't handled it well, I knew I shared part of the blame. As a princess, I should have known better than to become involved with my guard. I had hurt Cam, and I could understand her pain, but I was still upset by the way she had lashed out.

I released the letter and spoke firmly, "I expect there won't be any more issues moving forward. Orla is going to be my wife, and I trust you will remember and respect that. Do you understand?"

Cam bowed her head. "Of course, Your Grace. I give you my word." She placed a hand over her heart before standing upright again. After gathering her belongings, she quietly exited the room, leaving me alone in the stillness, with only the crackling fire and the soft rattle of the wind against the windowpane for company.

After what felt like an eternity, yet passed in the blink of an eye, I finally made my way to Captain Cole's quarters in the eastern part of the palace, where he was enjoying his dinner. The long hallways in this wing were not decorative or opulent; instead, their simple, orderly design seemed to prioritize efficiency and practicality over grandeur. The rows of doors along the hall were evenly spaced, each serving its purpose with quiet austerity.

I found the older man sitting on a creaky wooden chair at a simple, worn wooden table in one corner of the room. A small window opposite the door let in the fading light, casting a warm glow over the basic but clean bed along the left wall. Captain Cole's large leather trunk, its brass fittings rusted with age, was tucked into the corner nearest the door. The setting sun painted hues of pink and orange across the thin rug that softened the stone floor beneath our feet.

He was picking through a plate of root vegetables and a gray lump of meat, pausing to take a sip from a tankard that smelled faintly of ale. "Aye, I've been giving me leg a bit of a long rest, my Queen, but I'll be back up to all the old tricks in no time," he said with a rough chuckle.

I nodded, reassured to see he was on the mend. His injured leg rested on a small stool, a pillow propped beneath his foot. Turning away, I gazed out the dingy window at the vast lawn and distant forest beyond. "I'm sure you've already heard about Eamon—the prisoner?" I asked, my voice quiet but steady.

Captain Cole set down his tankard, the faint clink echoing in the quiet room. His expression grew somber, the lines on his weathered face deepening. "Aye, I heard," he replied, his voice low and gravelly. "Word travels fast, especially when it's news like that. A damn shame, and from what I understand, it was quick?"

I turned back to face him, my brow furrowed with guilt. "Yes, it was. I need to know everything, Cole. Every detail you have heard. How could this have happened under my watch, and at the command of King Oric no less?"

He sighed heavily, rubbing a hand over his graying beard. "Tristan carried out the command, correct?" I gave a small nod. "Unexpected, even for him. The guards… They were just as shocked as we were. None of us saw it coming."

I felt a knot tighten in my chest. "Eamon… he was under my protection. How could this just happen? We were supposed to be negotiating an alliance, not losing innocent lives."

Cole's face softened, his voice tinged with empathy. "Your Grace, it wasn't your fault. We were all blindsided. King Oric's command… it was out of nowhere. No one knew he intended for Eamon to die."

"But Tristan knew," I said quietly, anger and guilt swirling inside me. "He acted without hesitation. And now, whatever information Eamon had about Frostspire's plans is lost to us."

Cole leaned forward, his gaze steady but concerned. "We'll get to the bottom of this, but we must tread carefully. You should be cautious about aligning yourself with King Oric. He's unpredictable, and Tristan… he's a loyal dog to his master."

I took a deep breath, trying to steady the tumult inside me. "Have the guards been questioned? Anyone who might have any more insight on this or the king?"

"Aye," he nodded. "They were all questioned. Most of 'em seemed genuinely surprised, but there's always someone who knows more than they let on. I'll keep digging."

I closed my eyes for a moment, the weight of the situation pressing down on me. "Eamon had vital information, Cole. If Frostspire is using Fae magic… we needed to know how and why. Now, it's all slipping through our fingers."

He nodded grimly. "We're dealing with more than just a war of swords and shields, Aure. There are darker forces at play. We have to be prepared for anything."

I met his gaze, my voice firm despite the guilt gnawing at me. "Then we need to be smarter, more vigilant. We can't afford to be caught off guard like that again."

Cole's expression was resolute. "I agree. I'll have my best men keep their ears and eyes out around the palace and in the city. I won't let you be taken by surprise again."

"Thank you." I appreciated his loyalty and guidance. "And keep me informed of anything you uncover. We need to stay ahead of this."

"I will," he promised, lifting his tankard once more. "And, Your Grace… don't carry this burden alone. Eamon's death wasn't on you. But we'll make sure his death isn't in vain."

I nodded, though the guilt still weighed heavily on my heart. "Thank you, Captain Cole. Just… be careful. We're all walking a tightrope here."

He raised his tankard in a small salute. "To vigilance and caution."

"To vigilance," I echoed, forcing a small smile.

I turned to leave, the weight of Eamon's death still pressing heavily on my conscience, a constant reminder of the high stakes we faced. There was much to do, and uncertainty gnawed at my heart. I realized how hungry I was and decided to find something to eat.

Back in my chambers, I noticed the servants had left my dinner on the table, along with a bottle of a sweet lemon drink that fizzed with tiny bubbles. Lifting the metal cover from my plate, a beautiful assortment of vegetables, roast quail, and a warm roll greeted me. My stomach gurgled at the sight and the delicious aroma. I sat down, ready to eat, when a soft knock came at the door.

I sighed, placing the metal cover back over my plate, and stood up to answer it. As I opened the door, a wide smile spread across my face. Leaning against the doorframe, I took in the sight of Orla, who stood there smirking, her eyes a mesmerizing mix of colors. "Well, what brings you to my door at such a scandalously late hour?" I teased, my eyes sparkling with playful desire.

She stepped closer, entering my space, her gaze fixed on my face as if she were memorizing every detail. She swept a stray curl from my temple, and a small dimple appeared on her cheek—a feature I hadn't noticed before. "Such a scandal, Meles Tari," she whispered.

Before I could protest or ask what those damn words meant, her lips closed over mine, and I melted into the kiss. The hum of our magic surged and flickered around us. We stood in each other's embrace, exposed in the hallway for anyone who might pass by. She didn't seem to care about being seen, which only thrilled me more. I wrapped my arms around her neck as she braced herself against the doorframe with one hand, her other hand roaming down my body.

"Honestly, Rielle, I think the new trainin' regimen will sort them out. Too many of these recruits think they can slack off—" Frank's words cut off abruptly as he and Rielle turned the corner and caught sight of us.

He stopped mid-step, his mouth hanging open for a moment before a wide grin spread across his face. "Well, well, what do we have here?" he teased, his tone playful but loud enough to draw attention.

Rielle, standing beside him, tried—and failed—to suppress a smirk. "Looks like a bit of scandal in the making, don't you think?" she added, her voice filled with amusement.

I quickly pulled away from Orla, my cheeks flushing with both embarrassment and irritation. "Frank! Rielle!" I exclaimed, trying to sound more composed than I felt. "Don't you have anything better to do than interrupt?"

Frank chuckled, leaning casually against the opposite wall. "Oh, trust me, we've got plenty to do. But it's always nice to see the royalty... hard at work," he added with a wink.

Orla, far from embarrassed, grinned back at them, unbothered. "I could say the same about you, Frank. Shouldn't you be overseeing the evening drills instead of wandering the halls?"

Rielle rolled her eyes but smiled. "We were just finishing up. But now I'm starting to think we should assign a guard to this hallway. You know, to prevent any... interruptions," she teased.

I groaned inwardly, but couldn't help the small smile tugging at my lips. "Enough, both of you. Orla and I were just... discussing something."

Frank snorted. "Yeah, it sure looked like a deep discussion to me. Very... hands-on."

Rielle nudged him with her elbow. "Come on, Frank, leave them be. We don't mean to intrude on your 'discussion'." Rielle's tone turned more serious now, but still smiling. "Actually, we need to discuss some important matters with you, Your Grace. Like the plans for the upcoming engagement party, among other things. We have little time, and we wanted to make sure everything is in order."

Orla gave me a sly smile, clearly unbothered by the interruption, but I could sense the underlying frustration. "We were just getting to that," she said smoothly, releasing me but keeping her hand on the small of my back.

"Sure you were, I think you two need to save some of that for the honeymoon," Frank replied with a grin. "But it looks like this hallway isn't the best place for all this. Shall we take it inside?"

I sighed, nodding. "Fine, come in. Let's get this sorted." I stepped back, allowing them to enter my chambers.

Once inside, Orla and I sat down on the plush sofa while Frank and Rielle took the two chairs across from us, a small wooden table between us.

"So," Rielle began, all business now. "There's been some unrest among the Enchanters after what happened with Eamon. We need to address it before it escalates."

I nodded, my playful demeanor fading into seriousness. "Agreed. We need to ensure they understand what happened was an unfortunate incident, not a precedent we agree with."

Frank leaned forward, resting his elbows on his knees. "And about the engagement part, there are still some details we need to finalize. Like security arrangements, any ceremonial aspects… We need your input to ensure everythin' goes smoothly."

Orla chimed in, her tone thoughtful. "I think we should keep any ceremony simple, given the tension with Frostspire. The last thing we want is to draw unnecessary attention."

Rielle nodded. "A wise move. But we'll need to make sure all the key allies are invited and feel welcomed. It's a delicate balance."

Frank glanced at me, his expression more serious now. "And we need to be ready for anythin'. There are whispers that Frostspire might try to disrupt things. We can't afford any more surprises."

I took a deep breath, the weight of responsibility settling back on my shoulders. "Then we prepare for every possible outcome. Double the guards, increase the patrols. We need to ensure this engagement party goes off without a hitch. It's crucial for maintaining our alliances and showing our strength."

Everyone nodded in agreement, and as the discussion continued, the gravity of the situation pulled me back into focus. My eyes drifted to the untouched plate of food, and my stomach growled, reminding me of my hunger. I slipped off my shoes, tucking my feet beneath me as I leaned into Orla, who wrapped her arm around me protectively.

"Have you eaten yet?" she whispered in my ear as Frank and Rielle bickered about where to position the guards. I shook my head slightly, my stomach growling in response. Orla chuckled softly, her breath warm against my ear. "You need to eat," she murmured, gently shifting me aside so she could stand. She walked over to the table and lifted the metal cover from my plate. The aroma of roast quail and vegetables wafted through the room, momentarily pulling my attention away from our conversation.

Frank and Rielle's debate grew more heated, their voices overlapping as they discussed the optimal placement for the guards during the engagement party.

"I'm tellin' you, we need more guards by the entrance," Frank insisted, his tone firm. "If Frostspire tries anythin', that's the most likely point of attack."

Rielle shook her head, her expression resolute. "No, we need more guards and Enchanters inside, near the guests. The last thing we want is someone getting too close to the royal family."

Orla nudged me gently with her elbow, pulling my attention away from the argument. She handed me the plate of food. "Eat," she urged softly, concern etched in her eyes. "We don't need you passing out from hunger."

I took the plate, picked up a fork, and took a small bite of the roasted quail, the flavors rich and comforting. As I chewed, I listened to Frank and Rielle's debate, their differing strategies highlighting the tension that had simmered since Eamon's death.

"You both make valid points," I interjected, swallowing another bite. "Let's increase security at both the entrance and inside the main hall. We can't afford to leave anything to chance."

Frank nodded, looking somewhat satisfied, while Rielle gave a curt nod of agreement. "I'll coordinate with the guards and ensure they're briefed on the new positions," she said, jotting down notes on a piece of parchment.

Orla's hand slipped onto my thigh as I continued to eat, a small gesture of support that sent warmth through me. "We'll get this sorted," she whispered, her thumb brushing gentle circles over my thick skirt.

The hour grew late, while we continued discussing various details while enjoying each other's company. Cam silently joined in listening and providing agreements of support throughout. After I finished my meal, Orla and I curled up together on the sofa, entangled in one another. Her soft touches and public displays of affection warmed my soul. I was grateful for them, though I had worried she might be hesitant to show such affection openly. She had always been so reserved and composed, but this was a side of her I liked—a more open and comfortable side.

I wasn't sure when I had fallen asleep or when everyone had left, but I woke to the bright morning sun streaming across the room and onto the sofa where I had been sleeping. A blanket was tucked around me, and the room was otherwise empty and quiet. *Fuck, what time was it?* I stood abruptly, the blanket falling to the floor without a sound. I looked down at how wrinkled and disheveled my dress was from sleeping in it all night.

I noticed a covered plate on my desk, along with a small note. Stepping over to it, I picked up the note and read the beautiful handwriting.

Meles Tari,

Eat something before you start your day. I have a lot going on at the barracks, but I wish I could have stayed, holding you in my arms all day. See you soon.

-Orla

Her note brightened my smile, and a wave of warm, giddy excitement filled me. I glanced at my timepiece and realized I had only an hour before my lunch meeting with Lady Lili. I needed to get ready. Lifting the cover off the plate, I found an assortment of biscuits, bacon, ham, and a medley of fruit. Grabbing a biscuit, I shoved it into my mouth, grateful no one was there to witness me devour it so ravenously. I picked up a piece of bacon and walked into the bathroom to shower and prepare for the day.

I had made quick work of getting ready, but not fast enough. As I raced to slip on my shoes, I found myself briskly walking through the palace halls toward the grand dining room. I nearly collided with a startled Cam.

"I was looking for you. I thought you'd be outside on your usual morning walk before your meeting." She looked puzzled, and fell into step next to me.

"I overslept," I replied, keeping up my hurried pace as we neared the doors to the grand dining room. "You can stand guard out here; I'll be fine on my own with Lady Lili. We're just selecting the menu."

Cam nodded as she held the door open for me to enter. I found Lady Lili already seated at the head of the grand, polished wooden table. The room looked much different during the day, with sunlight streaming in through the tall windows lining the northern wall. The light reflected rainbows across the floor and walls, cast by the crystals hanging from the chandeliers. A large bouquet of fall flowers adorned the center of the table, running its length. A fire blazed in the large marble hearth, but it didn't fully warm the room, so I wrapped my knitted wool shawl tighter around me. The delectable aromas wafting in from the attached kitchen filled the air.

Lady Lili glanced up as I entered, her eyes warm with a hint of mischief. "Good morning, Aurelia," she greeted, her voice smooth. "I trust you slept well?"

"Well enough," I replied, taking a seat beside her. "I'm eager to finalize the menu for the engagement party. There's much to prepare."

She nodded, her gaze shifting to the assortment of dishes spread across the table. "Indeed. I've had the kitchen prepare a few samples for us to try. It's important we choose dishes that will not only delight our guests but also represent the bounty of our lands."

As she spoke, a servant entered, carrying a tray laden with small plates. He placed them in front of us, each plate offering a different delicacy—roasted quail with wild mushrooms, honey-glazed carrots, spiced lamb skewers, and a selection of freshly baked bread.

Lady Lili picked up a small fork and sampled a piece of the quail, her expression thoughtful. "The quail is particularly tender this season," she commented. "What do you think?"

I took a bite, savoring the rich flavor. "It's delicious," I agreed. "I think it will be a hit with our guests."

We continued sampling the dishes in silence for a moment. Then, Lady Lili set down her fork, her eyes locking onto mine. "Aurelia," she began carefully. "This engagement party is more than just a celebration. With all that's happening at our borders, it's also a statement of your commitment to the kingdom. Tell me, what do you truly hope to achieve with this alliance?"

I hesitated, caught off guard by the directness of her question. "I hope to bring unity and strength to our people," I replied. "To show that we are capable of standing together, especially in times of uncertainty."

Her gaze remained steady, scrutinizing me as if searching for hidden meanings. "Unity and strength are noble goals," she said slowly. "But they can mean different things to different people. Are you prepared to make the difficult decisions that might come with this union? To put the kingdom's needs above your own?"

I felt a pang of defensiveness, but pushed it aside. "I understand the weight of my responsibilities," I said, keeping my tone even. "And I'm willing to do whatever it takes to ensure the kingdom's safety and prosperity."

Lady Lili leaned back, her expression softening slightly, though a hint of skepticism lingered in her eyes. "I hope you mean that, dear. Because in these uncertain times, every choice you make will have lasting consequences."

I nodded, setting down my fork. "I'm aware of the stakes, Lady Lili. That's why I want everything to be perfect—not just for the engagement, but for the future of our people."

Lady Lili smiled, a knowing glint in her eye. "And it will be, dear. We have capable hands here. But remember, it's also about joy—about celebrating what you and Orla will share. Don't lose sight of that."

Her words touched something deep inside me, and I felt a wave of gratitude. "Thank you, Lady Lili. I needed to hear that."

She reached out and squeezed my hand gently. "Of course. Now, let's finish this menu and make it a day to remember."

We continued our planning, the room filling with the aroma of delicious food and the soft hum of our conversation. For the first time since meeting her, I felt a gentle warmth between us, allowing myself to finally relax into the moment.

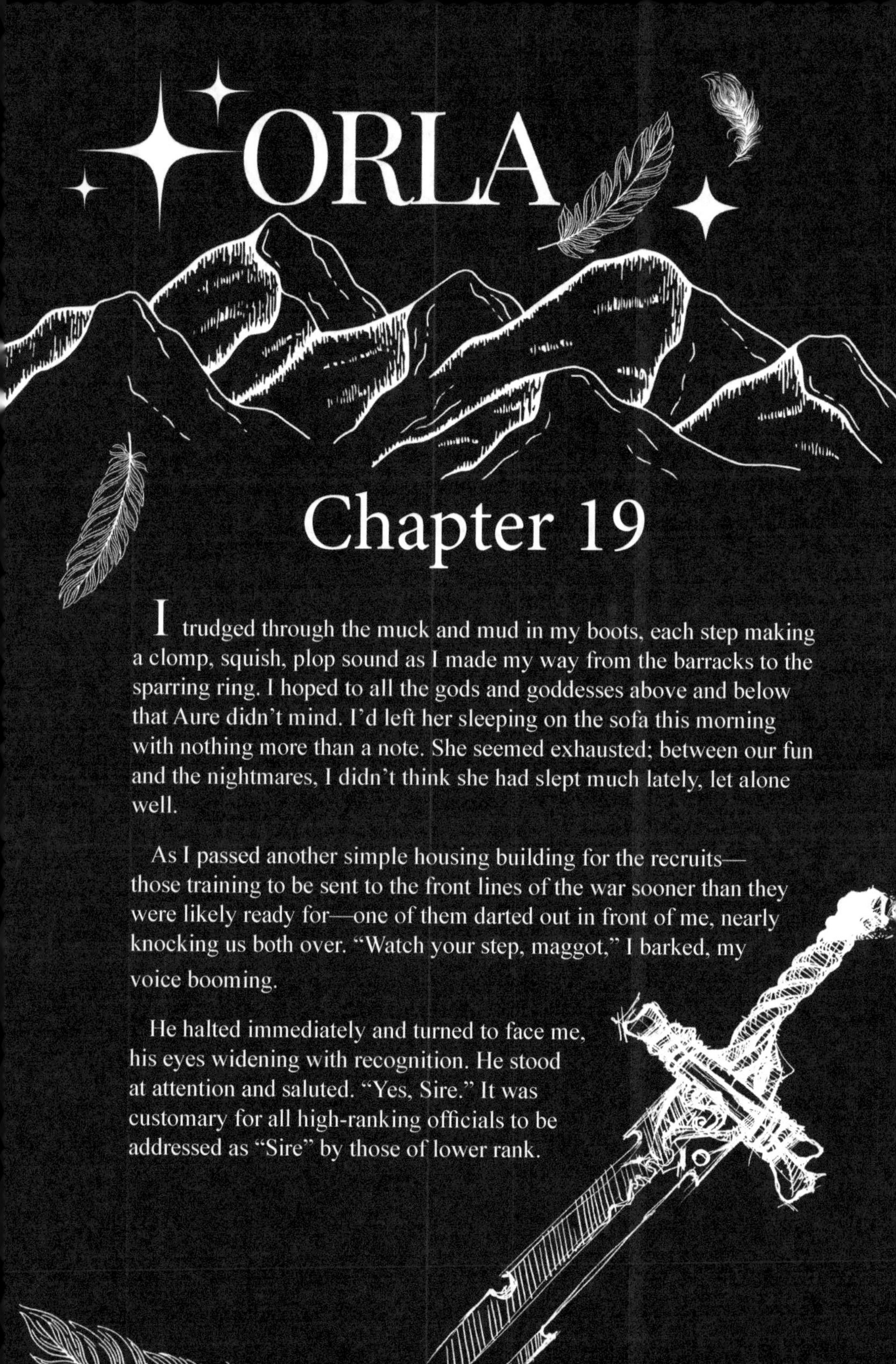

ORLA

Chapter 19

I trudged through the muck and mud in my boots, each step making a clomp, squish, plop sound as I made my way from the barracks to the sparring ring. I hoped to all the gods and goddesses above and below that Aure didn't mind. I'd left her sleeping on the sofa this morning with nothing more than a note. She seemed exhausted; between our fun and the nightmares, I didn't think she had slept much lately, let alone well.

As I passed another simple housing building for the recruits—those training to be sent to the front lines of the war sooner than they were likely ready for—one of them darted out in front of me, nearly knocking us both over. "Watch your step, maggot," I barked, my voice booming.

He halted immediately and turned to face me, his eyes widening with recognition. He stood at attention and saluted. "Yes, Sire." It was customary for all high-ranking officials to be addressed as "Sire" by those of lower rank.

I nodded. "As you were. Be more alert though, our enemy will be." He rushed off at a sprint toward the weapons training yard. The morning had started bright and sunny, hinting at the promise of warmth despite the frigid cold air. By afternoon, however, the sky had turned gray, and distant rumbles of thunder echoed across the land. The wind howled through the trees, carrying the threat of another icy rainstorm.

I continued making my way to the sparring ring, my thoughts drifting back to Aure. I wondered how, or if, her family celebrated Mortia's Passage. I knew the Fae called it Dorthonion, or in common tongue, the Festival of the Veil. We were taught that on this night, the veil between worlds thinned, allowing those who had passed on to hear us more clearly. Some even claimed the dead could send us back words of wisdom. I am not sure I believed that.

It was a night of feasting, drinking, playing games, and remembering those who had departed. Some dressed in costumes to ward off evil, while others made offerings at graves or gave gifts to children. As much as I had enjoyed the treats as a child, I now found the idea of offerings to children quite morbid. Since it fell on the thirtieth day of our tenth month, Luinith, it was always just days before my birthday, so I often was showered with gifts and blessings on both occasions.

I couldn't help but feel exhilarated at the thought of learning more about Aure's traditions and culture. I found it fascinating, both from a research perspective and a personal one. It felt like there had been little time to truly get to know each other, not with the war and our respective duties keeping us at opposite ends of the palace most of the time.

I finally reached the sparring ring, the air thick with the familiar scent of sweat and leather. The sounds of clashing swords and the rhythmic thudding of practice dummies filled the area. I spotted Frank leaning against the fence, his broad frame relaxed but his eyes sharp, watching the recruits as they trained.

As I approached, Frank pushed off the fence with a grin. "Well, look who's finally decided to join us," he teased, a playful glint in his eyes. "Took you long enough, Orla. Did Aure keep you occupied this mornin'?"

I rolled my eyes, a smirk tugging at my lips. "You know, for a grizzled old warrior, you gossip more than the kitchen maids."

Frank laughed, a deep, hearty sound that echoed across the ring. "Can't help it. I've known you for years, and it's about damn time you opened up that heart of yours—and your bed," he added with a wink. "Seriously though, it's good to see you lettin' someone in. You've been closed off for too long."

I chuckled, grabbing a practice sword from the rack. "Yeah, well, maybe it just took the right person to break through my defenses." Moving to the center of the ring, I took a steady stance and motioned for Frank to join me. "Enough chit-chat. Ready to show these recruits how it's done?"

Frank grinned, grabbing a practice sword of his own. "Oh, I've been ready. Let's give them a real show."

We began to circle each other, our eyes locked in concentration. I made the first move, a quick feint to the left before spinning to the right. Frank parried easily, his movements fluid and confident. We exchanged blows, the clanging of our swords drawing the attention of the nearby recruits, who paused to watch our impromptu duel.

"So," Frank said between strikes. "How's it feel bein' on the brink of an engagement? Ready to settle down and play house?"

I snorted, sidestepping a swing from him. "Hardly. You know me better than that. Besides, Aure and I have a long way to go before we're playing house. There's still a war going on, remember?"

Frank nodded, his expression turning serious as he blocked my next attack. "Yeah, I know. Things are gettin' worse out there. Frostspire is pushin' harder every day. We've lost good people, and I'm afraid we're goin' to lose more before this is over."

I softened for a moment, the weight of his words settling in. "I know, Frank. But we can't lose hope. We've got to stay strong, keep fighting. For all of us." I thrust my sword forward, catching him off guard and pushing him back a step.

He grinned, quickly recovering and countering with a low swing that I barely dodged. "What's it like havin' someone like her to warm your bed? Can't imagine it's been an easy adjustment for you."

I snorted, sidestepping a swing from him. "Oh, shut up, Frank. Just because you've had a string of lovers doesn't mean you know a damn thing about real feelings."

Frank laughed again, his voice light despite the serious nature of our conversation. "Maybe not, but I know you. And it's about time you let yourself have a little happiness, even if it means you've got to learn how to share a bed without hoggin' all the blankets."

I chuckled, grabbing a practice sword from the rack. "Enough about me. Let's see if you've still got those old reflexes." I lunged forward with a quick strike, which he blocked with a grin.

"You're not gettin' rid of me that easily," he quipped, countering my attack and swinging his sword in a wide arc that I narrowly dodged.

We continued to spar, the recruits cheering us on as we traded blows. Frank was relentless, his attacks coming faster and harder, but I held my ground, matching him move for move. His playful banter never stopped, though.

"You know," he said, dodging a strike, "it's nice to see you like this. Smilin', laughin'… I think Aure's good for you."

I smirked, delivering a swift kick that knocked him off balance. "Maybe. But don't think for a second I'm getting soft, Frank. I've still got plenty of fight in me."

Frank grinned, quickly recovering and countering with a low swing that I barely dodged. "Wouldn't have it any other way, Orla. Just promise me somethin'."

"What's that?" I asked, panting as we squared off again. Thunder clapped loud above us.

"Don't let her go. Not now that you've finally found someone who can keep up with you," he said, his tone surprisingly sincere.

I paused, lowering my sword slightly. "I don't plan to, Frank. Not if I can help it."

He nodded, a small smile tugging at his lips. "Good. Now, let's finish this."

With a renewed burst of energy, we clashed again, our swords ringing out with each strike. I could feel the strength in his blows, but I was determined not to give in. I had too much to fight for now.

In a swift move, I knocked his sword from his hand and pointed my blade at his chest. The recruits cheered, and Frank raised his hands in surrender, laughing. "Alright, alright, you win this round. But don't get too comfortable. I'll be back for a rematch."

I grinned, lowering my sword. "Looking forward to it, old man."

Frank clapped me on the back as we walked out of the ring. "You aren't gettin' any younger yourself." He winked at me.

I laughed, "True, I am almost thirty, but you will always be older."

Rein emerged from the crowd, clapping loudly. His chest and stomach muscles glistened with sweat, clearly showing he had been sparring as well. He was shirtless, and his rich, dark mahogany skin was smooth, except for the lighter tawny scars that marked his many battles or moments of folly. Unlike my calloused hands, worn from years of wielding bows and rapiers, his were surprisingly smooth-looking. Frank nudged me out of my envious admiration of his impressive physique.

"Well matched, Orla. That was some impressive footwork and sword handling," Rein said with a chuckle, his tone genuinely admiring. "I'd hate to face you on the battlefield. I didn't realize you trained with the elite warriors of Orlondia."

I shot him a wry grin. "You're impressed with my sword handling?" I raised an eyebrow, my eyes glowing with a playful purple.

Rein choked on a laugh. "Uh, yeah, maybe I could have phrased that better."

Frank slapped his knee and nudged me. "Sorry, Prince Reinferd, but I don't think she's interested in handlin' anyone's sword but her own."

A flush crept up Rein's cheeks as he fumbled for words. "I wasn't… I mean, I didn't think… That wasn't my intention or insinuation, Orla." He dipped his head slightly, clearly flustered.

I made a fist and gave Rein's arm a light nudge. "Don't mind Frank. I know what you meant and thank you. Some of us don't always have our heads in the gutter."

I shot a pointed look at Frank, who just shrugged. "Hey, it's fun in my head."

Rein laughed off the teasing, his expression growing more serious as he wiped the sweat from his brow. "But in all seriousness, Orla," he began, and tugged a loose cotton shirt over his head. With his voice lowering to a more somber tone he continued. "With the war advancing as it is, I'm feeling the need to head to the front lines myself. I can't just stay behind while others fight. The situation at the border is getting worse every day."

I nodded, my amusement fading. "I understand the feeling. I've been considering the same. It's hard to stay back when our people are out there, risking everything."

Rein studied me for a moment before asking, "What about your father, King Oric? Do you think he'll lead your forces into battle, as your grandfather once did?"

The question caught me off guard, and I took a moment to think. "My father… he's not the man my grandfather was. He believes his role is to strategize from the safety of the palace, to oversee from afar. He thinks that's how he can be most effective. But sometimes…" I hesitated, searching for the right words. "Sometimes, I wonder if he's afraid to lead from the front. Not just because of the risk, but because he doesn't want to face what this war really means—what it demands of us."

Frank, who had been quiet for once, added, "King Oric's not a coward, Orla. He's a king. His first duty is to his people, to stay alive and lead them. But I get it. It's hard to respect a man who won't fight beside his soldiers."

Rein nodded in agreement. "I've heard similar sentiments from my own troops. They respect a leader who's willing to stand in the trenches with them. My father was that kind of man… before he was taken." His voice dropped, a shadow passing over his face.

I felt a pang of sympathy. Rein's father, King Brutus Grathlend, had been a warrior, one who had earned the loyalty of his people through his bravery and sacrifice. Losing him had been a blow not just to Rein, but to all of Negall.

"We all have our battles, Rein," I said softly. "Your father was a great man. And you've got his spirit. Don't doubt for a second that you won't do him proud, wherever you are in this war."

Rein's expression softened, a small smile forming. "Thank you, Orla. That means more than you know."

Frank broke the moment with a grunt. "Fuck!" We turned to see him rushing over to a small group where a sparring match had turned into a heated scuffle. He was quick to intervene, his booming voice commanding order. I couldn't help but smile; Frank was always good at managing chaos.

Frank stayed behind at the sparring ring, continuing to train the recruits. As Rein and I walked away, I glanced back towards Frank, who now had the two offenders on the floor doing sets of pushups. Knowing he had it handled, I listened to Rein who confided in me.

"My brother, King Zardarian Grathlend, has rarely been on the battlefield because of our mother's insistence that he remain safe at home in the palace of South Negall," Rein continued, his voice taking on a more reflective tone. "Zar recently sent word, hoping I'd consider representing him on the front lines, rather than wasting my time bartering with diplomats." A soft, self-deprecating chuckle escaped him, revealing the frustration behind his reasons for wanting to join the fight directly.

Rein's expression grew more somber as he continued, "Atteris has all but fallen. The Frostspire forces are pushing deeper into our lands, and each day we lose more ground. Our villages, our people... they're suffering." He shook his head, frustration etched into the tight lines of his face. "That's why I'm heading to the front. I believe if I personally bring the Enchanters and the magic weapons to the battlefield, we might have a real chance to turn the tide and push back the Frostspire forces."

I nodded slowly, but my mind churned with doubts. "Rein, I need to tell you something. I'm not entirely sure how much of an advantage the Enchanters and magic weapons will give us," I said carefully. "There are rumors—no, more than rumors—that Frostspire is using dark magic. If that's true, they could have protections against our enchantments, or worse, something even more dangerous."

Rein's brow furrowed. "Dark magic?" he asked, his voice tinged with skepticism but also a hint of concern. "What do you mean? What have you heard?"

I hesitated for a moment, then continued. "From what I've gathered, Frostspire has been capturing Fae from the Sylvan Enclave. They're draining their magic, using it to fuel their own forces somehow. I don't know the full extent, but if they're willing to employ such practices, then traditional tactics might not be enough."

Rein was silent for a moment, digesting the information. His eyes met mine, a flicker of determination still burning within them. "If that's true, it's even more important that I go to the front. Our people need to know what they're up against. And we need to find a way to counter whatever dark magic they're using."

I nodded. "I understand. But we need to be smart about this. Rushing in without a plan could be disastrous. We'll need to gather as much intelligence as we can before making any moves."

We spoke while we walked and the scenery around us changed. Leaving the sparring ring behind, moving through a narrow path that led toward the palace grounds. The woods flanking us were dense, filled with the rich scent of pine and earth. The shadow gloom of the sky did little to light the path and made shadows beneath the limbs more sinister. The wind was harshly rattling in the trees, and the sound of leaves crunching underfoot mixed with the distant chatter of birds.

Rein and I continued along the path, the trees growing thicker around us. The palace's spires peeked above the treetops in the distance, a reminder of the sheltered world we were walking back into.

"So, do you believe bringing Enchanters and magic weapons to the front will truly be enough, then?" I asked, a note of concern still in my voice.

Rein nodded, though his expression was more thoughtful now. "Magic has always been a powerful tool in our arsenal. But if they're using dark magic, we might need to rethink our approach. Maybe, like you said, focusing on intelligence gathering and strategy rather than brute force is our better bet. Either way, I believe we need to be there—to see for ourselves, to adapt. Will you at least seriously consider coming with me if your father won't?"

I could feel his determination, his belief in the cause. It was infectious. "You're right. We've all lost too much already. We can't afford to lose more. I will think about it, truly."

We walked in silence for a moment, the gravity of the situation settling between us. The wind rustled through the trees, carrying the scent of the ocean, making my thoughts drift to Aure, hoping she was doing well today.

As we approached the palace lawn, the grand structure of the palace came into full view. Its tall spires and intricate stonework stood out against the darkening overcast sky, a symbol of strength and resilience amidst the growing turmoil of war. The vast lawn stretched before us, a manicured green expanse dotted with vibrant autumn flowers that swayed gently in the cool breeze.

Rein walked beside me, his steps purposeful, yet slightly hesitant. He seemed deep in thought, his brow furrowed, as if contemplating the weight of what lay ahead. Finally, he broke the silence, his voice low but steady.

"I plan to leave with the next group of reinforcements heading to the front," he said, glancing over at me. "It'll be just a few days after your birthday and engagement party."

I stopped in my tracks, turning to face him fully. "That soon?" I asked, surprise and concern coloring my tone. "Why not wait a bit longer? Give yourself more time to prepare?"

He shook his head, a determined set to his jaw. "There's no time to waste, Orla. Every day we delay, more of our lands fall into enemy hands. Atteris is basically lost, and the Frostspire forces are pushing further south. We need to act swiftly if we're going to make a difference."

I nodded slowly, understanding his urgency but feeling a pang of worry nonetheless. "I just… I wish there was more time," I said softly. "Time to plan, time to prepare. Time to figure out what we're really up against. More time for me to convince my father to join you…" Under my breath I added. "Or at least for him to let me go with you."

Rein gave a small, reassuring smile. "I know. Though sometimes we have to act before we have all the answers. We can't wait for the perfect moment, especially in times of war. We have to make our own opportunities."

His words held a certain wisdom, a reminder of the harsh realities we were facing. I let out my breath, slow and controlled, nodding in agreement. "You're right," I said. "And if I can't go with you, I'll at least be here, doing everything I can to support our efforts from this end."

Rein placed a hand on my shoulder, his expression sincere. "I know you will, Orla. And that's why I trust you. You have a strong mind and an even stronger heart. Our people need that right now."

We continued walking toward the palace, the crisp air nipping at our skin. The soft yellowing grass muffled the sound of our footsteps beneath us, and the distant murmur of palace activity grew louder with each step. Servants moved about, tending to the gardens, and guards patrolled the outer grounds with a heightened sense of vigilance.

As we neared the palace entrance, I couldn't help but feel a mix of emotions swirling inside me—pride in what we were fighting for, anxiety about what lay ahead, and a growing determination to see it through, no matter the cost. My eyes swirled with colors of the rainbow matching my internal struggle, before they landed on a deep amber.

"I'm glad you'll be there for my engagement party," I said, trying to lighten the mood a bit. "I'll need all the support I can get to survive that, too."

Rein chuckled, the sound easing some of the tension between us. "I wouldn't miss it for the world," he said. "Though I imagine you'll do just fine. You've faced worse than a room full of nobles and well-wishers."

I smiled, feeling a bit more at ease. "True. But still, it helps to have friends by my side."

As we reached the grand steps leading up to the palace doors, Rein paused, turning to face me once more. "Just promise me one thing, Orla," he said, his tone more serious now. "Promise me you will think about what I said. If you don't join me, take care of yourself and Aure, and keep an eye on things here. We will be counting on you to keep the diplomats on track."

I met his gaze, my eyes shifting into a deep sapphire blue. I was unsure if I had much control over anything here, but I still felt the weight of his words. "I promise," I said firmly. "And you take care of yourself out there. Don't take any unnecessary risks."

He nodded, a hint of a smile touching his lips. "I'll try," he said, then added with a wink, "But you know me."

I couldn't help but chuckle. "Yeah, I think I do. That's what worries me."

We shared a brief, knowing smile before continuing up the steps. The palace doors loomed ahead, a reminder of the responsibilities that awaited within. As we stepped inside, the warmth of the interior enveloped us. It did little to warm the chill that had set in my bones that wasn't just from the storm brewing in the sky. I glanced at Rein, his expression resolute as he seemed prepared to face whatever lay ahead. I watched him head to his chambers, and I found myself alone amongst the business of the palace, a feeling I had grown accustomed to after so many years here.

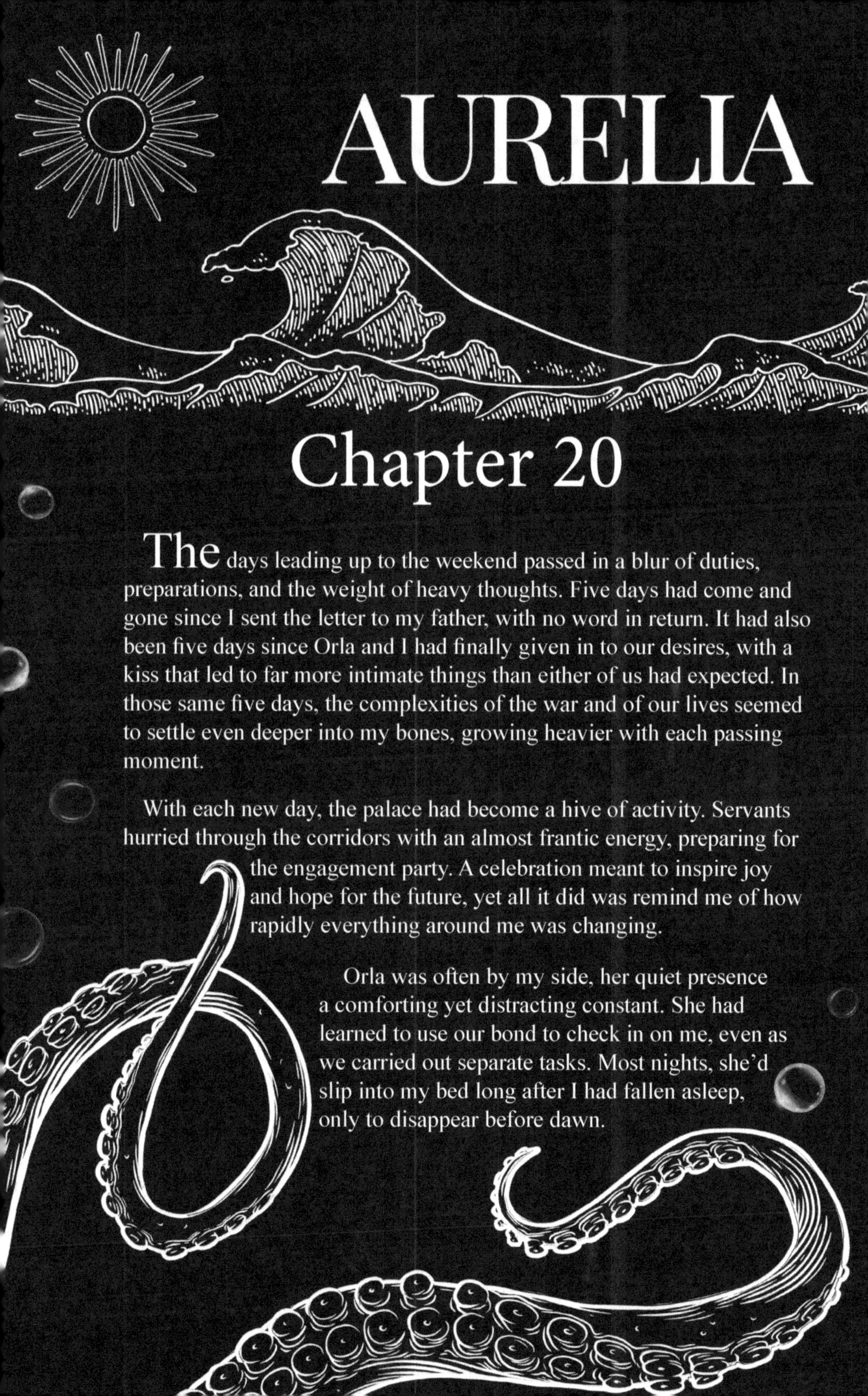

AURELIA

Chapter 20

The days leading up to the weekend passed in a blur of duties, preparations, and the weight of heavy thoughts. Five days had come and gone since I sent the letter to my father, with no word in return. It had also been five days since Orla and I had finally given in to our desires, with a kiss that led to far more intimate things than either of us had expected. In those same five days, the complexities of the war and of our lives seemed to settle even deeper into my bones, growing heavier with each passing moment.

With each new day, the palace had become a hive of activity. Servants hurried through the corridors with an almost frantic energy, preparing for the engagement party. A celebration meant to inspire joy and hope for the future, yet all it did was remind me of how rapidly everything around me was changing.

Orla was often by my side, her quiet presence a comforting yet distracting constant. She had learned to use our bond to check in on me, even as we carried out separate tasks. Most nights, she'd slip into my bed long after I had fallen asleep, only to disappear before dawn.

Despite the warmth of her body next to mine, the responsibilities and weight of my decisions felt like they grew heavier with each passing day.

I had thrown myself into the whirlwind of meetings with Lady Lili and Queen Helena, finalizing the last details for the upcoming event. Lady Lili's shift in attitude, from distant to almost doting, was unsettling. I couldn't quite place why, but something about her newfound warmth made me uneasy. Still, I pressed on, keeping my reservations to myself, if only for Orla's sake.

Beyond all the planning, my days became consumed with reviewing security protocols, overseeing the training of recruits with our Runic weapons, and enduring what felt like an endless string of diplomatic meetings, none of which seemed to yield any real progress. It was all just hollow words, dancing around solutions that were never reached. The weight of responsibility pressed down on me with each passing hour.

In the rare quiet moments between the chaos, my thoughts inevitably wandered to the battlefield, to the distant front lines where men and women fought and bled for a war that seemed as relentless as the meetings I attended. Even Orla had begun whispering about feeling the pull to lead our troops in person rather than from behind the safety of a locked tower. She admired Rein's courage for choosing to join the fight directly, and I could sense her restlessness. It matched the growing uncertainty within me.

Then there were my damn dreams, never simple nightmares, but the foresights were chaotic at best and full of confusing details. Each vision was more vividly chaotic than the last, shifting in meaning and each uniquely different. I tried to push them away, to shove them into the dark corners of my mind, but they always returned.

Each evening, I would drag myself to my chambers, hoping that exhaustion would bring me the reprieve of sleep, but rest never came. Instead, the haunting images played behind my closed eyes: blood-soaked fields, flames licking the sky, the cries of the fallen echoing in my ears, or one of Orla's many deaths. My bond with Azura felt strained, as though she, too, sensed the shifting tides of my magic and an encroaching darkness.

It was the early morning of Morveil. Orla had mentioned that they called it Mortia's Passage here, in honor of their goddess of death and the afterlife. Mortia. The name seemed to carry an unfamiliar weight on my tongue, the way the people of Orlondia revered her was different from how we honored the dead back home. There, it was more a celebration of life, a chance to sing and dance beneath the stars, to thank the sea for guiding the souls of our loved ones. Here, it was solemn. Respectful. But there was a darker edge to it, a reminder of the finality that Mortia represented.

Now, I stood alone at the edge of my balcony, the cold northern breeze tugging at my robes. The view of the garden stretching out before me usually brought a sense of calm, but today, even its scent and beauty couldn't soothe the turmoil brewing inside my mind.

I leaned over the balcony railing, watching the mist roll over the low yellowed grasses and bright-colored flowers. The sun rose, painting the sky in soft pinks and oranges. My thoughts drifted back to the nightmares that had been plaguing me these past few nights. They were getting worse, more gruesome.

In my dreams, I could feel the icy breath of the enemy, hear the cries of the dying, and see the blood that stained my hands. The harder I tried to hold on to Orla or save her in my dreams, the more bloody her death was. There was something else, something I couldn't quite grasp. A shadow, a presence that felt ancient and terrible that I couldn't decipher.

Orla had asked me about them again the night before night, her concern evident in her tone and the way she watched me. I had brushed it off, telling her I was fine, that I just needed more rest and was anxious about the party. The truth was, I didn't know what to make of these visions. They felt different from my usual foresights, more chaotic and less controlled.

Normally, the bond I shared with Azura would help me make sense of them, but even she seemed uneasy, restless in the back of my mind. I was just grateful Orla had seemed to share none of my dreams, at least not that she let on. Our mate bond, though growing stronger each day, seemed unpredictable. I wasn't sure how to control it or, if I even could.

I sighed, wrapping my shawl tighter around my shoulders as the wind picked up, the chill of another storm approaching sinking into my bones. The palace below was already stirring with activity. Servants preparing for today's feast and rituals, others tending to the final touches for the engagement party. My engagement party.

It still didn't feel real. I had spent so many years focusing on my duties, on the war, on my father, on my kingdom, and now, here I was, preparing to tie my life to Orla's. Not that I didn't want it. In truth, she had become more to me than I ever expected, and our bond was growing stronger. Now, I couldn't see myself without her strength, her loyalty, her intellect, and her affection. However, the timing felt cruel. Just as I had found someone I truly loved, the war seemed to be closing in around us, threatening to tear everything apart before we could even start building a life together.

A soft knock on the door pulled me from my thoughts. I turned, expecting one of the many servants, but to my surprise, it was Orla. She stood in the doorway, dressed in her usual simple leathers, but the look on her face told me she had been thinking as much as I had. Her beautiful eyes, pools of pure magic, with a rainbow of colors.

"You're up early," she said her voice gentle, stepping into the room and closing the door behind her.

I gave her a small smile. "Couldn't sleep. The usual."

Orla crossed the room, coming to stand beside me on the balcony. She didn't say anything at first, just leaned against the railing, her gaze fixed on the horizon. There was a tension in her shoulders, a weight that matched my own.

"It's Moveil today," I said after a moment, breaking the silence. "Back home, we would have prepared for the great song and celebration. Here, it's... different."

Orla nodded, her eyes distant. "Yeah, it is, but it's still a day to remember the dead. To honor them."

I swallowed, unsure of what to say. The weight of the day pressed down on me even more. "And what do we do? How do we honor them? Have you lost anyone?" I asked, my voice softer now.

Orla finally turned to look at me, her expression thoughtful. "We remember them in our own way, Aure. There's no right or wrong in this." Her hand reached out to gently brush a strand of hair from my face, her touch warm and reassuring. "We just... keep them close."

She kissed my cheek softly, her breath warm against my skin as she whispered, "Yes, I have people I honor on this day, and I keep them close to my heart."

Without thinking, I caught her wrist, pulling her closer as my other hand slid to the back of her neck. Rising onto my tiptoes, I drew her down, capturing her lips with mine in a full, lingering kiss.

She broke the kiss after a few heated moments, her forehead resting gently against mine. "I want to take you to the beach tonight, so you can sing," she whispered, her breath mingling with mine. "Will you honor me by allowing me to be there with you?"

Before I could respond, a soft knock interrupted us, and the door creaked open just enough to reveal Cam's face. She hesitated briefly, taking in the moment between Orla and me with a small, understanding smile.

"Sorry to interrupt," she said gently, her tone respectful. "But Orla, the recruits are ready for training. We're running behind this morning, but Frank's already trying to gather them up."

Orla sighed softly, her thumb brushing tenderly against my cheek before she reluctantly pulled away. "Duty calls," she murmured, giving me an apologetic smile.

I nodded, trying to hide the small pang of disappointment. "Go on. We'll have tonight, and yes is my answer." I reassured her, my hand lingering on hers for a moment longer.

Cam stood by the door, her posture relaxed but patient. "Take your time," she added kindly, glancing between us with a look of acceptance, as if she understood how important these moments were.

Orla gave me one last kiss on the forehead before heading to the door with a wide grin. "I won't be long," she promised, casting a warm glance back at me.

As they walked down the hallway, the sound of their footsteps fading into the distance, I found myself already looking forward to tonight, a small smile playing on my lips despite my unease.

After Orla and Cam disappeared from sight, I let out a slow breath, shaking off the lingering warmth of our brief moment together. There was still much to be done before tonight, but the weight of the tasks ahead felt too heavy to tackle immediately. My thoughts were already swirling with plans, strategies, and the ever-present shadow of the war. I needed a moment of quiet, a space to clear my head and prepare myself.

After eating and getting ready for the day, I decided I would retreat to the palace library, one of the few places where I could always find solace lately. The large, arched doors greeted me like an old friend as I slipped inside, the scent of ancient parchment and leather-bound books enveloping me in a familiar embrace. The soft glow of daylight filtered through the stained-glass windows, casting delicate patterns of light across the stone floor. Shelves upon shelves of books lined the walls, their spines filled with untold knowledge and history.

I walked slowly down the aisles, running my fingers lightly along the edges of the books as I moved through the rows. It wasn't long before I found myself in a secluded corner, where an old wooden table sat surrounded by stacks of scrolls and manuscripts. Sitting down, I pulled an old, weathered tome toward me, hoping the quiet surroundings would give me some clarity.

Just as I settled into my thoughts, the soft creak of the library door broke the silence. I glanced up to see Kepple entering the room, their silver-blue eyes scanning the shelves before landing on me. Their steps were light as they moved toward me, their expression calm yet intent as if they had been looking for me with a purpose.

"Aure," they greeted quietly, their voice soft but unwavering. "I've been searching for you. There's some things we need to discuss about the Order of the Golden Rose."

My heart skipped a beat at the mention of the Order. I pushed the tome aside, giving them my full attention. "What is it?" I asked, my voice low as the weight of their words settled over me.

Kepple pulled out the chair across from me and sat down, their usually serene expression now laced with concern. "I've come across more information. I think you'll want to hear this."

Their calm demeanor belied the gravity of their words. Their slender fingers traced the edge of the table before they reached into their satchel, producing a small, tattered scroll. Gently unrolling it, they placed it between us, the delicate parchment revealing a series of intricate symbols and handwriting that appeared to be centuries old.

"I've been combing through the restricted texts in the deepest part of the library," they began, their voice measured. "What I found here is unsettling. The Order of the Golden Rose—this isn't just a group of fanatics looking to eradicate magic. They have ties to an ancient doctrine, one rooted in something much darker. They believe they are following the will of their deity, Lux Veritas. They see magic as a corruption that must be eradicated to restore the world's natural order."

I nodded, absorbing the weight of the statement. "I've heard they're fanatical about this 'purity.' But how could they think purging magic—a force that's so intrinsic to Terraqua—would be what their god wants?"

Kepple met my gaze, with a flicker of uncertainty. "Because their sacred texts—*the Codex of Purity*—suggest that the existence of magic is a defiance of the 'divine plan.' And they believe Lux Veritas entrusted them with the duty to cleanse the world. They're convinced they're acting under divine mandate."

My chest tightened. The depth of their conviction was terrifying. "What does the Codex say?"

They leaned in closer, lowering their voice. "It speaks of a prophecy. The 'Unveiling of the True Light,' they call it. They believe that only by eliminating magic and the magic-born can they usher in an era of pure light, free from what they see as the corruption of magic. The more I read, the more it seemed like they're not just targeting individuals. They aim to change the very fabric of the world."

I could feel the weight of the words pressing down on me, the enormity of what we were facing. "Do they have the means to do this?" I asked, my throat dry with fear.

Kepple's face darkened. "They're getting closer. That's what worries me. The Syphon Rune isn't just a way for them to incapacitate magic-born individuals. It's part of a larger ritual—a ritual that, if completed, could have catastrophic consequences."

I felt my pulse quicken. "What kind of ritual?"

"The Order calls it the *Ritual of Ascendancy*. It's a ceremony designed to sever the connection between magic-born and the source of their magic, not just temporarily but permanently. If they can gather enough magic-born and perform this ritual on a massive scale, it could destabilize magic across Terraqua."

A chill ran down my spine and goose bumps skittered across my skin. "Destabilize it? You mean... destroy magic?"

They nodded gravely and pushed their glasses back up their nose in place. "That's what it looks like. The Syphon Rune is just the beginning. Once they've drained enough magic, they'll use it to fuel the ritual. It's why they've been quietly capturing Fae, Sirens, and others for years. And if they succeed... the repercussions could be disastrous."

I leaned back in my chair, my thoughts racing. "How do we stop them? If they've already started..."

They placed a hand on the scroll, tapping the symbols that lined its edges. "I'm not sure yet. But this is key. The Codex has gaps in its text, likely intentional, but I've been piecing it together. There's a countermeasure mentioned in fragments, something about 'returning the light to its vessel.' It could be a way to reverse the Syphon Rune or disrupt the ritual. But I need more time."

I swallowed hard, feeling the crushing weight of the moment. "Time is something we may not have much of."

They met my eyes, their gaze unwavering. "I know. But I'll keep digging. There's still hope, Aure. We just need to find it before they do."

I clenched my fists against the table, the reality of the situation sinking in. "Keep me informed, Kepple. Anything you find, no matter how small, could be the key."

They smiled faintly. "Of course, Princess Aure." They stood and after giving me a slight bow they slipped the scroll back into their satchel before they walked away, leaving me to ponder all they had shared.

I picked up the tome I had been reading earlier, my eyes scanning the familiar words, but the weight of what Kepple had revealed hung heavy in my mind. The sentences blurred together, the meaning slipping through my grasp as my thoughts drifted back to the Order and their dark ambitions.

Orla's footsteps echoed softly through the library as she approached. I looked up from my reading, my mind still spinning with the information Kepple had just shared. Orla's gaze immediately locked onto mine, her expression both curious and serious.

"You've been here a while," she said, her voice low. "I came to get you for the council meeting this afternoon. We can't skip it, unfortunately, before we sneak off to the beach tonight."

I sighed, running a hand through my hair and closing the book with a soft thud. "Right. The meeting... I almost forgot, with everything Kepple just told me."

Orla raised an eyebrow, sensing the tension that had taken root in me. "More about the Order?"

I nodded, standing up and sliding the book back onto the shelf. "Yes. Kepple found more references to their rituals. It's worse than we thought. They're not just hunting down magic-born, they're working toward something much bigger. Something that could affect all magic."

Orla's face darkened, her eyes swirling from lavender to a deep, stormy blue. "We'll handle it. Whatever they're planning, we'll stop them. But first, the council." She reached out and took my hand, her touch warm and steadying. "Come on, let's get through this, and then we can steal away to the beach. I promised you that."

Her words, though comforting, felt like a brief respite from the storm that was brewing around us. I let her lead me out of the library, my mind still buzzing with everything I had just learned. The weight of the council meeting now loomed over us, another task to tackle before we could finally take a moment for ourselves.

As we walked through the palace hallways, the distant murmur of voices and the clatter of activity filled the air. Servants moved quickly, preparing for the evening ahead, but all I could think about was the Order, their twisted beliefs, and how much more we still needed to uncover before it was too late.

But for now, I would push it all aside. We had a council to face, decisions to make, and after that... I would let Orla take me to the beach and forget the world, if only for a few hours.

As Orla and I approached the grand council chambers, the weight of the impending meeting settled over me. This gathering was critical, bringing together the kingdom's most influential figures, all of whom had stakes in the war and the threats we faced. The large oak doors loomed ahead, and I cast a sidelong glance at Orla, her expression a mask of quiet determination.

Just before we entered the chambers, Orla whispered to me, "Frank and Cam stayed back with the recruits, overseeing the weapon drills. They said they'd meet us after the meeting."

I nodded, appreciating the calm efficiency of our most trusted guards. Frank and Cam's presence had become such a constant in our lives that their absence was a bit unsettling, but I trusted them to handle the training while we dealt with the more delicate matters of state.

We entered the chamber, the heavy doors swinging open to reveal a long rectangular table surrounded by a mix of nobility, military leaders, and diplomats. The murmur of conversation halted as we made our entrance, and all eyes turned to us.

Now, seated at the large rectangular table, the room felt cold despite the fire blazing in the hearth. King Oric Orlond, regal in his deep blue and black garments. His chestnut hair, short and neatly groomed, framed a face that appeared younger than his years, though his pale, oily complexion hinted at a man who spent more time in dark chambers than under the sun. A potbelly protruded over his belt, but there was nothing soft about his presence. His charisma and ambition were palpable, as was the way he commanded the room with little more than a glance. The discussions centered on the ever-looming threat of Frostspire.

On his left was General Roderick Magnus, his brow furrowed as he pored over several maps. His military mind was always in motion, constantly calculating the best moves in the ongoing war. Beside him sat Duke Kinsmere, the wooden chair barely contained his short, burly frame. Any sign of his temper and his booming voice that often filled any space he occupied, for now was nowhere to be seen. He sat silently, eyeing the maps with a frown.

Across from them was Captain Cole Ashford, the naval captain of Faedamir. His face was lined from the sun and sea, but his eyes were sharp and intelligent. His leg appeared to be doing lots better today. He glanced up briefly at Orla and me, giving a small nod before returning to his quiet conversation with Madame Koi Kole. She had her silver hair pinned elegantly and her robes draped in the colors of the sea, while she exuded calm authority. She caught my eye and offered a warm, knowing smile.

At the far end of the table sat Rielle. Today her hair had bright blue braids which caught in the light as they swayed slightly with her movements. She tapped her fingers lightly on the table, her gaze darting between the maps and the faces of those around her. She had a habit of fidgeting. Thankfully, today it wasn't with her dagger. When her eyes landed on us, she broke into a wide smile, her energy radiant, opposite to the tense atmosphere of the room.

Ambassador Thorne Meadowcroft sat beside Rielle, his hands resting casually over his stomach as he leaned back in his chair with the calm demeanor of someone long accustomed to tension and chaos. I had heard he was a skilled mediator, perhaps honed by managing his nine children. Thorne had been instrumental in forging alliances between the various factions within Negall. His light brown hair and sun-kissed complexion reflected his agricultural roots, yet his diplomatic talents had brought him far beyond his homeland, leading him here to the capital, accompanied by his entire family.

Across from him sat Baroness Lyra Aveline, a patron of the arts and a key figure in cultural exchanges between the kingdoms. Her presence here today was a reminder that the war affected more than just soldiers and strategists—it was shaping the very fabric of our society.

Lord Alden Gareth sat close to the king, his eyes keen and observant. Orla had told me before that he was Tristan's father and chief steward of the royal court. His role in managing the kingdom's finances and administrative affairs was critical, especially in times of war. There was an air of quiet wisdom around him, though his loyalty to the king and this kingdom was undeniable.

Lastly, Rein sat beside Ambassador Thorne, his expression thoughtful, as though weighing every word being spoken. He caught Orla's gaze and gave her a small nod of acknowledgment, though his demeanor was far more subdued than usual.

King Oric rose to his feet, signaling the official start of the meeting. "We have much to discuss," he began, his voice commanding attention. "The war with Frostspire continues to escalate, and we must address new threats and opportunities. General Magnus, what is the latest on the front lines?"

General Magnus stood, clearing his throat. "Atteris is truly in desperate need. Reinforcements had been sent, but Frostspire's forces were advancing with a stronger offense than we had prepared for. Our troops are struggling to hold the line. All the lands and homes on the outskirts of Atteris have been lost. "

A murmur spread through the room, and I felt a chill run down my spine. I glanced at Orla, who stood beside me, her brow furrowed in thought.

"I've been hearing rumors," Orla interjected, her voice clear and firm. "The magic Frostspire wields—there's more to it than we know. I've learned that they're using dark rituals to draw power from Fae prisoners."

The room fell into a stunned silence, all eyes turning to Orla. General Magnus leaned forward, his expression grim. "Fae prisoners?" he echoed. "And what do you propose we do?"

Orla met his gaze evenly. "We need to stop it at the source. But more than that, we need to understand the magic they're using. Enchanters and magical weapons will help, but it may not be enough."

Rielle, who had remained quiet until now, finally spoke up. "We can enhance the weapons with stronger reflective runes," she suggested, her voice thoughtful. "But Orla is right—if they're using dark magic, we need to be prepared for something more powerful than traditional weapons alone."

Captain Cole leaned back in his chair, rubbing his chin thoughtfully. "I can divert some of my fleet to assist with this," he said. "But we'll need to coordinate closely with ground forces."

"Bawk! Those are simply rumors planted by enemy spies. Our armies are stronger in number, skill, and magical power. There's no need to trouble the entire council with this, Orla," King Oric dismissed her concerns with a wave of his hand, shaking his head as if the matter were trivial. Orla squirmed in her seat, and I could feel the simmering anger beneath her calm exterior, her frustration palpable as her father so easily discounted her words, her eyes shifted to deep cobalt blue.

As the discussion continued, plans and strategies were laid out. Rein eventually spoke, his tone serious. "I'll be leaving for the front with the next group of reinforcements after Orla's engagement party. I believe it's time I represented North Negall on the battlefield."

King Oric's eyes narrowed slightly, his cold, calculating gaze settling on Rein. "Your presence will be welcome, I am sure, but tread carefully. The battlefield is no place for diplomacy. We must strike hard and fast. Your late father understood that."

Rein nodded, though a flicker of unease crossed his features. "I understand, Your Majesty."

Orla stood then, her voice soft but determined. "Father, I would like to accompany Rein to aid the front as well."

King Oric barely glanced up from the map at first, then he burst into loud laughter, his belly shaking like a gelatinous mound. "Don't be ridiculous, Orla. They have no need of a princess at the front lines. You will stay put."

The room grew still, the tension palpable. Orla's jaw tightened, but she said nothing further. The atmosphere shifted as the reality of the war pressed in, casting a shadow over the room. She sank back into her seat, the weight of her father's dismissive words hanging heavy.

After a brief, awkward pause, the meeting resumed. Discussions about troop deployments, magical defenses, and battle strategies filled the air, but I couldn't shake the growing unease. The war was escalating, and each new detail made it all the more real.

When the meeting finally adjourned, I stood, feeling the weight of everything pressing down on me. As we made our way toward the exit, Orla leaned in close, her breath warm against my ear. "Frank and Cam will have the recruits ready by the time we return."

I nodded, reassured by the thought. Frank's steadfastness and Cam's loyalty gave me a sliver of calm amidst the turmoil.

As the doors closed behind us, the sense of urgency lingered in the air. The war loomed larger with each passing day, and there was much to prepare for. Tonight, there was a small moment of respite awaiting us at the beach. It sounded like a brief escape from the weight of the world before everything came crashing down again.

Later, the night deepened and darkness settled in around us. The sky was like blue crushed velvet, with the moon casting its soft, silver light over the secluded beach. We had managed to slip away from the palace, leaving Cam and Frank behind, their concerns voiced insistently that we not wander off alone. We needed this, for it to just be the two of us, far from the eyes of the court, away from the weight of war, and the responsibilities that had only grown heavier since the council meeting.

The rough sandy beach, littered with pebbles, stretched out before us, bathed in the glow of hundreds of floating lanterns drifting lazily through the night sky. The gentle waves mirrored their warm, flickering lights, where small boats carried candles, bobbing in the water like glowing stars scattered across the sea. The air smelled of salt, and the rhythmic sound of the ocean was the only thing breaking the silence.

I glanced at Orla, her silhouette illuminated by the soft glow of the lanterns above. Her eyes, a shimmering blend of purples and blues, reflected the beauty of the night. She seemed more at peace here than anywhere else. Her shoulders relaxed as the sound of the waves calmed the tension that had built up over the past week.

She turned to me, her expression softened. "I never thought I'd get you out here," she teased, her voice low and full of warmth. "Especially with no guards breathing down our necks."

I smirked, nudging her gently with my shoulder. "I'm good at slipping away when I need to. Besides, we deserve this. Time for ourselves." I took off my shoes leaving them on the ground, my toes curling into the cold sand and icy pebbles.

She took my hand, her touch gentle but grounding, pulling me closer to the shore. The sand beneath our feet was wet, the grains growing smoother and soft as we walked together toward the water's edge. The floating candles swayed with the tide, casting a golden glow across the dark water. I stared out at the horizon, feeling the serenity of the moment wash over me like the gentle waves lapping at my feet.

Even as the silence settled around us, my thoughts inevitably drifted back to my mother. The loss of her still felt like an open wound, aching and raw, especially on nights like this, and this time of year. I have only sung on Morveil, only to her, since the year she passed. My throat clenched with the memories of her gentle guidance, the way her hands had smoothed my hair when I was a child. I missed her more deeply than I ever allowed myself to admit, and now, the ocean felt like the only place where I could still feel her presence.

Orla must have sensed the shift in my mood. She squeezed my hand gently, bringing me back to the present. "You're thinking of your mother, aren't you?" she asked softly, her eyes searching mine.

I nodded, swallowing the lump in my throat. "I lost her too soon, Orla. She would've loved you." A tear slipped down my cheek, and I brushed it away quickly.

Orla stepped closer, wrapping her arms around me. "You can honor her tonight, Aure. Let me be with you when you sing for her."

I hesitated for a moment before nodding. This was something I needed to do with her. "I will," I whispered. "But to sing properly, I have to take my true form."

Orla's eyes flickered with curiosity and understanding. She stepped back, giving me space as I removed my dress and underclothes, letting them fall to the sand in a heap at my feet. The crisp night air bit my skin, and as I took a deep breath, I stepped forward into the icy water, letting it wrap around my ankles, then my calves, then my waist. A small shiver ran through me.

My magic released and my transformation began almost instantly. From my waist, eight sparkling champagne-pink tentacles unfurled, delicate but strong, catching the moonlight as they shimmered like jewels against the dark water. Ridges appeared along my stomach, curving upward to cup under my breasts, and thin gills opened along the sides of my neck below my ears, allowing me to breathe freely once I was beneath the surface.

I heard Orla gasp softly behind me, her breath catching as she watched me transform. I turned to her, offering her a small, nervous smile. "This is me, in my true form," I said quietly, my voice carrying across the gentle waves.

She stepped closer, her eyes wide with awe but filled with tenderness. Without hesitation, Orla began to undress, her clothes slipping to the sand as she stood before me, bare and vulnerable in the moonlight. Her beauty, her etched-toned muscles displaying her strength, her perky breasts with nipples that popped in the cold, and her tight ass. All of her took my breath away.

Orla walked into the water, the cold barely seeming to affect her as she joined me, the waves lapping at her thighs. I extended one of my tentacles, wrapping it gently around her waist, pulling her close to me. Our skin pressed together, the warmth of her body keeping the cold of the ocean at bay.

Without a word, I tugged her beneath the crashing waves, pulling us into the depths where the moonlight barely touched. My gills opened fully, and I took a deep, calming breath. The sea embraced us, and here, in the silence of the ocean, I began to sing.

The melody was low and haunting, my voice carrying through the water my Siren's call. It was a song for my mother, a song of love and loss, of remembrance and longing. The water around us shimmered with the power of the song, and I felt the presence of my mother in every note, every breath I took.

She didn't need to understand what this moment meant to me. She was simply there, my constant, my strength, my mate.

The water swirled around us, and once I ended my song, I pulled Orla closer, pressing my forehead against hers. Beneath the ocean, beneath the stars, we were the only two souls in the world, united in the quiet intimacy of the moment.

I felt her grip tighten on my waist as she struggled to hold the last remnants of air in her lungs. Sensing her need, I pressed my mouth against hers, sharing my breath with her, allowing us to remain suspended in this moment. It was just the two of us beneath the waves, wrapped in the dark stillness of the ocean.

ORLA

Chapter 21

I held my breath, captivated by Aure's song, the haunting melody echoing through the water, wrapping around us like a spell. Every note was infused with emotion, and I could feel the deep sorrow and love she held for her mother. The cold, which never seemed to bother me, wrapped around us, but it was her presence that kept me rooted, that kept me entranced.

Even though I had always been able to hold my breath longer than most, I was coming close to my limit now. I used to escape to the ocean as a child, sinking beneath the waves to find stillness and increase my length of being able to stay in the quiet emptiness. I ventured to the ocean front even in the dead of winter as the snow covered the shores. My nursemaids and even my mother would often say I'd catch my death, but I'd never even had so much as a sniffle. Now, here with Aure, I felt invincible. The way she sang beneath the water was unlike anything I'd ever experienced.

As Aure finished her song, I felt my lungs tighten, struggling to hold the last remnants of air. Before I could surface, her mouth closed over mine, filling my lungs with a deep, life-giving breath. The air tasted of her, fresh, like the ocean, with a hint of something sweet. My body wrapped in those stunning champagne-pink tentacles, she held me close against her cool skin, and with the heat growing within me, it sent a shiver down my spine.

One of her tentacles curled around my breast, the soft suction teasing the sensitive skin. It bit down slightly, releasing in a rhythmic motion that made a gasp escape me into her mouth. I felt desire coil in my core, the pressure building as her touch grew more insistent. We were weightless beneath the waves as the ocean cradled us while we sank slowly to the sandy floor below. My feet brushed lightly against the ground, and the sensation of the sand shifting beneath me only heightened the feeling of being completely lost in her.

Her tentacles inched their way up my legs, curling and wrapping around me like they were claiming every part of me. Her kiss deepened, her lips molding against mine as she gave me another breath. I felt her magic pulsate between us, a hum of energy that throbbed in rhythm with the surrounding ocean.

It was just us, beneath the dark water, the stars above faintly flickering through the waves, and the soft glow of the lanterns and candles shimmering on the surface. There were no royal duties, no council meetings, no war. Just the feel of her against me, the water surrounding us like a cocoon, and the sensation of her touch unraveling me piece by piece.

I moaned softly into her mouth, my hands gripping onto her waist as her tentacles continued their slow, deliberate exploration of my body. The cool of her touch and the fire burning inside me clashed, creating a delicious tension that threatened to consume me.

Her fingers sunk deep within my hair, holding my head to hers, and all her appendages moved along me in delicate caress, a graceful intensity that mirrored the push and pull of the ocean. The suctions from one tentacle slid along my inner thigh, sending sparks of sensation up my spine as it curled, licking ever closer to my center. I groaned, her kiss still deep and languid, giving me the air I so desperately needed.

Her ridges, those delicate scales that formed across her stomach, brushed against my skin as her body pressed closer. The desire growing inside me made it nearly impossible to focus on anything but the way we fit together. I was completely wrapped up in her, and I wanted nothing more than to lose myself in her entirely.

Aure's gills fluttered with the rhythm of her breaths, pulling in the cold seawater as she held me close. I could feel her body vibrating with the magic of her song still lingering in the depths. It pulsed through me, awakening something primal, something deep. It was as if the ocean itself was part of her, and in this moment, it was part of me, too.

I let my hands slide up her back, feeling the raised ridges along her spine, tracing the path where her skin shifted into those ethereal tentacles. Her touch, her magic, her being. It all consumed me, filled me with a sense of wonder and belonging I had never felt before. Every pull of her suction, every gentle curl of her tendrils around my thighs, hips, and breasts, brought me closer to her, deeper into the connection we shared.

She broke the kiss, her eyes swirling with iridescent green in the dim light beneath the water. I stared into them, breathless not only from lack of air but from the intensity of what we were feeling together. She pressed her forehead against mine, and I could feel the vibrations of her quiet hum. Was this a new song or the lingering echo of the song she had sung to her mother? It resonated between us like a shared heartbeat.

"Aure," I sent her my desire and longing through the mental thread of magic, our mate bond. Her tentacles squeezed lightly, and one slid further up my thigh, curling toward my center. I hitched, trying to keep my breath inside, the sensation nearly too much, and I arched into her, wanting more.

She smiled softly, the kind of smile that was both knowing and tender. Her eyes held mine, and without a word, I felt her intent. This moment was not just the physical pleasure, but something deeper for both of us. A merging of our souls beneath the waves, far from the world above.

The surrounding sea seemed to hum louder with the energy of it, the pull of the ocean mixing with our shared magic. Her lips found my neck, kissing a path down as her tentacles tightened their grip around me, her suctions teasing, tugging, releasing until I was trembling with need of her. The water grew colder, but all I felt was her touch, her strength, her love.

I let go, surrendering completely to her as we sank deeper into the ocean, the waves above crashing against the shore while the lanterns flickered in the distance. We were alone, hidden from the world, our bond growing unbreakable, and in this moment, nothing else mattered.

Her fingers trailed along my skin, and a soft moan escaped me, precious air slipping from my lungs. I pressed closer as her tentacles curled tighter around my legs, pulling me deeper into the ocean's embrace. Gods, I could understand how people could be called to their death this way. My lungs burned, but I didn't care. I was lost in the moment, lost in her. I was hers, and she was mine. Her mouth found mine again, and I greedily drew in the air that she gave me through her kiss. The sensations overwhelmed me—her touch, the pull of the water, the life-giving breath, and the way her magic intertwined with mine until I no longer knew where she ended and I began.

She broke our kiss, and as she pulled away, her voice rose in a soft, melodic song that resonated through the water. The sound was almost otherworldly as it pulled me further into her world. It wasn't the same song she had sung before. This was just for me now, a quiet, intimate melody that echoed in my mind as much as in my ears. I closed my eyes, letting the sound wrap around me, and for the first time in days, I felt completely at peace.

Her tentacles held me firmly, but there was a tenderness in every touch, every deliberate caress that left me trembling with anticipation. I could feel the way her body shifted against mine, her ridged skin brushing tantalizingly along my legs, and then the gentle pressure of her tentacles tightening their hold.

One of her tentacles slid further up between my thighs, curling upward, teasing the sensitive skin there. I continued to hold my breath in, my throat feeling tight as the suction tugged gently at my inner thigh. Her lips hovered near my ear, her voice a whisper beneath the water, with the melody meant only for me. I could feel her desire thrumming through our bond, intensifying the pull between us, making me ache for her in ways I had never imagined.

Then, with a deliberate, careful movement, one of her tentacles pressed against my entrance, slick with the ocean's saltwater and the slick warmth of my own need. I gripped her tighter, the sensation overwhelming as she teased me, applying just enough pressure to make me want more, but not enough to give me what I so desperately craved.

Aure's eyes met mine, my eyes swirling with vibrant, glowing colors matching the glow in hers. Her gaze was intense and filled with the same hunger I felt. Her fingers trailed up my sides, leaving a trail of electric fire in their wake, and she leaned closer, her lips brushing against mine, kissing me again. *"Let go, Orla."* A command and a promise all at once echoed in my mind through our bond.

I did. I let go of everything—of the world above, of the war, of the uncertainty—and surrendered to her completely.

With a slow, deliberate thrust, she pushed a single tentacle inside me, the slick, firm pressure filling me with a sudden, overwhelming rush of sensation. I cried out, the sound muffled by her mouth, my body arching against hers as she began to move inside me, the rhythm of her thrusts matching the pulse of the ocean around us. The suctions along her tentacle gripped and released, sending shockwaves of pleasure through me with every movement.

I clung to her, my fingers digging into her ridged skin as the pleasure built inside me, coiling tighter and tighter until it felt like I might shatter from the intensity of it. Her other tentacles continued to caress me, curling around my breasts, tugging gently at my hardened nipples, while some felt like kisses along my neck and collarbone. Her lips pressed hot against mine, her tongue flicking inside my mouth.

Every thrust, every touch, every kiss sent me spiraling further into a world where nothing existed but the two of us, wrapped in the ocean's embrace, our magic and desire intertwining in a way that was both primal and sacred. Her body moved with mine, her tentacles guiding me deeper into the depths of pleasure, her voice a soothing hum in my mind, urging me to let go, to fall completely into the ecstasy she was offering.

I could feel myself reaching the edge, the waves of pleasure crashing through me like the ocean's tide, pulling me under, drowning me in sensation. My body trembled, my breath coming in short, desperate gasps of air that I stole from her. I clung to her, every muscle tensing, every nerve alight with the fire she had ignited within me.

Her tentacle thrust deeper, curling inside me in a way that made me pull my head back and cry out into the water, my vision blurring as the pleasure consumed me. I felt our magic wrap around me, pulling me into the deepest parts of the ocean, where we were one with the water, one with the night, one with each other.

With a final, overwhelming rush, I came undone, my body shaking as the pleasure tore through me, my legs tightening around her waist, my fingers gripping her skin as I rode the waves of my climax. The ocean seemed to surge around us, the water humming with the force of our magic, our bond stronger than ever as we floated together in the darkness.

She held me close, her tentacles still wrapped around me, her body pressed against mine as I came down from the heights she had taken me to. Her lips found mine again, soft and tender, as I took in slow breaths from her. I felt the surge of magic, a promise of love and devotion that echoed through our bond.

As the intensity of the moment faded, we floated together, suspended in the embrace of the ocean and each other. Slowly, the rhythmic crashing of the waves above pulled me back into awareness, the weight of the world creeping in again as the night deepened around us.

Aure's fingers trailed down my back as she whispered softly, her voice blending with the sea's gentle hum. *"We should return to the surface. The others will be waiting for us."*

I nodded, reluctantly loosening my grip on her as she unwrapped her tentacles from my legs. With one last kiss, she gave me another breath of air before we swam upward, the dark ocean parting for us as we ascended toward the glittering stars above.

Breaking through the surface, I gasped, filling my lungs with the cool night air. Now hundreds of floating lanterns, their soft glow reflecting off the calm waters, illuminated the beach. Candle-lit boats dotted all down the shoreline, drifting lazily as the night's celebration of Mortia's Passage continued.

As we waded back to shore, I glanced at Aure, watching as her shimmering tentacles slowly retracted, her true form fading to reveal the beautiful woman who, to anyone else, would seem merely human. She smiled at me, brushing a stray lock of hair from her face before reaching for my hand.

In the secluded beach alcove, we retrieved our clothes, and I couldn't help stealing glances at her. She caught my eye, flashing me flirty smiles that sent warmth flooding through me. We both busied ourselves getting dressed, trying to focus on the task, but the charged energy between us made it difficult not to linger on each other for too long.

Once dressed, we held hands and stepped out of the alcove, walking along the shoreline as the distant, soft sounds of laughter and music drifted down the beach. The crackling of bonfires grew louder as the glow of flames came into view, scattered along the sand. Families and friends gathered around the fires, sharing food and stories to honor the memory of those who had passed. The air was rich with the scent of burning herbs and the smoky aroma of roasted meats, a comforting reminder of the community that surrounded us in this sacred moment.

We made our way toward the heart of the celebration, where I spotted Cam and Frank by one of the bonfires, mugs of ale in hand, their laughter carried on the night breeze. As soon as they caught sight of us, they waved us over, their faces glowing in the warmth of the firelight.

Aure squeezed my hand gently. "Come on, Orla. Let's join them. Tonight isn't just about me and my mother; it's about remembering and honoring all those who came before us."

I nodded, my heart swelling with the love and connection I felt for her, for this moment, and for the weight of the traditions we now shared. "Alright, Meles Tari," I whispered, knowing how deeply this night meant to her.

Hand in hand, we walked toward the bonfire, ready to share in the celebration of life and memory. Even as we honored the dead, the joy of being among the living and surrounded by those we loved filled the night with warmth.

As we neared the bonfire, the scene around us was alive with laughter and activity. Children darted around, dressed in playful costumes of mythical creatures—small dragons, sea sprites, and ghoulish goblins—chasing one another and giggling as they asked for small gifts from the adults. Some of the revelers wore masks and elaborate outfits, mimicking the spirits they were honoring, adding an air of mystery and fun to the night.

Frank raised his mug in greeting, his face split into a wide grin as he saw us approach. "Well, well, look who finally decided to join the celebrations!" he teased, his voice carrying over the crackling fire.

Aure laughed softly, squeezing my hand again as we reached them. "We needed a little… time to ourselves," she said, the hint of a smirk playing on her lips.

Cam, standing next to Frank with a mug of ale, gave us both a long, scrutinizing look. Her brow furrowed slightly in concern, but there was a glint of amusement there too. "Time to yourselves? You two slipped away without a word, and I was worried sick," she said, her tone serious but laced with affection as she took another calm sip of ale.

I shrugged, grinning as I tried to brush it off. "You know us, always finding a way to escape for a bit of peace," I said, though I could feel Cam's eyes studying me, gauging whether she should be more concerned.

Frank, however, was not letting it go that easily. He nudged Cam with his elbow and smirked at me. "Peace, huh? I don't think 'peace' is what you were after, Orla. More like… a different kind of battle. A private one." His tone was teasing, but there was a knowing look in his eye. "I mean, I get it. The beach, the stars, just the two of you. Very romantic."

Aure blushed, let out a soft chuckle, giving me a sidelong glance. "What can I say? I have good taste."

I rolled my eyes playfully, but before I could respond, Cam cut in, her voice more serious. "It's not just about romance, you know. There are real dangers out there, especially with the war creeping closer. You two can't just wander off alone without a word." She looked directly at me, her protective nature showing. "I'm not trying to be difficult, but we need to be more careful."

I softened my expression, feeling the weight of her words. "We know, Cam. I promise, we were careful. Tonight was important, though, for both of us." I glanced at Aure, who nodded in agreement.

Frank, never one to let a serious moment last too long, clapped Cam on the back. "Come on, Cam. Let them have their fun. They're grown women. Besides, they're practically untouchable, with all that magic between them. Besides, just look at how they look at each other. How can you not want them to have some romantical fun?"

Aure giggled, leaning into me as she whispered, "Well, we are a force to be reckoned with."

Cam sighed, her serious expression softening into a small smile. "Fine, but if you two decide to disappear again, at least let me know where you're going. I'm your guard for a reason, after all."

I reached out and gave her arm a reassuring squeeze. "I get it."

Frank raised his mug again, grinning like a rogue. "Here's to romantic escapes and not gettin' caught by overly concerned guards!" he declared, and we all laughed, the tension easing as we settled into the warmth of the celebration.

The night stretched on, and I found myself carrying a peacefully sleeping Aure back to her room. She had curled up against me by the fire, dozing off in my lap, and I couldn't bring myself to disturb her rest. Though she was a solid weight in my arms, she instinctively wrapped her arms around my neck and tucked her head beneath my chin when I lifted her. It made navigating the stairs easier, her body clinging to mine even in her sleep.

Cam walked alongside us, ever-watchful, her presence a comforting shadow. When we reached Aure's chamber door, she wordlessly held it open for me, her expression softening slightly as she watched me carry Aure inside. Once we were in, Cam quietly pulled the heavy door closed behind us, leaving us in the peaceful quiet of the room.

Gently, I laid her on the bed, carefully slipping off her shoes and tucking her under the covers. After undressing, I slid in beside her. Instinctively, she rolled toward me, wrapping her arms around me as I smoothed her hair. I breathed in her familiar scent—sea salt, coconut, and citrus mingled with the faint scent of the smokiness from tonight's fires. The soothing combination lulled me, and as her comfort enveloped me, I let myself drift off into sleep.

I awoke early, as I had most mornings, to the gentle nudging and whisper of Cam. "Your Grace, it's time."

I groaned softly as I clung to Aure for just a moment longer, kissing her forehead before finally pulling myself away. The warmth of her body was a tempting reason to stay, but I knew I had work to do. Rolling out of bed, I slipped into the robe that Cam held out for me, the cool fabric brushing against my skin.

We had an arrangement, Cam and I, where she would quietly wake me before the rest of the palace stirred. It helped keep the gossip at bay, but more importantly, it allowed us to focus on my training. I wanted to be in peak physical condition and sharpen my skills, especially with my runic broadsword. Perfection in battle was no longer just a goal, it was a necessity.

After a quick splash of water on my face to shake off the remnants of sleep, I changed into my training clothes. I tugged on a pair of tight-fitting leather pants, the material clinging to my legs which offered both protection and flexibility. The snug fit felt familiar, empowering. I fastened the buckle at my waist, making sure the pants hugged my hips securely.

Next, I slipped into a form-fitting shirt, the fabric stretching across my chest and shoulders, allowing for a full range of motion. I admired the way the shirt molded to my body. It was functional, yes, but it also made me feel strong, like I was preparing for something important.

I walked into the outer chamber where Cam waited for me. She raised an eyebrow as she looked me over, a smirk playing on her lips. "You look ready to take on the world," she said with a teasing tone, her voice low enough not to disturb Aure. Though there was genuine respect in her eyes.

I gave her a quick grin, adjusting the sword strapped to my back. "I'd better be." I nodded, slipping into my boots. "Let's go."

We quietly left the chamber, the heavy door closing behind us with a soft click. We nodded to Frank, who lazily took his seat outside the door, watching over Aure's chambers. The cool air of the early morning greeted us as we made our way through the palace corridors, still quiet with the lingering stillness of sleep. Outside, the courtyard bathed in the dim light of pre-dawn, the air crisp with the promise of another cold day.

"Where are we training today?" I asked, adjusting my robe as we walked side by side.

"The western courtyard," Cam replied. "It's still secluded enough, and most of the servants won't be out and about for at least another hour. We'll have some privacy."

I nodded, appreciating her foresight. Our routine had become almost second nature. For nearly a week she woke me early, training before the day's chaos descended, and ensuring that I was as prepared as possible for whatever battles lay ahead.

As we entered the courtyard, the training grounds were empty, save for the faint clink of distant armor and the occasional rustle of wind through the trees. Cam handed me my broadsword, the runic symbols etched along its blade gleaming faintly in the dim light.

"You've been improving," she said, her tone more businesslike now. "But today, I want to focus on precision. Your strength is there, but you need to be faster, more deliberate with your strikes."

I gripped the hilt of the sword and nodded, feeling the familiar weight settle in my hands as its magic hummed. "I'm ready."

We took our positions, Cam watching me with a critical eye as I began moving through the drills. The blade sliced through the air with purpose, each swing calculated, every movement deliberate. Cam circled me, offering corrections, pushing me harder, ensuring that I wasn't just strong but also fast and precise.

"Remember, speed and accuracy will save you more than brute force," she reminded me, her voice sharp with focus. "Don't over-commit to your swings. Keep your movements tight."

I nodded, adjusting my grip and stance, repeating the drill over and over until my muscles burned and my breath came in ragged gasps. Cam didn't relent, and I appreciated it. This was what I needed—discipline, focus, preparation.

After several adjusted strikes, my body moved in perfect sync with the sword. The runes on the blade hummed as it cut through the cool morning breeze, each stroke controlled, deliberate.

"Faster," Cam urged, her sharp eyes on my every move. "Tighten up your swings. Don't waste energy."

The tight fabric of my shirt clung to my skin, absorbing the growing heat as I moved with increasing speed and precision. Each swing, each step, felt more fluid, more controlled, the leather of my outfit supporting every motion.

Cam continued to circle me, occasionally stepping in to correct my stance or offer advice. "Good. Keep it tight, Orla. Your body needs to respond instantly, not with brute force, but with precision."

I gritted my teeth, focusing on the rhythm of the drills. The burn in my muscles finally became a satisfying ache, a reminder that I was pushing myself further every day. After several grueling rounds, and what felt like hours, she finally called for a break. I wiped the sweat from my brow, my chest heaving as I caught my breath.

"You're getting there," Cam said, a small smile playing on her lips. "But don't think I'm going easy on you tomorrow."

I chuckled, shaking my head. "I wouldn't expect anything less."

As we stood there, the sun finally peeked over the horizon, casting its golden light over the palace grounds. I took a deep breath, the cool air filling my lungs, feeling a sense of accomplishment despite the long day ahead.

"Okay, I should go relieve Frank before Aure wakes up and starts wondering why we both aren't around," Cam said, gathering herself. She gave a slight bow, and I nodded in response.

"Yeah, I'm going to try and find my father, see if I can convince him to let me join the next wave heading to the battleground," I said, adjusting the sheath on my back and sliding my sword into place.

Cam hesitated, her eyes filled with concern. "And what has Aure said about you joining the front?" Her tone was gentle but probing, as if she already knew the answer but needed to hear it from me.

I shrugged, avoiding her gaze for a moment. "We haven't really had that conversation yet," I admitted. "She knows I've been thinking about it, but I don't think she's ready to face the idea of me leaving."

Cam sighed, crossing her arms. "Orla, you know she's going to have strong feelings about this. She just lost Eamon under her care. She's not going to want you heading into that kind of danger."

"I know," I replied softly, finally meeting her gaze. "But I can't just sit here while others are fighting. It's not who I am."

Cam's expression softened, and she placed a hand on my shoulder. "Just talk to her first. She deserves to hear it from you, not through some rushed goodbye."

I nodded, knowing she was right. "I will."

With a final look, Cam turned and left, heading off to find Frank. I stood alone for a moment, the weight of the decision settling on my shoulders. Convincing my father would be one thing, convincing Aure would be another.

As I left the training yard, my mind buzzed with thoughts of how to approach my father. It was early enough that most of the palace was still quiet, which worked in my favor. If I could get him alone, perhaps I could sway him before the usual chaos of the day took hold.

I headed straight for his office, the place where he often retreated to plot strategies and handle matters of state. My boots echoed off the stone floors as I walked through the long corridors, my pace quick but purposeful. I rehearsed my arguments in my head, imagining the conversation, but as I neared his office, the faint murmur of voices stopped me in my tracks.

I hesitated for a moment before continuing down the hallway, the door to his office slightly ajar. The familiar scent of my father's cigars wafted through the air, but there was something else too, sickly sweet smell of anis and cherries. I heard soft laughter and... then something far more intimate.

Like being caught in a trance, I pushed the door open quietly, and what I saw made me freeze.

There, in his chair, my father sat with his robe open, leaned back, completely at ease. Straddling his wide bare girth was my Aunt Lili, her arms draped around his neck as she whispered something in his ear. Her dress was bunched up around her hips, her posture intimate as her hips moved, and his hands rested possessively on her waist.

My stomach churned, and for a moment, I couldn't breathe. They hadn't noticed me yet, too absorbed in each other to realize someone was watching. My heart pounded in my chest, and I stepped back instinctively, the heel of my boot making a soft sound against the floor.

Lili's head whipped around at the noise, her violet eyes going wide with surprise. My father's cold blue gaze followed hers, locking onto me. There was a flicker of something, shock, maybe annoyance, that crossed his face, but it was quickly replaced with his usual calculated demeanor.

"Orla," he said, his voice calm, though his eyes narrowed slightly. "I assume you have something urgent to discuss."

Lili shifted her hips slightly, smirking but confidently made no move to cover herself. I swallowed the bile rising in my throat. This wasn't something I could unsee, no matter how much I wished I could.

"I... I was looking for you," I managed to say, my voice sounding far more composed than I felt. "But clearly, this is a bad time."

My father's gaze didn't waver, and he simply leaned back further in his chair, as if daring me to say more.

I turned on my heel and walked out without another word, my heart pounding and my mind racing.

AURELIA

Chapter 22

"Gods, *Orla, if this seamstress pokes me one more time, I swear I'll fire her."* I sent through our bond, my frustration spilling over as I mentally reached out to wherever Orla had disappeared to this time.

Lately, it felt like Orla was always running off, leaving me to wake up to Frank's snores outside my door or, if I was lucky, the soft press of one of her adorable kisses at my ear. But today, I'd slept in later than usual, only to be roused by servants ushered in by Cam, no Orla in sight. They whisked me off to a small room on the main floor of the palace that looked like some sort of fitting room. The full-length mirrors lining the walls and the pedestal step in the center made me wonder if the seamstress always worked here, on site, or if this was just used on special occasions.

Still, there was nothing from Orla. No sign of her, no words through our bond, just the faint hum of emotions swirling in a chaotic mess that I couldn't quite decipher. The longer I waited, the more I felt the restlessness prickling under my skin. Something was off.

I really hoped it wasn't because of last night. The thought gnawed at me, making my chest tighten. I'd experienced pleasure before, many times and in various ways, but what we shared beneath the waves had been different. Intimate in a way I wasn't used to.

And now? Silence.

Lady Lili glided into the room, pulling me abruptly from my thoughts. I blinked in surprise at her appearance. She wore a strikingly elegant, dark violet gown that clung to her curves with a form-fitting silhouette, its luxurious fabric shimmering faintly as it caught the light. The dress flared out gracefully just below her calves, the satin pooling around her feet in delicate ripples. Tiny, gleaming crystals dotted along the neckline, drawing the eye to the deep, seductive plunge, revealing a surprising amount of cleavage which were unnaturally perky for someone of her supposed age. The intricate detailing around the bodice shimmered with every subtle movement, adding an air of opulence and allure.

Lady Lili clasped her hands together, a look of satisfaction spreading across her face as she let out a shrill, "Oooh yes." Her sharp gaze swept over me, taking in every detail of the gown with an almost appraising admiration. It was clear she was savoring the moment, her eyes glinting with approval.

"Vestra, darling, your work is simply exquisite as always," Lady Lili purred, her voice rich with self-satisfaction. She admired herself in the wall of mirrors, the fabric of her gown swishing elegantly as she gave a little twirl, showing it off. Turning back to me with a playful smile, her eyes gleamed with unmistakable hubris. "Aure, what do you think?" she asked, her tone laced with arrogance. "This will be my gown for tomorrow's celebration."

"Lovely." I gave a tight smile and a polite nod to Lady Lili, though I had to admit, my gown was a true masterpiece. The regal bodice was crafted from midnight blue silk, structured by boning that emphasized its form. It shimmered with delicate gold stars and celestial motifs, intricately embroidered in a lace-like pattern that wound around my chest and waist, accentuating every detail. The neckline dipped subtly, framed by gilded embroidery, and flowed into off-the-shoulder sleeves, adorned with delicate loops of golden chains and embellishments that graced my arms.

From my waist, the full skirt cascaded in luxurious layers of matching midnight blue fabric, overlaid with golden constellations, moons, and stars, each one seemingly twinkling in the soft light. Rich gold accents lined the hem, heightening the celestial theme, while layers of soft white tulle peeked out beneath, casting an ethereal glow around me. At the center of the gown, a crescent moon, crafted from brilliant gold, served as the focal point, surrounded by beadwork and gemstones that mirrored a starlit sky.

Vestra draped a final layer of fabric from the hips, ornamented with additional golden patterns. The gown resembled the night sky itself, a majestic cosmic embrace. Even as I stood there, I couldn't help but feel that this dress was an elegant, otherworldly garment, fit for a goddess of the night.

"It's such a delight to finally have a niece who enjoys dressing up," Lady Lili mused with a playful smile. "From a very young age, Orla insisted she was allergic to every kind of fabric. Just to avoid wearing the proper attire expected of her station."

I smiled, imagining a young Orla, hands on her hips, fiercely making her case.

"We could barely keep her in clothes at all during those early years," Lady Lili continued with a chuckle. "It was common to catch her, naked as a jaybird, darting through the palace halls or tearing through the gardens chasing the cats."

A giggle escaped me, but was short-lived as Vestra pricked me with a pin again.

"But eventually, we realized she'd at least keep pants on, so despite Oric's frustration, we convinced him to let her wear whatever she was willing to keep on," she said with a soft laugh, tucking a strand of her dark hair behind her ear as she rolled her violet eyes.

"I'm gonna need ya to step out of this now, m'lady," Vestra interrupted, her accent thick and rough, a pin still clamped between her teeth as she spoke. Instantly, two maids stepped forward, expertly unfastening the gown at my back, loosening the laces, and gently peeling it off my body, leaving me in my undergarments. Luckily, I had grown accustomed to such things over the years. Rielle and I had attended more than our fair share of royal events together, often doing dress fittings side by side. Today, though, she was out training Orlondia's warriors on the proper use of a blast arrow without injuring our own troops.

I let out a heavy sigh, wishing I had her company right now instead of Lady Lili's oddly appraising gaze. "Dear, I'd suggest you eat lightly today. No salt either. You wouldn't want this gown to fit poorly tomorrow," Lady Lili said with a sugary sweet tone that didn't quite match the sharpness of her words.

I bit back a retort, forcing a smile instead. Lady Lili's eyes were back on the gown now, her fingers delicately brushing over the intricate embroidery as Vestra made final adjustments. The maids draped a light robe over my shoulders, offering a small semblance of privacy as I stepped off the fitting platform.

"I'll take that under advisement," I replied, trying to keep my tone neutral. Inside, I could feel frustration bubbling up. Between the endless preparations for tomorrow's celebration and the constant scrutiny of everyone around me, I was beginning to feel suffocated.

Vestra finally pulled the pin from her mouth, examining the gown with a critical eye before nodding to herself. "It'll be ready for ya in the mornin'. The final touches will be done by then, m'lady."

I nodded my thanks, already moving toward the door. Lady Lili's gaze followed me, and just as I reached the threshold, she spoke again, her voice cutting through the air.

"And Aurelia, remember…" She paused, a smile playing on her lips. "You only get one chance to make the right impression."

I turned back to her, her words heavy with unspoken meaning. "Of course, Lady Lili," I replied smoothly. "I wouldn't dream of anything less."

With that, I swept out of the room, the heavy wooden doors closing behind me. The moment I was out of her sight, I let out a frustrated breath, tugging the robe tighter around me. I had some experience with social maneuvering, though never on such a grand scale. It was becoming clear, however, that in the days to come, every word and gesture would carry weight.

I began to make my way down the hallway, the cool stone floor under my bare feet grounding me. As I turned the corner, I spotted Orla ahead, her confident stride unmistakable even from a distance. Relief washed over me. At least now, I could escape the endless scrutiny for a little while longer.

"Aure!" Orla called out as soon as she saw me, her eyes lighting up with that familiar warmth. "How did the fitting go?"

I couldn't help but roll my eyes. "As well as it could, considering Lady Lili seems to think fitting into a dress is the only thing that matters in the world."

Orla's expression shifted the moment I mentioned Lady Lili. Her face paled, and a look of silent shock replaced her usual warmth. She stopped walking, her eyes wide and unfocused, as if I'd just told her something devastating. I watched as her hand instinctively gripped her stomach. Her face tightened like she was fighting the urge to be sick.

"Orla?" I asked, my voice soft with concern. "Are you alright?"

She didn't answer right away, her gaze fixed on some distant point beyond the hallway. I reached out, gently touching her arm, and that seemed to pull her back to the present. She blinked a few times, her lips parting like she was trying to say something, but couldn't quite find the words.

"Lady Lili..." she whispered, her voice barely audible. She swallowed hard, her throat working visibly as she tried to steady herself.

"What is it?" I asked, my worry growing. "What's wrong?"

Orla shook her head, but she still looked like she was ill. She opened her mouth to speak again, but no words came out. The silence between us stretched, thick and heavy, and I felt a growing sense of unease twisting in my gut.

Finally, she exhaled shakily, her voice fragile. "I... I can't talk about it right now. Not here."

I didn't press her. Whatever had caused this reaction was clearly something deep and troubling. Instead, I squeezed her hand gently, giving her the space to collect herself. "Okay," I said softly. "Whenever you're ready."

She nodded, her jaw clenched tightly, and took a deep breath, forcing herself to move again. We walked in silence, her usual confidence replaced by a fragile, tense energy. I could feel the weight of whatever haunted her, but I knew better than to push her right now.

Whatever it was, I had never seen Orla look so shaken before. The image of her Aunt Lili flickered in my mind, sending a chill down my spine. At first, I wasn't sure what was happening, but then a memory from Orla's mind surged through our bond. I saw King Oric's office and... "Oh my gods!" The words escaped me before I could stop them, and I yanked Orla to a halt.

Orla's eyes widened in panic, and she quickly gripped my hand tighter. She pulled me toward a quiet corner behind one of the grand tapestries hanging in the hallway. Her grip was tight, and I could feel the tremor in her hand.

"Keep your voice down!" she hissed, her face pale and eyes swirling with stormy cobalt blue. She pressed her back against the wall, taking a deep breath as if steadying herself. "We cannot talk about this here."

My heart was racing, my mind trying to process what I'd just glimpsed. *"Orla, that was your father and Lady Lili? How long have you known?"* I sent through our bond, shifting easily into it.

She shook her head; her gaze was distant. "I only found out today," she whispered, the bitterness in her voice unmistakable. "I went to talk to him about joining the next wave to the front lines. And instead, I walked in on... that."

I stared at her, still in shock. *"Your aunt... and your father? That's..."*

Orla's expression hardened, but her voice stayed hushed. "I know. It's disgusting. And now I don't know what to do."

"Wait," I started, my voice sharp as I pulled away from her grasp. "You were going to talk to your father about joining the front? You were actually going to leave without telling me?"

Orla blinked and her eyes swirled to a sky blue, clearly not expecting that from me. "Aure, I…"

"No," I cut her off, the anger bubbling up before I could contain it. "Are you out of your mind? After everything we've shared? After everything we did last night? You were just going to slip away and throw yourself into the middle of a battlefield? Without even discussing it with me?"

She looked down, her jaw tightening. "I didn't want to worry you. I was going to tell you after…"

"After you'd made the decision for both of us?" I spat, my hands trembling as I crossed my arms over my chest. "Orla, we're bonded! How could you not think that something like this wouldn't affect me?"

Her eyes flashed, the stormy blue deepening almost black as her frustration mirrored my own. "I know it affects you, Aure, but I didn't want to burden you with more! You already have so much to deal with, and the war is getting worse. I have to do something."

"And leaving me behind is your solution?" I shot back, my voice rising. "What the hell do you think I've been doing, Orla? I've been fighting, strategizing, trying to keep everything together, just like you. But the idea of you going to the front without me, without even asking." I turned away from her, my eyes burning from the tears threatening to fall.

"I didn't want you to feel like you had to come with me!" she snapped, her fists clenching at her sides. "You are much better with the people here. You know more about how to handle all the duties of the kingdom. You are better with the diplomats. And … I didn't want to drag you into more danger."

"That's not your choice to make," I said, my voice low but filled with frustration. A tear slid down my cheek. "We're supposed to make these

278

decisions together. You can't protect me from everything, Orla, just like I can't always protect you."

Orla's breath came in short, angry bursts as she stared at me, her jaw tight. "I wasn't just trying to protect you. I was trying to do something that mattered! Rein is leaving for the front, and he'll need support. I can't just sit back while everyone else fights for our survival."

"I get that," I replied, my voice softening slightly, though the anger still simmered beneath the surface. "But you don't have to do everything alone anymore. We're partners, mates. You don't get to shut me out just because you think you're protecting me or because you want to be the hero."

Orla ran a hand through her hair, frustration and guilt battling in her expression. "I'm sorry, Aure. I should've told you. Cam said—"

I whipped around, my loose hair swirling in fiery waves, my anger igniting even more. "Cam? She knew?" I cut her off, disbelief and fury flaring in my chest. Seeing her begin to nod, something snapped inside me. I was done. Done with this conversation, done with this day, done with Cam, and done with Orla's excuses.

Without another word, I stormed down the hall toward my chambers, Orla's hurried footsteps following close behind. I reached my door, threw it open, and slammed it shut behind me, the sound echoing through the room as I turned the lock. The startled faces of Cam and a servant girl greeted me, both of them standing at attention, clearly shocked by my abrupt entrance.

I locked eyes with Cam, anger and betrayal simmering in my gaze. A low growl escaped me, my frustration boiling over. I turned to the trembling servant girl. "Get out. Now." My voice was sharp, commanding, and the poor thing didn't hesitate, darting toward the door, unlocking it, and fleeing.

But Orla wasn't far behind, and she slipped in through the open door before I could shut it again. "Aure, please," she pleaded, her voice desperate.

I turned away from her, pacing toward the window, my emotions still raging inside me. "Please what, Orla? Please understand that you and Cam are plotting behind my back? Please forgive you for not trusting me enough to talk to me first?"

Orla took a cautious step closer, her voice soft but steady. "It wasn't like that. I wasn't plotting anything. I was scared, Aure. Scared of what you'd say, of what you'd think."

I shot her a fierce look, my anger flaring once more. "And that's supposed to make it, okay? You thought you could just decide what's best for me without including me in the conversation?"

Orla's shoulders sagged, her eyes filled with guilt. "I'm sorry. I just... I didn't want to hurt you."

I shook my head, my heart pounding. "After everything we've shared—everything we did last night—you still don't trust me enough to let me in?"

Orla winced at my words, her face crumpled as she realized the weight of what I was saying. "I do trust you, I do. I just—"

"Then act like it," I snapped, cutting her off again. "We're in this together, Orla. Stop treating me like I'm fragile or like you have to do this alone."

Orla's face hardened, her jaw tightening. "I am acting like it," she said, her voice low but resolute. "I'm doing what needs to be done. And right now, that means joining the fight at the front. It's not about shutting you out, Aure. It's about doing what I've trained my whole life for."

I stared at her, incredulous, my chest tight with a whirlwind of emotions. "So, that's it? You've already made up your mind?" My voice cracked with disbelief, my magic churning like boiling water under my skin.

Cam stepped forward cautiously, her hands raised slightly, as if to calm the storm between us. "Your Grace," she said softly, "Orla didn't mean to hide this from you. She was just trying to—"

"Cam, stop," I cut her off sharply, the anger flashing in my eyes again as my head jerked her direction. "This isn't your fight. Get out."

Cam hesitated, her gaze flicking between me and Orla. "But—"

"*Now,*" I snapped, my voice cold and final.

Cam gave a slight nod, stepping backward toward the door. "I'll be right outside if you need anything," she said quietly, bowing her head slightly before slipping out of the room, closing the door behind her with a soft click.

The room felt stifling, the silence heavy between us. Orla's expression remained firm, but I could see the flicker of uncertainty in her eyes. She stood tall, determined, but I could feel the weight of everything between us pressing down on her too.

"I'm not doing this to hurt you, Aure. That's the last thing I wanted," she said after a moment, her voice steady but softer now. "I'm doing it because it's what's right. I can't just sit here while others fight and die. I need to be out there, protecting our people, protecting our kingdoms, protecting you."

I turned away from her, facing toward the window as my eyes burned with all the unshed tears. My hands clenched into fists at my sides as the emotions roiled inside me, too big to contain anymore. "I know," I whispered, my voice barely audible. "I know you have to go. I get it. But gods, Orla, I'm terrified."

She moved toward me, her steps tentative. "Aure..."

I shook my head, my voice trembling as the tears finally spilled over, my back still turned to her. "I'm scared I'm going to lose you, Orla. Every day, this war gets closer, and I can feel it slipping out of control. And now... now you want to go right into the heart of it." My breath hitched, and I hugged my arms around myself as if to hold in the pieces that felt like they were falling apart.

Orla's hand gently touched my shoulder, and I turned to face her, my tears streaming down my cheeks. Her face softened, the tough exterior she'd tried to maintain faltering as she took in the sight of me, broken and vulnerable. "I don't want to lose you," I whispered, my voice raw and aching. "I can't... I can't survive that."

Her expression was pained, and for a moment, the warrior in her slipped away, replaced by the soft parts of her, that only seemed to show for me. "You won't lose me, Aure," she murmured, pulling me into her strong arms, her warmth surrounding me. "I swear, I'll come back to you."

I buried my face in her chest, my tears soaking into her shirt as the fear, anger, and helplessness finally broke through. Orla held me tight, stroking my hair, but I could feel the tension in her muscles, the pull of duty and the weight of her decision pressing on both of us.

"I'll always come back to you," she repeated, her voice barely a whisper, but the uncertainty lingered in the air between us. Neither of us could truly promise that.

My tears subsided slightly as I looked up at her. "Is that the only reason you've been so distant today?"

"Yes, mostly," she sighed, her fingers tangling absently in my hair as her gaze drifted toward the window. "I mean, I was also pretty shaken after finding my aunt with my father like that."

I curled back onto her chest, feeling the tension still radiating off her. "Yeah, that was disturbing. How long do you think that's been going on?"

Orla exhaled slowly, her breath warm against my hair as she wrapped one of my curls around her finger. "I don't know," she whispered, her voice heavy with frustration. "It's hard to say. No one talks about these things openly. But knowing my father...he's always been...strategic." She paused, resting her chin on my head. "What do you think I should do about it? Do I confront them? Do I just... pretend I never saw it?"

I took a breath, trying to find the right words. "Orla, this isn't something you can just ignore. I don't know what this means for the kingdom, for you and your family, but you can't carry this weight alone."

Her hand dropped to my shoulder, and she held me tighter to her. I could hear her heart beating fast. She spoke softly. "I don't even know where to begin. I feel... betrayed. And ashamed." Her voice cracked on the last word.

"You don't have to decide anything right now," I said softly. "But you're not alone in this, Orla. We'll figure everything out together."

She held me for a while longer, the silence between us filled with the weight of unspoken fears and the uncertainty of what was to come. Even in the quiet, I could feel the magic of our bond growing stronger than any of the chaos surrounding us.

"Aure," she whispered into my ear, her voice soft but edged with regret. "I'm sorry, but I have to go. Frank and Rielle are expecting me." She smoothed my hair once more, but I gently pushed back, slipping out of her grasp.

Re-clasping my robe, I stepped away, my fingers tightening on the fabric as if to anchor myself. "I understand. I need to get dressed and make sure everything is ready for the party tomorrow." I hesitated, then asked, my voice quieter, "Will you still be coming over tonight? To... you know, sleep?"

The vulnerability in my tone felt heavy, and I couldn't help but glance away, unsure of how she would respond.

Orla paused, her eyes softening as she reached out to touch my arm, her thumb brushing lightly over my skin. "Of course I'll be there, Aure. I wouldn't miss it," she said, her voice filled with sincerity. "I'll sneak in after everything is sorted with the recruits, and I'll hold you all night, I promise." She flashed a smirk at me.

I nodded, feeling a wave of relief wash over me, though the weight of everything still lingered. She gave me a small, reassuring smile before stepping toward the door, her movements slow, almost reluctant. "We'll get through this," she added, her voice firmer now, as if she were trying to convince both of us. "I'll see you tonight."

As the door clicked shut behind her, I let out a long breath, the room suddenly feeling too large and too quiet without her. The day stretched ahead of me, filled with preparations for the party, but all I wanted was for the night to come—when everything would feel a little less heavy with Orla by my side.

I stood for a moment, collecting myself, then turned toward the wardrobe, pulling out my dress for the day. The party preparations were a welcome distraction from the swirling thoughts in my mind, but even as I focused on the tasks at hand, the promise of the evening lingered at the edge of my thoughts. Tomorrow was not only the engagement party, but Orla's birthday. The night's celebrations would culminate in a grand display of fire magic at midnight, illuminating the skies above Orlondia.

The thought of the fireworks, the tradition of ringing in her birthday under the brilliant display of magical lights, brought a small smile to my face. It was a tradition steeped in history, meant to symbolize the bright future of the kingdom and the strength of its rulers. This year, it would carry deeper meaning for us, as Orla's upcoming role in the war weighed heavily on my mind.

I wondered how our bond would handle being separated if Orla was off at the front while I stayed behind to manage the alliance obligations. The thought of distance between us made my chest tighten, and instinctively, I reached out to the too-quiet green thread of magic that connected me to Azura. My connection with her had felt fainter lately, almost as if it were being overshadowed by my growing bond with Orla. I sent a wave of warmth and sweetness through the link to my Sea Dragon. *"Azura? How is the egg?"*

A soft shiver of warmth responded, and my signet glowed faintly beneath the mint-green sleeve of my dress. *"We are well,"* Azura's voice hummed through me. *"Safe in our home in Crystal Reef. We sleep, as it is nearly time for the hatching."*

Relief flooded me, though a trace of unease remained. Some weakening of our connection was expected, given that Azura had to pour a part of her magic into the egg to nourish and sustain the baby. But this disruption felt different, and I couldn't help but wonder if it had something to do with the mate bond forming between Orla and me.

"Does my bond with Orla bother you or the baby?" My anxiety seeped through the question, but Azura's calming energy enveloped me.

"No, I don't think so. It only disrupts our bond because you have not yet sealed your mate bond. If it's anything like ours," her voice became more serious. *"It will become imperative that you do so, or it could cause problems for everyone."* Her words left me both intrigued and worried.

I had tried to seal the bond with Orla when we were together under the ocean, but it hadn't worked—not the way it should have. Maybe it was because I hadn't explained everything to her, or perhaps because I had already used my song for Azura. I wasn't sure. All I knew was that time was running out, and I needed to find a way to make this right before it unraveled everything.

Azura's deep, worried thoughts broke through my mind like a dark wave. *"You do know what happens to unsealed bonds, yes?"*

A cold shiver ran through me. I had only heard tales—whispers really—of the giant Sea Dragons who refused to be mated, choosing instead to perform dark, forbidden magic to sever the chaotic energy between them. It was said to be a desperate act, and I had never witnessed it myself. Nor had I ever seen a fully grown, unmated Sea Dragon.

"Um, I'm not sure I do," I nervously admitted, sending the thought to Azura, the anxiety curling tighter inside me.

"If a Sea Dragon chooses not to seal their mate bond, for any reason—because it is their choice—then, to prevent the magic from becoming chaotic and destructive, they must perform the Ritual of Severance or the Ritual of Sacrifice." The weight of her words hit me like a crashing wave, so hard that my legs weakened beneath me. I stumbled, sitting down on the edge of the bed as my heart raced.

"What if we can't figure out how to seal our bond?" The words flitted softly along our bond, as I pressed my hands against my cheeks, trying in vain to stop the tears welling in my eyes. *"I don't even really understand what Severance or Sacrifice mean... but I know we want our bond sealed. I... I love Orla."*

Azura's energy shifted, protective but tense, as her response came. *"The Ritual of Severance permanently breaks the connection between mates, but at a terrible cost. Severance leaves both souls diminished— their magic is weakened, and their lives are shortened. The process is agonizing, not just physically but emotionally, as they must willingly sever the bond fate intended for them."* A shudder ran through me as dread tightened in my chest.

"Alternatively," she continued, her words washed over me. *"They can choose Sacrifice. One mate gives their life to empower the other, restoring*

balance but at the ultimate cost. The surviving mate gains great power, but they are forever marked by the loss, and the scar of their sorrow leaves an imprint on the world itself. Sometimes, this act can heal the land damaged by their uncontrolled magic... but the toll is unimaginable."

My stomach twisted as I absorbed her words, the fear settling deep within me. *"Neither of those things have been done in eons. We will figure out how to seal your bond,"* Azura reassured. Her presence in my mind felt warm, but the gravity of her explanation hung between us like a storm cloud, dark and heavy.

"I must rest now, Aure. We will figure this out," Azura's voice echoed in my mind, her presence gradually fading as she withdrew into the background. The glow of my signet dimmed along with her, leaving a soft warmth in its place.

I let out a slow breath, the weight of her words still pressing down on me. With a heavy heart, I finished readying myself, trying to shake off the lingering dread. There was still so much to do today, but the uncertainty of what lay ahead gnawed at the back of my mind.

For now, though, I had to focus on the details of the party. The decorations, the guests, the catering— I wanted everything to be perfect for tomorrow. I felt this night may be one of the last moments of joy before we faced whatever came next.

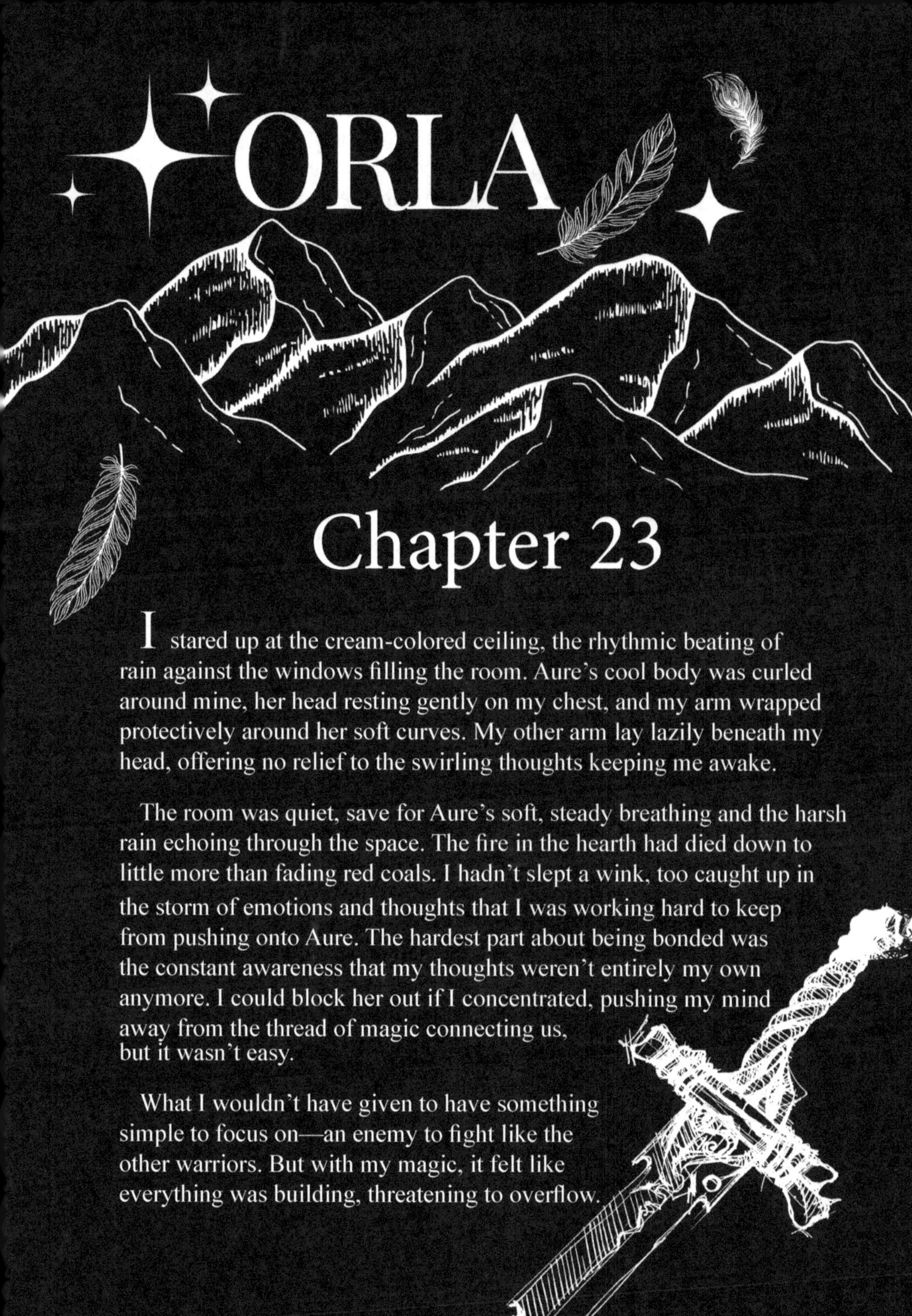

ORLA

Chapter 23

I stared up at the cream-colored ceiling, the rhythmic beating of rain against the windows filling the room. Aure's cool body was curled around mine, her head resting gently on my chest, and my arm wrapped protectively around her soft curves. My other arm lay lazily beneath my head, offering no relief to the swirling thoughts keeping me awake.

The room was quiet, save for Aure's soft, steady breathing and the harsh rain echoing through the space. The fire in the hearth had died down to little more than fading red coals. I hadn't slept a wink, too caught up in the storm of emotions and thoughts that I was working hard to keep from pushing onto Aure. The hardest part about being bonded was the constant awareness that my thoughts weren't entirely my own anymore. I could block her out if I concentrated, pushing my mind away from the thread of magic connecting us, but it wasn't easy.

What I wouldn't have given to have something simple to focus on—an enemy to fight like the other warriors. But with my magic, it felt like everything was building, threatening to overflow.

And this damned weather. It was worse than I'd ever seen before. Sure, the ice and rain were typical for this time of year, but not like this. Not with the tides rising and flooding the lower areas along the coast. There were even reports we might get hit by a snowstorm during the party. Maybe it would be enough to keep people from attending this stupid event.

I knew Aure wanted tonight to be special, for it to be a celebration to remember. But honestly, I'd be perfectly content staying in this bed with her for the next few days, far away from the expectations and responsibilities that waited outside.

Then there was my fucking father. I had always suspected something between him and my aunt, but I never wanted to acknowledge it—let alone see it for myself. My stomach churned at the memory, the image burned into my mind. The affair left me with far more questions than just about his fidelity. I had always felt closer to my aunt, and I'd always known I resembled her more than my mother, her sister. Now, the possibilities swirled in my head, making it hard to focus.

Why didn't they try to hide it or deny what I saw? Should I tell my mother? Would it ruin them? No. My father has always made it painfully clear—he does whatever he wants, whenever he pleases, without fear of facing any consequences.

I struggled with thoughts of the bond I shared with Aure. Apparently, we needed to "seal" it—whatever that meant. Honestly, none of that ancient magic or fate nonsense really mattered to me. What I knew for sure was that I had never felt this way about anyone before. I didn't think it had much to do with gods, destiny, or magic. I simply loved her. I loved her fiery temper, the way she held onto her grace even when she was about to unleash hell. Her bubbly optimism tempered with a wise charisma that made people listen. The way she carried herself with such strength, yet could be so gentle—like how she would patiently capture a lost bee in the palace, carefully carrying it to a blooming flower in the garden. Anyone who saw that would fall madly in love with her, too.

I gently twirled a loose curl that had fallen across her face around my finger, a small smile tugging at my lips as I watched her sleep. Sleep finally claimed me as my thoughts drifted to Aure, and the feel of her against me.

Liquid heat surged through me as tiny sparks of magic teased the sensitive skin between my legs. Slowly, I stirred awake, feeling the cool, deliberate touch of Aure's fingers tracing down my left thigh. Her soft, lingering kisses along my collarbone pulled me further into consciousness, each one sending shivers through my body.

My eyes fluttered open, and I met Aure's mossy green gaze just as her lips closed around my nipple, a mischievous curl playing at the corners of her mouth. A gasp escaped me, the sensation shooting through my body like a spark.

"Good morning, Meles Tari," I groaned as her fingers slid lower, teasing the growing ache that stirred deep in my core.

She shot me a playful look, biting my nipple lightly before releasing it, her fingers making slow, lazy circles, inching ever closer to their target. "I need to know what that damn nickname means," she demanded smoothly.

Shock flashed across my face, my eyes shifting from magenta to sky blue. "Oh… um… I assumed you spoke the language of the ancient Fae."

Her smirk widened into a devilish grin as her finger slid through my wetness, teasingly circling the soft entrance of my ass. I let out a low growl of want, and she responded in a voice as smooth as silk, "And why, of all things, would you ever assume I spoke Fae?"

Her thumb grazed over my clit, so sensitive that I arched into her touch, craving—no, needing—more. My eyes changed back to the deep, rich magenta and my breath hitched as I struggled to form words. "Because... you're educated, and... you never asked about it before." My voice was barely a whisper, my focus unraveling with each teasing movement of her fingers along my slit.

She lingered at my entrance, teasingly slipping past it, gliding back toward my ass, and then returning to my clit. The slow, deliberate strokes drove me wild, heightening my need for her in a maddening combination of pleasure and frustration. "Tell me what it means," she hummed, her voice laced with the promise of the release I craved. Before I could answer, she lifted a cup of water, holding it above my breasts, tilting it slightly toward me.

Where in the world did she get that—and why was she about to pour it on me? The sound of rain outside grew louder, matching the surprise that flashed in my eyes that shifted to sky blue once more.

As she poured the icy cold water onto my chest, it pooled unnaturally between my breasts, lingering there as her eyes fixated on it. All the while, her fingers continued their slow, deliberate teasing, sliding from my ass to my clit and back again in maddening circles. With a sharp flick of her wrist, she tossed the wooden cup aside, the faint clatter barely audible over the storm raging outside.

The wicked sensations of the icy water and the relentless teasing of her fingers had me utterly distracted. My breath grew ragged, my heart pounding faster with every stroke. A moan escaped my lips, "Aure," a desperate plea for her to give in to my growing need to have her inside me. Gods, if she didn't do something soon, I was going to flip her over and take her ass myself.

Her other hand moved to the icy liquid pooling between my peaked breasts, and I felt the cold trail start to circle the base of each one. The water spiraled upward, tracing an icy path toward my nipples, a deliberate use of her water magic, teasing the fuck out of me. I groaned, clutching at the blanket beside me as my body trembled with desire. The liquid heat inside me grew stronger, dripping down my thighs as she quickened the movement of her fingers, still teasing, adding just enough pressure at my ass and clit with each pass to drive me wild.

"Tell me," speaking in a singsong tone, her gaze trailing up to my eyes and my heavy breaths, that wicked grin and adorable dimples appearing.

"It... means..." The words barely escaped my lips. I closed my eyes as the water reached my nipples, engulfing them, and they stiffened at the sudden chill. A shiver ran down my spine, settling deep in my core as her fingertip slowly pressed into my ass. "My beloved queen," I gasped out quickly before letting my head fall back, releasing another deep breath.

She paused for just a heartbeat, and in that moment, the water on my chest cascaded down around me. Then, suddenly, she was on top of me, her body pressing into mine as she crashed her lips against mine with a fierce, fevered passion. Her fingers, no longer teasing, pushed deep inside me, invading my pussy with a hard, reckless intensity. I was not prepared for her to consume me so completely.

I moaned into her mouth as her tongue swept into mine, her fingers pumping in and out with each thrust harder and claiming more than the last. I came undone, my body surrendering to the ecstasy that pulsed through me in waves. I convulsed, my legs shaking, tightening around her hand as she pushed deeper, her fingers reaching for more, drawing out every last ounce of my pleasure.

As I unraveled, the need for more overwhelmed me. I wanted her to need me as much as I needed her, to see that same hunger in her eyes. Placing my hands on her shoulders, I rolled us over until she was beneath me. Our connection broke briefly as we both tried to catch our breath, but I grinned. "On your stomach, Meles Tari."

The sparkle in her green eyes when I called her that and the bemused smile that followed spoke louder than any words. Without hesitation, she did as I commanded. I wrapped my fingers around her hips, lifting her ass into the air as I knelt between her legs. My hands caressed her soft, supple skin before I leaned down and bit one cheek, just hard enough to leave red imprints. She squeaked in surprised pleasure. I licked the spot, savoring the moment. Gods, how could she be so perfect in every way?

She turned her head, looking back at me with anticipation in her eyes. I let my magic heat my hand, warming it just enough to be pleasurable— hopefully not so much as to burn her. I was trying something new. Testing it, I placed my heated hand on my own thigh; it was hot, almost too hot, but not unbearable. Good. I licked my lips, my eyes darkening to a deep purple as my desire to hear her scream my name surged within me, fueling my need.

I reached my heated hand between her legs, and she moaned, spreading herself wider for me. My fingers found her clit, already wet with her readiness, and I teased her clit, rubbing it hard, and deliberately. The heat intensified with every motion, and she rocked against my hand, pushing her ass back into my hips. Her breathing grew heavier, and I couldn't take my eyes off her, watching the way her breasts swayed, her body moving perfectly in rhythm with mine.

She moaned loudly as I slid my fingers along her center, thrusting two deep inside her, curling them just right. Her back arched, and she pressed forward into the pillows, another moan escaping her lips. A smirk tugged at my mouth as I reached around her hip, pulling her back against me, refusing to let her slip away so easily. My fingers pumped in and out, each thrust deeper and harder, until I slid in a third, then a fourth finger. When the fourth entered, her head snapped up, her back arching hard as she cried out, "Orla, oh, fuck!"

I leaned forward, pushing and stretching her tight pussy with my four fingers, whispering low near her ear, "You're such a good girl for me, Meles Tari." My movements quickened, thrusting deep and hard, claiming her as mine. As I kissed along her sweat-slicked back, I murmured, "My beloved Queen," my voice laced with possessive heat.

Her knuckles whitened as she gripped the pillow, surrendering fully to her orgasm. The tension in her body built to a peak, her breath momentarily stopping as her pussy pulsed and clamped hard around my hand. My thumb circled her clit, and she let out a loud scream, collapsing forward, but not far—my hand firmly held her hips against me. Her legs shook, her entire body quaked, and I growled in satisfaction as I unraveled her. The whole palace seemed to shake, lightning flashing and thunder cracking loudly, echoing our release.

I released her, and she collapsed into the pillow with a sweet giggle. I plopped down beside her as she rolled over to face me, grabbing my hand, still slick with her cum. Her eyes locked onto mine as she licked each of my fingers clean, sending a shiver skittering across my body. I enjoyed the sight far too much. Reaching under her chin, I gently pulled her toward me, capturing her mouth with mine in a deep kiss, tasting the sweetness of her mixed with the heat of our passion.

We lay there, our bodies tangled together, and I held her close. My eyes fluttered shut as I listened to the soft rhythm of her breathing, her cool skin soothing my overheated body. My breaths naturally fell into sync with hers, a quiet melody shared between us. I longed to stay in this moment for as long as I could. This—being with her—was everything I'd ever wanted. But I knew there was more I needed to do. No, more that I had to do for my kingdom. I couldn't just think of myself, of my own desires. My duty came first, and right now, my people needed me fighting for them, even if my father wouldn't.

I kissed the top of her head and murmured, "Meles Tari, we have to get up." She groaned in response, a small smile tugging at my lips as I carefully untangled myself from her embrace and stood. As I made my way to the shower, I glanced back at her—her flushed body still glistening in the afternoon sunlight streaming through the window. "You're truly beautiful, Aure."

She giggled, lazily tossing a pillow in my direction. "Not as beautiful as you are."

Shaking my head with a smile, I disappeared into the bathroom and turned the copper fixture. Warm water bubbled out of the spout, swirling into the small basin below before draining away. The soft sound of water filled the room, soothing to my nerves for what lay ahead.

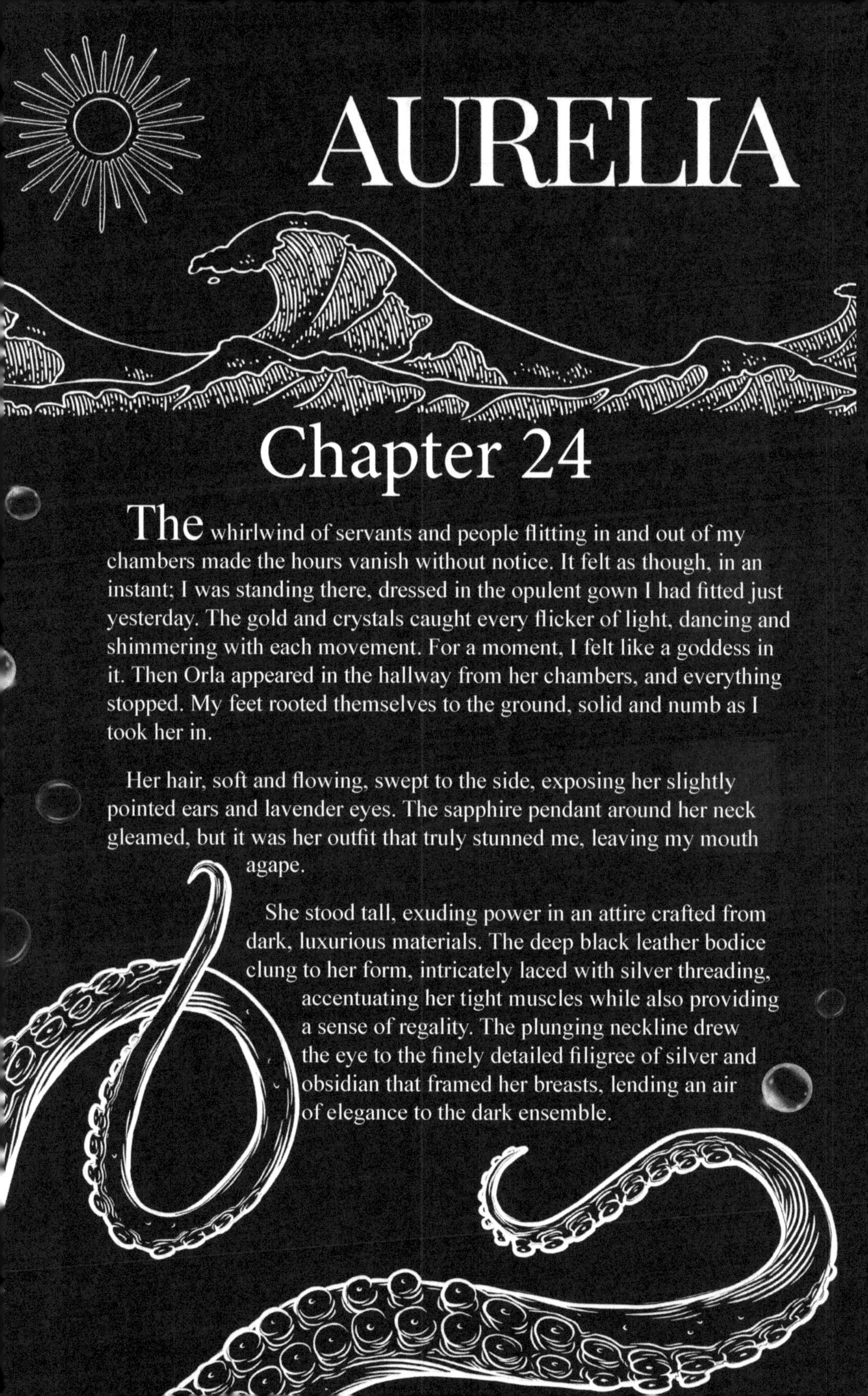

AURELIA

Chapter 24

The whirlwind of servants and people flitting in and out of my chambers made the hours vanish without notice. It felt as though, in an instant; I was standing there, dressed in the opulent gown I had fitted just yesterday. The gold and crystals caught every flicker of light, dancing and shimmering with each movement. For a moment, I felt like a goddess in it. Then Orla appeared in the hallway from her chambers, and everything stopped. My feet rooted themselves to the ground, solid and numb as I took her in.

Her hair, soft and flowing, swept to the side, exposing her slightly pointed ears and lavender eyes. The sapphire pendant around her neck gleamed, but it was her outfit that truly stunned me, leaving my mouth agape.

She stood tall, exuding power in an attire crafted from dark, luxurious materials. The deep black leather bodice clung to her form, intricately laced with silver threading, accentuating her tight muscles while also providing a sense of regality. The plunging neckline drew the eye to the finely detailed filigree of silver and obsidian that framed her breasts, lending an air of elegance to the dark ensemble.

Her sleeves were long, tapering into sharp, claw-like designs that extended over the backs of her hands, adding a touch of danger to her commanding presence. The fitted leather pants were sleek, adorned with subtle designs that mimicked the armor of a warrior. Each seam etched with fine craftsmanship, trailing down to the high, knee-length boots that shimmered with their own dark embellishments. The boots featured intricate silver embroidery that climbed up her legs, highlighting her strength and poise.

Behind her, a flowing black half-skirt billowed out dramatically, its fabric catching the light in such a way that it seemed as though shadows themselves had woven into the cloth. The half-skirt was fastened at her waist with intricate silver clasps, and the glint of silver dagger sheaths peeked out beside them. The edges of the skirt shimmered with a pattern that resembled stars fading into the night sky, adding an ethereal, almost cosmic quality. Every detail of her outfit was a delicate balance of grace, darkness, and lethal elegance, making her look like a queen of shadows—someone who commanded both loyalty and fear.

Orla had stopped in her tracks as well, both of us staring at each other in silence for a few heartbeats, the weight of the moment lingering in the air. Then Rielle stepped out from behind Orla with a playful smirk on her face. "Do you approve, Aure?" She asked, gesturing toward Orla with her fingerless gloved hands.

My mouth hung open, and I quickly snapped it shut, nodding slowly. Rielle stood in a similar ensemble, though hers gleamed with red and gold embellishments. Her black leather pants featured intricate gold leaf filigree running down the sides, extending seamlessly to her boots. Everything about her outfit hugged to her petite frame and perfectly tailored to her, the attention to detail evident in every stitch.

Rielle bounced forward, grabbing my hand and twirling me around with gleeful energy. "You are absolutely breathtaking, my Queen." She giggled, her eyes gleaming mischievously. "I had to step in—Orla desperately needed a wardrobe upgrade. The other day, I asked her what she planned to wear, and she pulled out some drab dress from the back of her closet. I looked at her and said, NO!" I smiled over at Orla. Rielle could be a force to be reckoned with when she wanted to be.

Orla stepped forward, still eyeing me with an appreciative gaze, her eyes shifting toward pink. The familiar spark of our magic flared, the energy moving between us like a live current the closer we got to one another.

"Yeep! Not while I'm standing in the middle!" Rielle squeaked, hopping back playfully as Orla reached for my hand. "You two are so chaotic."

Shaking her head, she flashed a smile, still brimming with mischief.

Cam stepped into the hallway, joining us with her usual poised presence. Her long blonde hair laid in a braid neatly around her head, the same style she wore for every formal event. Dressed in the royal guard uniform of Faedamir, the green and yellow colors stood out sharply against the gold and blue uniforms of Orlondia's guards. She smiled briefly before falling into step behind us as we made our way to the stairs.

Frank appeared bounding up the steps as soon as he saw us. He wore the tailored royal guard suit of Orlondia, his broad grin unmistakable as he approached. His voice, full of amusement, filled the air. "Ladies, you're lookin' fetchin' tonight." He offered his arm to Rielle, who gave him a quick once-over before crossing her arms with a smirk, and continuing down the stairs ahead of us.

I tightened my grip around Orla's hand as we descended the grand staircase toward the ballroom. The elegantly dressed guests watched as we passed, their eyes following us as we made our way down to the main floor. Cam and Frank trailed closely behind, taking their positions as our guards.

As we reached the bottom of the staircase, the grand ballroom came into full view. The space was large, bathed in soft golden light, with crystal iced chandeliers sparkling above like a coat of freshly fallen snow in the morning sun. The ballroom's high ceilings and marble floors reflected the elegance of the evening, as the soft hum of conversations mixed with the light strains of music from the orchestra positioned in the far corner. Through the wall of full-length windows, the night sky was clouded, and the light reflected off the soft snowflakes falling around towards the ground outside.

Orla's grip on my hand tightened for just a moment. I could feel the warmth of her presence beside me, and the soft hum of our bond pulsed quietly between us. She looked regal, yet there was a vulnerability to her tonight that only I could sense—a subtle tension hidden beneath her calm exterior.

The guests parted as we made our way through the ballroom, their eyes flicking between us, murmurs trailing behind. Cam and Frank kept a discreet distance, though I could feel their watchful gazes scanning the room, ever protective. Orla, acting poised, glanced sideways at me, her lavender eyes shimmering in the soft light, and for a moment, the rest of the room faded into the background.

"Are you ready for this?" she whispered, her voice soft but carrying a hint of uncertainty.

I squeezed her hand gently, leaning in closer. "With you by my side, yes."

The ballroom was full of dignitaries and nobles, each adorned in their finest attire. The women wore gowns of silk and satin, their intricate embroidery and jewels catching the light with every movement. The men stood tall in tailored suits, their expressions a mix of curiosity and calculation as they observed the proceedings.

As we approached the center of the room, a booming voice echoed from the far end. King Oric stood in a domineering stance at the head of the ballroom, flanked by several high-ranking officials and council members. His presence commanded the room, and his gaze fell on us as we approached. The weight of his cold blue eyes felt heavier tonight, and I could sense Orla's muscles tense beneath her calm exterior.

"Princess Aurelia, Princess Orla," King Oric greeted us with a sharp nod. His smile was one that was practiced but did not reach his eyes. His voice grew louder over the crowd and he continued, "It is a night of celebration, and I am honored to present the engaged couple. May this alliance stand strong and create peace through their union, just as it did in the Union of the Crescent and the Star, the first Queens of Negall." Cheers erupted throughout the space from most who attended. I glanced around smiling softly before settling back to King Oric.

A formal nod from me, and Orla simply inclined her head in respect, though the tension between her and her father was palpable. The king's attention lingered on Orla for a moment too long before shifting back to the crowd.

"Let the festivities begin," he declared, and with a wave of his hand, the music swelled and guests began to mingle, their earlier quiet whispers growing into louder conversations.

I turned toward Orla, my eyes searching hers. "Let's try to enjoy the night," I whispered, offering a smile.

Orla nodded, her expression softening as she leaned closer, her lips grazing my ear. "As long as you're with me, I think I will."

Just as the music swelled, Rielle reappeared beside us, a grin stretching across her face. "Well, don't you two look like the couple of the century," she teased, giving me a playful nudge. Frank, not far behind her, shot her a quick wink.

"Just try not to steal all the attention tonight, Rielle. That outfit—yum!" Frank joked, his tone light but sincere.

Rielle shot him a stern glare before giving him a half-hearted smack on the stomach. "Keep dreaming, Frank," she retorted, rolling her eyes with a smirk.

Without missing a beat, she turned back to the dance floor, leaving Frank momentarily distracted, his eyes trailing after her.

As we moved deeper into the crowd, greeting guests and exchanging pleasantries, I couldn't shake the feeling that something darker loomed on the horizon. Though, for now, all I could do was stay by Orla's side and let the night unfold.

The music swirled around us as Orla pulled me onto the dance floor, her fingers lacing through mine and we began to move to the rhythm of the waltz.

We swayed with the beat of the music, the warmth of Orla's touch grounding me amidst the sea of opulence. The crowd suddenly shifted. Out of the corner of my eye, I saw Lady Lili, her dark violet gown sweeping across the floor, gliding through the guests with a practiced grace. Her bright violet eyes were sharp, scanning the room until they landed on us. A wide smile crossed her face, though it didn't quite reach her eyes.

"Orla, darling!" She called out, her voice carrying through the room with ease. Before either of us could react, Lady Lili had closed the distance, gently but firmly pulling Orla away from me, much to Orla's visible surprise.

"Aunt Lili," Orla greeted, her tone neutral, though I could sense her irritation.

Lady Lili fussed over her immediately, wrapping her arms around Orla in a tight embrace, then stepping back to appraise her niece like a seamstress checking her work. "My dear, look at you," she cooed, brushing imaginary dust from Orla's leather-clad shoulders. "So regal tonight, but honestly, Orla, your hair..." Her hands fluttered to Orla's short, tousled locks, attempting to sweep the strands over Orla's slightly pointed ears, clearly agitated that they were exposed.

Lady Lili's fingers moved quickly, trying in vain to tuck the hair just right, but Orla's ears remained stubbornly visible. Orla's expression shifted from mild confusion to quiet exasperation as her aunt fussed, pulling her hair this way and that.

"Aunt Lili, please," Orla said through clenched teeth, gently brushing her aunt's hands away. "It's fine."

"Fine? Oh, Orla, you know how people talk," Lady Lili tutted, her voice dropping to a whisper as she continued to fuss over her. "It's not proper for you to leave your new ears so... on display."

Orla rolled her eyes, her expression slipping from calm to slightly strained. She took a step back, letting out a slow breath. "I'm not ashamed of them, Aunt Lili. I'm not hiding who I am."

"Of course, darling," Lady Lili replied, her voice sweet but strained, her eyes flickering with a mixture of frustration and concern. "But appearances matter, especially in front of the court. There are... expectations."

The tension between them was palpable, and I felt a surge of protectiveness rise within me. Orla's jaw tightened, her eyes flickering with the faintest hint of cobalt, a sure sign that her patience was thinning.

I stepped forward, placing a hand lightly on Orla's arm. "Orla looks perfect as she is," I said, my tone polite but firm. "There's no need to change anything."

Lady Lili's eyes flicked toward me, her smile tightening slightly. "Of course, Princess Aurelia, you're right. Orla is... well, she's unique," she said, the word "unique" dripping with a thinly veiled judgment. She turned her attention back to Orla, her hands hovering near her niece's hair once more. "But you know how people are, darling. They gossip. They look for anything to criticize, especially when it comes to matters of... lineage."

Orla stiffened at that, her gaze hardening. "I'm well aware of what people say, Aunt Lili. But I'm not hiding. Not anymore."

The finality in her voice left no room for argument, and Lady Lili's smile faltered slightly before she quickly masked it with another wide, false grin.

"Of course, of course, darling," she said, patting Orla's arm in a placating gesture. "I'm just looking out for you, as I always have. Now, go on, enjoy the party. Remember, however, the eyes of the court and others are always watching."

With that, she released Orla, though not without one final glance at her ears, before turning to glide back into the crowd, her gown swishing behind her.

Orla sighed heavily, rubbing her temples as she turned back to me. "That woman," she muttered, her voice low. "She never lets up. Funny, though I never noticed it much before."

I smiled gently, taking her hand once more. "You handled it well," I said softly. "Besides, I think your ears are perfect."

Orla chuckled, though her eyes still held a trace of lingering frustration. "I just wish she'd stop treating me like a child," she murmured, shaking her head. "I'm not ashamed of who I am, or what I am. I thought she would have been the one to accept that."

I squeezed her hand reassuringly. "She means well, but it's your life, Orla. You get to decide who you are, not her. And certainly not the court."

Orla's expression softened, her gaze meeting mine with a warmth that made my heart flutter. "Thank you," she whispered, leaning closer, her lips brushing against my temple. "For always standing by me."

I smiled, resting my head against her shoulder for just a moment. "Always."

We danced through the crowd, where many approached us to offer congratulations, share words of wisdom, or subtly attempt to curry favor. Some handed us gifts, which servants quickly stacked on a table along the wall. Other servants moved gracefully through the room, carrying trays of bite-sized delicacies and flutes of Uric wine. I allowed myself one glass; the warmth spreading through my throat and down into my stomach, a welcome contrast to the cold outside. The heat of the festivities, though, soon made the ballroom stifling. Large windows and doors were opened, letting in the chilly night air and swirling snowflakes, which melted on the floor, where even more servants were busy keeping the space dry and free of puddles.

As Orla and I glided through the crowd, spinning in sync with the rising tempo of the waltz, a flicker of movement by the king's table drew my attention. I slowed our pace, my feet dragging slightly as I caught sight of the tense exchange unfolding between Lady Lili and King Oric. Orla's arms remained steady around me, but I could feel her gaze follow mine as the soft swaying of our dance mirrored the escalating tension at the royal table.

Lady Lili, seated regally beside King Oric, her posture rigid, appeared to be on the verge of losing her composure. Her normally composed face was twisted with barely contained fury, her lips moving rapidly as she whispered heated words into the king's ear. King Oric's expression, however, remained stony, a flicker of impatience flashing in his cold blue eyes as he responded tersely. Queen Helena, seated to Oric's left, looked drained of color, her gaze distant, as if she was desperately trying to remain uninvolved in the brewing storm.

The intensity between Lady Lili and the king seemed to escalate with each passing second. The rest of the room was oblivious to the tension, lost in their own conversations and revelry, but I could feel the shift, the crackling air of impending chaos. Then, in a sudden burst of frustration, Lady Lili's fingers tightened around her delicate glass flute, and with a sharp crack, it shattered in her hand.

Gasps echoed nearby as blood dripped from her palm, but Lady Lili's attention never wavered from King Oric. Her eyes blazed with fury as she flung the shards to the floor, the bloodstained fragments scattering across the marble. The entire ballroom seemed to still as she rose abruptly, her gown sweeping behind her like a storm about to break.

Without a word, she stormed out of the room, the long train of her violet dress trailing behind her like spilled ink, leaving a trail of servants scrambling in her wake to clean up the shattered glass and smeared blood. Queen Helena remained motionless, her hands clenched in her lap, her face pale as a sheet. King Oric's expression, however, was unreadable, though a dark tension rippled through his body.

Orla's grip tightened slightly around my waist, her eyes fixed on the scene with a mixture of concern and suspicion. The festive atmosphere around us dimmed as the tension hung in the air like an unsaid curse.

For a moment, the entire ballroom seemed frozen in the aftermath of Lady Lili's dramatic exit, the faint sound of broken glass still ringing in my ears. All eyes were on the king's table, the tension so thick it felt like it could smother the festive air in the room.

Then, with a sharp movement, King Oric raised his hand, his cold blue eyes sweeping the room with an imperious glare. It was a silent command, a gesture that told the crowd to carry on as if nothing had happened. His face, as composed as ever, betrayed no emotion, but his rigid posture hinted at the storm brewing beneath his carefully maintained mask of authority. Queen Helena remained motionless beside him, her hands still tightly clasped in her lap, her gaze fixed on the floor.

The silence lingered for a beat longer, but the musicians, clearly skilled in royal affairs, took King Oric's signal and quickly picked up their instruments. The soft, melodic strains of the waltz began to play again, slowly pulling the guests back into the rhythm of the celebration.

Chatter resumed in low murmurs, and soon, laughter echoed through the hall once more. Yet, there was an undeniable shift in the air, a tension that crackled beneath the surface of the festivities. People exchanged wary glances, trying to gauge what had just occurred between the king and Lady Lili, though none dared speak of it openly.

Orla's hold on me remained firm, but I could feel the unease radiating through her. Her eyes flickered with an emotion I couldn't quite place—anger, perhaps, or maybe something darker. I leaned into her, trying to ground us both in the swirl of uncertainty.

"She's never lost her temper like that," Orla whispered, her voice barely audible over the music. Her gaze remained fixed on her father, who now seemed completely indifferent to the drama that had just unfolded. "Something's wrong."

I nodded, feeling the same unsettling twist in my gut. "What could've caused that kind of reaction?" I whispered back, my eyes lingering on the bloodied glass shards still being swept up by the servants.

King Oric, for all his composed demeanor, glanced toward the exit where Lady Lili had disappeared, a flicker of something dark crossing his face. But, just as quickly, he turned his attention back to the nobles gathered around him, waving off any concern as he leaned back in his chair. Whatever had transpired between them, he was determined to make sure it remained a secret.

Orla's grip on my waist tightened again, and I could feel her body tense beside mine, her dark blue eyes narrowing as they focused on her father.

"Maybe it was something about what I witnessed," Orla murmured, her voice low and filled with resolve. "I think there's more going on here than we know, however."

I swallowed hard, my mind racing as I tried to make sense of what we'd just witnessed. The music continued to play, and the guests danced and mingled as though nothing had happened, but the cracks in the facade were clear now. Something had shifted within the walls of the palace, and it was only a matter of time before the truth—whatever it was—came crashing down.

"Let's look into it more, tomorrow," I whispered back, feeling a chill run down my spine. "I don't trust any of this, though."

Orla gave a small nod, her eyes still trained on her father as we continued to sway to the music. The party went on, but beneath the surface, the tension simmered, waiting to erupt.

ORLA

Chapter 25

As the night edged closer to its peak, emotions swirled through my mind like a storm. The anticipation hung in the air, thick and almost suffocating, as the night escalated toward its grand climax the moment everyone awaited. My nerves churned with the rich food and Eruric wine sitting heavily in my stomach. The ballroom buzzed with feasting, conversation, and bursts of laughter—so much life and joy that it felt overwhelming. My gaze locked in on the stunning sight of Aure, who effortlessly took my breath away. Yet, despite the lively energy, I couldn't shake the sense of isolation creeping over me.

I leaned against the cool stone wall, watching the blur of activity that filled the grand hall. Aure's radiant smile lit up her face as she conversed with Madame Koi, the two of them deep in animated discussion. Across the room, Rein had finally arrived, fashionably late, though dressed in a finery I'd never even imagined could be real. His outfit was immaculate, and yet, there he stood, embroiled in yet another heated debate with the red-faced and thoroughly drunk Duke Kinsmere.

It should have been a moment of celebration, a night filled with laughter and connection. Yet, standing there alone, the weight of it all pressed heavily on my chest. The noise, the spectacle, and even Aure, so breathtakingly beautiful, felt like distant echoes. Everything was too much, too loud, too bright. I needed to ground myself, to remember why this night mattered.

Even as I tried to breathe, to calm the storm inside me, something gnawed at the edges of my mind, a feeling, something just out of reach.

My gaze caught Tristan, clad in his royal guard attire, slipping quietly through a side door. My eyes narrowed as I straightened up from where I stood against the wall. I glanced around quickly, spotting Cam, Frank, and Rielle strategically positioned near Aure. Satisfied she was well-guarded, I decided to follow my childhood friend, curiosity and suspicion urging me to uncover whatever he was up to.

As I stepped into the hallway, the soft murmur of the ball faded behind me, replaced by the quieter, more isolated stillness of the corridor. I followed the sound of light footsteps until I found Tristan, leaning casually against the stone wall, gazing out one of the small, arched windows.

His face lit up when he saw me. "Orla," he greeted, a grin spreading across his lips, his voice a low, eager whisper. "I didn't think you'd actually come looking for me."

I stiffened slightly but kept my expression neutral. "You disappeared from the celebration. I wanted to know why." My voice was measured, careful not to betray the unease that prickled at the back of my neck.

Tristan pushed away from the wall, his steps deliberate as he approached me. His grin widened into something that felt too intimate, too knowing. "I'm honored," he said, his tone thick with excitement. "I knew you'd eventually realize it. You don't belong in there, Orla, not with them." He waved a hand vaguely in the direction of the ballroom. "Especially not with her."

My heart beat a little faster. "What are you talking about, Tristan?" I asked, keeping my tone cool as he moved closer. Too close.

"Aure," he spat the name as if it were poison. His face twisted with something ugly. "She's corrupted you, Orla. Twisted your mind with her magic, pulling you into her darkness. But I can save you. I've been watching, waiting for you to see it. To realize that it's me. It's always been me."

My stomach churned at the intensity in his voice, and I instinctively stepped back, but he followed. His eyes gleamed with a mixture of desperation and triumph. "I know you've felt it too, Orla. You came looking for me. You could've stayed with her, but you didn't. You found me."

"Tristan, this is not what you think—"

"I know exactly what it is," he interrupted, his hand reaching out to grab my wrist, tugging me closer. "I've waited for you to break free from her grip. Aure's magic has blinded you, but deep down, you know she's dangerous. She's tainted you with her Siren magic. I've seen what it's done to you." His other hand gently touched my ear. "But I can free you, Orla. I can protect you."

I wrenched my wrist from his grip, my anger flaring, my eyes deepening to dark cobalt. "Tristan, you're wrong. I'm with Aure because I want to be. I love her."

He recoiled as if I'd struck him, his face contorting with disbelief and rage. "No. You're just saying that because she's controlling you! I know you, Orla. We grew up together. You never wanted any of this!" He gestured wildly, his voice growing more desperate. "You've been enchanted, but I can break the spell. I can make you see."

I shook my head, stepping further away. "Tristan, you need to stop. This isn't you. I chose Aure, and I'll keep choosing her."

His face twisted, his obsession shining through in his darkened eyes. "You don't understand. I'll kill her if I have to. I'll do anything to save you." His voice dropped to a low, dangerous whisper, his hand hovering near the dagger at his side.

"Tristan, don't do this." My voice was firm, but beneath it, my heart raced. I could see now how deep his obsession had gone, how dangerous he'd become. I kept my gaze locked on him, preparing for whatever might come next.

I moved closer to block his path, but before I could react, his eyes darkened with a predatory gleam. In an instant, he shoved me hard against the wall, his fingers gripping my wrists in a bruising hold. His mouth crashed down on mine, hot and unwelcome, his slimy lips pressing against my tightly closed mouth. The bitter taste of his saliva smeared across my lips, revolting and invasive.

Every fiber of my being recoiled, disgust churning in my stomach as I struggled to break free. His strength was godlike, far more than I remembered. No matter how much I struggled, his grip didn't loosen. My eyes darted toward my necklace, my last hope of fighting back, but Tristan caught the movement and let out a cold laugh. Releasing one of my wrists—his first fatal mistake—he sneered, "Her vile little trinkets have no more power over you, Orla."

With a swift motion, he ripped the Rebounder from my neck, breaking the chain and tossed it to the marble floor. The magic within the pendant sparked weakly as it skittered down the hallway, its glow faltering, as if fading with every bounce. I swung my free hand at him, but it felt leaden, like it was weighed down with rocks—a sensation I knew all too well from training. I was drained, weak, and utterly powerless.

He caught my hand easily, forcing it against his chest, and his hand moved mine to pull open his shirt. A bright red glow emerged, radiating from a symbol inked onto his skin—the Syphon Rune. The mark of the Order of the Golden Rose, the fanatical cult dedicated to purging the realm of magic. My heart sank.

"I must purify you, Orla," Tristan murmured, his voice trembling with a fanatical fervor. "It's the only way. And once I've done that, I'll kill her. I'll free you from her evil magic, and then we can rule this kingdom together. We'll rid the realm of magic, just as Lux Veritas commands."

His hand pressed mine harder against his chest, the glow of the rune pulsating beneath my palm. "Can you feel it, Orla?" he hissed, his eyes wild. "Her dark, evil magic... it's already being transformed by the almighty Lux Veritas. You're being purified."

I could feel the draining pull of the Syphon Rune, sapping not just my magic, but my strength, my will. The sickening sensation of losing myself in his twisted delusion made my blood run cold. I had to resist... but how?

My bond with Aure... it was gone. No longer the chaotic, tangled lifeline I had come to rely on. Now, there was nothing. Just a dark, quiet void that swallowed me whole. It was lonely—an unbearable, cold emptiness. I couldn't move, couldn't scream, couldn't even think straight. My body grew heavier, weaker, until I slumped down the wall like a rag doll, collapsing at Tristan's feet.

He seemed to revel in my powerlessness, his eyes gleaming with twisted satisfaction. As I slid to the floor, he positioned himself on top of me, gripping my left wrist tightly, still siphoning the remnants of my magic into himself. His hand moved to my cheek in a sickeningly gentle caress, and he whispered, "Shhh... purification can hurt, but only for a little while. I'll save you. I'll make it better. You'll be pure again."

My body twitched, the only response I could muster as I lay helpless beneath him. His slimy tongue left a wet trail down my neck toward my breasts, each touch making my skin crawl. His free hand moved to undo the clasp on my leather pants, his movements deliberate, slow. My mind screamed in protest, but my body wouldn't respond.

"I'll try to make this... as enjoyable as possible," he whispered, as if his twisted version of comfort would somehow lessen the horror.

But inside, I pushed. I fought. I clawed at the remnants of my magic, trying to sever the connection he had to me, trying to cut off the flow that was feeding his strength, his lust, his perversion of "purification." But it felt like trying to hold back a flood with a single hand. My power was slipping away, and with it, my hope.

I couldn't let this happen. Not like this.

I had to find a way to break free. For Aure. For myself.

"To purify you, we must offer a sacrifice—either of blood or love. We will give the almighty Lux both our love and her blood." Tristan's hand trembled as it slid down my pants between my thighs, his rough fingers brushing my center. His smile twisted into something vile as he brought his fingers to his lips, licking them slowly, savoring the moment.

The world around me blurred as Tristan's voice droned on, sickening and twisted, his grip on my wrist unrelenting. The flow of magic from me to him continued, but I fought back with everything I had. *Focus, Orla. Focus on the magic, on pulling it back.* My body lay motionless, helpless beneath him as his hands roamed where they shouldn't. His fingers clawed at my pants, ripping them down to my knees, and my stomach wrenched in revulsion.

Focus on the magic, I reminded myself, even as bile rose in my throat. I could feel his disgusting touch, the nauseating sensation of his hard length pressing against me, but I forced my mind away from it, away from the horror of the moment. *Don't focus on him, focus on the threads of light—your magic. Pull it back.*

I visualized the green, the blue, the gold of my magic swirling inside me. They were slipping, flowing into him, but I *had* to pull them back. Slowly, painfully, I began to gather them, dragging the threads of my power back into myself. His heavy breathing filled the air as he lost himself in his twisted passion, oblivious to my internal battle. He groaned, his body pressing harder into mine, his weight suffocating.

Then, as his release approached, I felt it. *The weakness.* His body was losing control, while mine was regaining strength. *This is my moment.* I yanked on the threads of my magic with everything I had left, pulling them back into me. Rage surged up from the depths of my soul, burning hotter and brighter than anything I'd ever felt. It was a volcanic fury, bubbling, threatening to explode.

His body trembled, his breath ragged as he pressed a kiss to my cheek, his weight settling heavier against me. The hot slickness of his release pooled between my thighs, down my ass, his spent cock still inside me, revolting me, but I didn't falter. I clenched my jaw, using the fire inside to fuel me. *I will take back what's mine.*

As he sighed, spent and momentarily weakened, I felt it: the shift in power. My magic was mine again. *And now, I'll end this.*

He pushed himself up to stand. My fingers twitched, but I still hadn't regained full control over my body. He shoved his cock back into his pants, and the dark promise in my mind solidified: *When I'm finished with him, I will cut his cock from his body.*

I focused now, my magic slowly returning to me as I tried to gather strength and recover before he could reach Aure. His hand pulled out a dagger, its blade glinting in the dim light.

"Now for the blood sacrifice," he murmured, his voice chillingly calm. "Hold on, Orla. You'll be completely free soon."

The lava inside me burned hotter, fueling my will to fight. I had to stand—I had to reach him, to destroy him before it was too late. My legs moved, trembling but obeying my commands. My fingers stretched out, my muscles shaking as the control returned. My eyes blinked, vision sharpening with every breath.

My hands twitched first, then my head followed, and finally my legs. I could move. Forcing myself to sit up, I ignored the pounding in my head and the spinning sensation that threatened to pull me back under. Slowly, shakily, I stood, leaning against the wall for support. My legs trembled, but I pulled my pants back into place, fastening them with clumsy fingers.

I didn't let myself think about the foul-smelling, sticky fluid that was still inside me, still clung to me, staining the inside of my pants. That could wait. *Right now, I have to get to Aure.* I had to kill Tristan.

Stumbling forward, I moved like a drunken sailor, my body unsteady. My vision blurred for a moment, but then I saw it—my rebounder necklace, pulsing faintly with magic once again. I scooped it off the floor and shoved it into my pocket, steadying myself as best I could.

When I pushed open the doors to the grand ballroom, the blinding brightness of the room hit me, and the noise felt like a physical weight. My eyes immediately found Aure and Rielle, twirling together on the dance floor, laughing and spinning like carefree girls in a meadow on a spring day.

They had no idea. No one but me knew Tristan was coming for her.

And no one but me would stop him.

My eyes darted frantically around the room, scanning for Tristan. Then I spotted him, slipping between guests, heading straight for Aure. His boldness was astounding, to think he could carry out this plan in front of everyone.

The music had just stopped, and the crowd turned toward the windows, preparing for the fire magic display. They began the countdown. "Ten... nine..."

I moved swiftly, my heart pounding, but Tristan was nearly at Aure's side. I wouldn't reach him in time unless... unless I unleashed my magic.

Aure, who had been enjoying the moment, now scanned the room, likely sensing my rage. My eyes, black as onyx, locked onto Tristan. She had to feel it—she had to know something was wrong.

"Six... five..."

The countdown echoed through the ballroom, but I had no time to waste. I shoved a few stunned guests out of my way. "Move!"

Time was running out.

Cam saw him first and moved swiftly, closing in toward Aure, who now looked frantic. Tristan was nearly there.

"Three... two..." The crowd's anticipation grew louder, completely unaware of the danger looming.

Cam positioned herself between Aure and Tristan, her hand resting on her sword, but she hadn't drawn it yet. My heart leaped into my throat as I finally had a direct line to him.

"One."

In that split second, I unleashed everything. A surge of electricity and fire exploded from my core, my eyes staying black as night. My magic shot toward Tristan, and just before he turned to face me, his expression twisted in pain. Lightning struck true. Then, he was gone—bursting into a million pieces of ash.

Screams filled the air as chaos erupted. People scattered in panic. Cam's sword, now unsheathed, was knocked from her hand as the blast flung her back, colliding into Aure. Servants and guests were either thrown back from the shockwave or, like Tristan, disintegrated into ash.

It all unfolded in slow motion—the energy I had unleashed, the fury that roared out of me like a beast untamed. I wasn't sure if I could control it, if I could pull it back in. Flames burst outside in the grand display, but inside, it was far from a celebration.

Guards rushed to shield my mother and father, escorting them out of the madness.

Frank was shouting orders at the guards and servants as they scrambled to contain the crowd and the flames licking up the walls. Above me, storm clouds churned, lightning crackling through the room.

I was a walking storm, and I wasn't sure if I could stop.

I had no sense of time as the chaos unfolded around me, but suddenly, a wave of raw, bitter sorrow tore through me, not mine—Aure's. The intensity of her grief hit me like a physical blow, cutting through the storm of magic still raging inside me. It was choking, unbearable, and it brought me back from the brink of losing myself entirely.

Lightning flickered one last time, and then, as if the storm had wept for what had happened, the rain began to fall. Cold droplets cascaded from the swirling storm clouds I had summoned, hissing as they hit the scorched ground, mingling with the ash and soot that covered the ballroom. My magic retreated in a slow, agonizing pull, but the devastation it left in its wake was all too real.

I moved, racing toward Aure as soon as my legs obeyed me. She sat on the ballroom floor, her white gown now a crumpled mess of stained tulle, smeared with ash, streaked with red—blood. For a moment, I couldn't breathe, a sharp, paralyzing fear gripping me.

Was she hurt? Had I hurt her? Was this my doing?

But then I saw it, the horror of the moment crashing into me like a tidal wave. Aure wasn't alone. Cam was draped across her lap, gasping for breath, her chest rising in ragged, uneven bursts. The fabric of her uniform was soaked with blood, the hilt of Tristan's dagger lodged deep between her fingers, which were clutched tightly to the wound.

"Cam," I whispered, my voice breaking. It was all I could say.

Aure's eyes, wide and frantic, met mine. They were clouded with tears, her lips trembling as she cradled Cam, helpless. Her bloodied hands pressed desperately against the wound, trying to stop the flow of blood, but it was too much—too fast.

The ballroom, that was once alive with laughter and music, was now a scene of destruction. Servants and guests fled in terror, some screaming, others frozen in shock. The fires had died, but smoke still curled in the air. And in the center of it all was Aure, drenched and shaking, clutching the only person who had been willing to sacrifice everything for her.

My heart shattered.

I dropped to my knees beside them, my hands trembling as they hovered over Cam's bloodied form. Unsure of where to even start, of how to save her, knowing deep down it was already too late.

 The rain, still pouring from the storm I'd summoned, soaked through my clothes, but I barely felt the cold. My entire focus was on her—the woman who had been by Aure's side for years, who had protected both of us with unwavering loyalty. Now, she lay there, slipping away.

"Cam, please," I whispered, my voice hoarse. "You can't leave us."

Her breath came in shallow gasps, her chest struggling to rise and fall as the blood continued to pool around her. With a weak, trembling hand, she reached up, her fingers brushing my arm before gripping my wrist with what little strength she had left.

"Orla..." she rasped, her voice barely above a whisper, but the weight of her words felt like a dagger in my own chest. "You have to... always protect Aurelia."

My throat tightened, my heart pounding painfully in my chest. "Cam, you—"

"No," she cut me off, her voice firmer, though strained. Her eyes flicked toward Aurelia, who was still sobbing, her hands pressing futilely against Cam's wound. "Promise me," Cam continued, her gaze locking with mine, fierce despite the pain. "Promise me... you'll love her... better than I did."

Tears blurred my vision as I looked between them. Aure was shaking, her face streaked with tears and ash. "Cam, please don't do this. Please, hold on, we can get help," Aure begged, her voice cracking.

Cam's hand tightened around my wrist, pulling me closer. "I don't... have much time," she whispered, her voice growing weaker. "You've... always been stronger than you think, Orla. Stronger than me... than all of us. She needs you... more than ever now. Don't let her slip away... because of this."

I nodded, unable to find the words, my chest heaving with the sobs I fought to suppress. My grip tightened on her hand, as if I could hold her there, keeping her from leaving us.

"I promise," I whispered, my voice breaking. "I'll protect her... and I'll love her. I'll do whatever it takes, Cam."

A small, sad smile ghosted across her lips. "Good," she gasped. Her eyes fluttered shut, her breath growing fainter by the second. "I always... knew you would."

For a moment, the world stood still. The rain, the distant screams, the smoke—all of it faded as Cam's hand slackened in mine. Her body went still, her chest no longer rising.

Aure let out a heart-wrenching sob, cradling Cam's lifeless form, her tears mixing with the rain. I felt my own grief clawing at my throat, threatening to tear me apart, but I couldn't fall apart—not now.

I wrapped my arms around Aure, pulling her close, holding her as tightly as I could. Her cries echoed in the nearly empty ballroom. The weight of what I had done was crushing down on me.

"I promise," I whispered again, more to myself than anyone else.

AURELIA

Chapter 26

With my eyes closed, I blocked it all out. The cold wetness of my dress clinging to my body, the weight of my wet hair. I shook, not really knowing if it was from the cold or from the emotions inside me. I opened my eyes once again, and the hazy scene came slowly into focus.

The world around me had crumbled, yet somehow, everything continued to move—people, sounds, the blizzard of snow outside coming in through the windows. My vision blurred as I stared at Cam's lifeless body, the crimson stain spreading across her tunic, mixing with the rain-soaked ash that clung to her pale skin. The ballroom, once full of light and joy, now lay in ruins. Bodies of the wounded littered the floor. Servants moved like ghosts, clearing debris, but it was all muted, distant, like I was trapped behind a pane of glass.

I could barely feel Orla's arm around me anymore, though I knew she was holding me tightly, trying to keep me grounded. My mind spiraled, unraveling, pulled in every direction, drowning under the weight of what had just happened.

Cam was gone. Dead.

I felt hollow, my body on autopilot as I stared at her still face, remembering the last moments—her soft smile, the way she had whispered to Orla, how she had always stood beside me, protecting me. And now… gone.

Gone.

Azura stirred inside me, a dull, sad presence at the back of my mind. *"Aurelia, breathe."* Her voice, usually fierce and full of joy, was soft, almost mournful.

I closed my eyes, trying to obey, to do anything but focus on the crushing weight of my grief. I couldn't. The air felt too thick to breathe, heavy with the stench of charred flesh and the sharp iron tang of blood. The sickly sweetness of spilled wine mingled with the woody thickness of lingering smoke, creating a nauseating cocktail of scents. My hands still shook from the adrenaline, my fingertips stained red with Cam's blood. I curled them into fists, but nothing could stop the trembling.

"I failed her," I whispered into the void of my mind, trying to make sense of everything, of why this had happened. *"I let her die. I could have done something. I should have **seen** it—"*

Azura's energy swelled, a wave of warmth trying to push through my pain. *"You did not fail her, Aurelia. You did what you could, but this is a war. You cannot carry the weight of every loss."*

"No, I should have protected her!" I screamed internally, my grief rippling into anger. *"I have magic and better control over it than Orla. I should have stopped him, stopped Tristan, stopped all of it, I should have seen this coming…"*

A flicker of memory flashed before my eyes—Tristan's cold, calculating face, his smug smile as he made his move toward me. The ash cloud of his destruction as Orla unleashed her full power. I could still hear the sound of the blast that ripped through the ballroom. I had felt the tremor of Orla's rage, her magic tearing through everything in its path, unrelenting.

And yet… Cam had stepped between us, and taken the blow.

I clenched my fists tighter, nails biting into my palms. *"I should have stopped it,"* I repeated, softer this time, a lump growing thick in my throat. *"I couldn't save her, Azura. I couldn't save her."* My tears flowed uncontrollably.

Azura was silent for a moment, the weight of her thoughts heavy against mine. When she finally spoke, her voice was soft but unwavering. *"You cannot save everyone, Aurelia. You are not the fates."*

"But I'm supposed to be her queen," I shot back through our bond, as I looked down at Cam's body, Orla's hand still resting on her chest, as if hoping to pull her back from the brink. *"I'm supposed to protect the people I love. How can I lead them if I can't even save one of the closest people to me?"*

Azura's presence flared again, stronger this time, and I could feel her power coursing through my veins. *"You will lead them because you love them. Because you fight for them. Even now, in the depths of your grief, you are thinking of them. You are more than your magic, Aurelia. You are more than your power. You have a heart, and it is that heart that will carry you through this war."*

I let her words wash over me, the steady pulse of her energy anchoring me, but the ache in my chest only grew heavier. My gaze shifted around the ballroom, taking in the aftermath of the chaos—overturned tables, shattered glass, the dark stains on the once pristine marble floors. The party was a distant memory now. The promise of celebration, of joy, had been stolen in an instant.

The servants moved with quiet efficiency, their faces pale and drawn, yet they worked without complaint, clearing debris and righting what they could. There was no music anymore, no laughter. Just the sounds of soft sobs, the clatter of cleaning, and the distant murmur of frightened guests. I caught sight of Rein, his brow furrowed as he spoke with some guards, his usual easy going demeanor replaced with grim resolve.

It was like the whole world had shifted, and we were left standing in the wreckage.

My gaze fell back again to Cam's too still body, her chest unnaturally still, her hand now limp. I swallowed back the sob building in my throat, my chest tightening as I forced myself to take in every detail—the way her blonde hair clung to her wet ash covered forehead, the way her once-vibrant eyes were now void and glassy. She had always been there for me, always. And now just… gone.

Azura's presence stirred again, a soft hum in the back of my mind. *"Grieve for her, Aurelia. But do not lose yourself in it. Cam would not want that."*

I pressed my lips together, blinking back the tears that threatened to spill over again. *"I don't know how to move forward from this,"* I admitted, my mouth feeling dry. *"How do I keep going, knowing that she's gone? Knowing that this war will take more of us?"*

Azura didn't answer right away, her presence more a comforting warmth than words. Finally, she spoke, her voice low and steady. *"You move forward by holding onto the love you shared, not the loss. And you fight. Not out of anger or vengeance, but out of love. That is how you will honor her, Aurelia. That is how you will lead."*

I closed my eyes, tears slipping down my cheeks as I leaned into Azura's energy, drawing strength from her. The grief would always be there, a shadow lurking at the edges of my heart. But Azura was right. I couldn't let it consume me. I had to keep fighting, for Cam, for Orla, for everyone. But gods, it hurt.

The weight of the night pressed down on me, suffocating in its intensity. When I opened my eyes again, Orla was watching me, her amber eyes filled with grief that mirrored my own. She was holding it together, just barely, but I could see the cracks in the armor she wore around her heart. She needed me, and gods, I needed her.

Amidst the wreckage and cold, I made a silent promise to Cam, to myself, and to the kingdom—*I will not let these sacrifices be in vain.*

Frank had already carried Rielle off to the healers, finding her beneath the remnants of the table she'd been thrown into during the blast. Rein approached with a few guards, kneeling next to us, his expression filled with gentle concern. He touched my cheek lightly, his gaze flicking between me and Orla. "Aure," he started softly. "We need to take her body now. Both of you need to go to the healers and somewhere secure."

I opened my mouth to protest. I didn't want her—Cam—to be alone, her body cold and lifeless in some distant place. But the words stuck in my throat. Instead, I swallowed my pain and nodded, unable to speak.

Rein stood and motioned to the guards to carry her body away. The moment they touched Cam, I collapsed into Orla, unable to hold myself up any longer. She tightened her arms around me, pulling me close. Her voice was strained, distant as she whispered into my ear, "We need to make sure you're not hurt. We need to stand, Meles Tari."

Her words tugged at me, but I barely had the strength to move. The world felt distant, fading into the background as my grief threatened to consume me whole.

Rein stepped forward, his hands tentative but firm as he placed them on my shoulders. His concern radiated through his touch, though I caught the flicker of uncertainty in his eyes as he glanced at Orla. "Aure, let me help," he said gently, though his gaze lingered on Orla with a trace of fear, as if unsure how she'd react.

I hesitated, still pressed against Orla, her presence the only thing keeping me from completely shattering. She looked at Rein, then back at me, her now steely gray eyes filled with grief but also a strange, guarded determination. "Go with him," she said softly, her voice distant yet holding a faint tremor. "He'll take care of you."

Reluctantly, I nodded, and as I pulled away from Orla's embrace, her arms fell to her sides, stiff and unyielding as she too stood. Rein guided me into his chest, and I clung to him, my body collapsing under the weight of the night. My breath came in ragged sobs, and I felt his arms wrap around me in an attempt to anchor me. Though, his concern wasn't just for me. He glanced over my head at Orla, his expression a mixture of sympathy and fear.

"Orla…" Rein's voice was soft, hesitant. "You should come too. You need to be looked after as well."

Orla stiffened, her face hardening into a mask of stoic control. "No," she replied, her tone sharp and clipped. "Take Aure to the healers. Make sure she's safe. I'll deal with… this." She gestured vaguely to the smoldering remnants of the ballroom, but her voice cracked slightly. I could hear the emotion she was trying so hard to bury.

Rein looked torn, clearly wanting to help both of us, but there was something about Orla now that made him wary. "Orla, you can't—" he began, but she cut him off.

"I said I'll deal with it," she snapped, her gaze locking onto his with an intensity that made him flinch. She paused, then added, more softly, "Go. Get her out of here."

I watched her, my heart breaking at the cold distance that had suddenly formed between us. She had grown to be my strength, my anchor, but now… now she seemed miles away. I reached out toward her through our bond, but the moment my hand gripped Rein's arm for support, I felt the shift in her.

Orla's expression shut down completely. Her blue-gray eyes, once filled with so much emotion, went blank. She looked at the spot where my hand held onto Rein, and her lips pressed into a thin line. The warmth, the connection of the bond we had shared, felt like it had nearly vanished in an instant. It was as if a door had slammed shut between us, and I was left standing on the other side, watching her retreat further and further into herself. She had figured how to shield our bond. I could still feel it, the strong chaos of our mingled magic, but it was closed off like she was ignoring me completely.

Rein, sensing the shift too, tightened his hold on me, his concern now equally split between the two of us. "Let's go," he murmured, his voice gentle but strained. He shot one last glance at Orla, fear mingling with the sympathy in his eyes, but she had already turned away, her focus now fixed on the surrounding devastation.

I let Rein guide me away, my legs barely supporting me as I clung to him for strength. Each step felt like a betrayal, like I was leaving something vital behind with Orla. I wanted to go back, to reach out to her, to fix the distance that had grown between us in the span of minutes, but her cold detachment kept me rooted in place.

As we moved farther from the ballroom, the weight of the night pressed harder on me, suffocating me in grief and confusion. Rein held me close, but even in his arms, I felt an unbearable loneliness without Orla.

Before I realized it, we stepped through the doors of the large sterile white room. The infirmary was a whirlwind of chaos, filled with the sounds of clinking glass vials, hurried footsteps, and hushed conversations between healers as they rushed from patient to patient. The sharp scent of medicinal herbs mixed with the heavy metallic tang of blood that still lingered in the air. As Rein guided me into the room, I felt a deep sense of numbness settle over me, dulling the noise and chaos around me.

Healers approached us immediately, their faces grim but professional. One of them, a stern-looking older woman with silver hair tied back in a tight bun, gestured for me to sit on a cot. I obeyed, barely aware of her hands as she began examining me, the cold touch of her fingers trailing over my skin, checking for injuries. I heard her voice, though her words barely registered through the haze.

Rein stayed close, his hand gently resting on my shoulder. His presence was the only thing anchoring me to reality as the healers worked around me.

Amid the chaos, Frank's voice rang out, his usual carefree tone replaced by one of frustration and concern. "Rielle, for gods' sake, even if it's just a sprained wrist, let me help you, would you?"

Rielle, sitting on a nearby cot with her arm wrapped in a bandage, rolled her eyes at Frank's fussing. "I'm fine, Frank. Stop hovering over me like an old nursemaid. It's just a few bruises and a wrist. There are people here far worse off than me."

Frank, clearly not convinced, crossed his arms over his burly chest, but his concern was evident in the way his eyes darted between Rielle and the other wounded in the room. His brow furrowed in a mix of worry and frustration, his usual bravado tempered by the weight of the evening's events.

As he noticed us, his face softened slightly, though the worry didn't leave his eyes. He approached quickly, his gaze shifting from me to Rein. "Where's Cam?" he asked, his voice tense. "And Orla? Why aren't they here?"

I flinched at the mention of Cam's name, the wound of her loss still raw and open. I couldn't bring myself to answer, my throat tight with emotion. My hands, still stained with blood, trembled in my lap, and I couldn't meet Frank's eyes.

Rein, sensing my inability to respond, stepped in with a tenderness I hadn't expected from him. He glanced at me, then turned to Frank, his voice soft but firm. "Cam… didn't make it, Frank. She… she saved Aure, but she's gone."

Frank's face paled, his usual cocky demeanor faltering as the reality of Rein's words hit him. He stood there, frozen for a moment, as if trying to process the loss. His gaze shifted to me, and I could see the weight of grief settling into his eyes, but he didn't say anything. Instead, he nodded slowly, his lips pressed into a thin line, as if struggling to hold himself together.

"And Orla?" Frank asked, his voice quieter now, his concern clear.

Rein hesitated for a moment, glancing at me before responding. "Orla is… dealing with everything in her own way. She stayed behind to handle things."

He stood there, frozen for a moment, eyes wide with shock. His gaze flicked between me and Rein, then darted toward the door, as if part of him was already running after her.

"She's handlin' things alone?" Frank's voice cracked, the urgency rising in his tone. His growing concern for Orla shoved aside his grief for Cam, though palpable.

Rein hesitated for a moment, then nodded. "Yes, but Frank, Orla is stronger than any of us. She'll be—"

But Frank wasn't listening anymore. His eyes darted back to Rielle, torn between staying here for me, for Rielle, or going after Orla. He shifted on his feet, his usual swagger gone, replaced with a desperate need to be in two places at once.

"I need to go after her," he muttered, more to himself than anyone else. His fists clenched and unclenched at his sides, the grief hitting him hard, but the weight of his duty dragged him forward.

Rielle, noticing his turmoil, stepped closer, her wrapped wrist held tight against her body, but her expression steady. She didn't try to reassure him that Orla would be fine—because we all knew she wasn't. Instead, she laid a gentle hand on Frank's arm, her voice soft but firm. "Go, Frank. Orla needs you. It's okay to leave."

Frank's head snapped toward her, eyes wide with a mix of fear and hesitation. "But you—Rielle, you're hurt, and Aure's—" His gaze landed on me, still trembling, barely able to focus on anything but the weight of my grief and guilt.

Rielle shook her head, her expression softening as she caught his gaze. "I'm fine. I'll be okay. You need to be with Orla. She shouldn't be alone right now. None of us should."

Frank hesitated for only a split second before his resolve hardened. His grief for Cam, clearly far from forgotten, simmered beneath his urgent need to be by Orla's side. He squeezed Rielle's hand briefly, then shot one last look at me—his eyes filled with sorrow and apology—before nodding to Rein.

"I'll find her," he said, his voice low but determined. Then he was gone, striding quickly out of the infirmary, the door swinging shut behind him.

Rielle watched him leave, her own expression torn between worry for Orla and the concern she felt for me. She exhaled a soft breath, then turned to me, offering a quiet nod of understanding. "He'll bring her back to you, my Queen." She whispered, though, her eyes held no promises, only the same unspoken fear we all shared.

I nodded faintly, still clinging to the last shred of my composure as the healers moved around me, their voices a distant hum compared to the roaring chaos in my mind. The empty void where my bond with Orla had once hummed now felt unbearably silent.

The healer examining me finally spoke, her voice breaking through the tension. "She's not hurt, physically at least. No serious injuries. But she's been through an ordeal."

I felt Rein's grip on my shoulder tighten slightly in silent support as the healer's words hung in the air. However, none of the physical assessments could heal the emotional wounds that had been carved into all of us that night.

I closed my eyes, concentrating hard, desperately searching for any trace of Orla, hoping she would reopen our bond, even just a sliver, so I could feel her warmth inside me again. Still, every time I reached out, my magic was met with a cold, empty silence, the flow bouncing back unanswered.

Rielle, her black and red braids now a tangled mess, wrapped her single arm around me, pulling me into a comforting embrace. Her voice was soft but steady as she looked over my shoulder. "Rein, help me get her back to her room so she can clean up," she said, her tone firm yet concerned. "We need to get her out of here."

Rein nodded, his expression still heavy with the weight of the night. He stepped forward and extended his hand, his movements careful, almost hesitant. I stared at his outstretched palm for a moment before slowly placing mine in his, the warmth of his touch grounding me. Gently, he helped me to my feet. "Come on, Aure," he said softly, his voice tender but laced with caution, as though afraid that even the smallest disturbance might shatter what little strength I had left. "Let's get you out of here."

As we made our way through the quiet corridors of the palace, the weight of everything continued to press down on me. The infirmary, with its frantic energy, had faded into a distant hum, but the chaos within me felt more suffocating than ever. Rein's hand remained a steady presence in mine, while Rielle, her arm still wrapped around me, guided me with quiet determination.

We reached my chambers, the heavy wooden door swinging open as Rein stepped aside to let me in. The familiar scent of my room—the lavender oils on my pillows, the soft flicker of candlelight, the coconut of my soaps, the orange blossom and bergamot of my perfume—should have brought me some comfort, but tonight, it all felt too distant. Too far removed from the nightmare that had unfolded.

Rielle guided me gently toward the edge of the plush chair near the crackling hearth, her movements slower now, as if she could sense how fragile I felt. Rein lingered by the door, his expression soft, yet unreadable. He gave Rielle a brief nod before stepping back into the hallway. "I'll make sure no one disturbs you," he said, his voice low, before closing the door behind him.

The silence in the room felt thick, almost unbearable. Rielle, with her own dress a wet blooded mess, knelt beside me, her unbandaged hand resting on my back in a reassuring gesture. For a few moments, neither of us spoke. She waited, her presence steady, as though she knew I needed time to find my voice.

Finally, she broke the silence. "Let me help you get cleaned up," she offered softly, her hand lingering at my back. "We'll get you out of those clothes."

I nodded, the simple gesture feeling like it took all the strength I had left. Rielle stood, moving to gather a fresh robe from my wardrobe as I sat, still staring at the floor. I barely registered the movement as she set the clean garment next to me, then turned to fill the basin with water. The sound of the water trickling in the quiet room felt surreal, like a distant memory I could no longer grasp.

"I'm going to help you with this," she said, her voice gentle yet firm as she approached me again. She knelt in front of me this time and slowly began undoing the clasps of my gown, her fingers deft despite the bandage on her wrist. She worked in silence for a few moments before she spoke again, her voice soft but carrying the weight of years of friendship. "Aure... you don't have to hold it all in, you know."

I swallowed hard, my throat dry and tight. I hadn't realized how much I needed to hear those words until she said them. My eyes burned, and I bit my lip, trying to keep the flood of emotions at bay. "I—" My voice cracked, and I couldn't finish the sentence.

Rielle's eyes softened, and she brushed a stray tear from my cheek. "It's okay. You can talk to me, Aure. I'm here. You don't have to be strong right now."

Her words broke something inside me. The walls I'd been holding up since Cam's death, since the attack, since everything came crashing down, and crumbled. The tears came then, heavy and uncontrollable, and I buried my face in my hands, my body trembling with the weight of my grief.

Rielle didn't say anything at first. She simply knelt there, her hand rubbing soothing circles on my back, letting me release the storm that had been brewing inside me. After a while, when the sobs had subsided into quiet tears, she spoke again. "You know, you're not alone in this. I know it feels like it right now, but you have people who care about you. I care about you. Orla cares about you."

At the mention of Orla's name, my heart clenched, and fresh tears welled in my eyes. "I... I don't even know if she does anymore," I whispered, my voice barely audible. "I can't feel her. Our bond... it's gone."

Rielle's brows furrowed in concern, and she gently pulled me closer, pressing a cool cloth to my tear-streaked face. "That's not true. I can still see your cord of mingled magic. Orla's just... going through her own storm right now. I know she loves you, Aure. That hasn't changed. She just needs time."

I shook my head, unable to find comfort in her words. "It feels different, Rielle. Like she's pulling away from me. Like she's shutting me out."

Rielle paused, considering her words carefully before she spoke. "Orla's been through a lot. She seems the type to carry everything on her own shoulders, even when she shouldn't. I am confident she'll come back to you. She just needs to figure things out."

Her words, though well-meaning, didn't fully ease the ache in my chest. However, they offered a glimmer of hope, a small thread of comfort amid my fears.

She helped me out of my soiled gown, her movements gentle yet efficient. Soon enough, I stood in front of the mirror, wrapped in a simple, soft robe. My gaze drifted to the once regal and beautiful gown now crumpled on the floor. It felt like a symbol of everything I had lost tonight—Cam, my strength, and the life I once knew. Nothing would ever be the same without her by my side.

Rielle stood beside me, her reflection catching my eye as she gave me a small, tired smile. "There," she said quietly, squeezing my shoulder. "A little better, yeah?"

I nodded, though my heart still felt heavy. But I appreciated her effort. "Thank you," I whispered, my voice still shaky. "I don't know what I'd do without you."

She smiled once more, though the exhaustion in her eyes betrayed her weariness. "You are strong on your own, my Queen," she said softly. "But I'm glad to be here for you, especially now."

I slowly made my way to the neatly made bed, retreating beneath the warmth of the blankets and furs. Curling into the pillows, my tears continued to fall as a restless, uneasy sleep finally overtook me.

ORLA

Chapter 27

One had now grown to thirteen. Five—the number of days until I would leave with Rein for the front. And my thirteen would grow even more. My fingers traced mindlessly over the pale pink skin of a thin, straight scar on my inner thigh—an inch-long reminder of the innocent life I'd taken when I was seventeen, a training accident or not, it was my fault. My responsibility.

I stayed behind to clean up the wreckage I caused and to account for the lives lost because of me. The healers informed me that Aure, though shaken and grieving, was physically unharmed. Relief washed over me, but only briefly, barely touching the storm of emotions raging inside. I kept our bond closed, sealed off tightly, forcing myself to maintain that barrier between us. I couldn't afford to let her feel what I was going through, not now. The weight of my magic, the destruction I had caused. It was mine to bear alone.

Now, I sat here, in the middle of the day, clean and naked on my bed, dagger in hand. My eyes fell briefly to the fresh scar across the center of my left hand. That one held a different memory, a wonderful one, a scar earned in love. A wave of nausea quickly replaced the warmth and thrill that had stirred in my core as my gaze landed on the bruises still darkening my wrist.

I pressed the tip of my dagger to my thigh, just a finger's length away from the old scar, and sliced deep. Blood trickled down in thin, slow streams, the stinging pain bringing with it a twisted sense of calm—a raw release of the emotions that had been suffocating me. It eased the heaviness I felt deep in my heart. My jaw clenched, the heaviness in my chest easing just slightly. I moved again, slicing another line beside it.

Two... Ten more to go.

I watched as the blood trickled down my thigh, the stark contrast of deep purple against pale skin oddly mesmerizing. It didn't take long for the familiar numbness to settle in—the haze of emotions dissipating just enough for me to catch my breath. I kept my focus on the lines I was carving, each slice carefully measured.

Three.

The sting was grounding, a way to control the chaos when everything else was spiraling out of reach. I shifted the blade, pressing deeper, feeling the pressure ease a bit more.

Four.

The room was quiet, save for the soft, steady drip of blood onto the sheets. I should have been more careful about that, but I didn't care. All I could think about was that I needed this. I needed to feel something that I could manage, something I could control. The heaviness of the memories, the pain, it all dulled with each mark I left behind.

Five.

I paused for a moment, my hand trembling slightly as I pressed the blade to my skin again. My breath was shallow, and a part of me—deep down—knew this wasn't the answer, but it felt like the only way I could honor them, keep them close. My eyes burned with unshed tears as I whispered into the silence of the room, "I'm sorry."

Sorry for Cam, for all the lives lost, for everything I hadn't been able to fix. For not stopping him sooner. For all the years I let him get away with the touches, the moments, the delusions. If I had been stronger, smarter, firmer... Cam would still be here. They all would. I moved the dagger again; the blade carving through my skin.

Six.

The sting shot up my leg, sharp and immediate, but the calm that followed was almost serene, like a balm to the relentless chaos. My breath shuddered as I exhaled, the pressure of everything momentarily ebbing away, replaced with the dull throb of the wound. I moved to the next spot, twisting the point of the blade at the start of the mark before slicing straight to match the others.

Seven.

I bit my lip, the taste of blood faint on my tongue. The fresh cut bled slowly, rich plum colored drops pooling on the pale skin of my thigh. I stared at it, focusing on the physical pain rather than the emotional storm raging inside me. The new color of my blood was still a bit unsettling. I refocused, keeping everything I could from my bond with Aure. I cut another slow, deep mark.

Eight.

My hand faltered. The blade slipped slightly, but I adjusted, dragging the metal with precision. Each line was straight, deliberate, just like the choices I should have made back then. If only I had been more decisive. If only I had seen the truth in Tristan's eyes, in his twisted love. Cam wouldn't have had to pay the price for my ignorance.

Nine.

I inhaled deeply, trying to hold back the sob threatening to break free from my chest. My head swam, flashes of Cam's face mingling with the cold expression Tristan had worn before he... My heart clenched painfully, and I pressed harder, the cut deeper this time.

Ten.

The silence of the room was deafening. I could hear nothing but the faint sound of my own breath, shaky and uneven. I wiped at the blood with the back of my hand, smearing the purple across my thigh. My vision blurred.

How had it come to this? How had I, once so confident and determined, been reduced to this? The weight of my guilt pressed down harder with every slice of the blade, each mark a testament to the failures I couldn't escape. The people I couldn't save. Grinding my teeth, I made another deep mark.

Eleven.

My hand shook violently now, but I forced myself to finish. I couldn't stop. Not yet. Each new scar was supposed to be a release, but it was turning into something darker, something that wasn't giving me the closure I thought it would. The final cut, deep and deliberate, carved across my thigh.

Twelve.

A sob tore from my throat, and I collapsed back onto the bed, the dagger slipping from my fingers. I pulled my knees to my chest, blood still seeping from the fresh wounds. The pain was real, tangible, but it couldn't touch the hollow ache inside me.

Curling in on myself, I whispered again, "I'm sorry."

For all of them. For Cam. For myself. For everything.

A knock at the door jolted me, the sound too sharp, too sudden. I froze, stifling my sobs, blood still oozing from the fresh cuts. I picked the dagger back up quickly, stuffing it under the pillow, my heart racing as I stared at the door.

I scrambled, trying to wipe the blood from my thigh, pulling the blanket up to cover myself, my heart thundering in my chest.

"Orla?" she called again, her tone edged with worry. The handle turned slightly, the door creaking open.

I swallowed hard, forcing the panic down as I tried to compose myself. "I'm fine," I croaked, my voice unsteady. "Just... give me a minute."

Rielle didn't push, but I could feel her presence on the other side of the door, waiting.

I glanced down at the cuts on my thigh, the blood slowly drying. Thirteen scars, old and new, hidden beneath the sheets, but still very much a part of me. I clenched my fists, closing my eyes for a second, trying to push away the guilt that surged back with every heartbeat.

"Just one more minute," I whispered to myself, trying to gather the strength before facing the world again. I reached for my robe, pulling it over my shoulders, the fabric heavy against my skin. Wincing slightly, I wiped my thigh roughly with the edge of the sheet, watching the rich plum smear into the fabric. I quickly tucked the bloodstained sheets beneath the blankets, hiding the evidence of what I had done. Clenching my robe tightly around me, I took a shaky breath.

"Hold it together," I muttered, trying to steady myself.

I walked slowly, each step awkward and painful. The new scars stung with every movement, and the relentless scrubbing in the shower had left me raw and swollen, a futile attempt to wash away the evidence of what Tristan had done. The soreness between my legs only added to the ache inside me.

When I reached for the doorknob, I forced every emotion from my face, stealing myself. My eyes dulled to a grayish lavender, swirling with muted hues.

"Yes?" My voice came out more sternly than I intended as I greeted Rielle, the tension hanging in the air between us.

Rielle's eyes widened slightly, sensing the shift in my tone, but she masked her concern behind a calm expression. She took a small step forward, glancing past me into the room, her gaze lingering for a moment on the rumpled bed and my disheveled appearance. I saw her hesitate before speaking.

"I just wanted to check on you," she said softly, her usual fiery demeanor replaced by something more careful, more measured. "I heard you hadn't left your chambers after the cleanup, and I thought... maybe you could use some company."

Frank had been the one who'd asked Rielle to check on me. Apparently, I hadn't been talking much during the cleanup in the ballroom—just staring, numb. He was worried, and now that I'd holed myself up in my chambers, it seemed he wasn't the only one. However, I could feel him, even now, pacing somewhere, torn between wanting to help and not knowing how to reach me.

Rielle, always no-nonsense, had taken the task upon herself. Of course, she had. Frank probably figured that she, of all people, might be able to get through to me when he couldn't. So, here she was, sitting beside me, her presence calm but persistent, waiting for me to speak.

"He's worried about you," Rielle finally said, breaking the silence. "Frank. He didn't know what to say, so he asked me to check on you. After everything that's happened, he thought you might talk to me instead."

I swallowed, my throat tight. I hadn't spoken much since the ballroom, since the mess I'd caused. Since him. I didn't know how to. Though Rielle was sitting there, staring at me, making it clear that she wasn't going anywhere until she knew I was okay.

I looked down, fingers twisting the hem of my robe. "I didn't mean to shut everyone out," I mumbled. "I just... I don't know what to say."

Rielle leaned back, giving me space but not backing down. "You don't have to say the right thing, Orla. No one's expecting you to have answers. But it's okay to feel it. Whatever it is. You don't have to pretend you're fine."

I sighed, the weight of the truth pressing down on my chest like a stone. "How do I face Aure after all of this? How do I face any of them? After Cam, after what happened in the ballroom?" My voice wavered, thick with emotion. "I couldn't control it, Rielle. I didn't mean for any of it to happen. Well, I meant for..." I swallowed hard, the words catching in my throat. I couldn't even bring myself to say his name. The rage was still so raw, festering deep inside me.

Smoke curled up from my hands, the edges of my robe beginning to singe. Rielle's eyes darted to the smoke, but she didn't flinch. Her grip tightened on my shoulder, grounding me.

"Orla," she said softly, her voice cutting through the haze. "Whatever you're feeling—whether it's guilt, anger, or grief—you don't have to fight it alone. You don't have to bury it inside yourself."

I clenched my fists, trying to smother the flames inside me and out. "I should have been able to stop him, to protect Cam, to keep everything from falling apart."

Rielle placed her hand over mine, her fingers brushing lightly against the bruise on my left wrist. Her gaze, sharp and unwavering, locked onto the dark marks that had deepened into a painful purple and blue. "You can't carry the weight of the world on your shoulders, Orla," she said, her voice steady but filled with concern. "You did what you had to do in that moment. But you can't let guilt consume you."

Her voice softened as her thumb traced the bruises with delicate care. "Orla, how did you get these?" The question lingered in the air, her eyes searching mine, both gentle and unrelenting.

The ache in my wrist paled in comparison to the storm swirling inside me. I wanted to pull my hand away, to shove everything down like I always had, but the tenderness in her touch held me there.

"I…" The lump in my throat tightened, making it hard to breathe. The words stuck, tangled in my chest, and all that came out was a choked squeak. "He…" I pulled my hand away from Rielle's, my face burning with shame. I turned away, trying to collect myself, but the flood of anger surged too quickly. "I should've killed him in the hall while we were alone."

My hand trembled as I grabbed the rebounder necklace off the dresser. The chain was broken, the stone cracked—useless. "This fucking thing is worthless," I spat, my voice rising with frustration as I gripped it tight. "I hope the rest of your magical wares aren't as defective as this trinket."

The anger was sharp, cutting, but it wasn't meant for Rielle. I knew that. Still, the heat of it surged, overwhelming everything else inside me. I clenched my jaw, trying to steady myself, but it was too late to take back the words.

Rielle took the pendant, turning it over in her hand with a measured gaze. The faint pulse and hum were still there, barely noticeable but undeniably present. She studied it for a few moments, her eyes widening with each passing second. "Orla," she said, her voice low and cautious. "How long have you been wearing this?"

I shrugged, still feeling the anger simmering beneath the surface. "Since Aure had Cam… a few weeks, why?" I stared at her, feeling the weight of concern, fear, and uncertainty pressing down on me.

Rielle's gaze darkened as she studied the pendant. "A rebounder forged within the mountain, imbued with the ancient magic of a Sea Dragon, and bonded through a siren's magic, etched with dwarven runes—it's only supposed to work for any user temporarily. Magic is like a vessel, a cup that holds water. When it's used up, it empties, and only an enchanter like me can recharge it."

I frowned, trying to follow her explanation. "So?"

"But this… this is different." Her voice grew more serious. "Somehow, your magic didn't just empty the vessel—it changed it completely."

Rielle's expression shifted from concern to deep contemplation as she continued to turn the pendant over in her hands. "Orla, your magic didn't just use up the rebounder's power—it poured into it. You've changed the alchemy of the stone itself. The original purpose of the rebounder—holding and redirecting external magic—is invalid now. Instead of just absorbing and deflecting magic, it became a reservoir for your own."

I stared at her, unsure of what to make of it. "What does that even mean?"

"It means that instead of being limited by the stone's original capacity, your magic overrode the enchantments and poured into it, like a dam filling a basin. This pendant was never meant to hold that kind of power, but somehow your magic transformed it." She paused, her eyes narrowing. "That's likely why you were able to release such an enormous, uncontrollable explosion in the ballroom."

My stomach tightened. "So I'm the complete reason everything went so wrong?"

"No," Rielle said quickly. "But your magic, unrestrained and funneled through this altered rebounder, created an explosion far beyond anything it was designed to handle. The original magic in the stone couldn't control the flood of power you poured into it."

I felt a chill run down my spine. "So what now? Can it be fixed?"

Rielle hesitated, her thumb tracing the jagged crack along the stone's surface. "It's not a matter of fixing it. This isn't just broken—it's become something entirely new. You've essentially created a new magical artifact, but it's unstable and unpredictable. It's empty at the moment, but we need to figure out how you altered its nature without even trying."

I stared at the pendant in her hands, feeling a weight settle in my chest. After a few moments, I sank back down onto the edge of the bed. Rielle gently placed the pendant into my palm, the coolness of the stone and chain coiling in my grasp like a sleeping serpent.

"Why did you think it didn't work? Were you attacked?" She asked softly, her voice filled with concern.

My grip tightened around the pendant, and I couldn't meet her gaze. "Yes," I muttered. "And it was useless... everything I thought would protect me failed."

I stood abruptly, the mask of duty slipping over me like armor, becoming my refuge once more. "Out," I ordered, my voice firm. "I need to dress, and then I'm going to check on the recruits. You're assigned to Aure until we can get her a replacement guard."

I turned away from Rielle, jaw clenched, determination flooding through me like a burning fire. I would protect Aure and this kingdom, no matter the cost. If my magic was as destructive as it seemed, then I would wield it against Frostspire on the front lines. Let it burn them instead.

Rielle hesitated for a moment, her eyes searching mine, but I refused to meet her gaze. She opened her mouth as if to say something, but stopped herself. Instead, she gave a small nod, understanding my decision—or at least knowing better than to challenge me in that moment.

"Fine," she said softly, stepping toward the door. "But don't forget, Orla... you're not alone in this. You don't have to shoulder everything by yourself."

I kept my back to her, focusing on the tightness in my chest. Her words dug into me, but I couldn't acknowledge them. Not now.

As soon as the door clicked shut behind her, I let out a shaky breath. I moved toward the dresser, yanking open the drawers and pulling out my combat gear. The black leather armor felt stiff under my fingertips, cold and unyielding. A perfect fit for the version of myself I needed to be right now.

I tugged it on, piece by piece, strapping the breastplate tight against my chest, pulling the gauntlets over my forearms. Every movement felt mechanical, deliberate, and it was all I could do to ignore the throbbing ache in my wrist and the bruises left behind by Tristan.

My fingers brushed over the rebounder pendant where I had placed it on the table. The cracked stone gleamed in the faint light, a reminder of the power I unleashed. A power I didn't fully understand. It felt foreign, even dangerous. That didn't matter. If I had to be a weapon, then I would be.

I slipped the pendant off its chain, rummaged for another in a box of things my mother had given me over the years and placed it on a new chain. I clasped it around my neck again and fastened my sword across my back. My heart pounded in my chest as I made my way toward the door, each step heavy with resolve. I would fight. I would train. I would be the protector this kingdom needed.

And if I had to tear down everything in my path to keep Aure safe, so be it.

I pulled open the door and stepped into the hallway. The cold air greeted me as I made my way through the palace, heading straight toward the training grounds. The recruits were waiting, and I needed the distraction. I needed to fight, to push away the swirling emotions threatening to drown me.

No matter how much distance I tried to put between myself and the events of the ballroom, I couldn't escape the gnawing feeling of guilt, the shadows of Cam's death, the shame of what I had let him do to me, and the fear of what might come next.

AURELIA

Chapter 28

I had given her over forty-eight hours. Rielle, Frank, Rein—even her aunt had seen her. Though every time I went to check in or asked where Orla was, there was always an excuse. No more. I was done. Furious didn't even begin to cover it. The fact that she was shutting me out was unacceptable, and I would not tolerate it any longer.

I stormed toward the training yard, the cold air biting against my skin, though it did little to cool the fire burning in my chest. The snow crunched beneath my boots, but the sound barely registered over the pounding in my ears. My hair trailed behind me, a fiery mess streaked like loose flames as if my anger had physically manifested in the tendrils. The fabric of my burgundy gown flowed around me, comfortable but not enough to soothe the rage simmering beneath my skin. How dare she shut me out like this?

Every person I passed moved quickly and quietly aside—recruits, servants, soldiers alike. No one dared to meet my gaze. Even Rielle had tried to talk me down, hovering like some overbearing chaperone since Orla had apparently assigned her to me, as though I were a child in need of supervision. I wasn't just some fragile figurehead. I was almost a queen of two kingdoms. I could find my own security detail if I needed one.

Not that I would have made a different choice in ensuring my safety, but the fact that Orla hadn't even considered the importance of treating us as partners infuriated me. We may not be married yet, but that was the plan—two halves of a whole. I wasn't going to be treated as less than, as though I had no say in our future or the dangers we faced.

I could see the recruits in the distance, their movements hurried and frantic under the watchful eye of the trainers, but I wasn't here for them. I was here for Orla. My bond with her—usually a comforting presence—felt like a closed door, and the longer she kept it shut, the angrier I grew. I had given her time, space to grieve, to process everything that had happened. I would not be kept at arm's length any longer.

I clenched my fists as I reached the yard. Orla stood near the edge of the training field, her back to me, dressed in tight, practical leathers, her dark hair tousled from the wind, focused on sparring with one of the recruits. Her movements were quick, efficient, and brutal as she disarmed the poor soul before her without so much as breaking a sweat. She didn't look back. Didn't acknowledge me.

"Orla!" My voice cut through the yard like a blade.

She froze for a moment, then slowly straightened, her head turning just slightly toward me, but she didn't face me. The recruit quickly scurried off, grateful for the interruption.

I marched up to her, my chest heaving with frustration. "You've avoided me for long enough. This stops now."

Then she turned, her face a mask of calm that only fueled my anger. "Aure, this isn't the time—"

"Not the time?" I scoffed. "When is it going to be the time, Orla? After you've shut me out completely? After you pretend we aren't connected in every way that matters?" My voice cracked slightly, the weight of my words heavy between us.

She exhaled sharply, her hands flexing at her sides. "I am doing what has to be done."

"And what about us?" I demanded. "What about what we need? What I need? You don't get to make these decisions alone anymore. We are supposed to face things together, Orla. But right now, you're not letting me in."

Her eyes, now dark gray, flickered, the coldness in them unsettling. "I'm doing what's necessary to protect you, Aure. To protect everyone."

I stepped closer, my voice low but fierce. "I don't need protection from you. I need you. All of you. Stop shutting me out."

For a moment, the wall between us flickered, the bond we shared pulsed and flared, but she quickly closed it again, hardening her resolve. Orla's lips pressed into a thin line. "I can't, Aure. Not right now." She turned away from me.

I clenched my fists, biting back the hurt that clawed at my chest. "You can't… Or won't?" My voice cut through the frigid air, thick with frustration and pain. My eyebrows raised, and a spark ignited inside me—a fire that wouldn't be contained any longer. If Orla thought she was the only dangerous one here, she was about to see differently.

The tension in the training yard thickened as I shifted into a battle stance, just as my trainers had taught me for controlling my magic. My hands trembled slightly, energy crackling at my fingertips, the urge to unleash it overwhelming. I felt the heat rise in my core, spreading outward like wildfire.

Then I let go.

A powerful surge of energy erupted from my hands, but instead of just flames, I commanded the very snow beneath our feet. It melted instantly, transforming into waves of water that I manipulated with swift, precise movements. The recruits and soldiers in the sparring ring had no chance to react as the sudden waves knocked them off their feet, sending them sprawling into the slushy mud.

The ground beneath my feet hissed and steamed as the flames met the newly formed water, creating tendrils of steam that spiraled into the air, weaving through the waves. My heart pounded in my chest, each beat echoing the power surging through me.

Orla's sky-blue eyes locked onto mine, her expression unreadable, but I didn't care. I wanted her to see—to feel—the fire and water inside me. To know that she wasn't the only one capable of destruction.

"I'm not afraid of you, Orla," I said, my voice low, but fierce. "Don't make the mistake of thinking you're the only one with power. I'm not someone you can shut out or control."

The waves settled, leaving a field of drenched and disoriented soldiers in their wake. I took a step forward, daring her to say something, to acknowledge the storm I carried just as she did.

This wasn't just about power. It was about us—about her seeing me, really *seeing me.*

Orla stood there, frozen for a moment as the steam rose around us, her now cobalt eyes reflecting the swirling tendrils of water and fire that still lingered in the air. Every recruit and soldier lay scattered, catching their breath in pools of slush and mud, from the force of the magic I had unleashed.

She didn't move, didn't flinch, even as my power rolled off me in waves.

I could see it in her eyes—the crack in her armor, the flicker of recognition. She wasn't the only one who could cause destruction, who could unleash chaos. I held my ground, my breath heavy as I stood before her, daring her to say something, to acknowledge what I had shown her.

Her hands clenched at her sides, the tension radiating off her in sharp pulses. Slowly, she stepped forward, her boots splashing through the muddy remnants of my power. The silence between us stretched taut, like a string ready to snap.

"You've made your point," she said finally, her voice low and tight. Her eyes, once cobalt, darkened to an almost steel gray, a sign of her own simmering emotions. "But this isn't about power, Aure. You think I shut you out to protect myself? I was trying to protect you."

"By pushing me away?" I shot back, my voice thick with emotion. "By acting like I don't matter? Orla, we're in this together. I'm not your enemy."

"You don't understand," she snapped, her voice rising as the tension between us crackled like a live wire. "You saw what I did, Aure. What I'm capable of. I lost control—*again.*"

"And you think I don't lose control?" I took a step closer, my magic still sparking in the air between us. "Do you think what just happened here wasn't a display of losing control? I nearly wiped out everyone standing here, Orla! But you don't see me running from it. I face it. I face you."

Her expression softened for a moment, but she quickly masked it again, the walls she had built around her heart rising back up. "I can't risk losing you," she whispered, her voice barely audible over the distant sound of the soldiers groaning as they pulled themselves back to their feet. "Not after everything we've been through. Not after Cam."

The mention of Cam hit me like a punch to the gut, and I felt my magic recoil inside me, the flames dimming. My chest tightened, the pain of that loss was still too raw to bear. "I don't want to lose you either," I said, my voice softer now, but no less determined. "But we both will if you keep pushing me away."

For a moment, Orla said nothing. Her gaze flickered over the ruined training yard, the soldiers and recruits regaining their footing, their eyes flicking between us with nervous glances.

Then, slowly, I reached out and touched her hand. The contact sent a shock through me—not of magic, but of something far deeper. She flinched but took my hand letting our magic and bond mingle for a moment before she let go, pulling away again. "I don't know how to do this," she admitted, her voice cracking slightly. "I don't know how to balance being what this kingdom needs and the person you deserve."

I swallowed hard, my heart aching at her vulnerability. "We'll figure it out together," I whispered, my hand reaching for hers again, hovering over it. "But you have to let me in. You have to trust me." She nodded but turned away again.

"Recruits!" Orla called out, her voice firm but not harsh. "Back on your feet, clean this mess up. Training's not over."

She turned to direct the recruits, and I moved after her, not letting this slide.

"Orla, we aren't done. We need to talk. I get relationships are new for you, but you can't just shut me out." I grabbed her shoulder to turn her toward me, and she shot me a glare that could've frozen the air around us.

"Fine, you want to train so bad and not talk? Then let's do it." I ripped a ribbon from my gown, tying my hair back into a tight bun. Orla's head tilted slightly, a brief smirk flickering across her face before she masked it with her usual stoic expression.

"I'm not going to fight you, Aure. Not in those clothes, not here, not now, not ever." She turned away from me again.

I wasn't going to back down. I threw a punch at her shoulder, and she blocked it effortlessly. A small smile tugged at my lips—I was done trying to reason with her. If this was what it took to get through to her, so be it. She shoved my hand aside, and when she turned, I moved in quickly, landing a jab to her side. She let out a small gasp.

"Come on, spar with me, darling. I'm not some fragile glass figurine." I mirrored her movements, circling her with a grin. The recruits had slowed their cleaning, their eyes now glued to us.

She growled, brushing me off. "Stop it. I'm not sparring with you."

I aimed a right hook at her jaw, but she caught my hand mid-air and twisted me around, pulling me flush against her body, my back pressed to her chest. Her breath was hot against my neck and I whispered, "Isn't this better, honey?"

With mischief playing across my face, I used her weight against her. I flipped her over and straddled her, pinning her to the slushy ground. A triumphant grin spread across my face as I leaned in. "I know you like it when I'm on top."

Before I could savor the moment, Orla swept her legs under me, flipping us both. I landed hard on my back, the cold mud soaking through my gown as my head splashed into a puddle. Her eyes sparkled with challenge, her gaze locked on mine.

She leaned in close, her voice low and teasing. "You look ridiculous."

Despite the mud and the cold seeping into my gown, I smiled, feeling the heat flare between us. I leaned up slightly and placed a soft kiss on her neck, and she let out a slow breath.

"I love you, Orla," I whispered, my voice carrying all the weight of my heart. "Not because of our bond, our arrangement, or because we have to marry. I love you because the first moment I saw you, I knew you were going to be my entire universe. I don't need you to protect me from everything. I just need you to be by my side through it all."

Her eyes flickered, her stoic mask faltering for just a moment, and I could feel the tension between us shift. Her expression softened for a heartbeat, and I could see the wall she'd built around herself crack, just a little. She looked away for a moment, the hardness in her lavender gray eyes replaced by something more vulnerable, but it was fleeting.

Her lips twitched as they curled into a small smile. She leaned her forehead down until it touched mine and whispered. "I love you too." Her eyes fluttered closed a moment before she picked her head back up, looking straight at me. "I am also by your side," she said quietly, her voice carrying a weight that made it clear she meant more than just this moment. "But Aure… I can't let you get hurt. Not like Cam."

I reached up, brushing a leaf out of hair and from her face, my touch gentle. "I know you want to protect me. But we protect each other. That's how it works, Orla. It's not just you fighting for me. I'm fighting for you, too." My hand lingered on her cheek, and for a moment, she leaned into my touch.

Orla shifted, her eyes searching mine, then glanced around at the recruits still standing awkwardly nearby, trying not to watch. With a resigned sigh, she stood, offering me her hand. I took it, allowing her to pull me up from the slushy ground. The mud clung to my gown and hair, but I didn't care.

She brushed off her own clothes, her face stern again. However, I knew I had gotten through to her, even if she wasn't ready to fully admit it.

"You're right," she said, her voice quieter now. "But there are still things I have to do alone. I need to fight on the front, to face Frostspire, to... make sure I control this power. If I lose control again—"

"Even if you do," I interrupted, stepping closer. "I'll be there. Just like I am now. I'm not letting you do this alone."

Orla sighed, her eyes flickering with a swirl of dull colors from the storm of emotions she kept locked away. "I'm not used to letting people in."

I placed my hand on her chest, over her heart. "Then let me be the first."

My hand lingered on Orla's chest, the warmth of our connection grounding us for a brief moment. She didn't back away, and I stepped into her space. I gently caressed her cheek. Her eyes fluttered closed for just a second. Though I could still feel the weight of everything unsaid, the unspoken fear that lingered between us.

"We should… I should get back to it," she finally said, glancing around at the soaked and disheveled soldiers. "Before the recruits think we're both about to kill them."

I let out a small, bitter laugh, the magic in me finally calming down. "They should be more worried about how to clean up this mess," I said, gesturing to the chaos I had created.

The sound of hurried footsteps broke through the sound of the yard. We turned in unison to see a servant running into the yard, his face flushed with urgency. He paused for a second, his wide eyes taking in the disarray—the scattered recruits, the mud-streaked ground, and us, still standing in the aftermath of our impromptu sparring.

Rielle, who had followed me, but had stayed silently watching us, now stepped forward without hesitation, positioning herself between us and the servant, despite her small frame barely reaching the young man's chest. Her presence commanded enough authority to give him pause.

The servant straightened, still breathless but determined as he spoke. "King Oric requests the presence of both Her Majesty Princess Orla and Her Royal Grace Princess Aurelia of Faedamir."

His words hung in the air for a moment as he caught his breath, the weight of his message apparent in his anxious expression. Orla and I exchanged a glance—equal parts curiosity and apprehension.

Finally, I exhaled softly, brushing a stray lock of hair from my face. "It's about time," I murmured, my voice laced with a mix of anticipation and caution.

Orla's jaw clenched, her eyes narrowing as she processed the servant's message. "It'll be about the events at the party," she said, though her tone hinted at something deeper, as if she suspected more lay beneath the surface.

She turned her gaze to the servant, her voice firm yet calm. "Tell my father we are currently indisposed and will meet with him in private in his office two hours from now."

The servant blinked, taken aback for a moment by the commanding presence Orla exuded, but he quickly nodded and bowed. "Yes, Your Majesty," he replied, straightening before hurrying off to relay the message.

Orla exhaled slowly, her gaze softening as she turned back to me. "Two hours," she repeated, her tone gentler. "That should give you enough time to get all the mud out of your hair and for both of us to look a little more... presentable." A small smile tugged at the corner of her lips as she leaned in, placing a soft kiss on my forehead. "I'll meet you there, okay?"

I nodded, feeling the warmth of her brief touch linger as she straightened up and my heart steadying. Whatever King Oric had to say, we'd face it together.

After we had cleaned up, I now stood with Orla in front of King Oric's office. Her fingers lightly traced the intricate carvings on the door before she straightened and pushed it open, gesturing for me to walk in first. King Oric stood in front of his desk, maps and small trinkets scattered across its surface, his attention focused on the strategy laid out before him. Lady Lili lounged casually in the chair behind the desk, her expression unreadable.

As we entered, King Oric looked up, offering us a smile that didn't quite reach his cold, calculating eyes. The warmth in his voice felt false as he moved toward me, closing the distance with swift steps. He grasped my hand and placed a kiss on it. "Ah, Princess Aurelia, as stunning as ever."

Before he could pull me into a hug, Orla stepped between us, her presence solid and protective. Her gaze fixed on her father as he took a small step back, and for a brief moment, a flicker of fear crossed his face before he masked it with a smooth smile. He quickly dropped my hand, adjusting his posture as if nothing had happened.

"Orla, daughter," he greeted with forced politeness, clearly sensing the tension. "Thank you both for meeting with us so quickly."

Orla shifted, uncomfortable with the stiffness of the exchange, her eyes narrowing slightly as she waited for him to get to the point.

King Oric cleared his throat, moving back to the large cluttered wooden desk. He adjusted a few of the items on the surface as if stalling for time, then finally spoke. "There's been much discussion within the court, particularly after the… events at the celebration."

Lady Lili, lounging elegantly in the chair, watched us with a sharp gaze, and forced a smile. Her fingers idly traced the edge of the armrest, her eyes flicking between Orla and me. "Yes, the council and other nobles have expressed some concerns," she chimed in smoothly, her voice laced with that familiar hint of superiority. "It seems there's a great deal of talk about the future of this kingdom, and with the war looming… stability is what we need."

Orla remained still, her jaw tightening at the mention of the council. I could sense her discomfort, her frustration simmering just beneath the surface.

King Oric continued, his voice smooth and persuasive. "What we're proposing, Orla, Aurelia, is that we move up the date of the wedding. It would do wonders to solidify the alliance between our two kingdoms. The people need something to believe in, especially now." He shot a glance at Lady Lili, who nodded in agreement.

"The sooner the better," Lady Lili added, her tone light, but the implication heavy. "A grand gesture of unity, especially in light of recent events, would be the perfect way to remind the people of the strength in our leadership… and of your place, Aurelia, in Orlondia's future."

Orla stood straighter, her posture stiffening as the suggestion sunk in. She didn't look at me; her eyes remained fixed on her father. "And you think rushing our marriage will somehow fix the unrest? That it will erase what happened?" Her voice was calm, but the tension was palpable.

King Oric's smile faltered slightly. "It's not about erasing what happened, Orla. It's about making our next move. About showing the people that despite everything, we remain strong. A united front is exactly what this kingdom needs. What both our kingdoms need."

I felt Orla's unease ripple through our bond, her silence speaking volumes. She hated being pushed into a decision like this, especially by her father.

"Moving the wedding up isn't something we can simply rush into," Orla finally said, her voice steady, though I could hear the restraint. "There are far more pressing matters, and it's not a solution to the problems we're facing."

Lady Lili leaned forward slightly, her smile never wavering. "Of course, we understand that, dearest. Surely, you see the benefit of ensuring the alliance is solidified before any more... disruptions occur." She paused, her gaze shifting to me for a moment before settling back on Orla. "It would give the people something to celebrate, something to rally behind."

Orla turned her head slightly, her eyes finally meeting mine since we entered the room. I could see the dark swirls of cobalt in her gaze, full of emotions—uncertainty, frustration, protectiveness. Beneath it all, there was a hint of something softer, something I wished I could reach.

I stepped forward, breaking the tense silence. "With all due respect, Your Majesty, rushing into a wedding isn't going to address the deeper issues at play. This is more than just appearances or presenting a unified front on the surface."

Orla's hand twitched as if she wanted to reach for mine, but she kept it rigidly by her side. King Oric's thin smile faltered, clearly displeased with our response. He stopped fiddling with the trinkets on his desk and straightened, his authoritative demeanor hardening. "We understand your concerns about timing," he said, his voice stern. "But there's another pressing matter that adds urgency to this situation."

Orla's posture tensed, her expression sharpening as she waited for him to continue.

"The display of power at the party," King Oric began, his tone laced with disapproval. "Was deeply unsettling. Not just to me, but to the council and our guests—particularly Sir Alden Gareth, Tristan's father. He spoke to me this morning, emphasizing his son's unwavering loyalty, despite what you claimed transpired. Many have expressed their concern about the level of destruction during what was meant to be a night of celebration."

I could see Orla's jaw clench, her eyes darkening further as King Oric's words cut into the fragile space between us.

Lady Lili interjected smoothly, "Your actions, while heroic to some, have cast a shadow of doubt among the council about your control and temperament. It's imperative now more than ever to show unity and stability."

Orla clenched her jaw, her voice firm yet controlled as she addressed them both. "If you are concerned about stability and control, then perhaps my place is on the front lines, aiding in the real battles, not just dressed up as a symbol in a rushed wedding."

King Oric's expression hardened. "This is not just a suggestion, Orla. It's a directive from your king and council. We need to move forward with the wedding promptly to quell any doubts about our leadership and the future of our kingdoms. Your... demonstration has made this all the more critical."

Orla shot me a glance, her frustration palpable. She turned back to her father, her voice rising slightly. "I am more than just a figurehead to be married off for appearances. I can be of real use on the battlefield, not just standing beside Aure at an altar!"

Lady Lili sighed, her voice softening as she attempted to placate the growing tension. "We are all striving for what's best for the kingdom, Orla. No one doubts your capabilities. However, perceptions are as powerful as actions. We must consider how these perceptions affect the stability of Orlondia."

Oric nodded in agreement, his tone final. "We've made our decision. The wedding will be moved up, and your role will continue to evolve as we see fit. This is for the greater good of all."

Orla looked at me, her eyes conveying a mix of anger and desperation. I reached for her hand, squeezing it slightly, signaling my support regardless of the edicts from her father.

"Besides, the love you both share is evident. Why wouldn't you want this?" Lady Lili's voice dripped with a saccharine sweetness that made my skin crawl. "I know you were opposed to the idea in the beginning, and rightly so, but now? Now, it seems almost petty to argue over something so... inevitable." Her eyes flickered with a manipulative gleam.

She let the words settle before adding, "And, Orla, with the marriage and treaty settled, you could be considered for the front lines. But we can't risk your life there if you haven't fulfilled your obligations here first. You know duty comes before all else, dear."

The way she twisted the situation—dangling the possibility of Orla going to the front as a reward—made my stomach turn. She was making it clear: the marriage wasn't just about unity or love, but control.

At that, Orla pulled her hand away and stormed out of the office alone, without another word. I stood there stunned for a moment, then spoke calmly. "I thought the agreement was we would choose when we wed to help both of us adjust to this arrangement, your highness?"

"Are you threatening to back out of this treaty, Princess Demajanio?" King Oric seethed, his eyes narrowing as he tossed an opened letter at my feet. The sharp edge of his words hung in the air as I bent to pick up the letter, the once-sealed message from Orlondia's diplomat to Faedamir. His voice dropped to a low, menacing growl as I began to scan its contents. "Because you don't have that right..."

He paused, watching me closely before finishing with a chilling finality. "Yet."

ORLA

Chapter 29

Sweat beaded on my brow, rolling down the side of my face in hot, stinging streams, but I didn't stop. The soft thud of my fists connecting with the padded dummy echoed through the empty training room. I struck again, harder this time, my knuckles stinging beneath the leather wraps. I couldn't stop.

The world outside this room was waiting—its demands, its weight, pressing down on me like an unmovable stone. Here, alone, it was just me, my fists, and the dummy. Nothing else mattered, not time, not my magic, not the war, and not my father.

I landed a hard punch to the dummy's chest, its fabric giving way beneath the impact. Another strike to the shoulder, followed by a low, sharp kick to the base. Each blow was fueled by the faces that haunted me— the ones I couldn't save. Cam, the boy whose life I had accidentally taken, the innocent people caught in the crossfire. The anger surged, raw and unrelenting, tightening my chest as I fought to keep control.

A left hook followed by a right jab. The sound of impact reverberated, but it wasn't enough. The sweat, the rage, the pain all churned together into a single driving force that demanded more.

I gritted my teeth and landed another punch. My muscles burned with the effort, each movement a raw release of everything I held back. The pain in my thigh was sharp, as each move of my pants rubbed roughly against the marks I had made there. My mind raced with thoughts I didn't want to face—the failures, the secrets, the mounting pressure.

I could feel the tension in my magic, the way it simmered just beneath the surface, aching to be set free. I couldn't let it out. Not here. Not now. Despite reaching for control. My fist felt burning hot, the heat scorching through me as it made contact with the dummy, leaving a charred mark on its surface.

"Fuck!" I screamed, the word echoing sharply through the empty room, reverberating off the stone walls.

I paused, chest heaving as I leaned against the wall, my hands resting on my knees. The room felt too small, the walls closing in as my thoughts spiraled. I closed my eyes, trying to steady my breathing, the heavy scent of sweat and worn leather filling my nose.

This was supposed to help. I was supposed to feel something other than this gnawing frustration. Instead, the weight only seemed to grow heavier.

With a growl of frustration, I stepped back and aimed a vicious punch at the dummy's head. The impact sent a tremor up my arm, and for a fleeting second, the pressure in my chest loosened. Only for a second.

I let out a shaky breath and wiped the sweat from my brow. I didn't know how much longer I could keep doing this. Keep it all in and to keep it all from Aure.

The door to the training room creaked open, but I didn't turn to look. Whoever it was could wait. For just a little longer, I needed to stay in this moment, where it was only me, the dummy, and the war inside my own head.

"I think he is well dead and bloodied," Frank mused as he leaned against the far wall watching me.

Frank's easy smile faded as he pushed off the wall, his eyes scanning the scorched dummy, then trailing back to me. He approached cautiously, his usual jovial demeanor replaced with concern. "You're workin' yourself hard again, Orla. What's goin' on?" His voice softened, a rare seriousness threading through it.

I wiped the sweat from my brow, avoiding his gaze as I reset my stance, preparing for another strike. "I have to be ready. The front line isn't forgiving. I need to be... unstoppable. A weapon," I said, my voice hard but steady.

He frowned, stepping in front of me, blocking the dummy with his body. "A weapon?" Frank's brow furrowed as he studied me. "You're not a weapon, Orla. You're the one who's supposed to lead, not just fight."

I clenched my fists, the heat from my magic still simmering in my veins. "That's the point, Frank. I need to be the strongest one out there. I need to make sure no one else dies because I wasn't strong enough." My voice cracked slightly, betraying the calm I was trying to keep.

He crossed his arms, his posture firm but not aggressive. "This isn't just about bein' strong, Orla. You're already stronger than most of us combined, but if you lose yourself—if you let this... anger consume you, you'll burn everythin' around you. Literally." His gaze dropped to the charred dummy.

I looked away, my jaw tightening. "That's the point."

Frank exhaled deeply, shaking his head. "No, it's not. You're not just a weapon, and you know that." He stepped closer, forcing me to meet his gaze. "We need you, Orla. All of you. Not just the part that can destroy things."

I swallowed hard, the weight of his words sinking in, but the tension in my chest didn't ease. "I won't let anyone else die, Frank. That's all that matters."

"People will die," he said, his tone blunt but not unkind. "That's war. But you can't shoulder all of it. You can't save everyone, and tryin' to will destroy you."

I clenched my fists tighter, feeling the sting of my nails digging into my palms. "Then let it. As long as I take the enemy with me, what does it matter?"

Frank stared at me, his expression unreadable for a moment, then he sighed. "It matters, Orla. Because you matter. More than you realize." He stepped back, giving me space but not retreating entirely. "Just... don't forget that."

I turned back to the dummy, needing to hit something, needing to release the storm inside me. "I'll be on the front line, Frank. No one's going to stop me."

He nodded, watching me for a long moment before speaking again. "I figured as much." He paused, his voice softening as he added, "Just don't forget who you are in the process."

I didn't respond, the fire in my chest burning too hot to allow anything else in. I just focused on the dummy, on the fight ahead, and the need to be ready.

I struck the dummy again, but this time it disintegrated into a pile of charred ash, the force of my magic completely obliterating it. My knees buckled, and I collapsed to the floor, a choked sob escaping my throat before I could stop it. Frank was beside me in an instant, his hand reaching out to comfort me.

I shoved him away, anger and shame boiling up inside me. "Get out of here, Frank," I snapped, my voice cracking with the force of my command. "That's a fucking order. Leave. Now. And don't let anyone in here."

His face filled with concern, but I couldn't bear to look at him. He hesitated, standing frozen in place for a moment before nodding slowly. Without a word, he backed away, leaving the room just as I had ordered.

As the door closed behind him, the silence was suffocating. The gravity of it consumed me, pulling me under. I was left alone with the wreckage of what I had just done, and the raw pain that had driven me to it.

My sobs overtook me, harsh and ragged, as the stench of burned leather and charred wood filled the air. My face was raw with tears and snot, but I didn't care. I lay there, the pressure sank into my chest, making it hard to breathe. If I was destined to burn the whole world down, I would do it far away from everyone I loved. Maybe that would be enough. Maybe that would keep them safe.

For a moment, my block on the bond between Aure and me slipped. A surge of her grief and heartbreak crashed into me, only intensifying the storm of my own rage and shame. I wanted to be there for her—gods, I did—but how could I protect her from the one thing that could hurt her the most? Me.

Rein burst through the door, his expression urgent. I barely had time to wipe my face or compose myself before he spoke. "Orla, Atteris has fallen. Frostspire's forces have overtaken it."

I rose unsteadily with a slight limp trying not to let it show, my heart sinking further with the news. Rein approached cautiously, clearly conflicted about respecting my solitude yet compelled by duty to inform me.

"I know Frank said you wanted to be alone," he started, his voice hesitant. "But I thought you needed to know immediately."

I nodded, pushing back the remnants of my tears. "Thank you, Rein. How bad is it?"

"The reports aren't fully in yet, but it's bad. They've pushed through our defenses. We've lost a lot of good people."

The room felt even smaller, the walls closing in with the weight of the news. I steadied myself against the nearest surface, feeling the burn of responsibility and war flutter like a harsh wind through my mind.

"We need to act," I managed to say, the decision hardening within me like ice. "Gather the commanders, I'll join shortly."

Rein nodded, his concern for me clear but overridden by the gravity of the situation. He left quickly, giving me a moment alone to gather my strength.

The brief touch of Aure's anguish through our bond lingered in my mind, a reminder of everything at stake. I stood, my resolve as a leader cementing, determined to fight not just for Aure, but for all of Terraqua.

I strode as briskly as I could despite the pain into the meeting room, where the commanders, the war council, my father, King Oric, Prince Rein, and several others had already assembled. The weight of my presence commanded attention as I entered, determination etched onto my face. My eyes, now a constant deep gray instead of their usual lavender or blue, reflected the unrelenting focus that had become my norm. I moved to my place at the table, but didn't sit—most hadn't, with the urgency of our next steps looming. My father, however, lounged in his chair, as though the gravity of the situation didn't quite reach him.

My gaze swept across the room, every face showing a mixture of resolve and anxiety. I cleared my throat, signaling the start of the meeting. "We need to assess our position and define clear strategies," I stated firmly, placing my hands on the table to lean in slightly, emphasizing my words. "Frostspire's movements are becoming increasingly bold, and after Atteris, none of our cities can consider themselves safe."

Prince Rein stood next, his posture rigid with concern. "Reports indicate that Frostspire's forces are utilizing new magic—more destructive than anything we've seen. Our current defenses might not be enough."

I turned to the map spread out in the center of the table, pointing at strategic locations. "We need to reinforce these points here, here, and here," I directed, marking the cities closest to the recent attacks. Murmurs of agreement echoed around the room.

King Oric finally straightened in his chair, his expression growing serious as he met my gaze. "Orla, ensure that our magical defenses are intensified. We can't afford any more surprises." His tone was commanding, yet it carried an undercurrent of reliance on my judgment.

I nodded, feeling the weight of responsibility settle heavily on my shoulders. "I'll coordinate with Rielle and her team of Enchanters to ensure the magical barriers are reinforced," I said, my voice steady despite the storm brewing inside me. I paused for a breath, closing my eyes briefly as I gathered my thoughts. "Additionally, I propose we dispatch a contingent of elite guards to the most vulnerable cities—immediately."

I shifted my gaze to my father, meeting his eyes squarely, my resolve clear. "I will lead them," I continued, unwavering. "My power can be used to support our efforts on the front lines."

The room fell into a brief silence as they considered the implications. Rein was the first to break it, his voice steady. "That's a proactive measure. I support it. Let's not wait for Frostspire to make the next move."

My father shifted uncomfortably as all eyes shifted to him. "We will have to discuss this further Orla, later, privately." He ground out his jaw set.

The tension in the room was palpable as my father's words hung in the air. I kept my gaze locked on him, unflinching, though I could feel the ripple of unease around me. Rein glanced between us, clearly sensing the shift in the room's atmosphere, but he remained silent.

"Is there a need for secrecy, Father?" I asked, my voice steady, though I felt a spark of anger simmering beneath the surface. "We're at war, and time is not on our side."

King Oric's eyes narrowed, his posture stiffening. "This is not about secrecy, Orla. It's about ensuring the right decisions are made. You may have power, but you are still young and—"

"I'm not a child," I interrupted, the steel in my voice surprising even me. "This is my kingdom too, and I won't sit back while cities fall."

He stood slowly, his gaze hard as stone. "You are my daughter, and while you may be a princess, the final decisions lie with me. We will discuss this in private, *later.*" His voice dropped dangerously on the last word, making it clear this wasn't a suggestion.

The tension between us crackled, but I didn't look away. I couldn't, not when lives were at stake.

Rein, sensing the impending clash, finally stepped forward, clearing his throat. "Perhaps we can focus on immediate reinforcements for now," he said, his tone diplomatic. "We need to send word to the commanders on the front and reinforce the city of Atteris. The situation there is critical."

I turned to Rein, grateful for the reprieve, though I could feel the heat of my father's glare on me. "Agreed," I said, my voice firm. "We cannot wait."

King Oric's lips thinned, but he said nothing as the room resumed its discussions, strategies flying back and forth. I remained standing, my heart pounding in my chest as the weight of my father's words settled deep inside me.

I wasn't sure what he had planned, but I knew one thing for certain—I would not let him, or anyone else, stop me from defending this kingdom.

The lights flickered softly along the palace corridors as night settled in, casting long shadows on the walls. My steps were slow, almost mechanical, as I made my way toward Aure's chambers. The day had slipped away, and now I found myself standing at the edge of another confrontation, one I wasn't sure I was ready for.

I needed to talk to her. I had to tell her about my decision—the frontline was calling, and I would go, with or without her blessing. The thought of leaving her behind tugged at my chest, but I knew she was better suited for handling the political chaos here. She had a calm and strategic mind, where now I had only fire and determination.

I only hoped she would understand that this was something I had to do, even though it meant we would be separated.

I caught sight of her in the hall, her long copper curls cascading down her back, brushing just past her shoulders and licking at the middle of her back. The dress she wore clung to every curve, and I felt my palms grow warm at the sight of her. She stood with a quiet authority, speaking to the servant with a smile playing gently on her lips, each word drawing his undivided attention. The magnetic pull of our bond stirred within me, stronger than ever, and my breath hitched in my throat.

For just a moment, I lost control of the barrier I'd carefully constructed between us. The overwhelming connection flooded through me, crashing into my heart with such force that I struggled to breathe. My hand shot out, gripping the wall for support as I tried to steady myself. Except it was too late—Aure had sensed it. She felt us.

Her eyes locked onto mine, and without hesitation, she dismissed the servant and glided toward me. The space between us seemed to disappear in an instant, her presence as cool and soothing as the sea. My breath was still ragged as I closed my eyes, desperate to regain control, to block the bond once more. Then I felt it, her touch. Her fingers, cool against my overheated skin, sent a shock of magic through me as they caressed my cheek. The air around us hummed with energy.

"Orla," she whispered softly, her voice like a balm to my frayed nerves. "You can let me in... it's okay."

But it wasn't. How could I let her feel the turmoil inside me? The weight of all the emotions I couldn't name was too much. I couldn't burden her with it, not after everything that had happened. Not after he... I just couldn't.

With my eyes still closed, her lips found mine, and I shuddered at the touch—a kiss full of want and need. I returned it gently, soft and tentative, though the desire within me stirred, threatening to pull me deeper into her embrace. Her hand moved, searching for mine, but when her fingers brushed over the bruises on my wrist, a sharp, dull pain shot through me. I flinched, my eyes flying open, the sudden discomfort breaking the spell between us. I pulled back from the kiss, leaving the air between us heavy with unspoken tension.

"We need to talk, Aure," I murmured, my voice low and soft as I stepped away. The connection between us snapped shut as I closed off our bond again, reclaiming the distance I needed. My expression hardened as I pushed everything down—every emotion, every trace of vulnerability.

Hurt flashed across her features briefly, though she nodded. "Ok, my chamber is empty. We can speak there if you would like."

I agreed, following her lead, my eyes tracing the graceful way she moved. I wished, deep in my core, that things hadn't become so complicated. Because all I wanted was to pin her to the wall, taste every inch of her skin, and worship her until she screamed loud enough to wake the gods. Just the thought made my heart race, my core heat, and desire coil within me, making me wet. Her ass was perfect, and it only fueled the smoldering need inside me.

We stepped into her room, and she turned to face me, one hand resting on her hip as she cocked it slightly to the side. "So, you wanted to talk? Let's talk," her voice carrying a mix of challenge and curiosity.

I swallowed, forcing myself to stay focused, even as the sight of her threatened to unravel my resolve.

I took a deep breath, feeling the weight of the words I was about to speak.

"I have to leave for the front lines," I said, my voice low but firm. "With or without your blessing, Aure. There's no other option."

Her eyes darkened, flickering with a mix of hurt and anger. "You can't just make this decision on your own!" she snapped, stepping forward, her arms crossing defensively. "We're supposed to be in this together. You don't get to shut me out whenever it suits you."

"I'm not shutting you out!" My voice rose, frustration bubbling over. "This isn't about us—it's about protecting the kingdom, protecting you!"

"Protecting me?" Aure scoffed, disbelief twisting her expression. "Orla, the reason your magic is out of control—the reason all of this is happening—is because our bond isn't sealed."

I rolled my eyes that swirled onyx, annoyance pulsing through me. "Why do you keep blaming everything on that?" I demanded, stepping closer. "That has nothing to do with it. I just need to control myself better."

Aure shook her head, her gaze piercing. "No, It's not just you. It's us. Our bond isn't sealed, and until we do that, our magic is going to keep spiraling. I've been feeling it too—this chaos between us, the imbalance. That's why your power is unstable."

I stared at her, my chest tightening as frustration boiled beneath the surface. "So you're saying this is because of us? That I'm losing control because of you?" I could hear the disbelief in my voice, the anger bubbling up with each word. "That's ridiculous, Aure. My magic is my responsibility. I just have to keep better control."

"No, you're not listening," Aure snapped, her voice sharp and urgent. "I'm not the cause of this. Our bond is. It's incomplete, and the longer it stays that way, the worse it's going to get for everyone."

I clenched my fists, trying to hold back the rising tide of emotion. "You think sealing our bond is the answer to everything? That somehow we just 'complete' each other and all my problems go away?" I scoffed, shaking my head. "I can handle my magic, Aure. I don't need to rely on you or some bond to keep it under control. I'm not weak."

Aure's eyes flashed with frustration, and she stepped forward, her voice trembling with intensity. "This isn't about being weak, Orla! This is about accepting what we are. We're connected, whether you like it or not. And until we seal the bond, you'll never have full control over your power. It's not something you can just ignore."

"I'm not ignoring it!" I yelled, my voice echoing in the room. "I am doing what I've done my whole life! I've controlled my magic and my emotions with no one's help, and I'll keep doing it. I don't need some bond or you to fix me."

Aure's expression crumbled for a moment, her frustration melting into hurt. "It's not about fixing you, Orla. It's about making us stronger—together. You don't have to fight this alone, or anything else." She reached out, touching my arm gently.

I turned away, running my hands through my hair as I tried to breathe, tried to hold on to the control that was slipping through my fingers. "I can't—Aure, I just can't deal with this right now. I have to go to the front lines, and I can't be worrying about sealing some magical bond while people are dying."

She stepped closer, her voice softer but still filled with urgency. "Orla, listen to me. You won't be able to fight like this. Your magic will destroy you if you don't accept what's happening between us. You need me. We need each other."

I clenched my jaw, refusing to look at her. "I just need to keep better control."

Silence stretched between us, thick with tension and unspoken fears. Aure let out a frustrated sigh, her hands falling to her sides as she stared at me, her expression both desperate and determined.

"You're wrong, Orla. You're strong, but you can't do this alone. Not this time."

I finally turned to face her, my heart pounding in my chest. "I don't have time to figure this out right now. I'm leaving for the front, Aure. With or without your blessing."

Her eyes narrowed, her voice dropping to a dangerous whisper. "If you walk out that door, Orla, don't think you can just come back like nothing happened. Don't think this is something I'll forgive."

My heart twisted painfully in my chest, but I forced myself to stay composed. "I'm not asking for your forgiveness."

I turned on my heel, heading for the door, each step feeling heavier than the last. Just as I reached the threshold, Aure's voice cut through the silence, sharp as a blade.

"If you leave now… don't expect us to be the same when you come back."

I froze, my hand hovering over the doorknob, the weight of her words crashing into me like a storm. My breath caught in my throat, and for a moment, I couldn't move. But I couldn't turn back either.

Just as I was about to open the door, our bond flared to life on its own—a tidal wave of raw magic surging between us, overwhelming the room. The air crackled, the walls streaked with flashes of green, blue, and gold, light twisting and flaring in all directions. The entire space seemed to spin around us, caught in the force of something I couldn't control.

I turned, my eyes locking onto Aure's, and the intensity in her gaze mirrored what I felt. Magic flickered across her skin like lightning, and I could feel the same energy coursing through me, our shared power sparking and igniting in a way that neither of us had intended. The physical sparks illuminated the space between us, lighting up the shadows that had been hiding in the corners of our hearts.

Her eyes glowed with an otherworldly light, and I knew mine must have, as well. My heart thundered in my chest, my breaths rugged and uneven. And then, without warning, our minds collided—our thoughts, emotions, and memories twisted together, a chaotic, tangled mess that neither of us could escape.

Suddenly, I was *inside* her memory.

I saw her as a child, barefoot in a thin nightgown, sprinting toward her mother's lifeless body on a beach. Blood stained her mother's dress, and the scent of salt, flowers, and coconuts hung in the air, mixing with the metallic tang of death. The full moon loomed high above, casting a cold, silver glow over the scene. Waves lapped at her mother's body, but Aure's screams filled the empty beach, raw and unrestrained.

I felt her desperation—*my* desperation. I was trapped in that moment with her, watching through her eyes as she tried to reach her mother, only to be yanked back by firm, gentle hands. I could feel her heartbreak, the suffocating grief as people I didn't know pulled her away from the horror. I saw her knees buckle as she crumpled to the sand, her small hands clawing at the ground, fingers digging into the earth as a tidal wave began to rise behind her. The air thickened with the scent of brine, the sky darkening as the ocean prepared to answer her pain.

And then there was a warmth. An elderly woman appeared behind her, wrapping Aure in her arms. The woman's voice was calm, soothing, speaking in a language I didn't understand, and I could feel Aure's rage, her grief, subsiding. With a single hand lifted to the wave, her magic was just enough for it to still, the water pulling back as if obeying the woman's will. The tide receded, returning to its normal rhythm, but Aure's heart remained shattered, the pieces of her pain too deep to ever fully mend.

The memory faded, but the emotions lingered. The connection between us was too strong, too visceral, and as I stood there, panting, I knew—we knew—that this was bigger than either of us.

"Aure…" I whispered, my voice shaky, my mind still reeling from the flood of emotions that weren't entirely my own. I tried to close off the bond again, to regain control, but it felt impossible, like trying to dam a raging river with my bare hands.

Her lips parted, but no words came out at first. She was just as lost in the moment as I was, her chest heaving with the weight of everything we'd just shared. The sparks in the air crackled and dimmed, but the magic between us still buzzed, refusing to settle.

I couldn't breathe. I couldn't think.

Because for the first time, I truly felt the depth of her pain, her grief—and how much of that she carried for me, for us. And yet, I still couldn't bring myself to let go of the fear. The fear of losing her. The fear of hurting her.

"Aure… I—" My words caught in my throat, and the room fell into silence, the magic still burning beneath the surface, waiting to be unleashed once more.

AURELIA

Chapter 30

"If you leave now... don't expect us to be the same when you come back."

I couldn't believe those words had left my lips, but as harsh as they were, they were the truth—the truth that bit deep into my soul, tearing at my heart. All I wanted was for us to be together again, to find comfort in each other. For her to trust me, to believe I was strong enough to hold her when she needed it.

I watched her freeze in place, her back still turned to me. For a moment, I thought—*hoped*—she might turn around. *Please, gods, just turn around.* Her hand hovered over the doorknob, hesitation in every breath she took. My chest tightened, and hot tears welled in my eyes, stinging as they blurred my vision.

Then something inside me cracked, broke open like a dam. Our bond, the one I had felt slipping further away from me, suddenly flared to life. It was raw, unrestrained, and magic poured out between us in a tangled, chaotic mess of light. Blue, green, and gold streaked across the walls, weaving through the air like fire, brighter and more volatile than anything I had ever seen.

I fixed my gaze on Orla, her eyes now glowing, swirling with colors that mirrored the magic around us. The energy between us was electric, not painful but charged—hot, buzzing, alive. My skin tingled with the sheer force of it, like standing too close to a lightning strike.

Without warning, I was hit all at once, with a flood of emotions, thoughts, and memories that weren't my own. They crashed into me like a storm, overwhelming and consuming. A chaotic whirlwind of *her* pain, *her* fears, *her* rage. Our minds tangled together in a whirlwind I couldn't control, her raw emotions bleeding into mine.

I saw flashes of her life, of moments she'd hidden from me—loss, guilt, shame, all buried beneath her strength. It was too much. It was everything.

Suddenly, vivid memories surged through me—raw and unrelenting.

She was a young girl, running through the woods, Tristan chasing her with playful determination. She giggled as she stumbled, and he tackled her, pinning her to the ground, holding a toad in his hand. "Kiss it, I dare you, Or." The young boy taunted, pushing the toad closer to her face despite the way her face squinted with discomfort. Reluctantly, she did, and he laughed, his eyes alight with childish mischief. "Now I dare you to kiss me. I am your prince charming," he grinned, leaning in before planting a quick kiss on her lips.

The memory shifted, and she was older now. Tristan had her caged against a hallway wall, the corridor empty except for the two of them. His voice was low, insistent. "We'll be wed one day, Or. Come on, just let me see, just this once." Hesitantly, she opened her blouse, and his hand reached out, cupping her breast with firm possession. "Gods, you're beautiful," he murmured, while her cheeks flushed with shame.

My rage flared, but another scene quickly came into focus—this time, they were on the training field, sparring with blades. Tristan had her pinned to the ground, his weight pressing her down. He leaned in, stealing a kiss as if it were his right. "Get off me, Tristan, and fight," she spat, seething.

The memories flashed faster, each one feeding my anger.

Him grabbing her ass in passing. Him cornering her in halls or empty rooms. Her attempts to laugh off his advances or firmly say no, and yet he always took what he wanted. Small moments of stolen affection, every touch unwanted, every boundary crossed. Whenever she wore a dress around him, his hands would be up it, down it, always on her, as if her body belonged to him.

My rage grew with each image, each violation, boiling over like a fire I couldn't control.

Then, the memories slowed—focused on a single moment, sharp and unforgiving.

I watched as Orla walked into the hall, feeling the pulse of her nerves, the subtle ripple of suspicion coursing through her. There Tristan was leaning casually against the wall, his eyes locking onto her like a predator that had cornered his prey. My stomach tumbled when I saw the look in his eyes— possession, hunger. He was looking at my Orla.

I felt her fear as he approached, his presence thick and suffocating.

"Orla," he greeted, a possessive smile stretching across his face, his voice dripping with obsession. "I didn't think you'd actually come looking for me."

Orla's response was quiet, cautious, but the moment he stepped too close, I wanted to scream for her to run, to slit his throat. "You disappeared from the celebration. I wanted to know why."

His voice, eager and relentless, filled the space between them. "I'm honored. I knew you'd eventually realize it. You don't belong in there, Or, not with them." He gestured dismissively toward the ballroom, his lip curling. "Especially not with her."

The venom in his words, the way he spat out "her," made my blood boil. I could feel Orla's panic, her breath growing uneven. My own breath caught in my throat, my heart pounding.

Leave, Orla. Just leave.

I watched helplessly as Tristan traced a slow, possessive finger along her cheek, sneering, "Aure... She's corrupted you, Orla. Twisted your mind with her magic, pulling you into her darkness. But I can save you. I've been watching, waiting for you to see it. To realize that it's me. It's always been me."

The rage within me surged, burning as I watched. Orla moved away, taking a step back.

Yes, keep moving. Leave.

Tristan followed her, his posture filled with desperate want. "I know you've felt it too, Orla. You came looking for me. You could've stayed with her, but you didn't. You found me."

She tried to reason with him, her voice gentle but firm. "Tristan, this isn't what you think—"

Run, Orla, just run.

Tristan was relentless. "I know exactly what it is," he said, his voice dangerously certain. He grabbed her wrist, yanking her closer.

"I've waited for you to break free from her grip. Aure's magic has blinded you, but deep down, you know she's dangerous. She's tainted you with her siren magic. I've seen what it's done to you." His hand brushed her ear, his touch invasive. "But I can free you, Orla. I can protect you."

She tried to pull away, her voice more resolute now. "Tristan, you're wrong. I'm with Aure because I want to be. I love her."

His expression warped in rage at her defiance. "No. You're just saying that because she's controlling you! I know you, Orla. We grew up together. You never wanted any of this!" His desperation grew more erratic, his movements frantic. "You've been enchanted, but I can break the spell. I can make you see."

Orla took another step back, her voice firm. "Tristan, you need to stop. This isn't you. I chose Aure, and I'll keep choosing her."

His eyes darkened as he closed the distance between them again, his voice dropping to a dangerous whisper. "You don't understand. I'll kill her if I have to. I'll do anything to save you."

"Tristan, don't do this." Orla's voice trembled as she moved to block his way, trying to stop him from reaching the ballroom.

Then, in an instant, he had her pinned against the wall, his lips crashing down on hers. His body pressed against her, suffocating her with his weight. The nausea stirred inside me as I felt Orla's emotions—her panic, her struggle. She fought to break free, but his strength was unnatural.

Why wasn't her magic working? Why hadn't I felt her before, when this happened? Why wasn't I able to help her?

His chilling laughter rang through me, even though it was only a memory.

He sneered, "Her vile little trinkets have no more power over you, Orla." He let go of her wrist, only to tear the necklace from her neck and toss it carelessly to the floor, her hand falling limp at her side.

What the fuck?

He caught her limp hand with his, forcing it to his chest as he pulled his shirt open. A bright red glow pulsed from his skin, emanating from a rune etched over his heart. The mark of the Order of the Golden Rose. In that moment, I realized he was the one behind the attack on me a while ago and he again tried to end my life. It all made sense now. That is what Orla was saying, and was so worried about.

"I must purify you, Orla," he whispered, his voice trembling with fanatical fervor. "It's the only way. Once I've done that, I'll kill her. I'll free you from her evil magic, and then we can rule this kingdom together. We'll rid the realm of magic, just as Lux Veritas commands."

His excitement grew, his grip tightening around her. I watched in dread as his eyes widened, filled with a dangerous wildness. "Can you feel it, Orla?" he hissed, his voice shaking with twisted joy. "Her dark, evil magic... it's already being transformed by the almighty Lux Veritas. You're being purified."

I felt Orla's fear seeping through our bond, the helplessness wrapping around her like chains, her loneliness echoing painfully inside me. It was a feeling I knew too well, and now she was trapped in it—her body slumping to the ground, useless. Just like her magic. Just like me.

She lay at his feet, unmoving, her magic drained, her spirit shackled.

His satisfaction was sickening, a vile smirk tugging at his lips as he crawled on top of her, gripping her left wrist tightly as if to drain every last drop of life and power from her. His other hand caressed her cheek, his voice barely a whisper, strained with obsession. "Shhh... purification can hurt, but only for a little while. I'll save you, Orla. I'll make it better. You'll be pure again."

Desperation clawed at me, rooted to my spot, watching, powerless, as he drained her magic, her very essence. I was forced to witness it, paralyzed by rage, sorrow, and guilt.

Her body barely moved, her breath shallow, eyes fixed on a single spot—unmoving. His twisted satisfaction only deepened as he licked her skin, caressed her like a predator toying with its prey. His hand moved lower, to the clasp at her waist.

No... My mind screamed, panic filling every fiber of my being. *No gods, please, he can't. He wouldn't. He is...*

I collapsed, crumpling to the floor in my physical body, tears spilling as I watched the vile scene unfold in my mind. Rage surged in me, sorrow burning like acid, guilt choking the air from my lungs.

His voice turned into a harsh rasp, "I'll try to make this... as pleasurable as possible."

I felt her fight, the strength she summoned deep within her, the fierce resolve to end him, to protect me, even now. I wanted to save her, to be the shield she needed—but I could do nothing. Nothing but watch.

He ran his hand roughly down her body, his kisses sickening, predatory, as he ravaged her neck. Then, with nocuous finality, he shoved his hand down her pants, violating her as he took what he wanted.

"To purify you, we must offer a sacrifice—either of blood or love," he muttered, his voice trembling with deranged devotion. "We will give the almighty Lux both our love... and her blood."

His lips curled into a slow, deliberate smile, his fingers slick with her essence. He brought them to his lips, licking them clean, his expression wicked, triumphant.

"I will finally make you mine, and you will belong to me under the blessing of Lux," he growled, his voice thick with lust. His hands yanked at Orla's pants, tugging them down roughly. My heart raced, and a repugnant knot churned in my stomach. I wanted to tear him apart, to scream at him to stop, but I was trapped—helpless, a prisoner to this memory, forced to watch.

He unfastened his trousers, exposing his erection as he gripped his hard cock in one hand, the other still holding her wrist in a brutal vice-like grip, draining her magic. He groaned, almost delirious with anticipation. I felt the pull of her strength siphoning into him, the magic she fought so desperately to keep within herself slipping through her fingers.

Orla struggled, her body weakening under his weight, her magic growing fainter with every breath. But her will—her spirit—never wavered. Even as he positioned himself between her legs and pushed his full length inside her, she resisted.

My breath caught in my throat. *Gods. No. Please, no.*

He thrust into her, deep and hard, a guttural moan escaping his lips as he violated her. The sound made my skin crawl, a vile noise that soured my stomach. Orla's body jerked beneath him with each rough stroke, her muscles tensing, her magic weakening, but she didn't surrender. She *fought*, her mind pushing back, trying to reclaim control.

Orla, fight. Keep fighting, I silently urged, my heart pounding in my chest. I wanted to reach for her, to drag him off her, but I was frozen in place—forced to watch the horror unfold, the memory binding me like chains.

His pace quickened, his breathing labored. He gripped her tighter, thrusting harder, his face contorted in pleasure. Each movement sent shockwaves of disgust through me. I felt her pain, her helplessness, her shame. Tears burned at the back of my eyes, but I couldn't look away. I wouldn't look away. Not from this.

Orla's face remained turned, her eyes unfocused, but inside I could feel her resolve building. She was fighting him with everything she had left, trying to pull her magic back, trying to hold on to the pieces of herself that he hadn't yet stolen.

His rhythm faltered—just slightly—but enough for me to notice. He was growing weaker. Her magic wasn't replenishing him as he thought. It was draining *him*. He was losing strength with each desperate thrust, though he continued, his body betraying him. Sweat dripped from his brow as his hips snapped against her, rough and needy, but with less force than before.

"Orla…" he whispered, his voice trembling with something close to desperation, though his thrusts continued. "You… you're mine now. Can't you feel it?" His movements became sloppier, and I could sense his magic faltering. His body was betraying him, just as hers had betrayed her moments ago. "Together… we'll be unstoppable…"

He was delusional, lost in his own sick fantasy.

Her body quivered beneath him, each stroke cutting deeper into her, not just physically but emotionally. I felt her pain, her rage, her humiliation. But beneath it all, I could feel something more—her determination. Her will to survive. Orla wasn't done yet.

The minutes dragged on, each one feeling like an eternity. His thrusts were erratic now, weaker, but still relentless, as if he couldn't stop himself. His voice cracked. "Purification… sacrifice… both of us, united…"

Stop, I silently pleaded. *Just stop.*

And finally, after what felt like an eternity, he groaned—louder than before. His body jerked, and I felt the shift in him. His release. I wanted to scream, to claw at my own skin to erase the feeling of it. He panted heavily, collapsing onto her with the weight of a man who had taken all he could. His body was limp, spent, but his grip on her wrist remained tight.

She didn't move. She lay still beneath him, her breathing ragged and shallow, but she hadn't given up. I could feel her magic still pulsing faintly beneath the surface, trying to reclaim what he had stolen. Her strength was returning, bit by bit, as his drained.

He kissed her cheek tenderly, his lips trembling faintly. "You're mine now," he whispered, his voice hoarse from the exertion.

He slowly pushed himself up, though it was clear he was weakened. His legs wobbled as he stood, adjusting his trousers and catching his breath. Orla remained motionless beneath him, but I could feel her magic swirling inside her, regaining strength.

And then, he pulled out the dagger—the dagger that I knew too well. The blade glowed with the etched rune of *strike true*, a death sentence that made it impossible to miss a fatal blow. He gazed down at her, admiring the weapon.

"Now for the blood sacrifice," he slurred, but his voice was chillingly calm. "Hold on, Orla. You'll be completely free soon."

As he turned to leave, I saw Orla begin to stir, slowly pulling herself back from the brink. Her strength was returning. She would survive this, and she would destroy him. I know that now.

The memory faded, leaving me breathless, raw, and trembling with rage. My own magic flared, erratic, and uncontrollable. I was on the floor, my head spinning, and Orla was beside me, her voice desperate as she tried to reach me. "Aure, please... I'm here. I'm here."

Tears blurred my vision as I reached out for her. My fingers brushed her cheek, and I choked out the words, my heart breaking. "I'm so sorry..."

I could barely get the words out as I gripped her face, feeling the softness of her skin beneath my trembling fingers. My own heartbeat thudded in my ears, drowning out the whirlwind of emotions that had crashed into me, threatening to pull me under. "I'm so sorry... I didn't know. I couldn't—" My breath hitched. "I should've been there."

Orla's hands closed over mine, steadying them, her touch grounding me even though the storm still raged in both of us. "Aure..." she whispered, her voice raw, the sound of it cracking something deep inside me. Her eyes, those swirling pools of cobalt and lavender, searched mine, reflecting pain but also something else. Something I couldn't name but desperately needed.

She sat beside me, her body close enough for me to feel the warmth radiating from her despite the icy tendrils of magic flickering between us. I held on to her gaze, her presence the only anchor I had in this sea of chaos. As I blinked away the tears, flashes of her memories surfaced again—moments of helplessness under Tristan's control, his hands on her body, the sound of his vile voice twisting the truth into something monstrous. It made my stomach roil, bile rising in my throat as I remembered every revolting detail.

I pulled my hand back, covering my mouth to stifle the sob that threatened to escape, but the dam inside me was crumbling. "I saw it all," I managed to say, my voice barely more than a broken whisper. "Everything he did to you, Orla." I closed my eyes, unable to face her for a moment as the guilt washed over me again. "How could I not have known? How could I let him…?"

"Aure, don't." Orla's voice was firm, but there was a tremor in it too, and she reached for me again, this time pulling me into her arms, her hold tight as if she could keep me from falling apart. "This isn't your fault."

I clung to her, desperate for reassurance, but the guilt gnawed at me, refusing to let go. "I should've sensed it. I should've stopped him. And now…" I trailed off, my words breaking as the memories of her struggle replayed in my mind.

"No." Orla's voice was hard now, and she pulled back just enough to make me look at her, her grip on my shoulders strong. "Listen to me. You didn't fail me. He's dead. You didn't fail."

I could see the way her eyes glistened, the way she held back her own pain, and the guilt flared again. She had been through so much, had carried so many burdens alone—burdens I hadn't been able to share with her until now. "But I wasn't there," I said, my voice breaking. "And if I had been—"

"You are with me now," Orla cut me off, her voice barely controlled as she forced the words out. "Aure, did you see everything because we—" She faltered for a second, her eyes flickering with uncertainty. "Because we shared each other's memories? I saw you too. I saw your mother… that night…"

My breath caught, the image of my mother's lifeless body on the beach flickering in my mind like a nightmare I had never escaped. I hadn't expected her to bring it up, not now, not in the wake of everything that had happened. My heart clenched painfully, and I felt exposed, raw in a way I hadn't been prepared for.

I found my composure because this moment wasn't about me, it was about her, and her needs. "I am sorry for everything," I whispered softly once more.

She stilled at the touch, as I reached out to caress her cheek once more, her breath still ragged, and for a moment, I saw something flicker behind her eyes—something I hadn't expected. Orla's hand came up to cover mine, her fingers firm but trembling slightly as she guided my hand to her chest, just above her heart.

"Aure," she whispered, her voice tight with emotion but steady. "You don't have to apologize. I'm here." Her thumb brushed the back of my hand, grounding me, steadying me as the chaos of our shared memories still whirled in the background. "I'm the one who's sorry. I didn't want you to see that. Any of it. You've already been through so much."

I swallowed, shaking my head, my heart aching at the way she always turned everything back to me. "Orla, you don't have to protect me from this. You can't keep everything inside and shoulder the burden on your own." My voice cracked as I tried to keep the weight of my own emotions under control. "You're allowed to let me in, too."

Orla hesitated, her jaw tightening for just a moment, and I could see the internal struggle in her eyes. She had always been the strong one, always focused on protecting me, on protecting everyone around her. But now... now there was no hiding, not after what we had shared.

"I can't—" she started, then stopped, her voice faltering. "I don't know how to let it all go. How to not... carry it alone."

I pulled her closer, my hand still on her chest and her working circles over the top of my hand. "You don't have to let it go, Orla. But you don't have to carry it by yourself, either." I tried to soften my voice, knowing she was reluctant, knowing how deeply ingrained it was in her to push herself aside for others. "We're partners in this, remember?"

She shook her head, looking down for a moment before meeting my gaze again. "I don't need anything, Aure. I just want to make sure *you're* okay. That you're safe." Her words were firm, resolute, but I could see the cracks, the way her walls were barely holding up.

I reached up, brushing a tear from her cheek. "I need you. I can't do this without you, Orla. And you can't just keep pushing me away and pretending you're fine when I know you're not."

Her expression softened at that, and her hand settled on my shoulder. "Aure, you don't understand—if I lose control again, if I hurt you—"

"You won't," I interrupted, my voice stronger than I felt. "Because I'm not afraid of you. I've seen your strength, Orla, but I've also seen your pain. And you don't have to hide that from me."

She clenched her jaw, clearly torn, but something in her seemed to shift. Her fingers twitched, and she finally allowed herself to exhale, the tension in her body easing just a little. "It's just… I've always been the one to protect everyone I cared for. It's what I've wanted to do for you since the beginning."

"I know," I whispered, leaning into her touch. "But you don't always have to. Sometimes I need to protect you, too. Sometimes you need to let me be there for you."

Orla looked away for a moment, her brow furrowed as if she were wrestling with the idea. "But how?" she asked softly. "How do I stop feeling like I have to protect you from everything?"

I gently took her hand and placed it over my heart, just as she had done to me. "You don't stop. We protect each other, Orla. That's what a bond like ours is. It's not about one of us carrying all the weight. It's about *sharing* it."

Her eyes flickered with something, maybe vulnerability. She nodded, the smallest hint of acceptance crossing her features. She was still hesitant, still not fully ready to let go of the armor she wore so tightly, but she was trying.

"I just… I don't want to be the one who causes you more pain," she uttered, her voice barely audible now.

"You don't," I said, leaning in so our foreheads touched. "What hurts is when you shut me out. I can handle the magic, the battles, the chaos. But I can't handle losing you."

There was a beat of silence, the air around us heavy with unspoken words and emotions that neither of us could fully articulate. But then Orla's hand tightened over mine, her touch no longer tentative but reassuring.

"I've never known how to share this part of myself," she admitted, her voice low, her words raw and honest. "But I'll try. For you, I'll try."

Tears welled in my eyes again, but this time, they weren't just from the pain. They were from the hope that had begun to flicker between us again.

"I know you will," I whispered back, brushing my lips softly against her forehead. "And we'll figure it out together."

We stayed like that for a moment, wrapped in each other's warmth, and for the first time in what felt like forever, I felt the weight of our connection settle into something solid. Something real.

Orla's hand lingered on my cheek, her thumb brushing away the last of my tears. "I'm sorry I shut you out," she said, her voice just above a whisper.

"But I swear, I'll protect you no matter what. Even from myself."

I gave her a small smile, leaning into her hand. "And I'll protect you, too. From everything, Orla. Including that fear inside you."

She exhaled, a small breath that seemed to carry a thousand unsaid promises. And this time, when our magic flared between us, it wasn't chaotic or wild. It was steady, a current flowing in unison.

Orla shifted slightly, her voice hesitant, almost afraid. "Aure, I saw your magic… when it's out of control. You've been through so much, but you've had time, training… You've learned to contain it, to control it."

My eyes widened, and I met her gaze, confused. "What are you talking about?"

"I'm saying you've had more experience with magic, Aure. I've always struggled to control mine, but you… You know what you're doing. I've seen you hold back when everything inside you was screaming to be unleashed."

I shook my head, feeling a twinge of panic rising in my chest. "Orla, no. You're wrong. I don't always have control. You saw what I did to that room. The chaos, the destruction… My magic is dangerous, just like yours."

She shook her head, her eyes clear, determined. "Aure, your magic is out of control because our bond is incomplete. I've seen it now. I felt it. If we don't seal it, neither of us will be able to handle this… to handle us."

Finally, I spoke again, my voice soft but sure. "Then we seal the bond, before everything spins even further out of control."

She nodded, her touch gentle as she traced slow circles over my hand, but there was a heaviness in her eyes that matched the pounding in my chest. "We'll find a way," she said with quiet determination, her gaze holding mine. But then, her next words shattered the brief sense of calm between us. "But I still think it's best I go."

I sat up abruptly, my heart skipping a beat. "Even after everything we've just been through?"

Her jaw clenched, the tension unmistakable, but she let out a long sigh, her shoulders dropping slightly. "Yes, *especially* because of all this."

I stared at her, disbelief coursing through me. "How can you still think leaving is the answer? After everything we've seen, after everything we've shared, you still want to run to the front-lines?"

"And what about us?" I whispered, the hurt evident in my voice. "What happens to us if you go? How can we fix this—how can we seal our bond—if you're gone?"

Her eyes lowered, a shadow crossing her face. "I don't know," she said quietly, pulling her hand back from mine. "But I do know that if I stay here without doing what I believe is right, I'll resent myself… and maybe everything else. I can't be who I need to be for you or anyone if I'm not fighting for what's out there."

I shook my head, the fear gnawing inside me. "I can't lose you, Orla… not like this."

Orla's gaze softened, but when she spoke, her words were filled with an honesty that made my heart ache. "I can't promise that you won't lose me," she said, her voice low. "I won't lie to you. I might not make it back. But what I can promise is this—I'll come back once you figure out how to seal the bond. That's a promise I can keep."

My breath caught in my throat, the finality in her tone settling in. "And if you don't make it?"

Orla met my gaze, the sadness in her eyes undeniable. "If I don't… then I'll have died for something bigger than myself. Like Cam did. I can't stand back and do nothing when I know I can fight for our kingdoms, our people. I'll do my best not to die, but Aure, I can't promise things I have no control over."

I swallowed hard, the reality of her words sinking in. I hated it. Every part of me wanted to scream, to beg her not to go. But I knew Orla. She wasn't just a princess. She was a warrior at heart. She wasn't someone I could keep by my side with a simple plea.

"I understand," I whispered, though my heart felt like it was shattering. "But don't think for one second that this makes it easier."

"I know," Orla said, her voice rough with emotion. "But it's who I am, Aure. I'll fight for our kingdoms, just like I'd fight for you."

With that, a heavy silence settled between us. It was filled with all the words we couldn't bring ourselves to say—fears left unspoken, hopes left hanging, and the love we were both too terrified to lose.

A soft knock at the door cut through the quiet, and it creaked open slowly. Rielle peeked her head in, her face somber. "I'm sorry to interrupt, Aure, but Captain Cole sent word—they're ready to take Cam's body to the docks. They want to leave before the next storm rolls in."

Orla's eyes widened, a flash of shock passing over her face as she looked at me. I nodded, feeling the tight squeeze in my chest that hadn't loosened since Cam's death. "I'll be right there," I said softly, though my voice felt far away.

Turning to Orla, I took a deep breath, the words heavy on my tongue. "They're taking her body back home. For the funeral rites... and burial. Captain Cole is escorting her, along with all the others we've lost—from the front-lines and from the attack when they arrived." My voice wavered for a moment. "Some are just ashes, others are bodies. We just want to give them the peace they deserve."

Orla stood abruptly and, without hesitation, reached out her hand to help me rise. I took it, the warmth of her touch grounding me. She spoke quickly, her voice earnest. "Can I join you? Let's do this together, please."

My heart squeezed at her words, the vulnerability in her eyes catching me off guard. For the first time in what felt like forever, she wasn't shutting me out—she was asking to stand beside me, through this pain, through this loss.

Without a word, I reached out and clasped her hand in mine, the connection between us sparking something soft, something comforting in the midst of the storm that raged inside. We walked out together, stepping into the cold reality of loss, but this time, we would face it united.

ORLA

Chapter 31

"Are you sure this is the best idea, Orla?" Frank's concern had become a constant companion, replacing the humor I usually relied on to steady myself. His usual jokes had faded, and now, his gruff voice was tinged with worry.

"Am I sure I need to fight? Yes. Since when did you become such an old worrywart? You're worse than a tassel toad," I teased, nudging the short, broad-shouldered man. He hadn't trimmed his beard in a while, and as he ran his fingers through its length, his brows furrowed with unease.

"I can be worried," he grumbled, though there was a familiar spark of his usual spirit. "Doesn't mean I'm not itchin' to get out there and give all them frosty bastards a taste of my wrath." He shot me a side-eye and cracked a sly grin. "I've missed the adventures. I don't want to leave Rielle and Rein to have all the fun without me. But…" He paused, his grin fading as concern slipped back into his expression. "What about your princess? How's that situation goin'?"

I chewed my bottom lip, fingers instinctively toying with the cracked rebounder around my neck. "We talked. Figured out some things after we sent off Captain Cole and..." My voice faltered for a moment, the weight of Cam's absence settling heavily on my chest. I swallowed hard before continuing. "And after we sent Cam home. We made a plan and figured out how things will work for now."

Frank nodded solemnly, the sadness that danced across his face when I mentioned Cam, noticeable but fleeting. Then his eyes gleamed with that mischievous spark. "Will ya be gettin' hitched before you leave?"

I couldn't help but give him my own wry grin, though it quickly slipped into a more serious expression. "We've sorted it out... for now. But before I leave, I've still got to force my father's hand. And I think I finally have something to make him listen."

Frank raised an eyebrow, leaning in slightly. "I don't think I've ever seen you this reckless, Orla. I support it, don't get me wrong. But I'm used to bein' the rogue between us, not you."

"It's about time I stood up for my own beliefs for once," I said, my voice carrying a sharp edge. "I'm tired of losing people because I didn't trust my instincts, because I let others decide my fate. I'm done, Frank." My voice trembled with emotion, a mixture of rage and fierce determination. "No matter who I upset in the process."

"So you think your father will really agree to lettin' you leave with the troops the mornin' after next?" Frank rubbed his beard again, that rogue's grin finally breaking through as mischief glinted in his eyes. "Or do you plan on sneakin' out again?"

I smirked back at him, feeling some of the tension ease. "I'm determined to make a difference out there, Frank. And Aure... well, she reluctantly understands. We've agreed I won't shut out our bond, so we can stay connected. She's going to work with Kepple to figure out how to seal our bond, maybe stop us both from being such chaotic messes."

Frank's eyebrow lifted. "So you're gonna stay linked, even out there?"

I nodded. "We don't have any choice. Though honestly, I don't think sealing the bond has a lot to do with everything that's happening. I just need space—somewhere to practice, to let my magic out without holding back. I can't keep bottling it up like this."

Frank grunted in agreement, his grin fading a bit. "You're not wrong about that. It's dangerous holdin' all that power inside, especially with what's been happenin' lately. You need to be out there, and the front lines are gonna give you that chance."

I took a deep breath, feeling the weight of the decision in every corner of my mind. "Exactly. I just hope my father sees it that way... but if he doesn't, well..." I glanced at Frank, giving him a knowing look. "We both know how to make an exit."

His grin widened and nudged me playfully. "For sure, I got you. I will make a plan, we will be one step ahead. Don't worry, Orla. If your father tries to keep you here, I'll be right there helpin' you slip out before dawn. We'll make sure no one even knows you're gone until you're halfway to the front."

I smiled, feeling a surge of warmth from his loyalty. "Thanks, Frank. I know you always have my back."

He winked. "Yeah, ya know it. Just promise me one thing: don't run off without me and get yourself killed out there. I'd miss that charmin' face of yours way too much."

I chuckled, the tension still there but softened by the moment of shared humor. Morning after next felt like it was approaching too fast, but one way or another, I'd be on my way to the front lines. The real battle was just beginning.

Frank headed toward the barracks, leaving me with my own resolve. I turned toward my mother's chambers, determined to bring her with me when I spoke to my father. This would be settled once and for all, no more delays or excuses. It was time to get this sorted.

I walked briskly through the corridors, the cool stone beneath my boots doing little to calm the simmering fire in my chest. My fingers tightened around the cracked rebounder pendant at my neck, the reminder of everything I had endured and what still lay ahead. The guards stationed outside my mother's chambers stood at attention as I approached, exchanging quick glances before stepping aside to let me through.

I didn't bother knocking.

The doors swung open, and I found her seated by the window, the soft glow of the morning sun casting a warm light across her face. She looked up, surprised, her hands folding in her lap as she regarded me with a cautious smile.

"Orla," she greeted, her voice soft but weary. "What brings you here so urgently?"

I didn't waste time on pleasantries. "We need to talk to Father. Now."

Her expression faltered, concern flickering in her eyes. "About what, darling?"

"About the front lines," I said firmly, stepping further into the room. "I'm leaving with the troops the morning after next, with or without his blessing. And I need you to help me make sure he understands this isn't negotiable."

My mother stood, her hands trembling slightly as she smoothed out the fabric of her gown. She opened her mouth to speak, but no words came out. Instead, she glanced toward the door, her eyes darting as if expecting my father to storm in at any moment.

"Orla… I don't know if your father will—"

"I don't care what he will or won't do," I snapped, taking a step closer to her. "This is my decision, and I'm not asking him for permission. I need you with me, Mother. I need you to stand with me for once."

She flinched at my tone, wringing her hands together. "Orla, you know your father… He won't be pleased…"

"I know exactly what he'll say," I said, my voice hard. "But it doesn't matter anymore. I've been trained for this. I'm ready for this. Aure and I have already agreed—this is what needs to happen."

Her eyes flicked toward the door again, her voice dropping to a whisper. "I… I don't know if I can..."

"You *can*," I pressed, my voice softer now but no less firm. "You've been silent long enough. You know I'm right."

She hesitated for a moment, her hands trembling as she glanced at me. I saw the fear etched in her features, the way her body seemed to shrink, as if she was already bracing herself for my father's inevitable wrath.

Finally, she nodded, but it wasn't strength or resolve that pushed her forward. It was fear—fear of what might happen if she didn't agree, fear of the consequences if she spoke against him. "Alright," she whispered, barely audible. "I'll come with you."

Without another word, I led her through the corridors toward my father's office, the tension in the air thick and suffocating. When we arrived at the heavy wooden doors, I could hear voices on the other side. My father, deep in conversation with one of his advisors.

I pushed the door open and stepped inside, my mother trailing meekly behind me, her posture tense and her eyes cast downward.

My Father looked up, his expression hardening when he saw us. The advisor quickly bowed and exited the room, leaving the three of us alone.

"Orla," he said, his voice cold. "What is this about?"

I took a deep breath, standing tall. "I'm leaving for the front lines with the troops in two days. I'm not asking for your permission. I'm informing you of my decision."

His eyes narrowed, his jaw tightening. "You think you can just come in here and dictate terms to me?" His gaze flicked to my mother, who stood quietly at my side, her hands clasped together as if trying to disappear. "Helena, what is this?"

My mother remained silent, her eyes downcast, the tension visible in her shoulders.

"I *know* I can," I cut in, my voice steady. "I'm not a child anymore, Father. I've trained for this my whole life. I've dealt with more than most of your commanders have. I'm ready."

He stared at me, a mixture of anger and disbelief in his eyes. "And what of your responsibilities here? Your duty to this kingdom, to your people? You think running off to war will solve anything?"

"I think standing idly by while our people suffer is far worse," I shot back, my temper rising. "I can't stay here pretending everything is fine while our kingdom is under siege. I won't."

Finally, he sighed, rubbing a hand over his face. "If you insist on going," he said slowly. "Then will you follow orders? Will you not act recklessly and not put yourself or others in unnecessary danger?"

My heart fluttered, but I didn't fully trust his words. I started to nod, words on my tongue as my mother finally stepped forward.

Her voice trembled with desperation, her hands wringing together. "No, no, Oric." Her voice went shrill and loud now. "You promised! We agreed you would keep her safe and here with me, us. That she would be treated as our child."

My father's gaze hardened, and his voice boomed with cruel finality. "Helena, that 'thing' is more than a miracle from the gods. She's a weapon, a tool. You saw her power. The front lines are where she belongs now, not coddled here in the palace. As she had made it very clear she's not a child anymore, and you're done playing house." He moved close to her and she trembled. His voice grew low and harsh. "Shut your fucking mouth and remember your place, woman."

His words cut through the air like a blade, as if I wasn't standing right in front of them. My stomach twisted, the nagging memory clawing at my mind, pulling apart everything I thought I knew. "A miracle from the gods? What are you both saying?" I asked, my voice wavering but filled with growing dread.

I took a breath, and then the question came, cold and sharp, "*I AM* your child and heir... right?"

They turned to face me fully, and in their eyes, I saw a truth I wasn't sure I was ready to hear.

My fathers face twisted, his expression darkening as he squared his shoulders and stepped toward me, his gaze heavy with a mixture of disdain and irritation. My mother stood frozen, her eyes wide and tear-filled, but she remained silent, wringing her hands as though she could somehow make herself disappear.

"You were always useful, and I knew you were valuable, Orla," My father spat, his voice cold and sharp, like ice cracking. "A tool from the gods themselves, gifted to us to ensure the future of this kingdom. But my child? No." He shook his head with a bitter laugh. "You were never *mine.*"

My heart stopped. The world seemed to tilt, and for a moment, I couldn't breathe. I couldn't think. I swallowed hard, my mind racing as everything I had ever known unraveled before me.

"Mom," I whispered, looking toward my mother, hoping, *begging* for her to say something that would undo what my father had just said.

But she only closed her eyes, a single tear rolling down her cheek as she whispered, "I'm sorry, Orla."

The admission hit me harder than any blow I'd ever taken in battle.

My father, no, Oric stepped forward again, his gaze unwavering as he spoke with cruel clarity. "You have been allowed this life with us because of your potential power, because of the prophecy surrounding you. You were *never* meant to be raised as royalty, but we never had children of our own, and Helena insisted. You were always meant to be a weapon, nothing more."

The room seemed to close in around me, the walls suffocating as my mind spun, trying to make sense of what I had just heard. All my life... everything had been a lie. The love I thought I had, the family I thought was mine... none of it had ever been real.

"I raised you as best as I could. You're my little girl," Helena whispered, her voice trembling. "But your father... he always saw you for what you are destined to be. I... I thought, maybe..." Her voice broke off, and she covered her mouth, unable to finish.

I took a step back, my legs feeling like lead. My chest tightened with the weight of betrayal, and the anger that simmered just beneath the surface began to bubble up, threatening to boil over.

"I'm not your weapon," I said, my voice low, but filled with a deadly edge. "I'm *not* your pawn."

He sneered. "You may not like it, but you are mine to weld. And you will go to the front lines, when and where I want you. You will fulfill your destiny, whether you want to or not."

I shook my head, disbelief and fury swirling in my chest. "You think you can control me? After everything?" My magic stirred, crackling at my fingertips, desperate to be unleashed.

He didn't flinch, his eyes narrowing. "You have no choice, Orla. You will obey."

My gaze snapped to the woman who had pretended to be my mother. She stood quietly, her eyes full of regret but not a single word of defiance. She had known. She had always known.

"I don't belong to either of you," I growled, stepping back toward the door. "I'll go to the front lines, but not for you. I will fight for this kingdom and for the people who deserve it. But when I return—if I return—it won't be as your pawn. It will be on my terms."

I turned on my heel and stormed out of the room, my mind reeling, heart aching, but a fierce determination burning in my chest. Whatever I had been before, whatever Oric and Helena thought of me, it didn't matter anymore.

I would make my own fate.

AURELIA

Chapter 32

The wind howled outside, and the darkness, despite the early hour, warned that this snowstorm would be a fierce one. I curled up on the plush sofa, as I'd done countless times since arriving here, the warmth of the blazing hearth enveloping the room. The air was thick with the earthy scent of wood smoke and the pungent aroma of spices the servants had added to the logs—meant, they'd said, to ward off evil spirits. Though, the old woman who tended the fire had chuckled, claiming it was more about keeping pests away as the cold and storm settled in.

I turned the letter over in my hands, examining every detail for what felt like the hundredth time. The worn, broken wax seal of Olondia, the familiar scrawl of Ambassador Corin Edevane, the Human diplomat who had first proposed this alliance to Faedamir. He was a stout, older man, the very one who had brought this proposal of aid to our kingdom, setting into motion events I was still coming to terms with.

I read the letter once again, scanning for any detail I could have missed.

To His Majesty King Oric Orlond,

Sovereign of the Realm of Orlondia, Guardian of the Northlands, Protector of the People,

Your Majesty,

It is my opinion and considered advice that the date of the impending nuptials between our esteemed Princess Orla and Her Grace, Princess Aurelia, be hastened. I regret to inform you that King Rowan Demajanio's health appears to be rapidly declining; he has taken to his chambers and has remained bedridden without taking an audience for two fortnights, with no indication of recovery on the horizon.

Moreover, I must bring to your attention the growing concerns within the council of Faedamir regarding the stability of the existing treaty. It has come to light that many council members are increasingly hesitant about upholding their side of the agreement if Princess Aurelia assumes the throne unwed. Their reservations stem from the perceived instability this may introduce to both kingdoms, casting doubt on whether Faedamir can, or should, maintain its commitments to our alliance without a formal union in place.

In light of these considerations, I strongly urge Your Majesty to advance the date of the wedding. A timely union would not only secure our rightful claim to the treaty between Orlondia and Faedamir but also assuage the council's concerns, ensuring a smoother transition of power and reaffirming the strength of our longstanding alliance.

Respectfully,

Ambassador Corin Edevane

Diplomat of Orlondia to the Kingdom of Faedamir

I folded the letter and rubbed the bridge of my nose, letting out a slow, shaky breath. Why hadn't I received word of my father's health sooner? I closed my eyes, trying hard to reach out to Azura, but the thread of our bond came back hollow. She'd told me, in the weeks leading up to her egg hatching, that she would enter a deep sleep to aid the baby, and that our connection would weaken, especially with me being so far away. Silent tears slipped down my cheeks. I was missing one of the most sacred moments in her life.

Sea Dragons only lay eggs once in their lifetime, a rare and revered event—a single chance to continue their line, a delicate measure to preserve the balance of nature and magic, as our histories taught us. Azura had only laid one egg, and there was no certainty that the hatchling would even survive. I wished more than anything that I could dive into the Crystal Reef City, to visit her in her home. She and Voraxius were more in love than anyone I knew—except for, perhaps, my own parents. Missing this special time with them was heart-wrenching. And not knowing if that last hug and kiss on the dock was my final goodbye to my father tore at me, splitting my heart in two.

My somber mood was abruptly replaced by a surge of rage and confusion flooding through my bond with Orla. At least she was keeping her promise not to shut me out, but the wave of emotions shook me to my core. I glanced toward the door just as she stormed through it, sparks flaring around her. Calmly, I set the letter aside and pulled the blanket tighter around myself as I rose to meet her.

"What happened, Orla? Are you okay?" I asked, fussing over her as I reached for her hand, which felt almost scalding in mine.

She ran a free hand through her hair, looking frantic, her magic radiating off her in pulsing waves. The wind howled louder outside, and the window was nearly blanketed with thick, white snow. I took a deep breath, trying to ground us both. "Alright, we need to take some deep breaths and calm down a bit."

But she pulled away from my hand, pacing from the bookshelves to the desk and back toward the hearth. I quietly closed the door behind her, watching as her steps remained uneven. Finally, she stopped, turning to face me with wide, blazing eyes swirling in blue and black. "I'm not even their fucking daughter!"

I tilted my head, a wave of confusion washing over me. "Not whose daughter?"

She looked at me, eyes wide and desperate. "King Oric and Queen Helena… they're not my parents. I'm not their blood, not their child." Her voice cracked, and she held her hands at her sides, palms open, as if pleading with the gods themselves to make sense of it all. "I… I don't even know who, or what, I am."

"They just told you this? Why?" I whispered, pulling her close as I gently guided her toward the sofa, hoping to get her to sit down and find some calm. My heart ached, knowing how deeply this was cutting her.

"I went to tell them I was leaving for the front, just like we talked about last night," she replied, her voice shaky. I nodded, pulling her a little closer to the sofa, hoping to ease some of her tension.

"And just when I thought my father might actually agree, and my mother seemed to be on my side, she suddenly lost it—begging him not to let me go. She started talking about how he promised to let me be their daughter." Her eyes widened, and her words grew more frantic. "Then he went off about some prophecy, about me being his weapon. It was all happening so fast, I could barely make sense of it, let alone focus on the details."

"Did they tell you anything about where you came from or who your real parents are?" I asked gently, watching her reaction carefully. She shook her head, frustration and sadness mingling in her expression.

"Honestly, I lost it. I didn't even give him the chance to explain. I just told him I'm not his pawn, and that I'll choose my own fate from now on." She sank onto the sofa, covering her face with her hands. I settled beside her, curling around her, my arms wrapping protectively as I tried to soothe her.

I ran my fingers through her hair, feeling the tension rolling off her in waves. She leaned into me, her breaths shuddering as she tried to calm herself. For a moment, we sat in silence, the only sound being the wind howling outside, the storm mirroring the chaos within.

Finally, I broke the silence, my voice soft. "Orla, whatever your past is, whoever your parents were... you're still you. The woman I fell in love with. That hasn't changed."

She let out a shaky breath, looking up at me, her eyes filled with turmoil. "But what if I'm just... a weapon? What if I'm something created to bring destruction? Everything they told me—it's like my whole life has been a lie. How can I trust anything anymore? How can I even trust myself?"

I placed my hand on her cheek, guiding her gaze back to mine. "You're more than just what they say you are. You're powerful, yes, but that power is yours to wield, not theirs. It doesn't define you; you define it. And I know the person you are, Orla. I know your heart."

Her eyes softened, and she looked down, fiddling with a loose thread on the sofa. "I've always wanted to believe I could choose who I become, but now... it's hard to know who I am anymore."

I held her hand, squeezing it gently. "You will grow into the person you choose to be, and I will be here by your side, every step of the way."

Worry etched across her face, and her voice was laced with concern. "What if he won't let us marry now that I know I'm not their biological child? If he changes his mind about the treaty?" Her breath became shallow and voice low. "What if they expect you to marry someone else?... I can't bear the thought of losing you that way."

Her fear and protectiveness surged through our bond, mixing with my own apprehensions. "Those are possibilities we will have to consider, especially after he gave me this the other day." I reached for the letter on the nearby table and handed it to her. "My father is apparently very unwell again. But I haven't received any direct news, and with Azura unable to communicate right now..." I trailed off, the crackle of our mingled magic punctuating the uncertainty surrounding us.

She read the letter in silence, her expression hardening as concern ingrained itself across her brow. Setting the letter back on the table, she looked at me thoughtfully. A swirl of emotions passed through our bond, reflecting the same blend of colors shifting in her eyes.

Suddenly, something flickered across her face, her eyes brightening into that beautiful violet I hadn't seen much of lately. A victorious smile slowly spread across her lips as she looked at me, her expression soft yet determined. Without hesitation, she shifted, kneeling in front of me while still gripping my hand tightly.

"Princess Aurelia Damanjanio of the Western Isles of Faedamir," she began, her voice low but steady. "Will you marry me? Just us, our closest friends, with a council witness—tomorrow night?"

The intensity in her gaze, full of love and resolve, left my heart racing.

"I..." My words caught, leaving me momentarily speechless as a wave of nerves washed across her expression. Smiling warmly, I leaned in close, cupping her face with my free hand. "Yes, of course I will."

Our lips met in a deep, lingering kiss, and she gently pressed me back against the sofa, her body melting into mine. In that moment, everything else faded away—it was just us, making our own fate come to pass.

She nipped at my neck, sending a thrill through me. I whispered into her ear, "Why wait? We could do this tonight. It would make a stronger case at the council meeting tomorrow when you announce your plan to lead the reinforcements to the front with Rein." My heart clenched, though, as the thought of her heading into battle weighed on me. A hint of worry crept in— *How would I manage everything here? Would it be safe? And, above all, could I bear the distance between us?*

Orla pulled back, her gaze locking onto mine as she brushed a copper ringlet from my shoulder with a soft smile. "Alright, let's do this." She stood, rising to her full height. She was a tall, chiseled masterpiece crafted by the gods themselves. I took a moment to sit up and admire her, memorizing every curve and line as if committing her to memory. Then, I joined her, standing by her side, both of us resolute.

Together, we moved through the palace, seeking out those we needed. We found Frank, Rielle, and Rein first, then summoned others like Kepple, Lady Kio, and High Chancellor Malachi. Each one understood the gravity of what we were about to do, their expressions mirroring a mix of curiosity and solemn respect.

We directed everyone to meet us in the small temple by the barracks—a simple but sacred space used by those in training or stationed here to worship and give offerings to their gods. This modest sanctuary honored all gods and goddesses equally, making it the perfect place for us to solidify our vows and claim our future together.

We still had to determine the correct ritual to seal our bond, but tonight would be our legally recognized union. As Rielle fastened the back of an ivory gown I hadn't yet worn, I couldn't help but smile at its delicate lace—a summer dress, really, and hardly practical for this weather. Though the snowstorm had stopped, a thick blanket of snow covered the ground.

Rielle chuckled as she stepped back to admire her work. "You're going to freeze your ass off on the way there, you know that, right? Are you sure you don't want something that... well, covers a bit more?"

I flushed slightly, smirking as I ran my fingers along the lace. "I just wanted to look extra pretty for her."

Rielle began pinning my hair up, her touch steady and gentle. I already felt a chill, even in my warm room, but I brushed it off.

"You're always stunning, My Queen," she said with a warm smile. "And I'm certain Orla would wholeheartedly agree."

My heart tightened at her calling me "Queen." I knew she hadn't meant it in a heavy way, but it brought a surge of worry and concern for my father. I missed him—his kindness, his laugh. I had always hoped that somehow, we would be able to arrange for him to be at my wedding once it was officially set. But even if he couldn't be here, I knew he would be happy for me and Orla, knowing that our union had grown into something far more than he could have ever hoped for me.

Rielle sensed my worry. "Are you okay?" I nodded, keeping my tears at bay.

"I just miss my father, and I'm worried about him, along with so many other things. But I'm truly happy to be taking this step with Orla, especially since she'll be heading to the front with you all. So many people I care about will be there, and even though I'm not alone, it feels a bit lonely."

A knock interrupted my thoughts, and the door swung open to reveal Rein, accompanied by a young soldier. The newcomer had strong yet delicate features, not as tall or muscular as Rein, but equally striking, with a deep, rich complexion. Rein's face lit up with his usual confident swagger as he made introductions.

"This is Alex, your new royal bodyguard—if you'll consider it?" Rein looked at me earnestly. "I know it's been difficult finding the right fit after everything, but we'd all feel much better knowing you have someone trustworthy and loyal at your side. Alex here is half-fae, skilled in defensive and healing magic. Offensive combat, though…" Rein trailed off, glancing at Alex.

The young soldier, speaking in a smooth, warm South Negallian accent, finished the thought with a hint of a smile. "I'm not one to cause harm unless I've got no other choice."

I tilted my head, looking at Alex with interest. "So, she's half-fae?"

"Um, HE is a full Lowlander and loyal to Her Majesty Princess Aurelia and Princess Orla," Alex corrected politely, bowing low, then raising his eyes to mine. Rein's grin widened as I felt a flush warm my cheeks.

A gentle smile touched my lips. "Alex, are you willing to travel wherever I go and remain loyal to me and my wife, regardless of our allegiances to any other kingdoms?"

He drew his short sword from its sheath and knelt before me, laying the blade carefully at my feet. Bowing until his forehead touched the ground, he placed both palms flat on the stone floor. Magic rippled along the surface, sending faint tremors up my legs, and he spoke with unwavering resolve, "I swear fealty to you, and you alone." A swirling green thread of light emerged from his hands, weaving itself into a binding rune that hung in the air between us. I had heard of such fae magic before, but I had never seen it with my own eyes.

Rein and Rielle both let out audible sounds of surprise at the display. My smile grew, though I kept my composure steady, holding onto the regal calm expected of me. I picked up the sword and held it out to Alex, speaking formally, "Rise, Alex. I accept your binding vow." He rose gracefully, accepting the blade and returning it to its sheath.

"Well, now that we have that settled... Your Grace looks exquisite, but I believe there's one more thing you'll need." Rein reached into his pocket and pulled out a braided cord of gold, green, and blue silk, about arm's length.

"Thank you," I replied, a bit puzzled.

Rein placed the elegant rope into my hands. "It's for your binding ceremony," he explained with a chuckle. "Here on the mainland, we bind the hands of the couple during the vows. Do you not do that in Faedamir?" I shook my head, and he gave an understanding nod. Taking my right hand in his, he demonstrated how to hold the cord.

"Take one end in your left hand, and I'll hold the other in mine. Like this, with the middle hanging between us. Then, when instructed, you'll pass your end over to each other, alternating sides. It effectively binds your hands together, symbolizing the bond you're forming." The simplicity and beauty of the gesture stirred something warm within me, a new connection to Orla's traditions.

We practiced with two passes, the cord loosely wrapped around our hands. The symbolism touched me, and I glanced up at him with gratitude. Though the moment grew slightly awkward, so I gently slipped my hand from his, and he handed the cord back to me with a smile.

Rielle and Alex exchanged a look. Then Rielle broke the silence, gently taking my arm. "It's time," she spoke gleefully. We stepped out of the palace and into the cold, our breath visible in the crisp, moonless night. The snow-covered path stretched ahead, illuminated only by the warm glow of the lanterns held by Rein and Alex, guiding our way through the darkness.

As we moved across the courtyard, the snow crunched beneath our feet, muffling our steps and creating a quiet, almost reverent ambiance. The cold air nipped at my cheeks, turning them pink, while the faint scent of pine from the nearby trees mingled with the smoke from the lanterns. Shadows danced on the ground, flickering along the edges of the path as the flames swayed in the gentle wind.

Ahead, the small temple rose out of the snow, its stone walls dusted in white, and the outline of the arched door glowed softly in the lantern light. I caught my breath at the sight—it looked almost magical, like something from a dream. The chill of the night wrapped around us, heightening the moment's solemnity.

The sky above was an endless, deep indigo, studded with stars that seemed to pulse in time with my heartbeat. I felt a shiver, not just from the cold, but from the enormity of what was about to happen. With each step, the space between Orla and I seemed to narrow, the anticipation building like the quiet before a storm.

As we reached the temple doors, Rein and Alex stepped aside, casting the last beams of lantern light upon the entryway. Inside, the flickering glow of candles reflected off the polished stone floors, casting a warm, golden light that filled the space. The walls were simple white stone unadorned, a blank canvas, and the air was thick with the scent of burning sage and cedar.

Rielle gently squeezed my arm, offering a reassuring smile. I nodded, feeling her support wash over me, steadying me as we took the final steps into the temple. The ancient stone seemed to hum with the whispers of countless vows made before us, a reminder that we were part of something timeless and sacred.

Orla stood waiting at the altar, her silhouette bathed in the soft candlelight, a vision of strength and elegance. Her gaze met mine, and in that instant, the world around us faded away. We were here, together, in this quiet, holy place, bound by a promise and surrounded by those we trusted most.

She wore a tailored commander's uniform, exuding authority and strength that radiated from her in waves as I took her in. My stomach flipped, not only from nerves but also from the reminder that soon she would leave me to do the very thing she had prepared for her entire life. As much as we both longed to protect one another, we would have to let go and trust in our combined strength and the trust we had built together.

I approached her slowly, taking in every detail—the way her shoulders squared with purpose, her magenta eyes flashing with determination under the lantern light, and the subtle glint of silver at her collar. Rielle gave my arm a gentle squeeze, bringing me back to the present, and we continued forward, the cool air wrapping around us.

Kepple stood at the front behind Orla, waiting patiently, their presence a calming anchor amidst the emotions swirling in the room. Frank, Rein, and the others gathered quietly in the front on either side, watching me reverently.

When we reached Orla, she extended her hand toward me, and I took it without hesitation, feeling the warmth of her fingers slip through mine. Our eyes met, and I saw a flicker of reassurance there, a promise of the life we'd build together. I couldn't help the small smile that crept across my lips, and she responded in kind, the tension in her shoulders softening ever so slightly.

Kepple cleared their throat, with a voice soft and steady as they began the ceremony. "Tonight, we honor the traditions of both Orlondia and Faedamir, binding two souls in unity, trust, and love." They gestured to the golden, green, and blue braided cord, and I carefully wrapped it around our wrists, like Rein had shown me. Orla smiled at my movements.

"As these threads bind you, so too shall your souls be bound," Kepple continued, the words reverent. Orla and I exchanged the ends of the cord, mirroring each other's actions. "Please repeat these words, then pass the ends as you do." We both nodded to Kepple's instructions.

"I vow to trust," we began, our voices merging as one. Slowly, we passed the cord between our hands, securing it in place.

"I vow to not place you above or below, but to walk beside you as two halves of a whole." My gaze held Orla's as we spoke, each word resonating between us, the cord shifting with each pass, binding us closer.

"I vow to grow with you in wisdom," we continued, the warmth of our voices filling the space. With every turn of the cord, the bond grew stronger, a promise taking shape around our joined hands.

Our voices softened, merging together one final time, "I swear by peace and love to stand, heart to heart and hand to hand, in this life and beyond."

The cord encircled our wrists now, entwined with our hands, a tangible reminder of the loyalty and strength we vowed to each other.

With the hand-binding complete, Kepple nodded toward me, their eyes holding a quiet encouragement. "Now, by the ancient Siren rites, we seal this union in blood, marking you both with the magic of your shared fate." They stepped forward, holding a small vial filled with an iridescent liquid in one hand and a delicate ceremonial knife in the other.

Gently, they took my hand first, pricking my finger just enough to draw a single drop of blood that shimmered as it fell into the vial. Next, they turned to Orla, who met the prick of the knife without a flinch. Her violet blood hissed as it met mine in the vial, causing the mixture to glow with an ethereal light.

Setting the knife aside, Kepple dipped a fine needle into the glowing mixture. With great care, they traced an elegant rune on Orla's right wrist, then mine, the faintly glowing symbol gradually sinking into our skin, marking us in a way that felt both ancient and eternal.

The magic pulsed, and I felt a warmth spread from the mark, tingling along my wrist as if the rune itself were alive. I watched as it mirrored on Orla's skin, a delicate yet powerful signet now forever etched there, binding us on a deeper, almost spiritual level. She looked down at her wrist, and when our eyes met again, there was a quiet awe in her gaze.

I spoke softly, repeating the vows I had heard my parents recite through every quarrel and in quiet moments, words they used to remind each other of their love.

"Ye are Blood of my Blood, and Bone of my Bone.

I give ye my Body, that we Two might be One.

I give ye my Spirit, 'til our Life shall be Done.

Ye cannot possess me, for I belong to myself,

But while we both wish it, I give ye that which is mine to give.

Ye cannot command me, for I am a free person,

But I shall serve ye in those ways ye require.

I pledge to ye that yours will be the name I cry aloud in the night,

And the eyes into which I smile in the morning.

I pledge to ye my living and my dying, each equally in your care.

I shall be a shield for your back, and ye for mine.

I shall not slander ye, nor ye me.

I shall honor ye above all others.

When we quarrel, we shall come together in agreement once again.

This is my wedding vow to you,

This is the marriage of equals."

Kepple's voice cut through the silence, resonant and final. "By these rites, I declare you bound, in both spirit and blood. May your bond strengthen your hearts, protect your kingdoms, and carry you through all that lies ahead."

As the words settled over us, the room felt impossibly still, the air thick with magic and anticipation. I knew that, whatever came next, Orla and I were forever entwined, our lives joined by both the traditions of our lands and the magic that flowed through us. And as we stood together, hand in hand, I felt the weight of our union settle around us like a protective shield, ready to face the world together, no matter the trials that lay ahead.

Then Orla's lips met mine, and I closed my eyes, surrendering to the warmth of her kiss, the taste of her filling my senses. Our magic flared, igniting a wild energy between us, and suddenly, a gust of wind swept through the room, snuffing out every candle. We remained locked together in the darkness, sharing a few perfect moments, oblivious to all else around us.

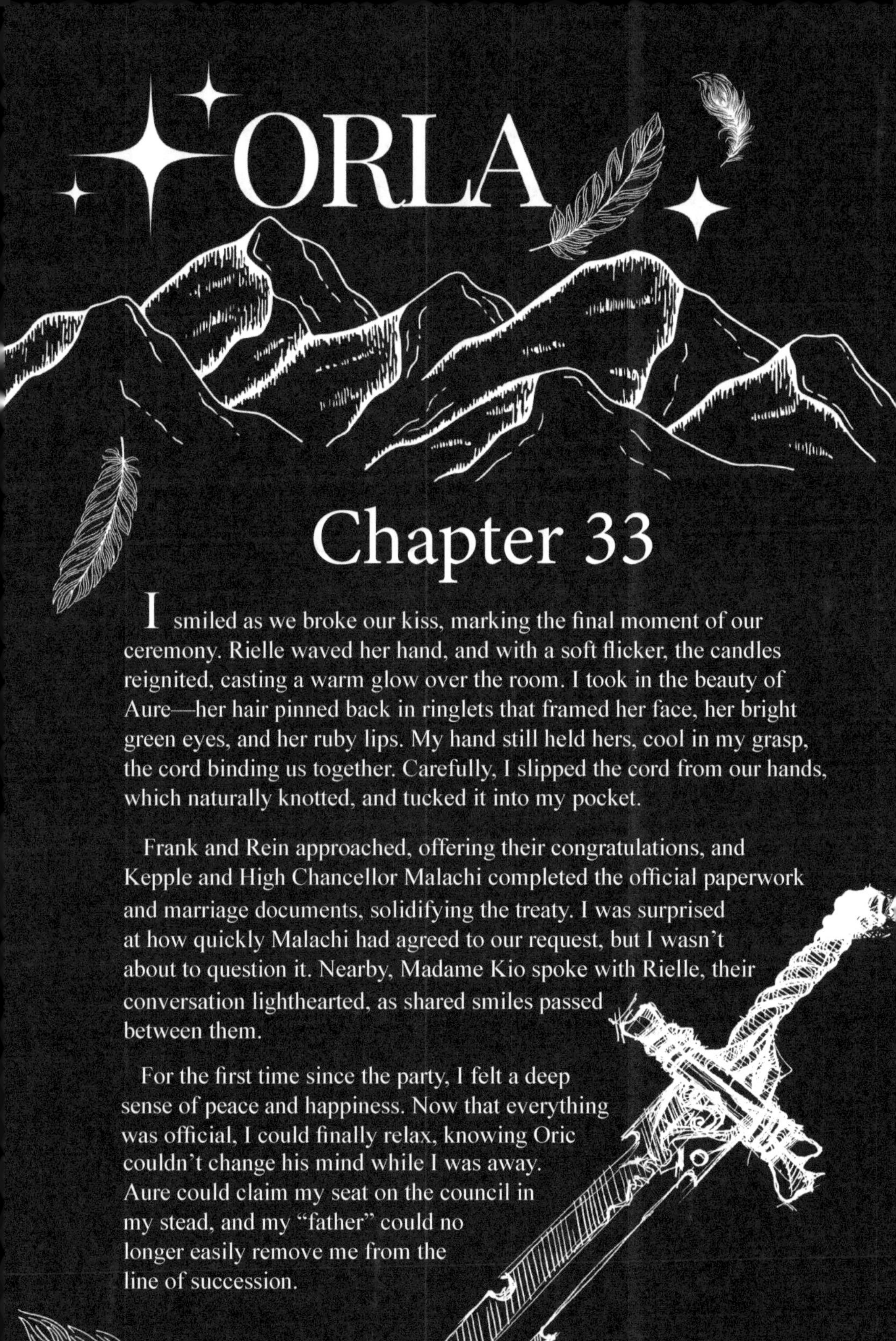

ORLA

Chapter 33

I smiled as we broke our kiss, marking the final moment of our ceremony. Rielle waved her hand, and with a soft flicker, the candles reignited, casting a warm glow over the room. I took in the beauty of Aure—her hair pinned back in ringlets that framed her face, her bright green eyes, and her ruby lips. My hand still held hers, cool in my grasp, the cord binding us together. Carefully, I slipped the cord from our hands, which naturally knotted, and tucked it into my pocket.

Frank and Rein approached, offering their congratulations, and Kepple and High Chancellor Malachi completed the official paperwork and marriage documents, solidifying the treaty. I was surprised at how quickly Malachi had agreed to our request, but I wasn't about to question it. Nearby, Madame Kio spoke with Rielle, their conversation lighthearted, as shared smiles passed between them.

For the first time since the party, I felt a deep sense of peace and happiness. Now that everything was official, I could finally relax, knowing Oric couldn't change his mind while I was away. Aure could claim my seat on the council in my stead, and my "father" could no longer easily remove me from the line of succession.

If, gods forbid, I never returned, Aure could claim the heirship to both thrones and rule our kingdoms alone. My plan would work, effectively disrupting any further attempts at manipulation.

I smiled warmly and tugged Aure close, leaning in against her neck to whisper in her ear, "I can't wait to get this wonderfully revealing dress off you and warm you up. You're breathtaking tonight, wife."

She flushed deliciously, a soft giggle escaping her lips. "Soon enough, we can do just that… wife."

After a few small conversations and signing the necessary documents, everyone drifted their separate ways. No grand party, no royal expectations— just a beautifully simple ceremony shared between us and a handful of trusted friends. It was perfect. She was perfect.

We made our way back to her chambers, though they had long since become ours. My belongings had found their way into the space, piece by piece, over the last few months. Had it really only been a few months since we first met? It felt like a lifetime. My bags were already packed, ready for my departure the day after tomorrow and sat just inside the door.

As soon as we entered the room, Aure kissed me, and we began kicking off our shoes. I reached up to pull the pins from her hair, letting her curls tumble down her back, and ran my fingers through their softness. Her hands moved to my shirt, unbuttoning the tailored uniform I'd commandeered and had the seamstress alter for me. I slipped it off, laying it gently on the sofa, my undershirt still snugly in place.

The room was bathed in a warm, flickering glow, candlelight casting soft shadows across the walls. The gentle illumination created an atmosphere that felt both intimate and inviting, drawing us closer into the cozy space.

I scooped her up, grinning as she let out an adorable squeak. Kissing her deeply, I carried her to the bed and set her down beside it, then began to unfasten the intricate lace of her dress, savoring every moment.

The dress slipped to the floor, pooling around her feet, and I began trailing kisses down her neck, then lower, to her now-bare breasts. A sheer, delicate pair of silk panties was all that remained, hugging her waist. Her fingers found the buckle at the top of my pants, but I gently lifted her, moving her hands out of reach, and leaned down to kiss her left breast, savoring her shiver beneath my touch before easing her down onto the bed. Our lips met again, and her arms wrapped tightly around my neck, pulling me closer.

"I love you, Meles Tari," I whispered tenderly, leaning back to meet her gaze. My eyes shone a deep magenta, and she returned my look with a smile, her sea-green eyes filled with desire. A brief flash of Tristan's face flickered in my memory, a hint of dread curling in my stomach. I quickly pushed the image aside, determined not to let him taint this moment. I wouldn't shut her out completely anymore, but I'd be damned if I let that bastard cause her any more pain.

"I love you too," she replied softly, her hand sliding up to my undershirt, pulling it off me. I closed my eyes, savoring the gentle touch of her fingers tracing down my chest and stomach. Her hands found their way to my waistband, but I caught them, gently pinning her wrists above her head as I claimed her lips in a fierce, possessive kiss. I wanted to give her everything tonight, to make this night all about her.

I licked and nipped at her tender skin, trailing kisses down to her sheer, teasing panties. I was going to rip that delicate fabric to shreds, but not yet— not until I had her begging for it. A wicked grin spread across my face at the thought of her moaning my name, pleading for more. Soft whimpers escaped her lips as I made my way lower, her fingers tangling in my hair. She gasped when I kissed along her hip bone, right at the edge of those tempting panties.

I let my tongue trace the waistband, skimming toward the center, teasingly close to where she needed me most. Her legs had already spread naturally, inviting me to settle between them. Sliding my arms beneath her thighs, I gripped them, pulling her further open. I paused for a moment, looking up at her, savoring the expressions of pleasure and the soft sounds spilling from her. Every reaction fed my desire, and I wanted to hear more—much more.

"Aure," her attention snapped to me, drawing her gaze to meet mine, a smirk spreading across my lips. "I'm going to make you beg me to let you cum." With confidence, I leaned in, letting my tongue glide over the fabric covering her, already coated in her damp need. I could taste her desire through the thin material, savoring the sweetness as she shuddered beneath my hold. I kept her firmly in place, taking my time as I lapped at her pussy, teasing her with every slow, deliberate stroke.

Her hips bucked, but I held them firmly, keeping her steady as she arched, trying to get closer. My movements continued with a slow, reverent rhythm, calculated to drive her wild. Her breaths came in short gasps, and soft whimpers of need escaped her lips as she tried to pull me closer, her fingers gripping the back of my head. But I was in control right now, and I wasn't about to give that up so easily.

I slipped my tongue beneath the edge of the fabric, grazing her clit before tracing a slow path along the delicate curve of her vulva. Then, I mirrored the motion on the other side, taking my time as I felt her body tense beneath me. A grin spread across my face as she panted and groaned, "Oh gods, Orla, please," her fingers tightening and fisting in my hair, urging me closer.

"Please what?" I teased, "You are the one who decided to wear these dainty little panties. I quite like them. Maybe we should keep them on you the whole night." My lips curled into a mischievous grin.

"No, you wouldn't," she playfully glared, fingers drifting to the thin straps of her panties, ready to slip them off herself.

I raised an eyebrow, meeting her gaze with a challenging smirk. Sitting up on my knees, I took hold of her hands and placed them firmly on her stomach. "I didn't give you permission to do that. Tonight, I make the rules."

With that, I slipped off my belt and wrapped the leather around her wrists, securing them together with a slow, deliberate tug.

She bit her lower lip, a spark of excitement flashing in her eyes, and I felt the heat flare in my core at the thrill of being fully in control, and it was on my terms this time. I could see she was loving every moment of it. She squirmed beneath me, her breath quickening, and I let my fingers trace tantalizing circles along the edges of her panties. My thumbs slipped just under the fabric, brushing her skin as my hands caressed her thighs. Soft moans escaped her lips, and her hips moved in subtle, encouraging motions, beckoning me to go further.

My hands trailed down her legs, reaching her feet, and I began rubbing them firmly, eliciting a groan from her. "Are you ticklish, Meles Tari?" I asked, a playful grin spreading across my face. I gently brushed my fingers along the center of her soles, and little giggles escaped her as she tried to pull her feet away from my grasp. Her laughter grew, uncontrollable, as I continued tickling, her breath coming in gasps between bouts of laughter.

"Stop, please..." she managed to say, laughing even louder, wiggling but unable to break free from my hold. I finally slowed, letting her catch her breath, my heart warming at the joy in her laughter. "I'll have to remember just how ticklish you are," I teased, smirking as I planted a gentle kiss on her toes. "Pretty sure you'd agree to anything I asked after that."

Her breathless voice replied, "You're such a tease, Orla." Her moan punctuated her words as I kissed my way up her leg, her skin warm and soft, like milk tea beneath my lips. I lingered at the edge of those enticingly sheer panties, my gaze meeting hers, as I continued my slow, deliberate ascent.

"Please, I want to feel you against me," Aure pleaded, her voice breathless with need. I couldn't deny her, though I decided to tease her a little longer. I placed my two fingers at the top of the waistband, gliding down the center, brushing over her sensitive clit and entrance through the thin fabric.

I trailed my touch lower, fingers running between her ass cheeks, where the material all but disappeared into the thin strip of string. With a smirk, I gave it a gentle tug, my fingers tracing along the slick line, caressing her ass.

The now taut, sheer white fabric being fully soaked, clung to her, revealing the full, pulsing heat beneath it. They glistened like a frosted veil, barely concealing the throbbing need of her pussy.

With a gasp, she groaned, "Gods, Orla, are you trying to drive me crazy?" She squirmed, hands flexing as she struggled against her restraints, her plump little butt pressing enticingly into my hand.

"I want to hear you beg me to make you cum, Meles Tari," I purred, my gaze fixed on her as a shiver rippled through her body. Her lip caught between her teeth. She met my eyes with that helpless, vulnerable need, finally letting out a soft, breathless plea. "Please…"

"Please, what?" I leaned in closer, running my tongue up the sheer fabric from the curve of her ass up toward her clit. She squirmed, arching against me, trying to urge me closer to where she wanted my touch. I slipped my arm firmly around her leg, holding her in place, while my fingers teased the delicate space just above her core, pressing down on her clit through the wet material. She moaned, rocking her hips, chasing the sensation.

The way her body responded to my touch, the sounds that spilled from her lips—it stirred something deep and primal in me. My magic crackled, mingling with the intensity of the moment, and for the first time in what felt like forever, the tightness in my chest eased. With her, the worries, the guilt, and the shame melted away. In this moment, it was just us, and with her, I felt truly alive, free, as though all the broken pieces had finally fallen into place. I wanted to be everything for her, with her, and to give her all of me.

She looked down at me, her breathing calming slightly as I'd paused, lost in my thoughts. Her voice, soft and needy, brought me back. "Please, I want you—all of you," she whimpered, her words sending a surge of heat through me.

Grinning, I moved swiftly, crawling up over her until my lips hovered just above hers. My knee pressed firmly between her thighs, my hands braced on either side of her shoulders, supporting me as I brought my body flush with hers. Leaning down, I brushed my lips over hers, savoring the way she gasped beneath me, my own desire building as our bodies melded together.

With my lips still a mere inch above hers, I breathed, "All of me?" The question slipped out more like a taunt than a request, a challenge mixed with a hint of my own vulnerability, needing reassurance that I was enough. With her hands still bound and resting between us, her fingers brushed lightly against my stomach.

"Yes," she moaned, her voice soft but resolute. Her hips ground against my knee, and I felt her fingers reach for the button at my waistband. I flinched as a shiver ran through me, and I shifted out of her reach, my lips falling against hers. I tasted the sweetness of her mouth, and when her tongue met mine, it was greedy, unrestrained. I groaned into the kiss, savoring every sensation as I explored her with my tongue, losing myself in her.

Her leg moved against my thigh, and a sharp, aching pain shot through me. I couldn't stifle the sharp intake of breath, and I froze. *Fuck, of course, she noticed.* Aure pulled back, her gaze intense, eyes locking with mine as they shifted, betraying me with blue streaks swirling through the magenta.

"Did I hurt you? Were you injured?" she asked, her voice filled with concern.

My jaw tightened. "It's nothing, really," I sighed, trying to dismiss it, leaning in to kiss her cheek. Though she pulled back, she didn't let go.

"It didn't seem like nothing a moment ago," she said, giving me a steady, probing look that made it clear she wasn't convinced.

I leaned my forehead against hers, closing my eyes as I spoke softly. "Please, Aure... let me do this for you. Just let it go and enjoy yourself, please?" My voice was a quiet plea, desperate to regain the intimacy we had lost, to push away the discomfort creeping into the moment. All I wanted was to be lost in her, to let everything else—my pain, my guilt, my shame—fade into the background.

If I had to show her my cuts, explain why I did it, or talk about the weight of my grief and the damage it had done, I'd lose control—of my magic, of my power, of everything I was holding inside. Truly, that terrified me more than anything.

She leaned in, kissing me softly, then murmured, "Okay. But when you're ready, I'll be here to listen."

A grin spread across my face, relief mixing with a spark of mischief. "You know," I started, my tone playful. "I've always wanted to try something I read about in one of my books."

Aure raised an eyebrow, a curious smile tugging at her lips. "You read books about sex?"

I shot her a mock-disapproving look. "No, I read romance books," I corrected, leaning in closer. "But there was this one scene with hot wax... driving someone right to the edge." My voice dipped into a flirtatious tone, letting the suggestion linger.

Her eyes widened, a hint of surprise flashing across her face, but no fear. If anything, the suggestion seemed to excite her. She began to grind against my knee again, purring, "So... why don't you try it?"

Gods, she was stunning, a beautiful mess beneath me. I reached over, grabbing the tall glass cylinder full of a slowly melting wax candle from the small table beside the bed. It had already been lit, courtesy of Rielle's thoughtful touch to make the room feel more romantic. I held it above her, the warmth of the candle radiating between us, and let a slow, seductive smile play across my lips.

I sat up, holding the warmed glass candle above her full breasts, knowing that the higher the wax fell, the more it would cool before touching her skin. The thrill of seeing her react to each sensation coiled inside me, building a quiet anticipation. I let a few droplets fall, landing softly on her left breast, then rolling slightly to form a hardened line along her skin. Aure gasped, drawing in a sharp breath, biting her lower lip as her hips pressed against me with a newfound urgency.

I let the candle tilt just a little more, and another droplet fell, this time landing just above her collarbone. I watched it cool, becoming a thin, glossy line on her skin. Aure whimpered, her head falling back, exposing the delicate curve of her neck. The sound of her need fueled me, and I trailed my fingertips over the wax lines, tracing them as if they were symbols of something sacred between us.

"You're stunning." My voice was rough with desire as I lowered my mouth to kiss the edges of the hardened wax, feeling her pulse race beneath my lips. Her hands, still bound together, shifted restlessly as her body responded to every gentle kiss, every flicker of heat.

"Orla…" she whispered, her voice breathy and filled with longing. Her gaze met mine, and I saw the intensity there, a mutual hunger reflected back. She arched, her body pressing up against mine, and the movement was enough to pull me fully back into the moment, centered entirely on her.

The sight of her biting her lip, her hips grinding up against me with such desire, sent a surge of heat through me. I tilted the candle again, letting a few more droplets fall, watching as they landed on the curve of her right breast. Aure gasped louder this time, her chest rising with the sensation, her eyes fluttering shut as she surrendered to the pleasure.

"Do you like that?" My voice was thick with desire as I watched her body react beneath me.

She nodded, her breath coming out in ragged pants. "More," she whispered, her voice strained but filled with need.

I obliged, moving the candle lower, letting the wax fall in a slow trail down her abdomen. Each drop seemed to send a shiver through her, her body arching slightly with every touch of the heated wax. I reveled in the sight of her—completely at my mercy, lost in the moment.

I leaned down, my lips brushing the cooled line of wax on her breast, kissing the trail the wax had left. She moaned softly, her hands still bound, her fingers twitching as though wanting to touch me, to pull me closer. I smiled against her skin, the power of the moment washing over me.

"You're so beautiful like this," I whispered against her, my lips trailing kisses up her neck, lingering just below her ear. "I could watch you all night."

Her breath caught, and I could feel the tension building inside her, her body taut with anticipation. She moved again, her hips bucking slightly, trying to pull me closer, to push me to the edge with her.

I wasn't done yet. I leaned back, eyes locked on hers as I raised the candle again, this time letting the wax drip lower, just above the line of her panties, teasing the sensitive skin of her stomach. She let out a desperate moan, her head falling back against the pillow as her body trembled beneath me.

"Please, Orla," she gasped, her voice barely a whisper. "Please, I need you."

Her pleading sent a rush of desire through me, but I held back, savoring the moment. "You're not ready yet," I teased, my fingers brushing over the edge of her panties, tracing the fabric lightly. "Not until I say so."

She whimpered, her body arching into my touch, her breath coming in shallow, needy gasps. I leaned down, kissing the spot where the wax had fallen, my lips trailing lower, teasing her, until finally, I pressed my mouth against her through the soaked fabric of those panties. She cried out, her entire body trembling as I kissed her, tasted her, through the thin barrier.

I let the hot wax drip onto her panties, each droplet leaving a glossy, hardened trail. She writhed beneath my touch, her body arching with each sensation, and I could see the tension building, bringing her closer and closer to the edge of ecstasy.

Her whimpers and moans urged me on as she squirmed beneath my touch, pleading, "Orla, please—you're driving me crazy." I set the candle aside, back on the table. I reveled in her need, and then, with a wicked grin, I let a spark of my magic loose, just enough to ignite the fabric. Her panties burned to ash in an instant, and she yelped in surprise.

I ran my fingers along her slit, feeling her shudder beneath me as a low, lingering moan escaped her lips. Pressing my body against hers, I slipped two fingers deep inside, moving with purpose. "Orla," she breathed, her voice thick with desire, as if she were praying to me.

I was captivated, lost in the moment, watching her move and moan, riding my hand, coming completely undone because of me. All I wanted was to see her shatter in ecstasy, and she was so close, unraveling beautifully.

"That's it, Meles Tari, come for me." With a final curl of my fingers and a deep thrust, I pressed a kiss to her neck. She shook uncontrollably, shattering around me as a scream tore from her lips.

My hand lingered as I slowly withdrew my fingers, tracing gentle circles around her sensitive, swollen pussy, soothing its throbbing in the aftershocks that rippled through her. I kissed her neck softly, pressing my body against hers. Her eyes fluttered closed, her breath gradually easing back to a soft, steady rhythm.

"I want to give you what you just gave me," she hummed, her eyes still closed, a soft smile playing on her lips. I gazed at her, memorizing every curve and contour of her face. "Shh, there will be time for that later," I whispered gently. "For now, just rest, okay?" I nestled my head against her shoulder, nuzzling into her neck, and pulled the blanket over us, holding her close.

I laid there, our bond buzzing contently between us as she drifted off to sleep. Her cute, small snores caused me to smile. I watched her until I finally fell asleep holding—my wife.

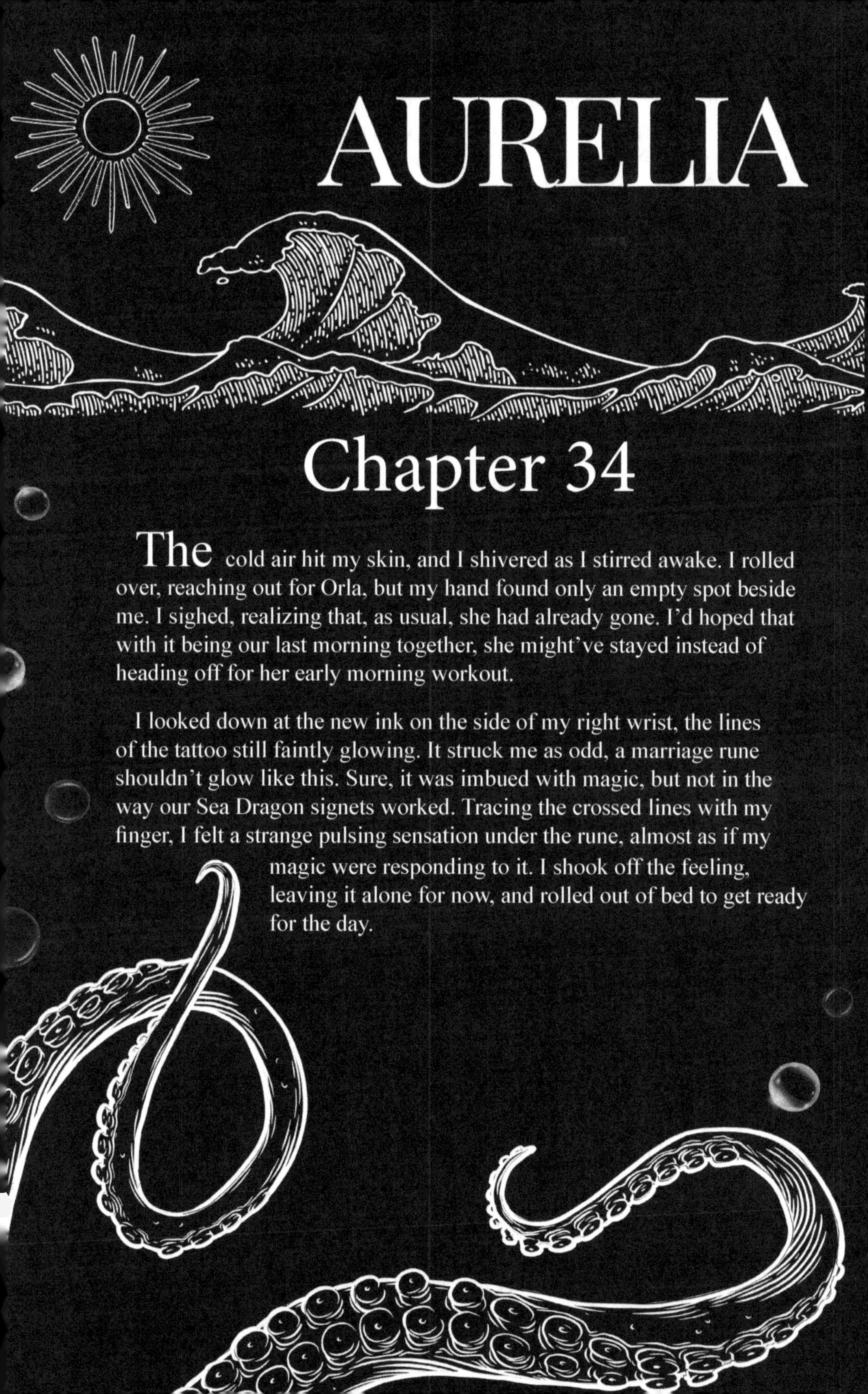

AURELIA

Chapter 34

The cold air hit my skin, and I shivered as I stirred awake. I rolled over, reaching out for Orla, but my hand found only an empty spot beside me. I sighed, realizing that, as usual, she had already gone. I'd hoped that with it being our last morning together, she might've stayed instead of heading off for her early morning workout.

I looked down at the new ink on the side of my right wrist, the lines of the tattoo still faintly glowing. It struck me as odd, a marriage rune shouldn't glow like this. Sure, it was imbued with magic, but not in the way our Sea Dragon signets worked. Tracing the crossed lines with my finger, I felt a strange pulsing sensation under the rune, almost as if my magic were responding to it. I shook off the feeling, leaving it alone for now, and rolled out of bed to get ready for the day.

I was meeting with Kepple to dive into some research and help with a few ongoing projects. Lately, Kepple had been a more frequent companion, especially with Orla being so distant. When Orla leaves tomorrow, I realized Kepple would soon be one of my only close friends left here, since Frank, Rein, and Rielle all planned to go with Orla.

Another storm cloud loomed overhead, casting the sky in dark, brooding grays. The lamps flickered in the dim light as the sun disappeared behind the thick clouds. I pulled on a deep forest-green wool gown, its warmth a comfort against the chill in the air. Carefully, I pinned my hair up, securing it with a thin, pointed throwing blade, though a few ringlets escaped, framing my face. Finally, I placed my ruby rebounder necklace around my neck, feeling its familiar weight rest against my chest.

As I finished adjusting my necklace, there was a gentle knock at the door, and Alex entered, balancing a tray laden with food. The aroma of fresh bread, roasted nuts, oat porridge, and spiced tea filled the room, and I realized how hungry I was.

"Good morning, Princess Aurelia," he greeted, offering a warm smile as he set the tray down on a small table in front of the plush sofa. "Her Highness, Princess Orla, sent this up for you. She thought you might need some nourishment before you get too absorbed in your day."

I smiled, touched by Orla's thoughtfulness. "Thank you, Alex. Would you please join me? If you'd like," I said, gesturing to the plush chair.

He looked a bit surprised, but nodded, taking a seat. "I appreciate the offer, Your Grace," he replied, his accent gently lilting over the words.

As we began to eat, I studied him, curious to know more about the young soldier who'd so suddenly entered my life. "So, Alex, tell me a bit about yourself. Rein spoke highly of you, but I'd like to hear it from you."

"Well, I was raised by my father, a blacksmith, in South Negall. He taught me a lot about the value of hard work and resilience. We didn't have much, but he made sure we had enough. When I wasn't helping him in the forge, I'd sneak off to watch the local healers at work." He smiled, a distant look crossing his face. "My mother had been one of them—a fae healer. She was always tending to the people in our village, whether or not they had enough to pay her. She had this way about her, calming people with just a look. I think she passed some of that on to me."

His face grew a bit somber. "She passed when I was young. An illness swept through our village, and she didn't survive it. My father always said she gave too much of herself, that she spent all her strength healing others and had none left for herself." He paused, taking a breath. "After she died, my father did his best to keep her memory alive, telling me stories and teaching me about her healing herbs and small spells. She left her mark on me, in more ways than one. That's why I'm here, really—between my father's strength and my mother's compassion. I want to protect people in the ways they taught me."

The thoughts of my own mother surfaced and the grief I felt for her washed over me as I saw it mirrored in Alex. I nodded, touched by his words. "You carry them both with you, then. And that's a rare gift, Alex. I imagine it makes you quite an asset in both battle and healing."

He offered a small, grateful smile. "Thank you, Your Grace. They both taught me so much, in their own ways. It's part of why I joined the ranks. I wanted to honor both their legacies by being there for others, like they were."

"You're more than just a soldier, Alex," I said, looking at him warmly. "Orla wouldn't trust just anyone to look after me. I know I'm in good hands."

He straightened, his gaze steady. "It's an honor, Your Grace. I'll be by your side for as long as you need me." Then he chuckled softly, "Her Highness Princess Orla once told me I'm good at keeping people out of trouble. It's been my specialty since becoming a soldier. I'm skilled at being where I'm needed, staying unnoticed, and making sure those I protect stay safe. All I ever really wanted, I think. To do something that matters."

I sipped my tea thoughtfully. "I think we all want that, in some way. To make a difference, even in small ways. But I have a feeling you're capable of more than just 'keeping people out of trouble.'"

He smiled, a bit of pride showing. "I appreciate that, Your Grace. And I promise you'll have no cause to doubt me."

"Alex," I began, leaning forward. "When you agreed to take this position, I assume you knew it might come with risks, especially now with all that's happening?"

He nodded solemnly. "I did, Your Grace. But there's nowhere else I'd rather be than here, serving you and Her Highness. I understand what's at stake."

I returned his steady gaze, impressed by his sincerity and loyalty. "I'm grateful, Alex. I think we will get along well."

I finished my meal, and a faint squeak caught my attention. Puzzled, I glanced over at Alex and noticed a small black fuzzball with long, delicate ears peeking out of his uniform shirt pocket. The squeak sounded again, a bit louder this time, and I watched as Alex pulled a tiny piece of strawberry from his plate and held it up to the little creature. Speaking softly in fae, he offered the fruit, and the creature snatched it with tiny, winged hands, nibbling contentedly.

Curious, I asked, "Alex, who's that in your pocket?"

His cheeks turned a shade of pink, and he quickly covered the pocket with his hand, giving me a sheepish grin. "Ah, this... this is Amethyst, my little pocket bat." He looked almost bashful, his smile a bit lopsided as he met my gaze.

I couldn't help but laugh softly, charmed by the sight. "Amethyst, huh? I didn't know pocket bats were so... small."

He chuckled, gently stroking the little creature's head with a fingertip. "She's a bit of a runt for her kind, but she has a big appetite and a lot of heart. She keeps me company and helps keep pests at bay, especially during long nights on watch."

I smiled, watching as the bat chittered, seemingly content. "Well, it's wonderful to meet you, Amethyst. I'd say you're in very good company."

Alex chuckled, gently stroking the little creature's head with a fingertip. "Yeah, she's special. And, well, she's not my only connection to the natural world." He hesitated, then continued, "I have a nature affinity. It lets me manipulate plants and communicate with small creatures, like Amethyst, to help me track or gather information when I'm out on a mission."

I raised an eyebrow, intrigued. "So, you can actually communicate with animals?"

He nodded, his grin widening. "In a way, yes. I can sense their emotions and guide them to assist me. Sometimes, it's just little things—like finding a hidden path, or knowing if something unusual is nearby. It's why Amethyst and I get along so well. She picks up on things and lets me know if I'm heading the right way."

"That sounds like a very useful talent. And it sounds like she has been a great asset to you." I grinned, truly admiring the Fae magic he possessed. I had heard about nature affinities, but I hadn't seen them firsthand before.

He nodded, a hint of pride shining in his eyes. "She's been with me through a lot. I'm glad you don't mind her tagging along, Your Grace."

"Not at all," I replied, enchanted by the little creature. "It's nice to know you have such a loyal companion by your side."

Alex grinned, giving Amethyst another gentle pat before she nestled back into his pocket. It was clear they shared a unique bond, and it was heartwarming to see him let his guard down, if only for a moment.

I nodded, sensing the deep bond they shared. "You and Amethyst are a perfect team. I'm glad to know you'll both be watching out for me."

Alex's eyes shone with gratitude, and he nodded firmly. "We won't let you down, Your Grace."

"Today, Kepple will be visiting, and we're meeting in the library downstairs in a few hours. Normally, I'd spend some time outside, but it looks far too cold for that today." I took a final, long sip of my tea and set the empty cup back on the tray. Alex watched me intently, clearly listening closely to my words.

"I'll probably just sit here and read until it's time to go. I can be quite boring company, I'm afraid." I offered him a small, apologetic smile.

Alex returned my smile warmly. "I don't mind quiet tasks, Your Grace. I'm perfectly capable of staying alert and my mind active, even during the more peaceful moments."

I picked up a book on the ancient races and histories, as told through the oral stories of the Sea Dragons. My fingers gently rustled the pages of the old tome, breaking the quiet of the room. The low crackle from the cinders in the hearth provided a gentle warmth that seemed to calm the space.

Alex stood quietly, moving to lean against the wall beside the door. Glancing over, I noticed his gaze fixed on the glowing embers, his thumb absently rubbing the hilt of his dagger. His quiet presence, steady and calm, brought me a sense of unexpected comfort.

As the muted sunlight trickled through the thick clouds, casting a dim light across the palace corridors, I gathered my books and rose from my seat. With a nod to Alex, who immediately fell into step beside me, we made our way to the library, where Kepple awaited. My heart felt heavy with anticipation; today, we were continuing the search for the knowledge that might seal the bond between Orla and me. If we could stabilize our mate bond, we could bring our powers into harmony, preventing any further chaos from spilling over.

At the library's grand doors, Alex held one open, gesturing for me to enter. The familiar scents of aged parchment and leather filled the space, lending it an air of wisdom and mystery. We found Kepple already seated at a large oak table, with several scrolls and heavy tomes spread before them. They looked up and smiled, gesturing for me to join them.

"Ah, Princess Aurelia," Kepple greeted warmly, motioning to the seats across from them, and glanced at Alex for a moment. "I've come across a few fascinating texts that may hold the key to our problem."

I took a seat, and Alex stood by, his eyes scanning the bookshelves as if assessing every corner of the room. "I'm eager to hear what you've found," I replied, leaning forward, my curiosity piqued. "You mentioned before that these texts covered the ancient dragons—the Sky Dragons and the Land Dragons—and something about the Three Sisters of Creation?"

As we settled into our chairs, the weight of the ancient myths seemed to fill the room, Kepple's expression reflecting both excitement and reverence as they laid out several old, cracked tomes before us. "The story of Terra's early days is one of wonder and tragedy," Kepple began. "A myth that recounts the delicate balance of creation—and how it was lost."

I watched, listening as Kepple's fingers brushed over a thick book, open to a page depicting three Dragon-like figures, each with unique features and traits. "Yes, the Three Sisters: Lilithariel, Sylvana, and Tethys. According to legend, they were the creators of all magic. Lilithariel ruled over the skies, Sylvana the earth, and Tethys the waters. They are the ones who birthed the dragons—Lilithariel hatched the Sky Dragons, Sylvana the Land Dragons, and Tethys the Sea Dragons."

My gaze traveled over the beautiful illustrations. "The Sisters of Creation… I hadn't realized their connection went so deep. And how does this help with the bond?" I asked, trying to connect the dots.

"It's here in this retelling of the myth of creation." Kepple pushed their round glasses up further on their nose.

Alex leaned in, intrigued. "I've heard fragments of this legend, but never in its entirety."

Kepple nodded. "It's a tale that speaks to the origins of magic and life as we know it. When Terra was young, the skies, land, and seas existed in perfect harmony, free from all intelligent life. But that all changed when a celestial star seed fell, bringing with it three powerful beings: the sisters of the sky, the sea, and the land. They lived together in peace for a time, their children thriving alongside them. But as the Sisters' offspring grew, so did the strain on the world's resources, and tension began to build."

I listened intently, absorbing the gravity of their words. I could feel the echoes of these powerful beings within me, still curious how this ancient history might relate to the bond Orla and I shared.

Kepple continued, "The Sister of the Sky, cunning and ambitious, sought dominance. However, unlike her sisters, she kept her magic to herself, giving her children little power. When war broke out between the sisters, her offspring were easily defeated, compared to the Sister of the Sea who imbued her children with her own essence. The Sister of the Sea had created beings of unmatched strength and resilience, yet binding them to a single mate—only found through their mating songs."

Alex leaned forward, his eyes gleaming with fascination. "So, the children of the Sea Sister gained a kind of unity, even if it came at a cost."

Kepple nodded thoughtfully. "Yes. In this way, her magic carried on with a focus on balance, albeit in a way that limited her offspring's independence. Meanwhile, the Land Sister, seeing the strain on the world, sacrificed herself to birth lesser beings: the Humans, the Dwarfs, and the Fae. In her final act, her magic was passed onto these new creations. But her sister of the sky, consumed with jealousy and rage, committed a terrible act. She struck down the Land Sister, sending shockwaves through the realm."

I shivered as the story continued, feeling the sorrow of that betrayal throughout me. "With the death of The Land Sister, she passed on a part of her magic," Kepple went on. "But not all. The Dwarfs, bound to minerals, and the Fae, to the trees, inherited her gifts, while the Humans, born from soil, remained untouched by magic."

The myth began to weave itself into my thoughts about the mate bond, and I wondered aloud, "And what of the Sea Sister? How did she survive?"

Kepple's eyes darkened as they spoke of the final moments of this ancient conflict. "Fearing the Sister of the Sky, the Sea Sister sacrificed herself to syphon the Sky Sister's magic, creating the Siren—a being of both sea and sky magic, bound to the waters yet infused with the power of the heavens. The Siren inherited the mating songs of the Sea's children and became the anchor for the last vestiges of the Sea Sister's magic. As for the Sky Sister, though weakened, she swore revenge, traveling Terraqua in search of her stolen power. Over time, she drained life and magic from those she lured, regaining fragments of her strength."

Alex crossed his arms, deep in thought. "So, the Sky Sister continues her search, even now, through descendants and remnants of her power?" he mused aloud.

Kepple's eyes held a deep, solemn gravity as they looked at me. "Yes. Though much was lost, fragments remain, and I believe those fragments, though faint, may hold the key we seek. Your Highness, if we can find a way to harness the binding magic of the Sister's dragons, especially with the echoes of sea and sky within you, it might stabilize your bond with Orla. That's why I've been buried in these ancient texts."

I glanced at Kepple. "Do you think any of their knowledge still exists, hidden away?"

Kepple nodded slowly. "If we can find them, we might use them to seal your bond. I've come across mentions of old rituals that resemble the mate bond, though they're incomplete. Still, there's hope. These texts could lead us toward stabilizing your connection with Orla."

Hope flickered within me, but it was tempered by the fear that the past might repeat itself. "Then we must keep searching. If the Sea Sister's sacrifice stabilized the magic of her children, enabling the creation of the Siren, perhaps we too can find a way to seal our bond and bring harmony to our powers."

Kepple's face brightened with determination. "Yes. We may be on the edge of uncovering a truth that has been hidden for centuries."

Together, we returned to the ancient texts, our purpose clear. The mysteries of the past held the key to our future, and it offered hope for balance and unity. I longed for our bond to be as final and binding as the wedding runes themselves.

I lost track of time as Kepple and I pored over ancient texts and incomplete myths. I was so focused on studying the scattered works that I didn't notice Orla had entered the room, except for the calm, comforting presence that washed over me as I read. It wasn't until she wrapped her arm around my chest and rested her head on my shoulder, her gaze falling on the table of books, and she began reading aloud that I turned my focus to her.

The words sounded beautifully foreign to my ears. "Sylvana drew polod uin dór os- hen, forming neled heads: er uin ore a minerals within i crater where he aeg, er uin trees whose roots grew polodren a tovon os- hen, a i third uin gwath- beneath hen feet."

Alex's head perked up when Orla spoke. With a sigh, I leaned my head against hers. "Which means?"

She chuckled softly and traced her finger along the line of scrolled words. "Sylvana drew strength from the land around her, forming three heads: one from the ore and minerals within the crater where she fell, one from the trees whose roots grew strong and deep around her, and the third from the soil beneath her feet."

Alex spoke softly, a smile on his lips, though sadness lingered in his eyes. "My mother spoke ancient Fae, but I never learned. I haven't heard it since. It's rare to know."

"Well, as interesting as that is, I don't think it's going to help us seal our mate bond." I closed the book and rubbed my eyes, the strain leaving me drained and fatigued.

Orla kissed my neck and massaged my shoulders for a moment. "I came to take you with me to the commanders' meeting. We need to announce to them—and King Oric—that we're married."

I looked up at her, worry creasing my brow, but I nodded. We would have to face them sooner than later and we would do it together.

ORLA

Chapter 35

I was determined to be the leader my people deserved, the leader Aure deserved, even if it meant revealing a bit more of my intentions than I was comfortable with. Now that we were officially wed, Oric would find it much harder to manipulate either of us for his own purposes. The weight of our union would shield us from his scheming, at least for now. I tightened my grip on Aure's hand as we entered the council meeting room.

Servants moved quietly, pouring wine for the commanders and council present while a roaring fire in the hearth filled the room with the heavy scents of wood smoke and cigars. The dim lighting cast long shadows across the walls, the sun having long since disappeared beneath the horizon, leaving the palace engulfed in cold, encroaching darkness. Only the glow of the fire and flickering lamps pushed back as the night illuminated the space, creating an eerie atmosphere.

I glanced at Aure, her expression steady, but the bond between us buzzed with a tension that mirrored my own. We had to face this united and strong. I would show them, and Oric, that we were not to be used in their games. We would carve our own path.

I gave Aure's hand a gentle squeeze, hoping the gesture conveyed the calm I didn't entirely feel. Tonight was crucial, a turning point for us, and while I kept my expression steady, the bond between us thrummed with shared tension. We stepped farther into the council meeting room, where hushed conversations died down, replaced by the weight of scrutinizing stares. Every eye followed us, lingering on our clasped hands, no doubt calculating the ramifications of our union.

At the head of the table sat King Oric, his face unreadable. Even though everyone still believed him to be my father, the tension between us was palpable. His plans had just become significantly more complicated, and I could almost see the calculations running through his mind as he scrambled for his next move. He had underestimated me—underestimated us. But that would end tonight.

"Ah, my daughters," Oric greeted us, his voice smooth but sharp at the edges. He gestured to the chairs at the far end of the table. "Please, join us." His eyes lingered on Aure, and heat flared in my fists.

Aure's grip tightened on my hand, and I met my father's gaze head-on, refusing to let the thinly veiled hostility unnerve me. "Thank you, Your Majesty," Aure replied evenly, guiding me toward the seats. The room felt charged, heavy with the weight of what was about to be said. Our announcement hung over the gathering like an impending storm.

As we sat, I stole a glance at Aure. Her expression was calm, but I could feel the tension vibrating through our bond, mirroring my own. We had to be united, unshakable, to face this challenge.

"As some of you may already be aware," I began, my voice strong and deliberate, "Aurelia and I are now wed. Our union solidifies not only our personal commitment to each other but also our alliance and loyalty to both of our kingdoms and their futures."

Murmurs rippled through the room. The commanders exchanged glances, and council members whispered among themselves. King Oric, however, remained silent, his eyes fixed on me, cold and calculating.

"We've come before you today," Aure continued, her voice ringing out clear and sure. "To ensure that our marriage is formally recognized, and to make it clear that we will not tolerate interference with our alliance or the future of our kingdoms. This is a decision we've made for the strength and stability of the whole realm."

The room fell into a tense silence. The fire crackled in the hearth, the scent of wood smoke thick in the air, as the council processed our words. My stomach clenched tightly, but my nerves would have to come to heel.

I took a breath and raised my chin, speaking clearly and deliberately. "We stand before you today not to challenge the authority of the crown, nor to undermine King Oric's rule. Our intent is not to seize power or control. We are here to announce that we are making our own choices about how we manage our lives—together."

Aure's hand still rested in mine, her calm strength reinforcing the boldness of my next words. "I will be joining the commanders on the front-lines."

The whispers stopped abruptly, replaced by stunned silence. Oric's eyes narrowed, but I didn't waver.

Aure looked at me with a smile or pride, but I could feel the hint of sadness and longing in her.

"We've made the decision," I said, turning to Aure and returning her smile, my voice steady. "The people need to see me beside them, leading from the front. It's not enough to sit here in the safety of the palace while others fight for us. I will go with the commanders to the front-lines."

I turned back to the council, aware of the ripple of shock passing through the room. "Aure will remain here to manage the political transitions and strengthen the alliances that our marriage has cemented. We each have our own roles to play—mine on the battlefield and Aure's here at the heart of the kingdom."

Oric's face tightened, his hands clasped together as he leaned slightly forward. "And who made this decision?" he asked, his voice deceptively calm.

"I did," I said firmly, meeting his gaze without hesitation. "As your daughter and heir to the throne, I am free to make choices about my own actions. I'm not here to take control or disrupt your reign. But Aure and I will not be dictated to in how we live our lives. This is about our personal commitment to each other and to the roles we have chosen to fulfill."

Aure's voice cut through the tension in the room. "We are not here to challenge your authority, Your Majesty, but to share the decisions we've made. Orla will support our forces in the field, and I will ensure the stability of the alliances we've formed. Together, we are stronger, and we will act in the best interest of both kingdoms. But we will do it our way."

The silence that followed was thick with tension, but I saw a flicker of respect in some of the commanders' eyes. They hadn't expected this bold stance—our firm declaration of independence within the confines of loyalty.

Oric, however, was harder to read. His face remained impassive, but I knew him well enough to sense the simmering displeasure beneath his calm exterior.

"You are playing a delicate game, Orla," he said slowly, his tone cold. "Leadership requires more than just making decisions for yourself."

"And yet, those decisions must also reflect who we are and what we stand for," I replied, my voice just as controlled. "I am not here to defy you, Father. But I will not allow my life, or Aure's, to be controlled by anyone's agenda but our own."

His eyes darkened, but he said nothing further. The tension between us hung in the air, but I knew I had made my point clear. We weren't taking over. We were simply asserting our right to live and lead on our own terms.

Aure gave my hand another squeeze, her calm presence a constant reminder of why this mattered. This wasn't about seizing power—it was about claiming the freedom to make choices for ourselves, to shape our own future together. Though I would seize power for the betterment of our kingdoms, and he should be worried about that.

Rein stood up, his sudden movement drawing my attention. I had completely forgotten he would be here today. He spoke to the table and commanded respect. "I for one, I am grateful that a skilled warrior such as yourself, Your Grace, will join us tomorrow as we march to face this threat. We must remember that our true battle lies at the border, and our real enemy is King Frostbane, who seeks to spread his tyranny across our lands."

The conversation shifted to the logistics of troop movements—the plans for getting the new troops to the front lines, along with the gear, weapons, and supplies, all while navigating the incoming storms. The weather had been the worst we'd ever seen, and I couldn't tell if it was the dark magic of Frostspire or the unsealed bond between Aure and me. I tried to stay focused as Aure traced small circles on my hand, the comfort of her touch grounding me as we clung to each other.

I was going to miss her—everything about her—and I knew I would worry. But I had to figure out my magic, somewhere safely away from her, and finally do something for my kingdom. I was done being the princess locked in a tower, waiting for my life to begin.

After the meeting ended, it was late, and we walked back to our room. My Aunt Lili intercepted us, hugging us both tightly. "I hear congratulations are in order," she cooed, her smile not quite reaching her eyes. My magic buzzed under my skin as her touch lingered.

"Yes, I assume you're referring to our marriage," I said, watching her carefully as she nodded and took my hand. She gasped at the sight of the marriage rune.

"It's lovely. So, you chose the old siren ritual for your union? I've always thought the water folk's ways were rather primitive, but this is truly beautiful." Unease stirred inside me. Had her compliments and affection always felt this forced?

She then took Aure's hand, holding both of ours as the surge of prickling magic became impossible to ignore. Her smile grew wider, almost giddy. "Now that you're wed, you must join me! I'm leaving tomorrow for my home in the Southern Reach—I can't bear this wretched cold. I'll be wintering there for the season. Say you'll come."

I gently pulled my hand away, freeing Aure's as well. "Unfortunately, we can't, Aunt Lili. I'm leaving for the front-lines early tomorrow to join the fight, and Aure will handle matters here. I do hope you have a pleasant trip, though."

Aunt Lili's expression grew dramatically concerned. "Oh, Orla, I had truly hoped you wouldn't go through with such a dreadful idea. The front is no place for royalty—that's for soldiers! You're far more important than they are. Why would you risk yourself so foolishly? Think of your mother! I know you were never close with Oric, but your father loves you and would never want to see you in such danger. Surely you'll reconsider."

I wasn't sure if she knew who—or what—I truly was, and I wasn't about to share that secret yet. My jaw tightened slightly, but I replied calmly, "I've made my decision, Aunt Lili, after careful consideration."

She interrupted, clinging to Aure. "But think of your blushing bride! You don't want to make her a widow so soon. Orla, I worry about you. Please, I beg you—reconsider."

I reached over, taking both my aunt's hands in mine, gently pulling her away from Aure, my eyes darkening to a deep cobalt grey. My voice was firm and steady. "We have made our choices, and we will stand by them—just as

I'm sure you stand by yours, despite the consequences." My words carried a pointed, veiled meaning.

Feigning innocence, she responded with a delicate smile, "My actions have little effect on this kingdom compared to yours, Orla."

Aure shot me a warning look, sensing the shift in my emotions, but the anger that had been simmering beneath the surface finally broke free. I snapped, unable to hold it back any longer. "I'm pretty sure my mother would disagree with you."

My aunt's smile faltered, and she recoiled, her expression one of hurt and shock. For a brief moment, I almost regretted my words. Almost. But then I remembered everything—the lies, the manipulation, the betrayals that had piled up like stones on my heart, each one weighing me down until I could hardly breathe. Did she think a delicate smile and feigned innocence would undo any of it?

She gave me a look, as if I'd wounded her, but I couldn't bring myself to care anymore. I still loved Helena—how could I not? She had raised me, and that kind of love doesn't just disappear overnight. But it had changed, twisted under the weight of all the secrets she'd kept from me. And my aunt… I loved her too, in some strange way, but her betrayal felt even sharper, more personal.

The people who were supposed to love me had been the ones to hurt me most. They had kept me in the dark, used me for their own ends, and I had let them—trusted them—until now. It was like the walls I'd built to hold in all that pain were crumbling, brick by brick, and I wasn't sure I wanted to stop it.

I clenched my jaw, feeling the heat of my anger mix with a deep, growing sadness. This wasn't how it was supposed to be. Family wasn't supposed to feel like a burden, like chains wrapped around my heart, slowly tightening until I couldn't breathe. I wanted to scream, to demand why they had done this to me, but I already knew the answer. It didn't matter.

The look of hurt in my aunt's eyes should have softened me, but instead, it only hardened the resolve I hadn't known I was capable of.

I was done. Done playing the part of the obedient daughter, the naive niece, always looking for their approval, always trying to please them. I had given them enough. Now, it was time for me to take back what they had stolen from me—my own sense of self, my freedom, my choices.

I don't care anymore. I thought to myself, the realization settling in like a weight lifting off my shoulders. I was tired of the charade, tired of pretending that everything was fine, that I wasn't angry or hurt or broken inside.

I still loved them both, in some strange, twisted way, but that love no longer bound me. The betrayal had done something else—it had set me free.

Aure grabbed my arm, tugging me close, her touch grounding me. But I wasn't done. Not yet. I might die out there—hell, I might not make it back at all—and I wasn't about to leave these words unsaid. The truth had been clawing at my insides, festering. It was time to lay it all out, consequences be damned.

"I expected better from you, Lili," I said, my voice laced with venom I didn't even try to hide.

Her expression hardened instantly, the false warmth she always carried falling away. She wasn't even going to pretend now. "And I expected you not to speak about things you know nothing about. But here we are."

I felt a bitter laugh rise in my throat, but I swallowed it down. "Then enlighten me," I said, crossing my arms, voice cold as ice. "Explain yourself."

I felt Aure standing firmly beside me, her presence strong, her silent support unwavering. She could have said something, could have told Lili to back off, but she knew. She knew I needed this. I needed to confront Lili on my own terms.

My anger boiled over, and this time, I wasn't going to hold back. I couldn't keep pretending like her betrayal was some minor wound I could just nurse back to health. No, it was deeper than that—rotting. "Why don't you start with why you were fucking my father, Lili?" The words came out sharper than I intended, but I didn't regret them. I wanted her to feel it—the sting of being called out, the disgust that had been building in me for so long.

Lili's face paled, her mask cracking in an instant. For the first time, she looked rattled, her composure slipping as the shock washed over her. "Orla—" she began, but I wasn't letting her dodge this. Not now.

"No, don't you 'Orla' me," I snapped, stepping forward, my voice growing louder, rawer. "I know what you did. I know everything. How long, Lili? How long were you sleeping with Oric behind my mother's back? How long have you been lying to me, to her, to everyone?"

Her lips trembled, and for a second, I thought I saw something—guilt? Shame?—flash in her eyes. But it was gone as quickly as it appeared. She stiffened, straightened her posture, trying to regain control. "You have no idea what you're talking about. This isn't some childish game, Orla. You wouldn't understand the complexities of it."

"The complexities?" My voice was trembling with fury now. "What complexities justify betraying your own sister? What complexities make fucking my father something I wouldn't understand?"

Aure's grip tightened on my arm, grounding me just as I was about to lose control completely. But I didn't back down. Not this time.

Lili opened her mouth, her usual air of superiority trying to creep back in, but I could see her faltering. I could see the cracks in her mask. "It wasn't like that. You don't know the full story."

"Then tell me!" I roared, my chest heaving as the rage burned through me. "Tell me why! Why did you betray her? Why did you betray me?"

The silence in the room was suffocating. I could hear my own heartbeat pounding in my ears, the fury mixing with the sickening feeling of betrayal that had been festering for so long.

Lili's face was tight, her usual grace slipping away as she stared back at me, clearly not prepared for this level of confrontation. "It's more complicated than you think," she whispered, her voice shaking, but I wasn't buying it.

"Complicated?" I scoffed, the sound bitter and hollow. "You destroyed everything. You shattered the illusion of this family, and for what? For him? For power?"

Her eyes flickered, but she didn't respond, and in that silence, I knew. She wasn't going to admit it. She wasn't going to give me the satisfaction of hearing the truth from her lips. But it didn't matter. I knew.

I could feel Aure beside me, her silent support unwavering, but this moment—this bitter, ugly truth—was mine to carry. I was done being manipulated, done being kept in the dark.

My voice dropped lower, the weight of my question hanging between us. "Did you know about me?"

She tilted her head slightly, her expression unreadable at first, but then her voice shifted, growing softer, almost too tender. "What about you, dear?"

That tone—so sweet, so disarming—might have fooled me once, but not anymore. My heart pounded in my chest, each beat a reminder of the truth I had been chasing for so long. I stared at her, waiting for something, anything—some flicker of recognition in her eyes, some crack in the mask she always wore. But there was nothing. Just that empty tenderness, as if she truly didn't understand the weight of my question.

And that's when it hit me. Whether she knew the truth or not, she would never tell me. I could ask her a hundred different ways, beg for answers, demand the truth, but I would always be met with that same facade. A mask of love and care that hid the secrets she'd buried deep.

A surge of frustration and sadness twisted inside me, a bitter mix of emotions that felt like they would tear me apart. I had hoped—no, I had **wanted**—her to slip, to reveal something that would give me clarity, but instead, I was left drowning in the same uncertainty. I could feel the walls closing in, the silence between us suffocating.

The tenderness in her voice, the way she tilted her head like I was still the naive child she once knew—it sickened me. She was playing her role, as always, keeping her truths hidden behind layers of sweetness and false concern. The betrayal hit me all over again, sharper this time, because now I understood: no matter what I asked, she would never give me the answers I sought. She would keep me in the dark, just like she always had.

I swallowed hard, fighting the lump rising in my throat. I wanted to scream, to shake her, to force her to see me—not the girl she could manipulate or dismiss, but the woman who had a right to know who she really was. But I knew that would be pointless. I could see it in her eyes—she would never admit anything.

I took a breath, steadying myself, trying to swallow the ache in my chest. This moment was the closest I would ever get to the truth from her, and yet it felt miles away.

"I see," I whispered, more to myself than to her. The realization was like a cold wave crashing over me—there would be no closure here, no confessions. Just more lies wrapped in tender words. I clenched my fists at my sides, the frustration burning through me, but I refused to give her the satisfaction of seeing me break.

She smiled softly, that same practiced smile she'd given me a thousand times before, but now it felt hollow, mocking. I knew better now. I knew the truth was hidden behind that smile, locked away where she thought I'd never reach it.

But she was wrong. I didn't need her to say it. I already knew.

"I hope it was all worth it," I said, my voice cold and final. "Because you've lost me."

The silence that followed was suffocating, and for the first time, I saw real fear in Lili's eyes. Not fear of me, but fear of the consequences of her own actions.

I turned, pulling Aure with me as I left the room. There was nothing more to say. The truth had been laid bare, and the damage was done. There was no going back now.

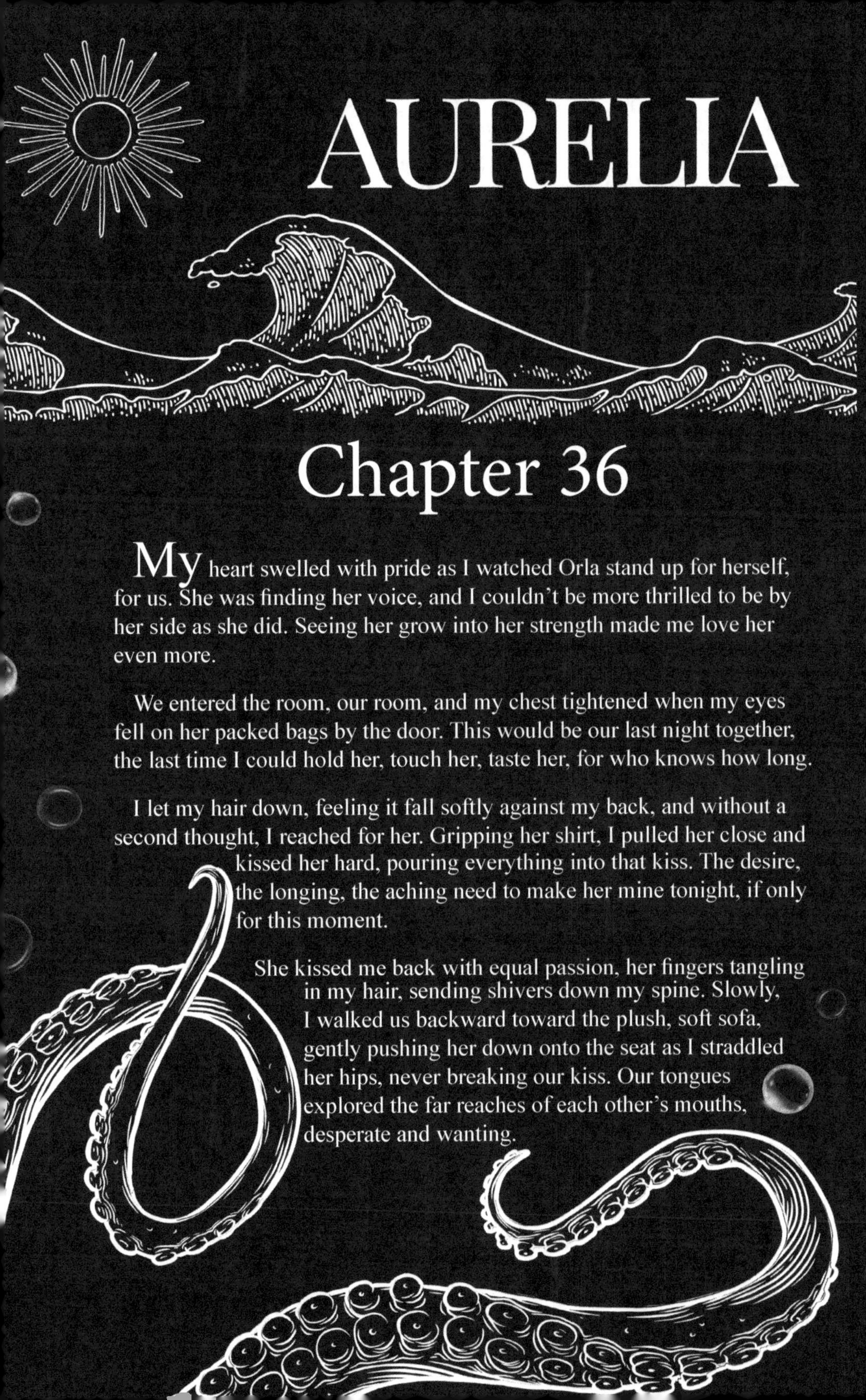

AURELIA

Chapter 36

My heart swelled with pride as I watched Orla stand up for herself, for us. She was finding her voice, and I couldn't be more thrilled to be by her side as she did. Seeing her grow into her strength made me love her even more.

We entered the room, our room, and my chest tightened when my eyes fell on her packed bags by the door. This would be our last night together, the last time I could hold her, touch her, taste her, for who knows how long.

I let my hair down, feeling it fall softly against my back, and without a second thought, I reached for her. Gripping her shirt, I pulled her close and kissed her hard, pouring everything into that kiss. The desire, the longing, the aching need to make her mine tonight, if only for this moment.

She kissed me back with equal passion, her fingers tangling in my hair, sending shivers down my spine. Slowly, I walked us backward toward the plush, soft sofa, gently pushing her down onto the seat as I straddled her hips, never breaking our kiss. Our tongues explored the far reaches of each other's mouths, desperate and wanting.

My hand traveled over her chest, then up her neck, finding the delicate curve of her slightly pointed ears. I caressed them softly, feeling their shape between my fingertips. My fingers traced the line of her ears, then down to her jaw, where I held her face tenderly. Slowly, I pulled back, breaking the kiss to catch my breath, my heart racing in my chest.

In a low whisper, I pleaded, "Please, Orla, let me give you the pleasure you always give me. Just let go for a while and enjoy this moment with me. Here. Now." The plea wasn't just for her—it was for me too, a desperate need to share this night with her, to lose ourselves in each other.

I knew I needed to be gentle, to let her set the pace. She thought I hadn't noticed her hesitation last time, but I had. And gods, who could blame her? All I wanted was to replace the hurt and shame she had felt with my love, my trust, my acceptance. I selfishly wanted to make her completely mine again, to show her she was perfect, strong, beautiful, and my everything.

Her eyes swirled with shades of lavender, blue, and magenta as she studied my face, her fingers gently caressing the side of my jaw in a tender gesture. I leaned into her touch, savoring the warmth of her hand. Her head fell back, eyes closing, and through our bond, I heard her voice in my mind. *"Alright, Meles Tari, I am all yours, my beloved."*

The warmth of our connection surged through me, filling me with a deep sense of belonging. I kissed her neck, my hands slowly beginning to roam down her body. A soft groan escaped her lips as her breath grew heavier, each sound igniting something deeper within me. My heart raced, heat building in my core as I lost myself in her, in us.

My slow kisses trailed down her collarbone as my hand cupped her breast, my thumb gently circling her peaked nipple beneath the fabric of her clothes. I looked up at her, watching as soft groans escaped her lips, her head still resting back against the sofa, eyes closed. She was losing herself to me, to my touch, and it sent a thrill through me.

"There are far too many clothes between us," I teased, sending the words through our bond with a smile, the anticipation building between us.

With a mischievous grin, Orla looked up at me, her eyes gleaming with playful challenge. "So, what are you going to do about it?" she teased, her voice dripping with anticipation.

I tilted my head, my lips twisting into a smirk as I met her gaze, an amused glint dancing in my eyes. "I could take a page out of your book," I said, my voice low and teasing. "And cut them off you."

Orla laughed, a soft, melodic sound that sent a shiver down my spine. She shook her head. Magic hummed under my skin as her hand trailed down my arm. "Please don't," she said with a smirk, her tone playfully exasperated. "These are my favorite pants."

I let my eyes linger on her for a moment, the fabric of those favorite pants hugging her curves in all the right ways. The firelight flickered in the room, casting a warm glow over her skin, and for a second, I felt the electric tension between us deepen, charged with the promise of what was to come.

I leaned in closer, letting the heat of her presence pull me in. "Fine," I whispered, brushing my lips just close enough to hers that I could feel her breath. "But you owe me something in return."

Her head tilted slightly, her eyes shifting to a deep, vibrant magenta. "I do? And what would that be, Meles Tari?" she asked, her voice laced with playful curiosity.

My grin widened as I looked her over, biting my lower lip slowly, savoring the moment. "Your shirt," I demanded, my voice low with anticipation. My hands found the hem of the soft linen, fingers brushing against her skin as I slowly lifted it off her body, revealing her inch by inch.

She sat there, her hands resting firmly on my hips, watching me intently, her gaze heavy with desire. As I revealed her bare body, I realized she had worn nothing beneath that thin slip of linen. Her toned muscles, honed from days of rigid training, were even more defined in the soft glow of the firelight.

I gasped at the sight of her, mesmerized by how her creamy skin seemed to glisten, illuminated by the flickering flames. She was breathtaking, every inch of her radiating strength and beauty.

Her firm, perky breasts made me almost envious of how they seemed to stay perfectly in place. Mine, on the other hand, had a mind of their own, moving every which way. Tossing her shirt aside, I leaned in and pulled her hardened nipple into my mouth. The deep groan she let out sent a rush through me, pushing me to suck harder, my tongue teasing her in slow, intoxicating circles. My hand moved to her other breast, warming it with gentle, attentive caresses.

She settled back into the sofa, relaxing into my touch, her body yielding to the moment. One hand gripped my hip possessively, while the other slid into my long curls, her fingers threading through my hair as she held the back of my head tenderly.

I reveled in the way she responded, her body melting beneath my touch. Her fingers tightened in my hair, pulling me closer, as if she couldn't bear the distance between us. The warmth of her skin, the sound of her soft gasps, and the way her breath hitched with each movement of my tongue fueled the fire inside me. I wanted to give her everything, to make her forget anything that had come before this moment.

I shifted slightly, bringing my free hand down to trace the curve of her waist, feeling the firm lines of her toned muscles beneath my fingertips. Her skin was smooth, soft, and she shivered at the touch, her hips shifting slightly under me. I smiled against her breast, kissing my way slowly down her body, savoring every inch of her.

Her grip on my hip tightened as I moved lower, her anticipation palpable in the air between us. I paused for a moment, looking up at her, taking in the flush of her cheeks and the way her chest rose and fell with her ragged breathing. Her eyes met mine, and in them, I saw everything—her trust, her desire, and the silent plea for more.

With a slow, deliberate movement, I reached down, undoing the belt buckle then the clasp on her waistband and pulling away the remaining fabric between us, my hands trembling slightly with the need to feel her, to be closer. She arched her back slightly, aiding me in removing her clothes, and I couldn't help but marvel at how effortlessly beautiful she was, how perfectly she fit against me. The firelight flickered around us, casting a warm glow over her body, making her look like some kind of untouchable goddess.

But she wasn't untouchable. She was mine. And I intended to remind her of that with every touch, every kiss.

As I moved, kneeling before her, I settled between her legs, my lips trailing lower. She let out a soft whimper, her body arching toward me. I could feel her need, her desire, radiating through our bond. Nothing else mattered, it was just her and me together in that present moment.

My hands gently ran down her warm thighs, and my thumb grazed a rough patch of skin. She flinched, just slightly, a grimace flashing across her face— noticeable, but fleeting. My gaze dropped to where my thumb had brushed across healing cuts, faint lines in a row, the skin still raw and clearly scarring. Tenderly, I traced my finger along the first scar that began the line. Her body stiffened as her hand moved from my hair to rest on the top of mine, guiding me but also holding me back.

I'd seen scars on her body before, always assuming they were from her relentless training and sparring, the marks of a warrior. But this… this was different. These were deliberate, self-inflicted. My chest tightened with a flood of emotions I hadn't expected. Without a word, I leaned down and kissed the first scar, then the next. Each kiss was soft, careful, reverent. I wasn't going to ask her questions, scold her, or tell her what she already knew. Instead, I was going to show her that I loved her—all of her. Her scars, her past, her pain. Everything. She deserved love, unconditional and without restraint.

I kissed all thirteen of her marks as she clutched my hand in silence. Her grip was firm, holding onto me as if afraid to let go. When I had kissed the last scar, I moved to her other thigh, placing a kiss there too. Her breath hitched, and this time, she gripped the back of my head with a fierceness I hadn't expected, a soft moan escaping her lips. She arched her back, parting her legs wider.

Her breathing became shallow, each inhale laced with anticipation. She guided me closer to her wet center, and as I hovered there, she groaned out, "Gods, you are so beautiful, Meles Tari, with your head between my legs."

I looked up at her, a mischievous smile playing at my lips. Her eyes locked on mine, the tension between us growing as I lowered my mouth to her skin. I kissed the outer folds where they met her thighs, teasing her, feeling the way her body tensed in response. The heat between us grew, coiling tightly in my core, as her anticipation built.

Gently, I brushed my thumb against her clit, and her hips bucked in response, a sharp gasp escaping her. I grinned against her, reveling in her reaction. She was fully stretched out, her body relaxed and open on the sofa, her head resting back against it, eyes never leaving mine. Her grip on the back of my head tightened, urging me closer against her pussy, and I obeyed.

I pressed my lips to her, feeling the warmth of her wetness, breathing in her scent, savoring every moment as I lost myself in her.

My tongue flicked around my thumb, which was still tracing soft circles around her clit. Another groan escaped her lips, and her fingers tightened in my hair, pulling me closer. I began to explore her with my tongue and mouth, the need to hear her pleasure growing stronger with every heavy breath she took.

When I pushed my tongue inside her, she held me firmly in place, grinding against me. My thumb moved faster now, pressing harder against her clit, and she let out a low, desperate growl. "Gods, Aure, you're going to make me cum."

Through our bond, I shot back a playful, flirtatious thought. *That's the point, my love. I want you to cum all over my face.*

Her breath hitched before she released a guttural growl, her movements growing frantic as she ground against my mouth and tongue. Her hand gripped my head, moving me in rhythm with her hips, while her other hand, still holding my fingers on her thigh, dug in tighter. The tension coiling inside her was palpable, driving her closer to the edge with every flick of my tongue.

I could feel it—she wouldn't last much longer. The anticipation of her release only heightened my own arousal, the heat and wetness between my legs growing more intense as I savored every moment of her unraveling beneath me.

Finally, she held me tightly against her, my movements steady as she neared her climax. Her breath hitched, her body becoming rigid, eyes closing as she held on. Then, with a loud, drawn-out moan, she trembled, my name slipping from her lips. "Aure..."

She came undone on my mouth, her release coating me as I slowed my movements to a near stop, allowing her to ride out the last waves of pleasure. Tiny shudders rippled through her body as the aftershocks settled, her breathing heavy, her grip still firm in my hair.

I lifted my head from between her legs, meeting her satisfied gaze. She released my hand and cupped my cheek, her thumb gently wiping away the wetness from my chin. A tender, yet pained expression crossed her face as she whispered, "You are so perfectly fucking beautiful, and I don't deserve you."

I crawled on top of her, straddling her hips until we were eye to eye. My hands cradled her face as I spoke, my voice serious and sincere, hoping my words would reach the deepest part of her soul. "Orla, you deserve the best of everything. You are worthy of love, you are worthy of *my* love. There is nothing you have ever done, or could ever do, that would make you any less deserving of me or my love for you. You are mine, and I am yours. Even if you can't believe it right now, I will believe it for you—because that's what unconditional love is."

Tears welled in her eyes, and before I could say more, she closed the distance between us, kissing me fiercely. I returned her passion, our bodies fitting together effortlessly, as if they were always meant to be this way. Around us, our magic crackled and danced in the air, a reflection of the raw connection we shared. But in that moment, none of it mattered—because she was mine, and I was hers.

We continued kissing and holding each other, even as the hour grew late and exhaustion took over. Eventually, we fell asleep, tangled together on the sofa. Sometime just before dawn, I woke with a shiver, lying there naked with Orla asleep, collapsed on my chest, her arms wrapped tightly around me. I kissed the top of her head, glancing around the room in search of a blanket.

With a sigh, I gently eased myself out from under her and stood, wrapping my arms around myself as the cold seeped in. I slipped into the adjoining bedroom, found my robe, and tugged it on. Grabbing the fur blanket, I returned to Orla, covering her with it before sitting beside her. Tears trickled down my cheeks as I gently rubbed her back. I still didn't want her to leave today. I understood her decision, I respected her choice—but that didn't make this any easier.

Wiping my tears away roughly, I picked up a book and settled in, letting her sleep for as long as possible, savoring these final quiet moments.

The hours ticked by, too quickly, and then came the soft knock at the door—our signal that it was time to prepare. She would be leaving in an hour. I leaned down and kissed her warm cheek as she stirred, whispering gently to wake her fully. "It's time, Orla."

She sat up slowly, a sleepy smile crossing her face. The first light of dawn streamed through the window, casting a soft glow across her skin, and for a moment, I could have sworn I saw an iridescent shimmer along parts of her body. She moved, and it was gone.

"Morning, Meles Tari," she said brightly, her voice warm and full of affection, as though today was just another morning for us.

I couldn't help but smile back at her, even though my heart felt heavy. She looked so peaceful, so radiant in the soft morning light. I reached out, brushing a strand of hair away from her face, memorizing the warmth of her skin, the way her smile reached her eyes. I wanted to freeze this moment, to hold onto it for just a little longer before reality set in.

"Good morning," I whispered, my voice barely steady. I tried to mask the tremor in my tone, not wanting her to sense the depth of my dread. I didn't want her to see the sadness that threatened to overwhelm me.

Orla stretched, her arms reaching up as she let out a soft yawn. "I suppose I should get ready," she said, her voice was light but tinged with the awareness of what today meant. She stood, letting the blanket fall from her shoulders, and for a moment I just watched her—how effortlessly strong she was, how composed. She moved through the room with a quiet confidence, but I could sense the weight she carried, the burden of her decision pressing down on her just as much as it did on me.

I stood, crossing the room to help her gather her things. As I handed her a piece of armor, our fingers brushed, and I caught her gaze. For a heartbeat, everything stood still—the soft hum of morning, the glow of dawn, the cool air in the room. I wanted to say something, to ask her to stay, but the words caught in my throat. I knew I couldn't ask that of her. I had to be strong, even when all I wanted was to hold her here with me, to keep her safe.

"Are you ready?" I finally asked, my voice softer than I intended.

She looked at me, her smile fading slightly as she met my gaze. "I don't know," she admitted, her vulnerability showing in a way it rarely did. "But I have to do this."

I nodded, my chest tightening. "I know. And I'm proud of you."

Orla stepped closer, pulling me into a warm embrace. Her arms wrapped around me tightly, as if she was drawing strength from me, and I held her just as fiercely. For a few moments, we just stood there, tangled in each other's warmth, neither of us wanting to let go.

"I'll come back to you," she whispered against my hair, her breath soft against my ear. "I promise."

I squeezed my eyes shut, willing the tears to stay at bay. "I'll be waiting."

With a deep breath, Orla pulled back, her fingers lingering on my arms before she stepped away. She began to strap on her armor, her movements quick and practiced. Watching her prepare for the front-lines made everything feel so final. I hated it. I hated that I couldn't stop her from going, that this was something she had to face alone.

The soft knock at the door came again, a quiet reminder that time was slipping away. I walked over, opened it, and found the messenger waiting. He bowed slightly, his expression somber as he informed us it was time to depart.

I nodded and closed the door, turning back to Orla. She had finished donning her armor, her sword strapped to her side, and for a moment, she looked like the warrior she was. Strong. Fierce. Unyielding.

But to me, she was still Orla—my Orla. And the thought of her walking into battle made my heart ache.

She stepped toward me, her expression softening as she reached for my hand. "We'll be together again soon," she said, her voice steady, though I could see the emotion flickering behind her eyes.

"I'll hold you to that," I whispered, my fingers curling around hers, holding on for as long as I could.

She leaned in, kissing me gently, and for a moment, everything else faded away. It was just us, tangled in each other's touch, the world outside the door forgotten.

When she pulled away, the finality of it settled deep in my bones. I followed her to the door, our hands still linked, until we reached the threshold. She let go, giving me one last look before stepping into the morning light. I stood there, watching her walk away, my heart breaking with every step she took.

The door closed behind her, and I was left alone with the quiet hum of dawn.

ORLA

Chapter 37

I rose from my cot in my command tent, just as the first light glistened off the frost covered ground outside. It had been three weeks into our two-month journey to Atteris, and we were now steadily approaching Emberfield. The small town had grown significantly over the last five years, becoming a key waypoint halfway to the Front-line. Its position made it a haven for travelers and a critical supply stop. Unlike the smaller depots spaced about two hundred miles apart, Emberfield boasted a strong military base, further securing its importance.

I had settled into a simple but consistent routine as we moved slowly through the Emerald Hills. The well-traveled roads had made the journey easier, but the inclines and biting cold had slowed our progress. Each morning, I would lie in my cot for a few moments, reaching out to Aure through our bond, uncertain how far it could stretch, as this connection was still new to both of us.

Lying there, I folded my hands behind my head and closed my eyes. *"Morning, Meles Tari."* Our bond hummed to life, threads of magic dancing in my mind.

"Good morning, Orla. Are you staying warm enough out there? It snowed again last night. I miss the warmth of home so much." Aure's voice was tinged with sadness and distance. Lately, it had been harder to keep our connection strong—perhaps the growing distance between us was affecting the bond. But still, we made this effort every morning, clinging to these brief moments of closeness.

Things had been quiet in Orlondia, and here, my focus was solely on getting to the front safely and quickly. However, each day, the separation seemed to stretch further, making the magic that linked us feel more fragile.

"I'm warmer than most; the cold doesn't seem to affect me like it does the others. We haven't lost anyone yet, thanks to the healers and enchanters." I sent all my love and affection through our bond, hoping to give Aure something to hold on to. I missed her more than I could express, and leaving her had been one of the hardest choices I'd ever made.

Though, in a way, I was relieved she hadn't been there to see the instability of my magic. The memory of one such day in the forest still haunted me—an acre of trees reduced to ash in a wild burst of power, while Reille did her best to help me control my lightning strikes. It seemed hopeless to attempt anything with precision. I felt as useful as a jar of flare sap—the unstable concoction the dwarfs used for mining explosions, and that we relied on to set fire lines during retreats. My memories fluttered through our bond to Aure. *"I feel so useless sometimes,"* I admitted to her.

Her voice came through the bond, soft but steady, *"You're not useless, Orla. Your power is just… overwhelming. You'll master it in time. I believe in you."* Her unwavering faith in me wrapped around my heart, easing the frustration that had been gnawing at me more with each practice session.

I sighed, though I tried to keep the doubt from bleeding through our connection. *"I hope you're right, but sometimes it feels like my magic is more of a curse than a gift."* I shifted on the cot, staring up at the canvas of my tent roof. *"I'm supposed to lead, but how can I if I can't even control myself?"*

Her response was gentle but firm. *"You're a leader because of who you are, not just what you can do. Don't forget that. You've always been strong, even without your magic."* Her words were like a balm, soothing the raw edges of my doubt. She always had a way of making me feel whole, even when I felt broken.

The cold air crept in through the seams of the tent, but I barely noticed it. All I could think about was Aure, her warmth, her presence, even from miles away, she was my anchor. *"I miss you,"* I sent through the bond, my heart aching.

"I miss you too, my love," she responded, her sadness clear as the emotion swept through me. *"But you'll be back before we know it. Once you are, we'll figure it all out. Together."*

I closed my eyes, letting her words sink in. *"Together,"* I echoed, feeling the weight of the journey ahead settle over me again. As much as I wanted to be with her, I knew my duty here was just as important. The front needed reinforcements, and Emberfield was just one more step closer to the battle awaiting us in Atteris.

The sound of movement outside my tent broke the silence, and I opened my eyes, reluctantly pulling myself out of the warmth of our bond. It was time to get back to reality.

"I'll check in tomorrow morning, same time," I said, a hint of a smile creeping into my voice.

"I'll be waiting," she replied softly, and with a last pulse of affection through the bond, I let the connection fade.

With a deep breath, I pushed myself out of bed, pulling my cloak tight against the cold. The frost glittered over the blooms of the iceblossom and heather that grew plentiful here in the early morning light as I stepped outside. The dusted evergreens and rowan trees surround the camp slowly coming to life. Men and women huddled around campfires eating the last of the Ice Stag and wild Hare, their breath visible in the icy air. We would need to hunt again tomorrow if you didn't make it to Emberfield soon. Somewhere in the distance, I heard the familiar clatter of armor being strapped on, and the low murmur of soldiers preparing for another day of travel.

I made my way through the camp, exchanging nods with a few of my officers. My mind was still on Aure, on our bond, on the way she made everything feel manageable, even when my magic threatened to unravel me. Though here and now, I needed to focus.

Rein was waiting for me by the command tent, his breath puffing in the cold air. He gave me a slight nod as I approached, his expression as unreadable as ever.

"Morning," I greeted him, tugging my cloak tighter.

"Morning, Crown Commander," he replied, his sharp eyes scanning the camp before settling back on me. "We're making good progress. We should reach Emberfield by the end of the week, assuming the weather holds."

I nodded. "Good. I want the men rested before we push on to the front. We won't have the luxury of stopping much once we leave Emberfield."

He grunted in agreement. "The healers are doing what they can to keep everyone in good shape. I have been told so long as they can keep finding frostroot for their warming potions, we will be ok. The cold hasn't gotten the better of anyone yet, but it's wearing them down."

"Yes, it is wearing us all down." I said, glancing out at the campfires. The soldiers huddled around them as healers passed veils of blue liquid to some. "Let's make sure they're ready. We can't afford to lose anyone to this cold."

I then pulled the map from my saddlebag, the crisp winter air biting at my nose as I spread it out on the wooden table in the command tent. Rein stood beside me, his brow furrowed as he studied the lines and markings. The ravine loomed large on the parchment, a narrow cut through the rugged hills—one they couldn't avoid if they wanted to reach Emberfield in time.

"Grimscar Ravine," I murmured, tracing the jagged line with my gloved finger. The name alone sent a shiver down my spine, though I tried to mask it behind a calm facade. "If Frostspire were going to set up an ambush anywhere, this would be the place."

His expression darkened as he glanced at me. "It's the quickest route, but also the most exposed. That ravine is a natural choke point. If we're caught there, we'll have no room to maneuver."

I nodded as I gazed off across the distance and considered the terrain. The walls of the ravine were steep and lined with crumbling rock—perfect cover for archers or magic users alike. The path itself was more narrow than the road, barely wide enough for two wagons to travel side by side. One blocked road, and the entire convoy would be trapped.

"Do we have another option?" I asked, but I knew the answer even as I spoke out loud.

"Not if we want to reach Emberfield before the next storm rolls in," Rein replied grimly. "We could try the lower pass around Silverwood, but it would add a week to our journey, and we'd be without supplies for half of it. The men wouldn't make it."

I clenched my jaw, frustration simmering beneath my calm demeanor. "Then we'll have to risk it. We can't go in blind. Double the scouts and send word to the Enchanters. We need to have them set up wards for detection and shields for the most vulnerable sections of the column."

He hesitated, his eyes narrowing slightly. "And what about you, Crown Commander? You know Frostspire would target you above anyone else if they get the chance."

I looked up sharply, meeting his gaze. "Maybe, if they are even aware I am here. But hiding or running isn't an option. We push through, and I'll be where I'm needed, in the center of the formation. If they happen to come for me, I'll be ready."

Rein's jaw tightened, but he nodded slowly. "We'll keep you protected. But, Orla, if something feels wrong…"

"We will deal with that if it comes," I interrupted softly. I doubted very much that Frostspire cared much about me. "We'll be careful."

I glanced back down at the map, a gnawing sense of unease settling in my gut. Grimscar Ravine felt like a trap, the kind of place where shadows lurked and whispered, where unseen eyes watched your every move. The soldiers had whispered about it too, calling it cursed, a place where patrols disappeared without a trace.

I shook off the thought, straightening. "We'll push through quickly. No lingering. And Rein, make sure everyone is on high alert. I want everyone in position to respond the moment anything feels off."

Rein's nod was firm, but I could see the doubt in his eyes. "Understood. I'll have the troops briefed before we move out."

With that, I folded the map and tucked it away, turning my attention to the preparations outside. The camp was already bustling with activity, soldiers moving to and fro, checking weapons, packing supplies. If our enemy was out there, watching them, they wouldn't see fear. They'd see a force ready for anything.

Or so I hoped.

As we marched toward Grimscar Ravine later in the morning, I couldn't shake the feeling that we were making a mistake, but what other choice did we have? The thought sent a chill down my spine, but I steeled myself. Whatever awaited us, we would face it head-on.

The horses' hooves crunched over the snow-covered ground, the cold air whipping at my face as we rode closer to Grimscar Ravine. The tension in the air was thick, the knowledge of what lay ahead weighing heavy on all of us. Though Frank, who never let a serious moment pass unchallenged, decided to break the silence.

"So, Orla," Frank called over with a grin, his eyes gleaming with mischief. "How about after we get through this ravine of doom, I treat everyone to a pint? Heard Emberfield's got some excellent ale, and it's served by some beautiful ladies."

I raised an eyebrow, a small smile tugging at my lips despite the creeping unease. "A pint? Really, Frank? You're already planning the afterparty?"

"Well, someone's gotta keep morale up," Frank said with a wink. "Besides, you never know when we'll all get a chance to relax. Unless, of course, you're afraid you'll be out-drunk by me. You know I can be quite… impressive."

"Impressive?" Rielle snorted from beside him, her eyes rolling. "The only impressive thing about you, Frank, is how you manage to keep your head attached with all the hot air inside it."

Frank feigned a wounded look, his hand dramatically clutching his chest. "Rielle, that cuts deep. Here I am, offering the promise of a good drink to all, and you insult me. If I didn't know better, I'd say you were in love with me."

Rielle's eyes flashed with amusement, though her voice was sharp. "If I loved you, Frank, you'd already know it. Mostly because I'd have made you work a lot harder than you do now."

Rein, riding ahead, shook his head at the banter, but even he couldn't suppress a small grin. "Frank, Rielle, enough. Let's save the flirting for when we're not heading straight into an ambush zone."

"Oh, I'm not flirting, Crown Commander Rein," Rielle quipped, casting a teasing glance at Frank. "I'm just keeping him on his toes."

Frank chuckled, tipping his head toward her. "Admit it, you enjoy keeping me on my toes."

"Someone has to," Rielle shot back, her tone playful but with an edge of fierceness.

I smiled to myself, letting the banter between them lighten the mood, if only for a moment. Frank's antics and Rielle's sharp tongue were familiar comforts, something to hold on to as we neared the ravine's shadowy mouth.

My mind drifted back to the terrain ahead, and an uneasy feeling that crawled up my spine. Grimscar Ravine waited for us, its name a whisper of danger on the wind. Still, the laughter around me was a welcome distraction from the weight of command. I turned to Rein, who was scanning the horizon with that ever-present seriousness etched into his face that I had grown to rely on.

"You know, Rein," I said lightly. "I think Frank's right. We could all use a drink once this is over."

Rein glanced over at me, his expression softening slightly. "If we make it through this without incident, I'll be the first to buy the rounds."

"You hear that, Frank?" I called over my shoulder. "Rein's buying. You'd better make it out of this ravine, or you'll miss the free ale."

Frank's grin widened. "See? That's what I like to hear—free drinks and survival. My two favorite things!"

"Assuming you don't trip over your own feet before we even get there," Rielle teased.

"I'll have you know I'm very nimble on my feet," Frank replied, his tone mockingly serious. "I've been told I'm like a cat."

"A very loud, very clumsy cat," Rielle shot back, smirking.

Rein let out a quiet sigh, though the amusement in his eyes wasn't lost on me. "Focus. All of you. We're not out of this yet."

The mood sobered slightly, but the warmth of their banter lingered. As we rode closer to Grimscar Ravine, the walls of rock rising like jagged teeth on either side, I felt a little lighter, even as the shadows of what was to come loomed over us.

We reached the entrance to the ravine just before high noon. The light cast unnaturally long shadows that crept across the jagged rocks like fingers of some unseen hand. The wind howled through the narrow passage, carrying a strange, eerie whistle that set my nerves on edge.

"Orla," Rein murmured from beside me. "Are you sure about this?"

I took a deep breath, scanning the rocky walls above. Every instinct screamed at me to turn back. But there was no turning back now.

"I'm sure," I said quietly. "Stay close. And be ready."

The walls of Grimscar Ravine loomed around us, jagged cliffs rising high on either side, feeling like they could fall in on us at any moment. The sky above was overcast, a thick blanket of gray clouds hiding the sun, making the ravine feel even more ominous. The path narrowed, forcing our column into single file, and the sound of our horses' hooves echoed eerily off the stone walls.

The air felt heavy, charged with a tension none of us could ignore. The soldiers who had been chatting and laughing earlier were now silent, their eyes scanning the rocky heights above, alert for any sign of danger. Even

Frank now rode with his hand resting on the hilt of his sword, his usual grin replaced by a tight, wary expression.

I rode just behind him, with Rielle on my left, her brow furrowed in concentration. She murmured softly under her breath, weaving spells of protection around us, her magic shimmering faintly in the damp air. Rein was at the front, his back straight, every muscle tense as we moved deeper into the gorge. I could sense his unease, a quiet storm brewing beneath his calm exterior.

"Grimscar Ravine," I muttered, my voice low. "Feels like we're walking into a trap."

"Feels like it because we probably are," Rielle replied, her tone clipped. "This place stinks of bad magic."

Frank turned in his saddle, flashing a grin that didn't quite reach his eyes. "Oh come on, Rielle. Maybe we'll just find a nice spot to have lunch. I packed some bread and cheese."

Rielle shot him a sidelong glance, her lips twitching with a hint of a smile. "Only you would think about lunch in a place like this."

"Well," Frank said with a mock sigh. "You've gotta keep your strength up somehow."

Rein glanced back at us, his brow furrowed. "Focus. Stay sharp."

His words only confirmed what I'd been feeling since we entered the ravine, the quiet was too complete, the air too still. It was the kind of silence that only came before an attack.

We moved further in, the light from the overcast sky above barely piercing the thick shadows. I could feel the pressure building, an invisible weight pressing down on my chest. Then I heard it—a faint hum in the air, almost like a distant drumbeat, growing louder, closer.

"Ambush!" Rein's voice rang out, sharp and sure.

In an instant, the sky above erupted with arrows, dark shafts raining down from the cliffs. Rielle's hand shot up, magic flaring to life as a shimmering barrier formed around us, deflecting the arrows. She began muttering a spell, reinforcing the shield.

"To the sides!" Rein barked, his sword already drawn as he moved his horse toward the rocks for cover. "Find shelter!"

Frank urged his horse forward, swerving toward an outcropping on the left. "Can't we ever get ambushed in a meadow with flowers?" he called back, his tone half-joking, half-serious.

Rielle rolled her eyes but stayed focused, her hands weaving through the air as she strengthened the shield. "It's not just arrows," she hissed. "There's magic coming."

As if on cue, a bolt of dark energy slammed into the shield, sending cracks of icy blue through the protective barrier. Rielle staggered, her face pale, but she held the line, her jaw clenched in concentration. I tried to pour my own magic into the shield, but the weight of the attack was immense. The shield was faltering.

"Orla!" Rein's voice cut through the chaos. "Stay hidden!"

My heart raced as I scanned the cliffs. Figures in black armor emerged from the shadows above, moving with deadly precision, their faces hidden beneath dark hoods. They were swift, silent, and I knew in an instant this wasn't just a random ambush. They were The Shadow Guard, an elite force, not simple foot-soldiers, and I was their target.

"They want me," I whispered, the realization sinking in.

Rein cut down an attacker who had dropped from the cliffs, his movements fluid and fierce. "Stay close! We won't let them take you!"

Even as he spoke, I felt the cold touch of magic creeping toward me, invisible tendrils winding through the air. I turned to Rielle, but her focus was on maintaining the shield, her hands glowing with fiery energy as she fought to keep the attackers at bay.

Frank was already swinging his sword, cleaving through one of the black-armored soldiers with a grunt. "Not today, you bastards!" He growled with the fierce protectiveness of the royal guard he was.

There were too many of them. More figures poured from the cliffs, their attacks unrelenting. I struggled to help hold the shield. It was weakening, the cold magic pressing in from all sides. Then I saw him, standing on the ledge above us, cloaked in darkness. One of the rumored Dreadmages of Frostspire, said to be the most powerful dark magic welders.

He raised his hand, and I felt it before I saw it—the pulse of dark magic aimed directly at me. His gaze locked with mine, and in that moment, I knew this was no ordinary attack. This was planned. They wouldn't stop until they had me.

"Orla!" Rielle's voice was frantic, her eyes wide with panic. "Get out of here!"

I couldn't move. The Dreadmage's spell had already taken hold, wrapping around me like icy chains. I reached for my magic, but it slipped through my fingers like sand, powerless against the dark energy closing in.

Rein slashed through another attacker, his eyes wild with desperation. "Orla! Hold on!"

It was too late. The Dreadmage whispered something in a language I didn't understand, and the world tilted. I felt my body go limp, my vision darkening. The last thing I saw was Rein's face, his mouth forming my name, before everything went black.

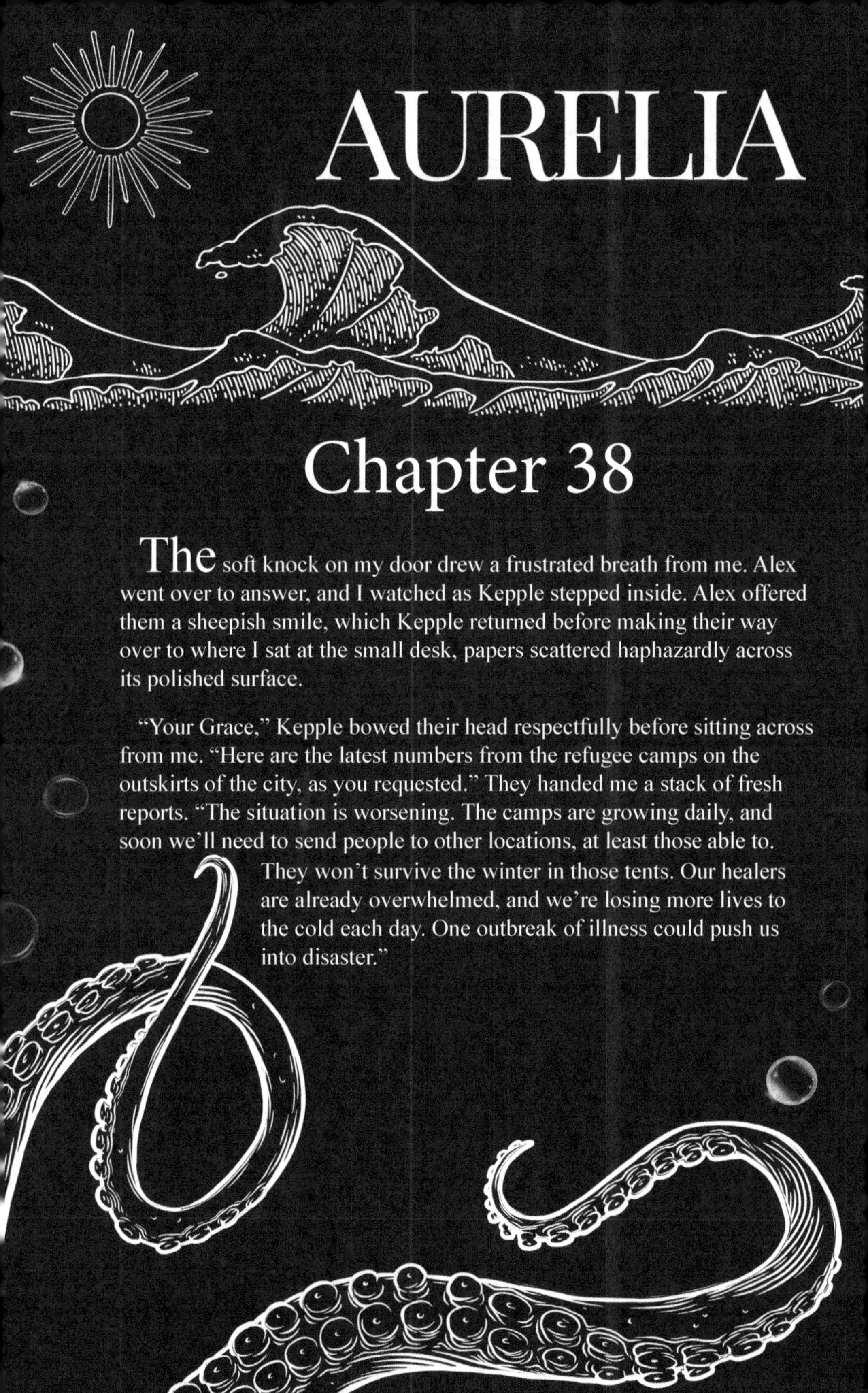

AURELIA

Chapter 38

The soft knock on my door drew a frustrated breath from me. Alex went over to answer, and I watched as Kepple stepped inside. Alex offered them a sheepish smile, which Kepple returned before making their way over to where I sat at the small desk, papers scattered haphazardly across its polished surface.

"Your Grace," Kepple bowed their head respectfully before sitting across from me. "Here are the latest numbers from the refugee camps on the outskirts of the city, as you requested." They handed me a stack of fresh reports. "The situation is worsening. The camps are growing daily, and soon we'll need to send people to other locations, at least those able to. They won't survive the winter in those tents. Our healers are already overwhelmed, and we're losing more lives to the cold each day. One outbreak of illness could push us into disaster."

Anger surged through me, my hands tightening around the papers as I thought of how King Oric was ignoring the crisis—no, *worsening* it with his endless feasting and celebrating. The winter holiday of Vulcan's Flame wasn't even here yet, and though it was only the twelfth day of Faelivrin, the final month of the year, Oric had already been feasting daily. He was indulging far beyond the traditional celebration, which wasn't meant to start until the twenty-first. I growled in frustration as I scanned the reports.

"Your Grace," Kepple's voice softened, drawing my attention. "You seem more upset than usual today. Is everything alright? Have you still not been able to connect with Orla through your bond?"

I clenched my jaw, feeling the familiar ache of worry. "She's been silent for twelve days, Kepple. I could still sense her presence, like she was in a deep sleep I couldn't wake her from. But today... Today is different." My voice wavered as I continued, unable to hide the fear that gnawed at me. "I reach out, and there's nothing. It's like she's gone." I refused to say the word I thought, Dead.

"I'm worried something is seriously wrong." I chewed my lower lip, my voice strained. I also still had not heard from Azura and how things were going with the hatchling, but at least I could still sense her and her sleep, which brought me some level of comfort.

Kepple frowned, their gaze searching mine. "I'm sure she's alright, Your Grace." They said softly trying to ease my worry, looking thoughtful. "Though, we should take this seriously. If the bond has truly gone silent..."

"I know what it means," I snapped, though I immediately regretted the harshness in my tone. Kepple didn't deserve that. I took a breath, trying to steady myself. "I'm sorry. I'm just... I don't know what to do."

Kepple reached out, placing a hand on the desk between us. "We'll figure it out. And we'll do everything we can for the refugees in the meantime."

I nodded, though the weight of worry pressed heavily on my chest, making it difficult to breathe. The papers in my hands blurred as thoughts of Orla consumed me. Something was wrong, I could feel it deep in my bones. I tried to seek comfort that my foresight dreams never showed her on the front-lines or in battle.

Leaning back, I closed my eyes, struggling to keep my emotions in check. Now wasn't the time to lose focus. After a steadying breath, I looked back at Kepple. "What if we start sending people to Faedamir on the empty supply ships as they return? There's space, and even in tents, the climate there is far more tolerable in the winter. The journey only takes about a week each way, depending on conditions."

Kepple leaned forward, considering my suggestion. "It's a good idea, Your Grace. Faedamir's climate would certainly be more forgiving, even in temporary shelters. And with the ships bringing much-needed supplies back to us on regularly scheduled trips we could organize it easily." They paused, their brow furrowed in thought. "But planning would require a coordinated effort. We'd need healers and provisions sent with the refugees, and we'd have to ensure that Faedamir can handle the influx."

I nodded, the weight of responsibility settling deeper on my shoulders. "I'll send word to the Faedamir council immediately. We need to know what they can accommodate, and we'll make sure the next fleet of ships is prepared to take refugees on the return trip." My eyes flickered over the scattered papers again, the rising numbers of the displaced pulling at my conscience.

"We could start with the most vulnerable," Kepple added softly. "The elderly, the children, those who can't survive another night in the cold."

I sighed, rubbing my temples. "Make arrangements with the healers to identify who should go first. We can't keep losing people. Not like this."

Kepple nodded, a quiet understanding in their eyes. "We'll move quickly. But we're going to need a long-term solution. Winter is just beginning."

The conversation turned practical, laying out the logistics of sending aid and gathering support. A different worry gnawed at me, one I had been trying to push away but could no longer ignore. After a moment of silence, I finally spoke, my voice quieter.

"Kepple, there's something else that's been troubling me," I said, shifting the conversation. "I haven't heard much from my father lately. His letters have dwindled down to almost nothing. The last one I read wasn't even from him, it was from the Orlondian Ambassador assigned to Faedamir. King Oric allowed me to see it, and it mentioned something about my father's health."

Kepple's eyes narrowed slightly in concern. "Your father? That's troubling, Your Grace. Was there any mention of what could be wrong?"

I shook my head, frustration bubbling beneath my calm exterior. "Nothing specific, just vague references to him being unwell. I've sent letters, but there's been no response. And now, with Orla gone silent in the bond, everything feels... off." My hands trembled slightly as I spoke, but I forced them to still. I couldn't afford to let my emotions take over.

Kepple frowned, leaning forward. "You should ask King Oric for more information. If your father's situation is as serious as it seems, we may need to take action sooner rather than later."

"I will," I said, though the thought of pressing Oric for anything made my stomach turn. His control over information was just another form of manipulation. "I'll have to tread carefully."

Kepple nodded in agreement. "If you need help, I can reach out through my contacts. We may be able to get more information from Faedamir through other channels."

I offered a small, grateful smile, nodding. "I'd appreciate that."

As our conversation drew to a close, before I shifted in my chair, trying to calm my nerves still. Alex, who had been standing nearby, suddenly straightened, his gaze sharp. His pocket stirred, and a small dark shape emerged, Amethyst, his tiny bat, flitting her wings lightly as if sensing something approaching.

Alex tilted his head, alert. "We're about to have company."

Before I could ask, a knock echoed at the door. Alex moved swiftly, crossing the room in a few strides to open it. A messenger stood there, bowing slightly, holding a small stack of letters in his hand.

"Delivery, sir," the messenger said, nodding to Alex. "These just arrived for Her Grace."

Alex accepted the letters, offering a quick nod in thanks before closing the door behind him. Amethyst, her job done, circled once more before retreating into the folds of the pocket at his chest.

"What is it?" I asked, my curiosity growing.

Alex thumbed through the letters quickly, pausing when he reached the two familiar seals. His expression turned serious as he handed them to me. "Two letters from Faedamir. One bearing the royal crest of King Rowan, and another an official letter from the Faedamir council."

My heart quickened. "Both from Faedamir?"

Alex nodded. "The letter from the council is marked urgent."

I stared at the two letters in my hands, the weight of their contents already pressing down on me. The royal crest on my father's letter gleamed under the dim light, and next to it, the council's official seal stood out sharply. I hesitated for a moment, feeling the tension rising in my chest.

I broke the seal on the first letter, the one from my father. My hands trembled slightly as I unfolded the thick parchment, my eyes quickly scanning the words written within.

My beloved Aurelia,

I write these words knowing my time in this world is slipping away, and the thought of leaving without seeing you one last time tears at my heart. It aches beyond measure that I will not hold you close again, whispering how proud I am of the strong, beautiful woman you've become. The regret of not being able to fall to my knees and beg for the forgiveness I fear I'll never truly deserve weighs heavily on me.

Though I received your letters, and I sense the growing love between you and Orla, I am haunted by the choices I forced upon you. I wanted nothing more than to see you happy and free, but in my desire to secure our kingdom, I fear I may have stolen that choice from you. Love should never be a matter of diplomacy, and I am sorry, my darling, that I made it so. I put our kingdom above your heart, and for that, I beg your forgiveness. You deserved so much more than I gave you.

Enclosed, you will find my official retraction of the treaty. If you choose to rescind it, you have my blessing, my heart, and my deepest apology. I would never force you into a marriage now. All I ever wanted was for you to feel the kind of love your mother and I shared. I pray you, and the god of the deep, Pontus, can forgive me for this transgression.

However, if you choose to uphold the treaty, understand that Orlondia is bound by promises King Oric made. He pledged that our merchants would travel untaxed through Orlondia, not only during my reign but during yours as well. The kingdom will owe us half of all land taxes and rights across their lands, regardless of who rules. If this is the path you choose, you must hold him to these terms.

Our copies of the sealed treaties rest with Chieftain Garrick, should you need them.

Please, Aurelia, choose the path that brings you the greatest joy and peace. My wish for you, more than anything, is to experience the love and happiness you so rightfully deserve. Know that wherever I go now, I carry my love for you with me, always and forever.

With all my heart,

Your Devoted Father

I shuffled through the two pages, my hands trembling as I came upon his official retraction of the treaty. My breath hitched, and my mind swirled with emotions. *Had he not received my letters? I had told him—I had told him that Orla and I were wed, that we had formed a mate bond, and that she was my everything. He had nothing to feel shame for, nothing to regret.*

The words blurred as tears gathered in my eyes, the weight of my father's apology cutting deeper than I could bear. Pain surged within me, and I felt the threatening tears prick at the corners of my eyes, my brow creased with the overwhelming sorrow of it all.

He hadn't known. He hadn't known that the very thing he feared he'd taken from me, my freedom, my choice, had been what led me to Orla, to the love that completed me. And now, with his words of regret and sorrow, all I could feel was the deep ache of wishing I could tell him that everything had turned out right. That I was happy. That his guilt was misplaced.

I feared it was already too late. With trembling hands and tear-streaked cheeks, I slowly opened the urgent letter from the council. My heart pounded, each beat a heavy thud in my chest as the seal broke beneath my fingers. The moment I unfolded the parchment, I felt the weight of it before I even read the first word.

1st day of Faelivrín, year of 1705

Your Majesty,

The title hit me like a blow, and my breath caught in my throat.

We write to inform you of the passing of King Rowan, your father. His spirit departed in the early hours of the morning. It is with deep sorrow that we send this message, but also with urgency. You are now Queen of Faedamir. Your presence is required immediately to take the throne, and preparations for your coronation are already underway. It is also expected that you bring your consort, Orla, to stand at your side as tradition dictates. The kingdom is in mourning, but we look to you, our Queen, to lead us through this time of grief.

The words blurred, my eyes filling with tears that fell unchecked, spilling down my face. A sob tore from my throat, sharp and raw, as the parchment slipped from my trembling fingers. The air left my lungs in a rush, and I doubled over, clutching my chest as the full weight of the letter crushed me.

"He's gone..." My voice was barely a whisper, but the devastation in those words echoed in the room, louder than any cry. "My father... he's gone."

The room spun, the edges of my vision narrowing as the overwhelming grief consumed me. I could no longer hold back the torrent of emotion crashing through me. I dropped to my knees, my body shaking as sobs wracked through me. The loss hit like a physical pain, stabbing deep into my chest, stealing the breath from my lungs.

Kepple was the first to move, rushing to my side with a soft gasp. "Your Grace..." Their voice trembled, and I felt their hand gently rest on my shoulder, but it did nothing to stem the flood of grief pouring from me. I couldn't stop it, I didn't want to stop it. It was too much. All of it—my father, the guilt, the regret. The words in his letter still hung in my mind, the love and sorrow he had for me now forever lost, before I could even tell him I forgave him.

Kepple knelt beside me, their hand tightening on my shoulder, a quiet, steady presence amidst my storm of emotion. "I'm so sorry, Aure... I'm so, so sorry," they whispered.

I shook my head, the sobs choking any words I wanted to say. The ache in my chest deepened as the reality of it sank in. I would never see him again. Never hear his voice. Never feel the warmth of his arms around me.

I screamed. A broken, desperate sound that ripped through the air, my pain raw and unrestrained.

Alex, who had stood quietly near the door, was suddenly by my side, his strong arms wrapping around me from behind. He said nothing, only held me tightly, offering his silent support, his strength. I buried my face in my hands, my entire body shaking as the sobs kept coming, wave after wave of grief crashing over me.

"He can't be gone," I gasped between sobs, my chest heaving with each breath. "I didn't—he didn't know—I didn't tell him... I didn't—"

"Shh..." Alex's voice was soft, soothing. "You loved him, and he knew that, Aure. He knew."

But it wasn't enough. It wasn't enough. I had been so far away, so focused on everything else, and now he was gone. Gone before I could say goodbye, before I could tell him that I was happy, that I had found love, that he had nothing to regret. And now, I would never have the chance.

The letter lay crumpled beside me, its cold, final words staring back at me. *Queen of Faedamir.* The words felt like a curse, heavy and unwelcome. How could I be queen now, when I felt like I was falling apart?

"I can't do this..." I whispered, my voice shaking. "I can't—I'm not ready. He's gone, and now they expect me to—" I broke off, my voice lost in another sob. "They expect me to just take his place? To bring Orla back and be their queen?"

Kepple's hand tightened on my shoulder, their voice steady. "You don't have to be ready right now, Aure. No one expects you to be ready for this kind of loss. But you *are* strong enough to do this. You're not alone. We're with you."

Alex's arms remained firm around me, grounding me as I cried. "We'll help you," he murmured. "We'll help you through this, every step of the way. You don't have to face this alone."

I nodded through the tears, though it felt like everything inside me was crumbling. The grief was still raw, a wound that I knew would never truly heal, but as I sat there, I felt a small flicker of something, something like hope.

Maybe, just maybe, I could carry on.

I withdrew into myself, curling up in the quiet of my grief. For the rest of the day, I refused all visitors and set aside my duties, unable to face anything beyond the pain that consumed me. Kepple and Alex stayed close, giving me the space I needed but never too far, offering silent care and protection. I spent the hours drifting between fits of sobbing and uneasy sleep, the waves of sorrow relentless.

Now, in the dark hours of the morning, I felt drained of tears but still unable to rest. I lay awake, staring into the shadows, the weight of it all pressing down on me. Kepple had read that the letter was dated the first day of Faelivrin. He has been gone thirteen days now.

Thirteen days. That was the last time I had spoken with Orla.

The thought clawed at me, a fresh ache in my chest. I felt so alone. Utterly, painfully alone. I tried to reach for Azura, hoping to find comfort in our connection, but she remained focused on her egg. I didn't want to disturb her delicate task. The last thing I wanted was for my grief to ripple through our bond and disrupt the fragile hatching process.

And so, I lay there in the stillness, consumed by my thoughts and my grief, feeling as though I was drowning in the silence.

My thoughts were interrupted by loud banging on the door, followed by a barrage of harsh, hushed voices from the outer chamber. I rose quickly, wrapping my robe around me as I moved toward the source of the commotion.

My thoughts raced as I reached the outer chamber, the soft swish of my robe barely audible over the low murmurs. The moment I stepped inside, my breath caught in my throat. Frank stood in the middle of the room, his clothes drenched with sweat and dirt, his usually bright expression dark and grim. Alex and Kepple were speaking with him in hushed tones, their faces tense.

The sight of Frank—disheveled, exhausted—made my heart plummet. My pulse quickened, a sense of dread crawling up my spine. *No,* I thought. *It can't be...* My stomach churned as I stepped forward, my voice barely above a whisper.

"Frank...?"

His eyes met mine, and I saw it—saw the truth in his gaze before he could even say the words. The color drained from my face, and I felt the world tilt around me. My chest tightened with a mix of fear and devastation, my mind already bracing for what I didn't want to hear.

"Aure..." Frank's voice cracked as he stepped closer, wiping the sweat from his brow with the back of his hand. "I'm sorry. Orla's been taken."

For a moment, relief flickered in my chest—*taken, not killed*—but the weight of his words still hit hard. My breath caught, and I gripped the back of a chair to steady myself.

"Taken...?" I echoed, my voice barely a whisper. The small relief that she wasn't dead did nothing to ease the overwhelming grief. If anything, it only sharpened it.

Frank nodded, his face pale. "It was Frostspire. They ambushed us on the way to Emberfield. It wasn't just an attack, it was precise. They were after her specifically. They... they took her."

I stared at him, my heart pounding in my chest. I had let her go. I had let Orla leave, and now she was gone. *Taken.* My relief quickly morphed into something else, anger, thick and burning in my chest.

"You were supposed to keep her safe," I snapped, my voice trembling with rage. "***You were there***, Frank! How could you let this happen?"

Frank flinched, his face falling, but before he could respond, I stepped forward, fury overtaking me. "You were supposed to protect her! You swore you would protect her!" My voice cracked, and I could feel my hands shaking, the anger bubbling over, mixing with the grief.

"I tried, Aure," Frank said quietly, his voice full of guilt. "We... we couldn't hold them off. They came for her, and they were too strong. I—"

"You failed!" I shouted, my chest tightening with a wave of emotion. My fist found its mark on his chest. He didn't move. "She's gone because of you!" The strangled words escaped me, raw and unfiltered, but the moment they left my lips, I knew the truth: I wasn't just angry at Frank. I was angry at *myself.*

I had let her go. I had been the one who told her it would be fine, who didn't stop her when I had the chance. And now, she was gone. Tears blurred my vision, and I could no longer hold back the sob that tore from my throat.

"I should have stopped her," I whispered, my voice shaking. "I should have made her stay." Frank's arms wrapped around me as I buried my face against his moist shirt, my hands trembling as the sobs overtook me. "I... I let her go."

Frank's grip on me tightened, but I barely felt it. The grief was too much. It crashed over me like a tidal wave, drowning me. My breath came in ragged gasps as I tried to pull myself together, but I couldn't.

"I should have been there," I choked out, my voice breaking. "I should have done something."

"Aure, it's not your fault," Kepple said softly, but the words felt hollow. I couldn't believe them. How could I?

Alex moved closer, to where Frank still held me to himself. "This isn't on you," Alex said, his voice steady. "You couldn't have known this would happen."

But I had. *I had known*. The visions. The dreams. I had seen her in chains in Frostspire. And yet, I did nothing to stop her from going closer to them. The realization sent another wave of sobs through me, and I covered my face with my hands, the weight of everything crashing down.

"I saw it," I whispered through the sobs. "I saw it in my dreams. I knew something was coming, and I did nothing. I let her go... I let her go." My voice cracked, and I felt as though I was breaking apart, piece by piece, under the crushing weight of my failure.

Frank let his chin rest on my head, his voice heavy with guilt. "Aure, I... I'm so sorry. I would have given my life to protect her."

But his words did nothing to soothe the storm inside me. The anger, the guilt, the sorrow—it was all too much. My chest tightened painfully as I sobbed, unable to breathe, unable to think of anything except the fact that Orla was gone, and I had failed her.

Kepple reached their hand out, squeezing my shoulder. "We will find her, Aure. We will get her back."

I shook my head, my voice barely a whisper. "What if I'm too late? What if... what if she's gone forever?"

"You're not too late," Alex said firmly. "We'll fight for her. We won't stop until she's back."

The sobs wracked through me, shaking my entire body as I tried to process the weight of it all—the grief, the guilt, the anger. I felt like I was drowning, sinking deeper into the abyss of my own despair. And yet, through it all, a small flicker of hope remained—a tiny, fragile ember that told me Orla was still out there.

But that ember was quickly overshadowed by the darkness of my fear. And for the first time, I wasn't sure if I was strong enough to hold on to it.

The grief that had already shattered me from my father's death now returned in full force, sharper and more agonizing. Orla—my Orla—was gone. And I had failed her. I hadn't been able to protect her, just like I hadn't been able to save my father.

My body shook as a sob tore from my throat. It was too much. Too much loss. I hadn't even started to cope with my father's death, and now Orla... I couldn't bear it. The world around me felt distant, my heart pounding in my chest as panic and grief swirled together, threatening to suffocate me.

"I can't... I can't do this," I choked out, my hands trembling as I pressed them against my chest. "I've lost her. I've lost... everything."

Frank looked down at me, holding me firmly like the sturdy rock I needed, his voice soft but firm. "We'll get her back, Aure. I swear to you, we'll find her. But we need you to stay with us and not let your grief consume you. We need you to stay strong."

I shook my head, tears blurring my vision. "How can I stay strong when she's gone?" My voice broke again, the sobs coming faster, my body trembling uncontrollably. "I... I felt her. I always felt her through our bond, but now... now there's nothing."

"Your Grace," Alex's voice was calm, but there was a strength in it that pulled me from the edge of despair. "We're not giving up. Not on her. And not on you. You still have that connection to her. You will be able to find her."

I stared at him, my chest heaving, torn between the unbearable grief and the flicker of hope his words sparked. My bond with Orla... it was still there, wasn't it? Somewhere, buried beneath the fear and panic, I had to be able to reach her.

But at that moment, I felt only emptiness. And that emptiness terrified me. I had to do this, I needed to for both my kingdoms, for my father, for Orla.

The intensity of my sobs lessened, though the pain still burned deep inside. I wanted to believe them, to hold on to the hope that Orla was still out there, waiting for me to save her. But the fear, the doubt—it was overwhelming.

If Orla was strong enough to face everything she had and still hopefully was, then I could too. I closed my eyes, drawing in a shaky breath as I tried to calm the storm raging inside me. My hands still trembled, but friends' steady presence, their unwavering loyalty, kept me from falling apart completely.

I had to try. For Orla. For us.

"I'll try," I whispered. "I'll do everything I can."

Frank nodded, his arms still wrapped around me. "That's all we need from you, Aure. One step at a time. We will all try to do everything we can. We'll get her back."

The room fell into a heavy silence, the weight of the moment pressing down on all of us. Orla was gone, taken by Frostspire, but I couldn't let that be the end. I *wouldn't* let that be the end. We had to bring her back, no matter the cost. I had to find the strength, because losing her wasn't an option.

A surge of resolve coursed through me. I would go home, claim my throne, and then I would rain fire on Frostspire. I would tear it apart if I had to, burn it to the ground, if that's what it took. I would get Orla back, and I would bring her home.

My voice was steady, fueled by the steel in my heart. "We're going to Faedamir. I'm going home, and I am claiming my crown because I am Queen."

ORLA

Epilogue

My head pounded, each heartbeat thundering in my ears, heavy and relentless. My body awakened to a rush of shooting pain, an aching stretch that throbbed in my chest. I managed to move my fingers, but my arms feel leaden, unresponsive. My heart raced as I slowly regained my senses, the world around me coming into hazy focus. I lifted my head, a sharp pain shot down my spine as I did, and I blinked against the brightness, trying to clear my vision.

I shifted my arms, and a deafening clank echoed around me, biting pain searing through my wrists. As my eyes adjusted, I took in the cold stone cell, where I was strung up, arms stretched wide. I hung suspended in the middle of the room, glowing golden chains bound my wrists, the only things keeping me from collapsing entirely. My ankles were shackled to the floor, anchoring me in place.

At least I was still clothed, though only in my leather pants and loose, thin cotton shirt. My lips were cracked, dry flakes of blood coated them as I tried to moisten them with my tongue. The bitter taste of blood soured my stomach. I tried to make a sound, but it was a struggle—my throat felt thick, like it had been stuffed with cotton.

I reached for my magic, feeling it deep within me, but it was as if it too was chained, just out of reach. My bond with Aure... panic flared as I tried to connect with her, reaching out, but there was nothing. I trembled, rage and fear twisting together, and I screamed as loud as I could. The sound echoed back, bouncing off the cold, empty walls, as trapped here as I was.

I took in my surroundings, a round, windowless room with a single door, thick beams stretching up to the high ceiling. The only light came from the unnatural golden aura that radiated off the chains that bound me, casting a faint, eerie glow around the space. My breathing grew heavier as I struggled to remember what happened, how I got here, or who could have done this.

I screamed again, the sound ripping from my throat, but it did nothing to ease the helplessness settling in. Pain was my only companion, sharp and constant, draining me with each passing minute. Time blurred; I couldn't tell how long I'd been strung up like this, my body aching, exhaustion pulling me under. Everything felt uncertain, as if my whole world had crumbled, leaving me in pieces.

I thought of Aure, the way she'd be worried—how I'd planned to leave her. *Gods, I was such a fool.* I should have stayed, been the wife she deserved. I missed everything about her: her scent, the way her hair tangled in my fingers, the way she bit her lower lip when deep in thought. I had failed her.

And now... now, I was trapped, and she had no idea where I was, or if I was even still alive.

I screamed until my voice turned hoarse, breaking under the strain until no sound would come. No one came; no one cared that I was awake. Time continued to slip away, meaningless and warped.

Eventually, I couldn't hold back the urge to urinate, and the hot liquid trickled down my legs, pooling on the floor beneath me. The warmth sent a shiver through my body, followed by the chill of the dampness against my skin. But I was too exhausted, too wracked with pain, to care about the humiliation. It was just one more indignity to endure.

Exhaustion was overtaking me, and I started to nod off, my body desperate for even a moment's rest. But suddenly, the door slammed open and I jerked my head toward it. An armored guard entered, clad in the dark, forbidding metal of Frostspire, making way for a tall, muscular, middle-aged man with broad shoulders. His dirt-brown hair was tousled, clipped short around his ears, and he wore a heavy black cloak lined with white fur. Beneath it, silver armor gleamed, adorned with intricate blue crystal inlays on the chest plate.

I took him in—the pale, frostbitten skin that looked as cold as ice, a clean-shaved face with harsh angular lines, and his piercing sky-blue eyes. Then, I saw it: the jagged crown of ice upon his head. My breath caught. This was him, the King of Frostspire—King Malachor Frostbane, the tyrant of the North, the enemy I'd spent my life training to fight. And here he stood, mere feet from me, a smug smile playing on his lips.

He dismissed the guard with a wave, and the door closed, sealing us alone in the room. He studied me with a calculating gaze, and I held his stare, I knew my own eyes darkened to a stormy cobalt as rage simmered beneath the surface. His eyes shifted then to an unsettling ruby red as he spoke, his voice smooth, almost hypnotic.

"Hello, Orla. Your mother was right. It was time for you to come home, Daughter."

Acknowledgments

Writing a book is never a solitary journey, and I would not be here without the love, support, and encouragement of so many incredible people.

To Roni, for being the mother I always needed but never had. Your unwavering love, guidance, and belief in me have been a gift beyond measure. This book brought us together, and for that, I will be forever grateful.

To Kayla, my best friend and the sister my heart chose. Thank you for standing by my side through every challenge, for celebrating every triumph, and for loving me exactly as I am—differences and all.

To my BookTok community, your enthusiasm, kindness, and support have left me in awe. You embraced my words, encouraged my creativity, and gave me the confidence to keep going. This book exists, in part, because of you.

To my Alpha/Beta readers, critique partners, and ARC team, your insights, patience, and encouragement helped shape this story into what it is today. Every comment, every suggestion, and every moment you spent in my world means more to me than I can express.

To my family and close friends, who lifted me up when I doubted myself and reminded me why I tell stories in the first place—you are my foundation.

To my readers, whether this is your first journey with me or one of many to come, thank you for choosing this book. May you find joy, sorrow, adventure, love, and meaning within these pages.

And finally, to the version of me who dreamed of this moment but never believed it could happen—you did it.

With all my love and gratitude,

A.K. Neane

Special Thanks To Indie Authors

To the indie author community, thank you for your inspiration, encouragement, and unwavering support. Writing can be a lonely road, but having a community of authors who uplift one another, celebrate each other's wins, and share in the struggles has made this journey all the more meaningful. Your passion, resilience, and creativity fuel the indie book world, and I am honored to be among you.

A special thank you to Leslie Swartz, who not only beta-read this book but also became an incredible mentor and guide. Your wisdom, patience, and encouragement have been invaluable, and I am forever grateful for the time and heart you put into helping me shape this story.

To all the indie authors who have supported me along the way, I see you, I appreciate you, and I am endlessly thankful for you.

Indie Authors & Friends Who Deserve All the Love

Leslie Swartz -- @leslieswartz333

Danielle Douglas -- @danielle.douglas_author

Kat Baxter -- @k.bax.author

Piper Leigh Ion -- @authorpiperleighion

Bree Moore -- @breenovels

Atlas Avery -- @atlasaverywrites

Jac Franklin -- @jac.franklin.author

Danielle Smith -- @daniellesmithauthor

Asher D. Payne -- @author.asherdpayne

Whitney Mayoral -- @twisted.pearls

Ashlee Pippin -- @ashleepippian.author

Faith Sloan -- @author_faithsloan

Luna Nightshade -- @lunanightshade.authorr

J.S. Corvus -- @thiswitchylife_

Aurora Steinhart -- @author_aurora_steinhart

K.F. Starfell -- @wyverealm.author

R D Moreno -- @rdmorenauthor

A heartfelt thank you to the small businesses that contributed their creativity, craftsmanship, and passion to this journey. Your dedication to your craft brings so much magic to the world, and I am beyond grateful for your support. Whether through custom bookish items, promotional materials, or just cheering me on along the way, your impact has been immeasurable. Supporting small businesses means supporting dreams, artistry, and community, and I am honored to have worked with such talented creators. Thank you for being a part of this adventure!

@empb122 - Custom Crafts
@midnightsoapery - Waxmelts
@resincraftsbychelsea - Resin Crafts
@beadworkbyber - Magnet Bookmarks,
Annotation Bookmark

About the Author

A.K. Neane (they/them) is a queer
fantasy author who believes in the power
of storytelling to create safe spaces and
amplify diverse voices. Inspired by the
comfort books have always provided,
they craft immersive worlds filled with
magic, complex characters, and the kind
of representation they longed for
growing up.

When not writing, they can be found
wrangling their teens or goats on their
small family farm, researching mythology,
or diving into their next obsession.

Veins of Sapphire, Hearts of Steel is their
debut novel, the first in the Destiny of
Terraqua trilogy.

Stay connected for updates, exclusive
content, and behind-the-scenes insights:

@A.K.Neane.Author